Finding Grace

Finding Grace

A Novel

BLACK
STONE
PUBLISHING

Dear
JANIS THOMAS —
Much love to you
and thanks for all
your support
and your
friendship,

Copyright © 2022 by Janis Thomas
Published in 2022 by Blackstone Publishing
Cover and book design by Alenka Vdovič Linaschke

The characters and events in this book are fictitious.
Any similarity to real persons, living or dead, is coincidental
and not intended by the author.

Printed in the United States of America

First edition: 2022
ISBN 978-1-7999-2141-7
Fiction / Thrillers / Suspense

Version 1

CIP data for this book is available
from the Library of Congress

Blackstone Publishing
31 Mistletoe Rd.
Ashland, OR 97520

www.BlackstonePublishing.com

For Penny Thiedemann, whose real-life Peepers inspired this story.
With a dear friendship like ours, we are never far from the home we love.

PROLOGUE

Louise

They found Grace on the George Washington Bridge wearing a tattered pair of Hanes boyshorts, a graying cotton underwire bra that could no longer support its cargo, and a worn, oversized fanny pack. According to witnesses, she'd been singing a Pearl Jam song. Of course. I'm betting on "Even Flow."

A cyclist saw her and dialed 911 on his cell phone. Although the first responders couldn't definitively determine that she'd planned to jump into the Hudson River, they were confident that a well-past-middle-aged woman on the GWB in nothing but her skivvies should be expressly deported to Bellevue.

When the hospital administrator called to inform me of the situation, I was only surprised Grace still had my number in her archaic address book. I assumed she'd ripped out that page. Our last interaction had been unpleasant. Catastrophically unpleasant.

Part One

ONE

Louise

"I have to go to Bellevue."

I'm sitting on the couch in my studio apartment in Hell's Kitchen. Jett sits in the worn leather recliner across from me, noodling on his acoustic guitar. He drags his eyes from the fretboard and gazes at me.

"Whoa. Seriously? Why?" Jett is a fortysomething musician who's never made it past wedding bands and Irish pubs. He tends to speak in one-word sentences. Which is perfect for me because I never hook up with anyone for the conversation.

I set my phone down and grab my beer. "They have my mom."

And that's that. Almost instantly, Jett peels off his newly designated "main squeeze" label and evacuates our fledgling relationship. One mention of Mom and the loony bin, and he's out the door, precious guitar in hand. He claims he's just going to a rehearsal, but I know I'll never see him again. No one wants to sleep with a woman who has a crazy parent. I'm not upset by his sudden departure. Jett's penis is as unremarkable as his musical chops. Whatever we had, which wasn't really anything, wouldn't have lasted long.

My apartment feels bigger without Jett. I don't have a lot of furniture, so it seems more spacious than it is. Couch, recliner, coffee table.

A card table in the corner of the galley kitchen with one chair. A shelf for books and knickknacks. No dresser. All my clothes are in the closet. Well, not *all* of them. Some are strewn on the radiator. Good thing it's May. Otherwise, the building might have gone up in flames days ago. A twin bed huddles in the far corner next to the window. A TV tray doubles as a nightstand on which my laptop sits. It's not much and it's not mine. Just how I like it.

I've been subletting for a couple of years from an older woman who moved in before the area became trendy, back when junkies and prostitutes littered the streets and getting home safely was anyone's bet. The neighborhood has been gentrified, but my landlady must not have noticed. She charges me a song. Still, she relocated to some Podunk town in Idaho, so my meager rent check allows her to live in style.

I polish off my beer and check the time. 2:04 p.m.

I decide to walk to Bellevue instead of taking the bus, which is a terrible idea since I have to work tonight. My leg will pay the price. But other modes of transportation would get me there too fast, and I don't want that. I'll walk slowly. I'll take ibuprofen. But first, I think I'll have one more beer. And a cigarette. I've been trying to quit, but today isn't the right day to go without nicotine. Maybe I'll take a shower, too. And maybe I'll stop at the Starbucks on my way, grab a latte, have a scone.

I'm definitely not in a hurry.

TWO

Melanie

CALIFORNIA—PRESENT

Delilah's making brownies again. It's like the third time this week. When I walk into the house, I can smell them, and my stomach rumbles appreciatively, even though I know I won't get any. Delilah is my foster mom. She makes brownies when she's upset about something. Mostly when she's upset about Ray—my foster dad. She makes them and then she cuts out a little corner, carefully so she won't hurt the pan, then she tastes the little corner. And then she spits her mouthful out and dumps the whole batch into the trash, like it's poison. I personally do not think anything that smells that awesome could be poison.

One time, after she dumped a batch, I went to the trash and tried to find a piece of brownie that didn't have trash skody on it. But before I could even reach in the bin, Delilah came in and caught me. She smacked my hand and told me not to even think about it. Which was very hard because when she makes those brownies the whole house smells like chocolate and chocolate is my absolute favorite flavor of all time.

I walk into the kitchen to find her staring at the oven, waiting. She doesn't look at me, just waves her hand to let me know she knows I'm there.

"It smells delicious," I tell her, and she waves at me again, but this wave is different than the first. This wave is impatient, like she doesn't believe me

"Can I try them this time?" I ask. I know what she'll say, that I can try them if they turn out okay, which according to her, they never do.

"If they turn out okay," she says. She still doesn't look at me, just watches the brownies through the dirty window of the oven, like she's trying to will them to bake up right. "Go do your homework, Melanie."

"I don't have any," I tell her. Seventh grade sucks less than sixth, but there's a lot more homework, so days like these, when none of my teachers hand out stupid worksheets or assign stupid notes, are days to be celebrated. With brownies, maybe, if I had a different foster family.

"Well, then, go read for a while," Delilah says. I notice that her roots are showing gray. She hasn't gone to Eileen's for a while. Eileen has a shop with five beauty chairs. She trims my hair every couple months, and when she does, she washes the gray out of Delilah's roots. We haven't been there for a while.

"Can I do tech?" I ask. "It's Friday." That excited me the most about having no homework on the weekend. That I could go straight to my iPad and draw on my cool new app, maybe listen to the new Billie Eilish single.

"Read first," Delilah says. "For an hour."

I'm not happy about this but I'm not surprised. I shrug, even though she's not looking at me, then turn and walk out of the kitchen.

I go to the back of the house, into my little room, set my backpack down, and go to my bed. My Warriors book sits on my nightstand and I grab for it.

This kid in my Core class, Reuben Meserve, he's reading it too. I saw him with it before the bell rang and it surprised me a little bit because I thought that mostly girls read the Warriors series. For a minute I forgot that I was a social misfit and I told him I was reading that book too. He gave me a kind of funny grin before turning away and tucking the book into his backpack and completely ignoring me for the rest of class. I guess I should have known better than to try and talk to a *normal* kid. Not that Reuben is normal either. He was held back in kindergarten and seems a little strange, but no stranger than me. The Meserves live in my same tract of houses, and I sometimes see him on his bike. But he's never said a single word to me before, so I don't know why I thought he'd strike up a conversation over a book.

My stuffed animals surround me as I get comfy on top of my bed. I'm probably getting too old for them, but I'm not ready to let them go. Some of them have been with me for a very long time. Mr. Chinchilla sits on top of my pillow, and Chauncy the Dolphin lays next to him. My first parents, the ones who adopted me when I was a baby, gave me Chauncy. He's worn in places but looks pretty good for twelve.

I tuck myself between him and Mr. Chinchilla, then find where I left off in the Warriors book and start to read. It's getting exciting, but before I can finish the chapter, I feel that feeling, the one that makes the hair on the back of my neck stand up straight.

I set the Warriors book down on the bed next to me, then reach under my pillow and pull out my journal. My black gel pen sits snugly in the leather loop on the side of the book, and I tug it free. I open the journal to the first empty page, then fit the pen into the fingers of my left hand. I can still feel my neck hair standing at attention. I take a deep breath and close my eyes, then lower my left hand to the journal.

A few seconds later, my left hand stops moving. I open my eyes and stare down at the page, at the four words that weren't there before, written in handwriting that isn't mine, but I recognize all the same.

Somebody's coming for you.

THREE

Grace

Louise will come. Oh, she'll take her time about it. Try to torture me, make me think she's not coming. But I know my daughter. I haven't seen her in five, maybe six years. Still, I know her in that way only a mother can.

The orderlies didn't put me in restraints, and I am greatly appreciative of that. They had no reason to. I was docile as a kitty cat, didn't want the straitjacket, which I've had the displeasure of wearing on more than one occasion. I made it clear to them that I had no intention of jumping into the Hudson. God, no. Someday, possibly not too long from now, I'll take my last breath, but it won't be after churning around in that filthy river. Although, I suppose the East River's worse, what with all the bodies that get dumped in it.

My being there wasn't about jumping into any river and it wasn't about killing myself. It was about getting Louise's attention. I figured the George Washington Bridge stunt and Bellevue was the way to do it. She won't be happy, but at least she'll come.

The room around me is small and gray. If I were claustrophobic, it might be a problem. But I'm not. I have many other challenges, but thankfully, claustrophobia is not one of them.

There's a guy in the next room. I can see him through the glass window. Kind of reminds me of my hero, Eddie Vedder: longish hair and a bit scruffy looking. The staff should have closed the privacy curtain, but they didn't. I don't blame them, it's pretty busy around here. Never a shortage of crazies in the old city of New York. But this guy, he's naked and he's strapped to a wheelchair and he's drooling all over himself and shaking like there's a 9.5 earthquake going on inside of him. And although I'm doing my best not to look at his you-know-what, it's very difficult not to because he's got a sizable you-know-what, and it's standing at . . . well . . . half-mast.

I was glad when the paramedics brought him in. Not that I enjoy looking at him. But there were a lot of people in this little room with me, asking questions, taking my vitals and generally checking me out, and as soon as that guy got here, they all left me alone to attend to him. I don't think they believed me when I told them I was just fine and dandy, but they could see I was doing a whole lot better than Mr. Naked-Shaking-Drool-Man.

A woman shrieks from somewhere outside the room. She's got a kind of rhythm going. She shrieks, then goes quiet for maybe two minutes, then shrieks again. I'm guessing no one's paying any attention to her, because this has been going on since I got here. I asked the doctor about her when he came in with those other people to assess me. Asked him if she was all right. He gave me that patronizing look, the one I've become familiar with over the years, then didn't answer me. I've been marking time by her shrieks. According to her violent vocalizations, I've been here for about two hours.

The shrink they sent in wasn't patronizing, but I swear, she didn't look old enough to have a degree in babysitting. She talked low and quiet, asking all the usual questions, did I mean to harm myself, and all that. So prim and proper, this young woman, with her hair scraped back into a bun and her blouse buttoned all the way up her throat and her black-rimmed glasses perched on the bridge of her pug nose.

But that girl has a dark side, yes, she does. She likes to get people committed. It gives her a sense of power she doesn't have anywhere else in her life. She'll get *me* committed if she gets the chance. So, I acted my part. Gave all the right answers, in front of the doctor and the social worker as well as the shrink so they could all bear witness to the fact that I am not, in fact, off my rocker, but just having a really bad day. I didn't mention any of my previous diagnoses, nor the long list of meds I've been put on over the years, or Dr. Brenner and his shenanigans. I didn't mention that other thing I've got going on. These people don't need to know any of that. And I cannot be committed.

I have places to go. People to see. And, God willing, Louise is going to help me.

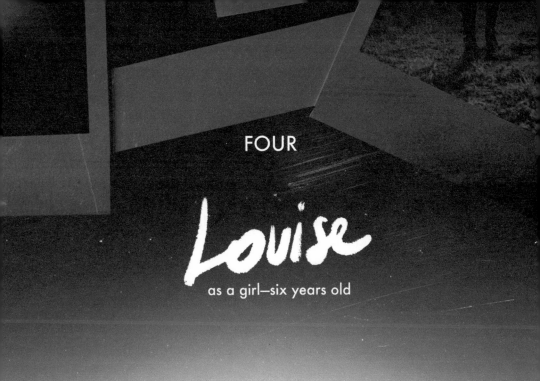

FOUR

Louise

as a girl—six years old

The back door of the restaurant stands open. Louise can hear the maria-chi music from the parking lot, and it makes her feel happy inside. She closes her car door and takes a step toward the restaurant. Her mom comes around the back of the car and grabs her hand, gives it a squeeze. She looks up and sees the big smile on her mom's face. A genuine smile. And that makes her even happier than the music.

Her mom peers down at her. "I'm thinking a big vat of guaca-mole to go with our chips and salsa. What do you think, missy?" She winks.

Louise nods enthusiastically and her mom leads her to the back entrance. The music grows louder in her ears, but she likes it.

"We can share a plate of chimichangas, too," her mom says.

"What's a chimchiyona?" she asks.

"Chimichanga. Just about the most delicious goldarn thing you can get at a Mexican place. In my opinion, at least."

They walk side by side into the restaurant, past the restrooms and the door to the kitchen. A waitress greets them before they can reach the hostess stand, and gestures to an open table. The waitress is pretty, Louise thinks, with olive skin and long shiny dark hair braided down the side of her face. She has a large pink flower tucked behind her ear, but Louise doesn't know what kind it is except that it's not a rose.

"Isn't this the best?" her mom says as they slide into the booth. "A mother-daughter date."

"I wish we could do this every day," Louise says.

"If wishes were fishes and cattle were kings . . ." her mother starts.

"The world would be full of wonderful things," she finishes.

"I suppose if we did this every day, it wouldn't be special, right? But we could sure do it more often."

Louise nods again. "Agreed."

Her mom laughs, delighted. "*Agreed*. You're pretty precocious for a six-year-old."

"What's *percoshus*?"

"That means, um, sort of like, more clever and smart than other kids your age."

Louise sits up proudly in her seat as the waitress returns. She sets a child's menu and a couple of crayons in front of her, and a regular menu in front of her mother.

"What can I get you to drink?" She glances back and forth between them. The restaurant is more than half full, but she shows no signs of impatience.

"Can I have a Shirley Temple?" Louise asks.

Her mother scrunches her nose. "Awful lot of sugar in a Shirley Temple. Not really too healthy, is it?" She looks up at the waitress for confirmation, but the waitress's expression remains neutral. "Oh, what the heck. We'll both have a Shirley Temple. And a vat of guacamole."

The waitress smiles. "A vat? Okay. I'll be back."

Her mom looks around the restaurant, and Louise mimics her. The table next to them has a large family, and everyone is laughing and talking at the same time. Louise wonders what it would be like to be in a family like that but she also knows she probably shouldn't wonder such things because it would hurt her mom's feelings. There's an older couple at a booth on the opposite wall, and behind them is a mom and two teenagers, and in the middle of the room are two empty tables and one table with three men wearing suits and ties and drinking beer.

Louise turns back to her mom and sees that her smile is gone.

"What's wrong, Mommy?" she asks. Before her mom can answer, a busboy comes over and sets down a basket of chips and some salsa.

"Thanks a lot," her mom tells him, then adds, "*Muchas gracias.*"

Louise goes to grab a chip, but her mother stops her. "What do we always do before we start eating?"

She grins. "We say your name!"

"That's right." Her mother closes her eyes. "May we always be grateful for our blessings," she says. She doesn't open her eyes right away. Louise watches her. Her lips are still moving, but no words are coming out, and she's frowning and shaking her head back and forth. Finally, her mother opens her eyes and looks at her. "Okay, dig in."

She grabs a chip, scoops up some salsa, then pops the whole thing into her mouth. Her mother follows suit, and they crunch in unison.

"Oh, that's spicy, isn't it? I hope they bring our Shirley Temples soon, right, missy?"

"Me too." Louise looks at her mom and can tell something's bothering her, even though she's trying to pretend there isn't. "What is it, Mommy?"

Her mom smiles again, but not the same way as before. She leans forward and fake whispers, "I just have to go to the ladies' room, that's all. You wait right here. I'll be right back." She gets out of the booth and starts to walk toward the restrooms, then stops. She turns and stares at her daughter, and Louise thinks she has never seen her mom look so sad. Then suddenly, her mom grins and winks at her. "Don't go eating all those chips while I'm gone, okay?"

She slashes an X across her heart with her index finger. "Promise."

"That's my baby."

As soon as her mom disappears around the corner, Louise turns back to the chips. She takes one and dips it into the salsa. Her mom's right, it's a little spicy, but she loves how it makes her tongue tingle. The waitress comes over and sets down two bubbling, pinkish drinks and a large bowl of guacamole.

"*Muchas gracias*," Louise says. She doesn't think she pronounces it just right, but the waitress smiles at her.

"*De nada*," she answers. "Where's your momma?"

"She went to the ladies' room."

The waitress nods then moves to another table. Louise grabs a chip and rakes it over the mound of guacamole. She should probably wait for her mom, but the dip looks so inviting. Surely, her mom won't mind if she has a little.

The guacamole is delicious. She doesn't like avocados, but this is different, like the avocados have been transformed into something scrumptious and smooth and wonderful. She wonders if she herself will ever transform into something wonderful, like a ballerina, or a princess, or a butterfly.

To keep from eating too much guacamole, she grabs a crayon and starts to do one of the puzzles on the children's menu.

After she finishes all the puzzles and the word search and the maze, Louise realizes it's been quite a long while since her mom left the table. She knows how long it takes to make a peepee, and that making a number two takes a while longer. But even if her mom had to make a number two, she still should have been back by now.

She sets the crayon down and takes a chip. She crunches for a moment, then tries to swallow it. She looks around and sees the mother at the table across the way glancing in her direction. The chip sticks in her throat, and she thinks maybe she's going to choke on it. She takes a long drink of her Shirley Temple, not even tasting it, which is a shame, but the gulping helps the chip go down, and she can breathe again.

She glances toward the kitchen and sees the waitress talking to the busboy. They're both looking in her direction. She shifts in her seat, suddenly uncomfortable. The waitress says something to the busboy, then walks toward the back door, where the restrooms are, and disappears around the corner. Louise takes another sip of her Shirley Temple, tasting it this time, and *oooh*, it's good. Sweet and bubbly and yummy. She watches the drops of condensation trickle down the glass of her mom's drink and hopes her mom will hurry up because she knows that ice can make a drink not as tasty if it melts too much.

A moment later, the waitress comes out from the hallway and shakes her head at the busboy. Then another man walks over to them. He wears a collared shirt and a tie and a name tag, but Louise can't read it from where she is. The waitress whispers to the name-tag man, and they all—the waitress, the busboy and the name-tag man—look over at her. Her heart starts beating really big and hard in her chest. *It's the salsa*, she thinks, but underneath that thought is another. A bad thought. So bad that she refuses to think it.

Now the man with the name tag walks toward her table. She grabs a chip and shoves it into her mouth, without salsa and without guacamole. Just a big chip that tears at the roof of her mouth when she bites down on it. The man stands next to the table and Louise looks up at him. She can read his name tag now. It says *J-O-R-G-E*. She sounds it out. *Jorg, she thinks*. Funny name. But she doesn't laugh.

"Hello, *bonita*," he says. He sits down in the booth across from her, in her mother's place, and smiles without showing his teeth. He has a round face, a nice face. He doesn't give her the creeps, like some adult men do. But even though he seems okay, Louise is worried. She doesn't know why he's sitting here. She doesn't *want* to know why he's sitting here. She turns the kids' menu over to the blank side, picks up a crayon, and starts to draw.

"I am Jorge, the manager of this restaurant," he says.

Louise knows what a manager is. Her grandma was a manager of a gift shop.

"How did you get here, *niña*?" he asks.

She doesn't hesitate. "In our car."

"Is it parked out there?" He nods his head toward the back door.

She can feel eyes on her. Eyes from the other tables. She doesn't look around, but she notices that the talking and laughter from the big-family table has stopped.

She keeps drawing. "Yup."

"Do you know what it looks like?"

She chuckles a little bit, even though her heart is still thudding. Grown-ups can be funny. Of course she knows what her mom's car looks like.

"Yup," she tells him.

"Do you think you could point it out to me?" he asks. And suddenly, the tingle on her tongue turns into a burning sensation that goes all the way down to her belly. Because she knows what's going to happen. She stops drawing and sets the crayon down.

She shrugs. "I guess."

He nods, then slides out of the booth. He puts his hand out to her, and she stares at it for a few seconds. She picks up her Shirley Temple and takes a couple of big gulps off it, then reaches out and grasps the man's hand.

All the people at the big-family table are looking at her, and the mom and her teenagers across the room are too, and also the older man and woman. The men in the suits are in a heated conversation, maybe about basketball or something, and aren't paying attention to her at all, which she's glad about.

The manager starts to lead her away from the table, but glances down and sees her drawing.

"That's a nice picture, *niña*," he says. "Is that your *mamita* and you?"

Louise shakes her head. "Those are your daughters."

He gives her a strange look but doesn't question her. He escorts her past the tables, past the kitchen door, and past the bathrooms. Louise wants to break away from him and run into the ladies' room, just to make sure her mom's not there, but she knows that the waitress with the pretty pink flower already checked.

The sunlight is blinding, and she puts her hand up to shield her eyes from the fiery rays.

"Where is your car?" the man named Jorg asks.

She scans the parking lot. Her heart, which has been thudding painfully for the last five minutes, suddenly stops beating and falls into her stomach.

Her mom's car is gone.

FIVE

Louise

I'm not from New York. I'm from a place where the weather is better and the people are worse. Weather is what it is. But the people where I come from—La-La Land—they don't know who they are. I know who I am, which is why I hate those motherfuckers. Manhattanites know who they are—good, bad, and ugly included. I like that. Plus, no one here seems to give a damn about anyone else. I like that too.

I didn't have some grand plan to come here. It just happened. I needed to be someplace where I could lose myself, and there's probably no better place in the world to lose yourself than New York City. And Grace always ranted about how much she hated the Big Apple, that she wouldn't be caught dead here, that hell would freeze over before she'd come back. Since I never wanted to see her again, that pretty much cinched the deal for me.

But now she's here.

A light breeze caresses my face as I walk toward Lexington Avenue. My hair is still damp from my shower, but that's okay; I don't mind the air-dried look. I didn't bother putting on makeup or dressing nicely. Pretense is not required when visiting a mental hospital.

There's a Starbucks up ahead. I decide against stopping for a latte.

I loitered around my apartment, finding any excuse I could to put this off, but now that I'm on my way, I just want to get it over with. I don't know what Grace wants or what condition she's in. The hospital administrator was not forthcoming with details. I know I don't have to do this. She's not my responsibility. But there's no one else. My grandma's been gone for years now. And my dad—not sure why I call him that—was gone before I arrived on the scene. He only spent three months with her before he took off. I can't blame him. Three *minutes* with my mom is about my max.

I've tried to pretend she doesn't exist. That doesn't work. The more I push her out of my mind, the more she infects my thoughts. I can go years without seeing her face-to-face, but not a day goes by when I don't think about her. Understandable since she's the reason I am how I am.

I walk past a hole-in-the-wall Mexican joint, and the aroma of chimichangas and flautas wafts out to the street. My stomach clenches. I haven't eaten Mexican food since I was six, and for good reason. I should have crossed to the other side of the street.

As I head down First Avenue, the hospital looms large before me. Despite the warmth of the May day, a shiver courses through me. I hook a left on Twenty-Eighth and make my way to the emergency room entrance. I stop at the sliding glass doors and take a deep breath. My leg is throbbing, but I try to ignore it. The pain is only going to get worse so I might as well put up with what it is now. I pull at the straps on my backpack, tightening them. The sudden pressure on my shoulder blades serves to ground me.

Okay. Let's get this done. I step inside.

I've never been to Bellevue before. Although it's been here since the early 1700s, the interior looks just like any other big hospital emergency room. There's a waiting alcove where several people sit in vinyl chairs, and a reception area with a glass partition and a couple of bored-looking clerks. I keep my focus straight ahead, don't want to see the angst on the faces of the people waiting for help. When I reach the glass partition, one of the clerks, an older woman with silver hair and a dour expression, looks up at me.

"May I help you?" she asks.

"I got a call from Marjorie Lipman," I say. "My mother was brought in earlier today."

"Your mother's name?"

"Grace Daniels."

The woman gives a curt nod then types on her keyboard. She nods again, then jerks her head toward the waiting alcove. "Okay, just have a seat and someone will be with you shortly."

I back away from the glass partition until I reach the opposing wall. I should sit down, take the pressure off my leg, but I don't want to become a part of the miserable masses.

I glance at the security door that leads to the patient area and cross my arms over my chest. I try for a smile, but it doesn't take. "I'll wait here, if that's all right."

"Suit yourself."

Five minutes later, a woman with black-rimmed glasses and a tight bun pushes through the locked door next to me. She introduces herself as Dr. Lisa Markham and ushers me into the bowels of the Bellevue ER.

Compared to the sedate waiting and reception areas, this side of the security door is bedlam. Someone is shrieking, and someone is crying, and I'm pretty sure the guy we just passed, strapped to a gurney, is speaking in tongues. Hospital staff scurry to and fro, phones ring from the nurses' station, and a bevy of raised voices echoes through the halls. I try to focus on what the psychiatrist is saying, but the frenzied activity around us makes it difficult.

"Obviously, due to the circumstances in which she was brought in," she says, "we have to evaluate her mental capacity and competence and determine whether she is a danger to herself and/or others."

The only person she's a danger to is me.

I keep the thought to myself, mostly because Lisa Markham rubs me the wrong way. She's younger than me and a lot more accomplished, but there's also an underlying malice to her words. She doesn't like my mother. I don't like my mother either, but she's mine to dislike. This stranger has no right to judge her.

The psychiatrist stops at the door of a small room. The curtains are pulled back, and through the window, I see Grace. She's sitting on an exam table, and even though I shouldn't care, I'm glad she's not in restraints. Her lips are moving, but she's not talking to herself. Not now, anyway. She's singing. I can't tell what the lyrics are.

I think of the last time I saw her, and my hands clench into fists.

If I never see you again, Grace, that will be fine. You are the worst part of my life. It's time I cut you out of it.

Her hair is longer than it was then, still full and thick and wavy, but the dark strands are woven with large patches of silver. She looks older, and not just because of her hair. She looks weary and used. It's not my problem, but it makes me sad. Because I see myself in her.

Dr. Markham opens the door. I follow her inside.

SIX

Melanie

CALIFORNIA—PRESENT

Somebody's coming for you.

Those four words stare up at me. I kind of want to ignore them and go back to my Warriors book, but when this happens, I can't pretend it doesn't. This is a message from my friend. I could call her an *imaginary* friend, because no one can see her, not even me. But I don't imagine her. She's real.

Her name is Penny, and she lives in my left hand. She started coming to me when I was five. I was too young to really understand what was happening. I thought maybe I was psycho or schizo or had multiple personalities or something.

When I was old enough to go on the computer, I looked it up on Google. There's this thing called non-dominant handwriting, or intuitive handwriting, where you're supposed to discover stuff about yourself or get therapy or whatever by using your other hand. But no one said anything about an actual *other person* telling you stuff, so I'm pretty sure it's not that.

I don't know how it happens or why. But every so often, I get this tingly feeling. I get my journal and I put a pen in my left hand, and Penny talks to me. She tells me all kinds of things, like when Hamish

Murphy was out of school for two weeks, she told me he had mono, and sure enough he did. Or when Ms. Landers barfed all over the administration office, Penny told me she was pregnant, and about four months later, her stomach started to stick out a lot. Sometimes, she writes old-time lyrics, like "I've got you under my skin," or, "You and me, we're the kind of people that people would like to be," and I think I recognize those songs from when I was with my first parents, but I'm not exactly sure. Sometimes, Penny talks about the world and politics and stuff, things I don't really understand or care about. She gives me advice on how to be and how to get by. Which is really good, because being me is pretty hard.

I've been with Delilah and Ray for three years. Before them it was Ingrid and Tom and their three *real* kids who were total weenies and did mean things to me all the time. Like putting mud cakes in my backpack and bugs in my food and always, *always* telling me I wasn't *really* a member of the family but was just there so Ingrid and Tom could get money from the government.

Before Ingrid and Tom, it was Pam and Andy. And before Pam and Andy, it was my first adoptive parents, Gladys and John. I think I called them Mommy and Daddy. They named me Melanie. Melanie isn't the name on my birth certificate, but I don't let myself think about that because then I start thinking about my biological parents and why they gave me up. And I *really* don't want to think about *that*. But Gladys and John are the first memory I have of a family. And I was with them until I was five. They were killed in a really bad car accident, and because they didn't have any relatives that could take me, I went into the foster care system. That's when Penny first showed up.

I stare down at my journal.

Somebody's coming for you.

I put the pen in my left hand. "Who's coming, Penny?" I ask, then close my eyes. But nothing happens. I wait a few minutes, but my left hand stays still.

Penny's like that. Here one minute, gone the next.

Footsteps sound in the hallway and I quickly tuck my journal under my pillow and grab for my Warriors book. I know better than to let anyone find out about Penny. She's the reason Pam and Andy sent me away, and Ingrid and Tom, too, and even though I didn't like Ingrid and Tom's real kids much, I really liked Ingrid's cooking. She made the best spaghetti ever.

I find my place in Warriors just as Delilah appears at the door to my room. She leans against the doorjamb and gives me a tired smile.

"How's the book?" she asks.

"Good. How're the brownies?" She frowns, and I know what that means. The brownies are in the trash. "Bummer."

"I'll get it right one of these days," she says. I don't respond. "It was my mom's recipe. She taught me how to make them. I used to make them perfect. It's how I caught Ray. Quickest way to a man's heart and all that."

She's said this exact same thing a ton of times before. I wonder if she realizes it and doesn't care, or if she's getting that brain disease that eats your memory. Delilah's a little young for it, but you never know.

"Anyhow, I might invite Lori and Audrey over this evening for a little girls' time."

"Can I do all your nails?" Sometimes Delilah lets me paint her fingers and toes when she needs a lift. I'm not as good as the manicurist at Eileen's, but I'm not bad.

"Not tonight," she tells me. "I was thinking I could set up the TV tray and you could have a movie dinner in my bedroom. Double feature even."

Ah. Delilah wants me out of the way so she and her friends can smoke pot. She doesn't think I know, but God, I'm twelve. Not six. I even know some kids at my school who smoke pot. I would never, and not because I'm a Goody Two-shoes, but because I think it would be stupid. My brain works funny without adding a drug to it. And if I got caught, I'd probably get sent away from here. Delilah and Ray are not perfect, not by a long shot. I could make a list of all the ways they're not perfect, starting with the whole weird Delilah brownie thing and ending with the way Ray hogs the bathroom every morning, reading his favorite blogs while he poops, knowing I'm standing on the other side of the door trying to keep my bladder from bursting.

But they treat me okay. Nobody says anything mean to me, nobody hits me. I don't think either of them really loves me the way a kid wants to be loved, but they don't hate me, and I think I mean a little bit more to them than the checks from the government.

"What do you think?" Delilah asks. "Does that sound good? Double feature in the big bed?"

"What about Ray?"

She bites her lip. "He's going out after work with his buddies."

Ray's been going out a lot lately. I get the feeling Delilah thinks if she'd just made a proper pan of brownies, Ray would come home, like her baking has some voodoo hocus pocus kind of magic in it. Which is totally ridiculous. And I know that sounds funny coming from a girl who has a person living in her left hand, but brownies are just brownies.

"Can I watch *Hunger Games* and *Catching Fire*?" My friends at school . . . Okay, they're not my friends. I don't have any real friends besides Penny. But these two girls, Kim Casey and Jenny Frank, they let me sit with them at lunch and then pretty much ignore me, which is just fine by me. I overheard them talking about these movies and saying how awesome they were. I haven't read the books yet. They're always checked out of the library.

"Can we get 'em free?" she asks, and I nod. "Well, I guess that's all right."

I could have asked for *The Texas Chainsaw Massacre* and she would have agreed. When Delilah wants to smoke up, she'll let me watch anything. She squints at me then walks over to my bed. She runs a hand through my hair and wrinkles her nose. "When was the last time you took a shower?" she asks. I shrug, and she chuckles. "That means it's been too long. Shower before movie dinner, okay?"

I roll my eyes, but then nod. I'm not crazy about taking showers. My hair is long and really thick, and it takes like a ton of conditioner so I can get the brush through it. But the longer I leave it, the worse it gets.

Delilah pats my head, then walks back to the doorway. She turns to me. "I'll make your favorite. Mac and cheese and hot dogs?"

"Thanks, D." Dinner of champions.

"But, Melanie. Make sure you don't interrupt us ladies, okay? We're going to be talking about grown-up stuff."

I keep from rolling my eyes again. "No worries, Delilah. I won't bother you one bit."

SEVEN

Grace

NEW YORK—PRESENT

There she is. My Louise. My baby girl. She's not a baby anymore, no. She's thirty-three, and weary ten years north of that. But I'll always think of her as my baby girl. It's a mom thing. I haven't been a great mom to her, not even a good one. But feelings are what they are. I remember the day she was born like it was yesterday, holding her in my arms and singing to her, and feeding her at my breast. And how she looked up at me with her wide blue eyes, really looked at me, not like most newborns who can't focus on anything. And her steadfast stare extracted a promise from me to be true and faithful and to always be there for her, like a mom's supposed to be. I've broken that promise more times than I can count.

She follows the shrink into the room and stops just beyond the door. Her expression is stony. She's probably thinking about the last time we saw each other. I feel bad about that meeting, and she likely does too, but there's nothing we can do about it now. Onward and upward, right?

"Grace," she says.

"I always preferred *Mom*," I tell her, and she winces. "But Grace is fine . . ."

Strained silence. Our usual.

Something buzzes from the shrink's pocket. She pulls out a cell phone and gazes at the screen, then clears her throat.

"I have an intake." The shrink turns to Lou. "Are you comfortable being alone with your mother?"

"Yes," she says, even though I know she's not. Louise has never been comfortable with me, alone or in a crowd.

The shrink nods and heads for the door, stops and gestures to a button on the wall under the window. *Panic button.*

"If you need anything, just push this. I'll be back in about fifteen minutes and we can discuss the next step."

"What does that mean?" Louise asks. "The next step?"

The shrink stifles a shrug, glances at her phone. "We'll talk."

Louise nods, not happily, and watches the woman leave. Turns back to me and frowns.

"I didn't know you were in New York," she says. "I thought you hated the Big Apple."

"Oh, I do."

She takes a step toward me. Stops. "Then why are you here? And what were you doing on the George Washington Bridge in your underwear? What the hell, Grace?"

I suppress the urge to stand up and rush at her and throw my arms around her. She wouldn't be open to my ministrations. She would reject them. So I hold myself still on the exam table, with the long, wide strip of parchment paper under my hind parts. They gave me a gown, but it doesn't wrap far enough around to cover my boyshorts. They took my bra, although I'm not sure why. Maybe it interfered with the stethoscope, or maybe it was so stretched out it had no place being called a bra anymore. Don't know, don't care. My tatas don't mind swinging free.

"I came here for you."

She glares at me. "How did you know where I am?"

"Facebook," I tell her, and her lips curl into a sneer.

"I'm not on Facebook."

I shrug. "Neither am I. How are you doing, Louise?" I ask, and she shakes her head.

"Don't change the subject."

"I'm not, missy. Is it a crime for a mother to ask after her daughter?"

She rubs at her eyes and shakes her head at the same time, then drops her hands to her sides and looks at me. "Okay, I have to be at work at six, so I can't stay much longer. I came to see if you're all right. You are. Now I'm going to go."

She unhoists her backpack, then yanks it open and rummages through it. A moment later she tosses two pieces of clothing at me; a pair of gray sweats and a black T-shirt. I grab them midair, set the sweats on the exam table and shake out the T-shirt. The legend Nirvana, with the stupid smiley face and X'd-out eyes, glares at me. I look at Louise.

"You know I hate Nirvana."

She gives me a mean grin. "Yeah, well, it's all I had clean."

We stare at each other for a long moment.

"Let Dr. Markham know I left," she says.

"Who?"

"Dr. Markham? The psychiatrist? The one who was just in here?"

"Oh, her." I nod. "I don't like her at all. Bad one, that girl."

Louise looks at me, pretends to be disinterested, but I can tell she's got a bad vibe about the shrink too.

Another round of silence. Louise pulls her cell phone out of her backpack. God, I hate those things. I have one, of course, but I feel like they are the downfall of mankind.

"I gotta go," my daughter says. She turns away and takes two steps toward the door.

"Wait!" I call to her. "Don't go. I need to tell you."

Impatience oozes from her pores. "What, Grace? What do you need to tell me?"

I try for a conciliatory smile, one that spreads my lips far and wide and exposes my veneers.

"Close your mouth," she says. "You look like a ghoul."

"That's a fine way to talk to your mother."

"What, Grace?" she presses. "What do you need to tell me?"

I don't smile this time, just keep my expression neutral. "I found her," I say. "I found Edie."

I watch as the color drains from my daughter's face. "Don't call her that," she snaps. "That's not her name. It never was."

"Doesn't matter, Lou. What matters is, I found her. And she needs us."

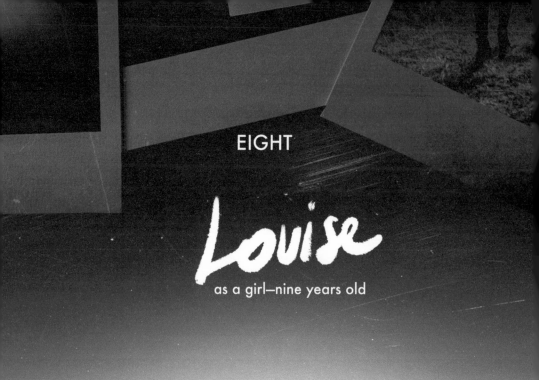

EIGHT

Louise

as a girl—nine years old

"Your mom's really old," Clancy Ludloff says.

Louise glances over at the bleachers, then shakes her head. "That's my grandma."

Clancy peers at her. "Where's your mom?"

She shrugs. Clancy's mom sits a couple of rows down from Louise's grandma, talking to some other parents. The fourth-grade Student-Teacher-Parent Picnic is underway, and the fourth graders are gearing up for an epic soccer battle.

"She's not here?" Clancy asks, and Louise shakes her head. "What about your dad?"

"I don't have a dad."

"Everybody has a dad," he says.

"I mean, I have a dad, but I've never met him."

Clancy gives her a look like he has no idea what she's talking about. *Of course, he doesn't*, she thinks. His dad stands on the side of the field with a bunch of other dads, cheering for the fourth-grade soccer team and talking about work.

"That's weird," Clancy says.

Yeah, well, welcome to my family.

The principal of the school and the vice principal and office manager are the refs for the game. Louise hears a whistle and she and her five teammates take the field. She is good at soccer. It appeals to her need to be present in the moment and not think about anything but the ball. She likes having something to focus on other than her absent mother and her father who is a ghost, not because he's dead, but because the void he creates looms large in her life.

And also, Louise runs like the wind.

The fourth-grade teachers stand on the other half of the field. Louise thinks it's funny to see them all in sneakers and sportswear, high-fiving each other and stretching and jogging in place, like this is the most important game in the world. But then, for the students, it kind of is. If the fourth graders win, they get out of homework for the rest of the year, and they all totally want that prize.

Ms. Blank is coaching the fourth graders. She's a fifth-grade teacher, and Louise hopes she gets her next year, because according to some very reliable sources, Ms. Blank gives out candy every Friday to everyone who gets an A on the vocab test. Louise has gotten 100 percent on all the vocab tests this year.

Ms. Blank calls Louise and Clancy to the middle of the field where her homeroom teacher, Mr. Johnson, is standing. She leans over.

"Okay, which one of you is going to get that ball?"

"I will!" Clancy shouts. Louise looks over at Mr. Johnson. He smiles at her and gives her a thumbs-up.

"I like your enthusiasm, Clancy," Ms. Blank says.

"He can do it," Louise says, nodding toward her teammate. She doesn't want to fight Mr. Johnson for the ball. She's done the opening scrimmage on her after-school team, and she knows how rough it can get trying to take control of the ball. Sometimes players get all tangled up with each other fighting for it. She likes Mr. Johnson. He tells funny stories and does weekly movie reviews that make her laugh. But she doesn't want to fight him for the ball. That would be too awkward.

"Okay," Ms. Blank says. She leads Clancy to the scrimmage and gestures for Louise to stand on his left side, at the ready. She calls the other fourth graders onto the field and sets them in their places, then jogs to the sidelines and nods to the principal. The principal blows his whistle as he drops the soccer ball between Clancy and Mr. Johnson. Clancy makes a mad dash for the ball and manages to kick it to Louise.

She gets her foot on it and presses forward, pushing it back and forth between her feet as she weaves through the fourth-grade teachers. Her movements are fluid. She seems to have a preternatural intuition about which way the staff opponents will go and dodges them with ease, falling into a rhythm.

She runs, picking up speed with each footfall. As she approaches the goal, where Mrs. Polk plays goalie for the teachers, she hears a loud voice cut through the air.

"That's my girl! Yes indeed, that's my baby! You go, Louise!"

She knows who that voice belongs to. And although she does her best to ignore it, she falters. Her cleat snags in the grass and she trips, losing her rhythm. She tries to right herself, to zero in on the goal.

"Go, baby, go!" her mother shrieks.

She pulls her foot back and swings it forward, but even before she makes contact, she knows the shot will go wide. The ball sails far left of the goal box. Louise stops and watches it roll out of bounds, then turns and scans the bleachers.

And there she is. Her mother, Grace, whom Louise hasn't seen for almost a week, standing next to her grandmother. Her grandma looks pained, but Grace looks gleeful. Louise notices the other parents staring at her mother and whispering to each other with mean expressions on their faces.

"That's okay, missy!" her mother shouts, unfazed by the other parents' scrutiny. "You'll get it next time! Goal, goal, goal!"

Louise looks down at her cleats, ducking her head to keep Mrs. Polk and Clancy from seeing her tears. She swipes at her cheeks, then stands up straight and marches off the field, past the bleachers, past her grandmother and her mother and the rest of the parents, straight to the girls' restroom. She stays there for the rest of the game.

NINE

Louise

NEW YORK—PRESENT

"Why are you doing this?" My hands are clenched into fists again and I force my fingers to relax.

"Lou, just listen to me—"

"No." I shake my head. "I don't want to hear it."

"She needs us."

"Stop."

The door opens, and Lisa Markham pokes her head in. "Everything okay?"

A harsh breath escapes me. Everything is *not* okay.

"Perhaps you'd like to step out for a moment, so we can talk."

I glare at Grace, then turn and walk from the room.

"The choice is yours," the psychiatrist tells me. "But it's my opinion that your mother would benefit from further observation."

"Seventy-two-hour psych hold, right?" We stand outside Grace's room. The curtains are still open, and through the window, I see my mother plucking distastefully at the Nirvana tee. Somewhere down the corridor, the shrieking woman continues with her regular outbursts. I'm surprised she hasn't gone hoarse.

"For a start," the therapist says. She glances through the glass and narrows her eyes at my mother. "Extended care is also a possibility."

Commitment. I don't say the word out loud. It wouldn't be the first time my mother was committed. Might not be the last. But something about how Dr. Markham looks at Grace makes me uneasy. I don't trust her as far as I can throw her. She has plans for Grace. I can see her brain working, and I can tell those plans might not be in her patient's best interests.

Not my problem, I remind myself, then check the time on my phone. "I have to go."

The psychiatrist nods. "If you'll just come with me, I have some papers for you to sign. Won't take long."

As I follow her down the hall, the screeching woman releases a bloodcurdling wail that echoes through my head and causes gooseflesh to erupt over my entire body. I'm suddenly sick to my stomach.

Grace needs help. Obviously, after the GWB and this nonsense about Edie. But maybe not the kind of help Dr. Markham will provide.

"Wait."

Markham turns and looks at me impatiently.

"Yes?"

"I'll take her with me," I hear myself say, and can't believe what I said.

The psychiatrist scowls. "Do you really think that's a good idea?"

No, I think it's a bad *idea. I think it might be the* worst *idea I've ever had.*

"Your mother is unwell," Markham says, arching a brow. "I highly doubt you have the tools to deal with her."

Of course I don't. But god damn it, her condescension pisses me off. I shrug. "I have duct tape. You know, for emergencies."

The psychiatrist is not amused. She crosses her arms over her chest. "I suspect you will regret this decision before too long."

Unfortunately, Dr. Markham is right. It only takes about seven minutes for me to want to haul my mother back to Bellevue, shove her in a padded room, and throw away the key.

As we make our way to the West Side, Grace points out all the reasons she hates New York, loudly.

"Too many people," she says. "Too many buildings," she says. "Too much traffic," she says. "It's just too much."

At the corner of Ninth and West Forty-Fifth, she stops dead in her tracks, puts her hands over her ears, and squeezes her eyes shut. Just stands there as passersby weave around her. This is Manhattan, so no one takes any notice of her. Not like when I was a kid in suburbia and Grace's particular brand of crazy stood out. Here, everyone is a little bit off their rocker, so Grace is just another fish in the sea of marine life that thinks to themselves, "Oh yeah, you're nuts? Me too."

I have no trouble shelving my empathy. I've been caught in the empathy trap too many times over the course of my relationship with this woman. But watching her as she desperately tries to disconnect with all the unwanted stimuli around her is unsettling. I walk over to her and place my palm on her forearm.

"We're almost there, Grace," I tell her. "Just a few more blocks."

She opens her eyes and locks her gaze onto mine. I don't smile. She hasn't earned that from me. But I need to get her to my apartment, so I force a welcoming expression. Not a smile. Just a calm look that says *it's going to be okay*. She takes it and responds with a nod.

We reach my apartment without incident, but as we climb the stairs to the second floor, my heart starts hammering in my chest. I've done everything I can to remove myself from this woman's orbit, yet here she is, infiltrating my life. And I'm allowing the infiltration. *Inviting* it. Maybe *I* should be committed.

Grace pauses just before we reach the second-floor landing. She presses her hand against her chest and takes a few gulps of air.

"You're not going to have a heart attack, are you?" My question comes out meaner than I intended. But Grace grins.

"If I didn't drop dead from putting this Nirvana T-shirt on, I'm not going to do it now."

Reflexive laughter threatens, but I stifle it. I lead her into the apartment. She looks around, keeps her expression neutral.

"It's smallish," she says. "And it could use some art on the walls. Lithographs, maybe, or a couple of landscapes. Brighten it up a bit."

"Yeah, well, I'm not much into art."

She narrows her eyes at me, a challenge. "Is that so?"

I don't take the bait. She drops the subject and continues to inspect my apartment. She notices the ashtray, which I failed to empty before I left, and wrinkles her nose. Before she can comment, I change the subject. "You've stopped coloring your hair."

She runs a hand through her shoulder-length locks. "I'm going for the Anne Bancroft look. What do you think?"

I consider how to answer. Decide not to. Instead, I pull my cell phone out of my pocket and glance at the time. "I have to go to work."

She nods. "I'll be okay."

I'm not comfortable leaving her alone, but I don't have a choice. My boss is a former one-night stand who regarded my blow job as one of the highlights of his life and declared his undying love for me post-ejaculation. Because I don't want to spend the rest of my days pleasuring him orally, he's tried to make my life at the bar a living hell, coming down on me for any and every mistake I make. I can't abandon him on a Friday night in May, when all the alcoholics in the city are gearing up for summer. I need my job.

But my mother is in my apartment. My *crazy* mother. She'll be unattended. On the heels of a brief stint at Bellevue and an appearance on the George Washington Bridge in her underwear.

"I can't call in sick," I say. "My boss has a small dick and a big temper. I'll get fired."

"Louise," she says. She lays her fanny pack down on my minuscule kitchen table. "I will be fine. I promise. Just give me another T-shirt, unless you want me to tear this one to shreds. And point me in the direction of your take-out menus. I'm about starved. Those Bellevue bastards don't feed their patients for crap."

I stand, unmoving. Because, as with Lisa Markham, I don't trust my mother as far as I can throw her.

"Louise," she says again. She catches my gaze and holds it. I can't look away. "I won't leave. I won't do anything to upset you. I'll be here when you get back from work."

I believe her. I *have* to believe her. What else can I do?

I walk to the radiator and grab an oversized tee, one I use as a nightshirt on occasion. I've had it for as long as I can remember, and it's practically worn through in places. I keep meaning to get rid of it, but somehow never do. Maybe because it's the only thing I have that belonged to my biological father. Other than half my DNA.

It smells fairly clean. I toss it to Grace. She shakes it out and looks at the front, at the legend Pearl Jam, then smiles.

"I can't believe you still have this."

"The take-out menus are in the drawer next to the fridge."

She nods. "When do you think you'll be home?"

"On a Friday night?" I muse. "Probably one or two."

"Okay. I'll be up. And we can talk about E—uh, we can talk."

I don't respond. She smiles at me, and her smile is full of knowing.

"You might want to tell that small-penised boss of yours that you're going to need some time off."

TEN

Melanie

CALIFORNIA—PRESENT

I wrap my hair in a towel and pull the belt of the bathrobe tight around me, then tiptoe into Delilah and Ray's bedroom. I hear giggles from the living room. Delilah and her friends have started smoking already.

My dinner waits for me in the master bedroom. There's a plate sitting on the TV tray in front of the bed with a heap of macaroni and cheese and a couple of hot dogs. I move closer and see that the cheese sauce is clumpy, like Delilah didn't stir it very well. But I'm going to eat it anyway. It'll still taste good.

There's nothing green on the plate. Delilah's not big on veggies because Ray doesn't believe in them. That's what he says. "I don't believe all this bullcrap about vegetables being healthy. My grandpa lived to a hundred and two and never ate a freaking brussels sprout in his life." I do believe in veggies because we had a whole unit in health class on them and all the good things they do for your body. So when I get to buy lunch at school, which is every Friday, I make sure to have salad or carrot sticks or whatever they have. I don't tell Delilah or Ray. Just one more secret I keep from them.

Luckily, Delilah believes in hydration and has placed a bottle of water on the tray next to my dinner.

I brought my pajamas in here before I got into the shower, laid them out nice and neat on the bed. I have two sets of pj's Delilah got for me, one with long pants and long sleeves, covered with rabbits. And these ones, fuzzy lavender shorts that almost reach my knees, and a lavender tank top with big soccer balls on it. I don't play soccer, never have, and I don't really like rabbits, but I'm not complaining. Anyway, these are super comfy. I've worn them so much, they kind of melt against my skin.

I take my bathrobe off, but before I put the pajamas on, I stop and look in the full-length mirror on the back of the bedroom door.

Delilah spends a lot of time looking in this mirror, and when I catch her doing it, I can tell she doesn't like what she sees. She frowns a lot, and poses, and tries to suck in her stomach, and sometimes, she pulls at her cheeks. I don't understand why, because Delilah is totally beautiful. She came to the school a couple months back when I was getting an award, and this boy, Randall Pierce, told his friend Brian Moore that she was a MILF. I had to google what that meant, and even though I'm not comfortable with the wording, I have to agree with Randall. Delilah is hot.

I stare at my reflection for a few minutes. I'm not totally hot. More like average, which is okay with me. I don't envy the really pretty girls at school because I don't think they know what to do with their prettiness. Maybe someday I'll be beautiful. Maybe not. But if I am, maybe by then, I'll know what to do with it.

I'm twelve. I haven't gotten my period yet, but I have a feeling I'm going to get it real soon. A couple of the girls at school have gotten theirs and they complain about it. I overhear them talking about maxi pads and tampons and what a total pain it is to have to worry about what you wear and bleeding through your clothes. I don't think about it too much—it'll happen when it's supposed to. But I have noticed that my body is changing. I was kind of chubby when I was younger, but my legs have gotten longer, and my belly has gotten smaller, and my . . . well, my boobs . . . I see them now. Before, they were just two stupid nipples on my chest that just sat there. But now, there's a kind of fullness underneath the nipples. I have a little hair *down there*, but none under my arms yet.

I don't have any feelings around these changes. I understand that this is growing up. It would be cool to be able to talk to someone about it, but Delilah is not a "talking about things" kind of person. At check-ins, my caseworker, Pearl, always asks if I want to talk "girl stuff" with her, but, *yuck*.

A full belly laugh sounds from the living room, and that gets me moving. I grab my pj's and hurry into them, then scoot behind the TV tray at the end of the bed. I grab the remote next to the plate and turn on the TV. We don't have cable—that's another thing Ray doesn't believe in. What he does believe in is this little box that he got from a friend that gets all the movies and shows for free. I'm pretty sure it's illegal, but I don't think the police will come after us. Too many other bad things keeping them busy. That's what Ray says, anyway. I turn on the box and search for *Hunger Games*.

I stretch out dinner for as long as I can, savoring every bite of the clumpy macaroni and cheese, and timing my bites of hot dog. I know I won't get dessert tonight. I'm kind of banished. I learned that word in fifth grade, and it stuck with me, maybe because it's happened to me so many times in my life.

I don't need anything sweet, but even if I did, I don't dare go to the kitchen to get something. Delilah would freak. But that's okay. I like my stomach being a little smaller.

When I finish everything on my plate, I pause *Hunger Games* and follow Delilah's instructions. I put the empty plate on the dresser, take the water bottle and set it on the nightstand, then fold up the TV tray and lean it against the wall next to the closet. I take the remote and climb onto the bed and scootch up to the headboard. I puff up the pillows behind my back, then push my feet under the covers and get nice and comfy. I'm almost at the good part of the movie, so I'm sort of glad about this whole being-banished thing. If I were Cinderella, locked in the cellar with nothing to eat and no pillows and knowing that she was never going to see her true love because of her evil stepmom, that would suck big time. But I don't have a true love, and we don't have a cellar because of earthquakes, and my stomach is comfortably full.

Just as I press play on the remote, the bedroom door opens and Ray walks in.

ELEVEN

Grace

NEW YORK—PRESENT

Louise didn't want to bring me here. I know that. And I can't blame her. But I'm awfully glad she did. Because it shows that even after everything we've been through—or, more specifically, everything I've put her through—she still cares about me. Enough to take me away from Bellevue and that shrink.

It's not difficult to keep my promise to Louise. I wouldn't step outside this apartment without her. Some folks think New York is the greatest city in the world, and that might be true for them. But for me, it's hell with a capital *H*. Like I said on the street, NYC's just got too much of *everything*. And all that *everything* pounds on my brain, trying to get in. Hurts like a son of a gun.

I know of people who fashion hats out of aluminum foil and place them on their heads to keep outside stuff from sneaking in. Alien communications, other people's thoughts and emotions, entreaties from malevolent spirits. Works for those people, too. I envy them. Because a tinfoil hat won't help me. And don't think I haven't tried it. I've tried a host of things. Valium, lithium, Prozac, Lexapro, Haldol, Risperdal, not to mention some treatments I've been subjected to over the course of my life, electric shock among them. *That* had about as much effect as the goldarn tinfoil hat.

Anyway, my point is, I won't go outside without Lou, not even if the building catches on fire.

The window's open, which is good because the lingering stink of cigarettes might otherwise be overwhelming. I didn't say anything about her overflowing ashtray. Choose your battles, and all that. But at some point, I'll have to butt in on that subject, no pun intended.

I sit at her poor excuse for a kitchen table and sort through the menus from the various local eateries. My choices are practically unlimited. I can get Greek, Indian, Italian, Ethiopian, Chinese, Japanese, or good old American fare. I set aside the Japanese menu—I don't go for that raw fish crap. Mercury is a killer. I scan the pink Chinese trifold. I used to love moo goo gai pan, but I don't think I have the stomach for it. Greek reminds me of Louise's dad—the few months I spent with him were filled with gyros and souvlaki and enough tzatziki to kill a horse—so I toss that menu on top of the Japanese one.

Pizza or a burger. That's where I'm heading. If I get a pizza, there'll be some left for Louise when she gets home. Food to sustain her for the conversation we need to have. Good choice.

I look around the apartment and realize that Louise doesn't have a landline.

I unzip my fanny pack and pull out my little red flip phone. It's not one of those newfangled smartphones. It doesn't get Wi-Fi, or Google, or radio signals from other planets. I could text with it, if I were to be very patient, but texting isn't something this old girl will ever do, thank you very much. I dial up the restaurant and order a large sausage and pepperoni pizza and a Caesar salad, and the girl on the other end tells me I'll have my food in forty-five minutes or less.

I stand and walk around the small apartment. Louise's laptop sits on top of a TV tray next to the bed. I run a finger across the touch pad and the screen comes to life. The screensaver is a picture of my mother and Louise when Lou was a girl. Louise is wearing a purple-and-black jersey and black shorts, her hair tied back in a purple ribbon. She holds a soccer ball in her hands and sports a close-lipped smile.

My heart squeezes in my chest. The photo was taken at a soccer match. I missed that entire season. I know I did because I have no memory of that particular uniform. I remember a black-and-white uniform—that season, the team named themselves the Killer Whales. And I remember a horrid neon-yellow uniform that defied naming. In the end, they called themselves the Predators, although I saw that movie and the monster was definitely not neon yellow.

I push these thoughts out of my head and sit on the twin bed, then gaze at the icons on the computer screen—the folders and apps that populate Louise's desktop. I could check her history, delve into her life, get to know what she's been up to for the past few years. I know how to do it thanks to a roommate I had a few years back at the hospital. Caroline Quinn. She told me that browser history is somewhat of a tell-all about a person. I didn't know what that was back then, but I do now. Caroline had discerned from her husband's browser history that he'd been cheating on her with someone called Dark Mistress, and also that he had a goat fetish. She killed him in his sleep, claimed she didn't remember doing it, and got an insanity pass. She wasn't insane, knew exactly what she was doing when she stabbed him in the chest and sliced off his ding-dong. I tried not to judge and learned a whole heck of a lot more about accessing browser history than I ever cared to. And even though I'd really like to find out more about my daughter, I don't want to be disrespectful of her privacy. I wait for the screen to go dark, then cross to the couch.

The coffee table is littered with take-out containers, gum wrappers, a couple of flyers, and that ashtray overflowing with butts. Two different kinds of cigarettes. Louise has had a recent visitor.

I can't stand the smell. And I can't stand the mess. I reach for the ashtray with two fingers, trying to touch it as little as possible, and carry it into the kitchen. I find the garbage can under the sink and dump the foul butts. The ashtray looks as though it hasn't been cleaned since the manufacturer sent it to the store. I set it in the sink and fill it with water, then look around at the kitchen. A decade's worth of dust films the counters. But this is New York, so it's probably only a few months' worth. I tear a wad of paper towels from the roll above the sink and set to work.

This is not spying on a browser history. Surely, cleaning up after one's own daughter is not an invasion of privacy. Louise might see it that way, but I can't help myself. If I don't eradicate the mess of this place, I'll need more than a tinfoil hat. I'll need a hazmat suit.

I begin to wipe the counters.

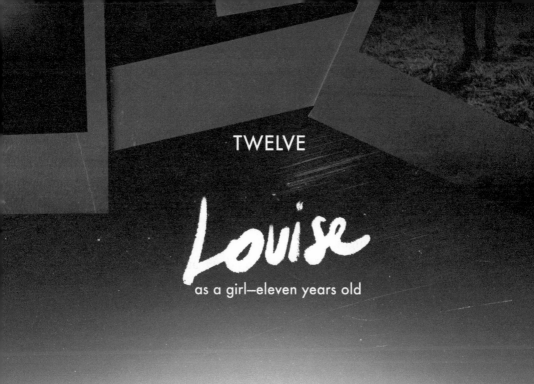

TWELVE

Louise

as a girl—eleven years old

Louise sits on the bench outside the cafeteria, her lunch sack next to her, as yet unopened. She doesn't know what her grandmother made for lunch today, but it will be a sandwich of some kind. Maybe turkey or tuna. But she isn't really hungry. She's trying to finish her sketch and can't think about food until she gets it done.

The playground is alive with the fourth and fifth graders playing foursquare, handball, basketball. A crowd of girls is jumping rope. A group of boys uses a game of football as an excuse to wrestle each other.

Louise blocks out the commotion around her. When she draws, her focus is so intense the rest of the world falls away, no longer exists, the only reality is that which she renders on the page. She doesn't notice the curious looks some of the other fifth graders give her as they pass by.

She's been working on this sketch for a couple of days, in the sketchbook her mom got for her. She's trying to draw a puppy. Louise wants a puppy more than anything else in the world, and she knows she will never *ever* get one. She's not old enough to take care of a dog, and her grandma is *too* old to take care of one, and her mom, although the perfect age, is gone too much to make that kind of commitment.

But, oh, she thinks, wouldn't it be wonderful to have a warm body to curl up with in the dark hours of night, when the thoughts come barreling into her brain, and the feelings overtake her, emotions she's not mature enough to understand, but that doesn't stop them from wrapping themselves around her.

A dog might protect her from these thoughts and feelings, and even if he couldn't, or *she*—Louise doesn't care about gender—the presence of another being, a loving, loyal, warm-hearted soul, might help her sleep through the night.

She bites her bottom lip as she stares down at the sketchbook. The puppy isn't right. The arms holding it are. They look like her own. But the dog is all wrong, perhaps because she doesn't know what kind of dog she wants, or maybe because she doesn't care what kind of dog she gets. Or maybe because she's a crappy artist. That's probably it.

She uses the eraser on the end of her pencil to make the snout, face, and ears of the puppy disappear.

"What'cha doing?" She looks up to see Parker McGovern standing over her.

"Drawing," she says. *Like, duh.*

"Let me see," the boy says, and Louise shakes her head. She knows that Parker is one of the popular kids, but he's also a little mean. No matter how good her sketch is, Parker will make fun of it.

"Come on! Let me." He reaches for the sketchbook and Louise smacks his hand with the spiral wire coil. The boy yanks his hand away and glares down at her.

"Ouch! Are you crazy?" His lips curl into a sneer. "I hear your mom is. Crazy, I mean. I hear she's totally bonkers and, like, lives on the street half the time like a homeless person."

Louise swallows hard as tears threaten. She pushes herself to her feet and tries to walk away, but Parker steps closer, boxing her against the bench. A couple of his friends have gathered around them, backup for the bully. They listen and chortle in agreement.

"You do know crazy runs in families," Parker says, his voice loud in Louise's ear. "That means you're bonkers too!"

She grasps her sketchbook so tightly her fingers ache. "Leave me alone," she whispers.

"Why? You gonna go all wacko on me?" He turns to his cohorts. "Oooh, I'm scared."

The boys laugh. Before Parker can turn back to her, she sidesteps away from him, then hurries across the playground toward her homeroom.

"Where you going, wacko?" he calls to her. "Hey! You forgot your lunch! Wackos need to eat, too."

She glances back just in time to see Parker McGovern drop her lunch sack to the ground and stomp on it with his sneaker while the kids around him cheer.

THIRTEEN

Louise

Work is a major suck-fest, from beginning to end.

I work at Zelda's, a bar and grill on the Upper West Side. Patrons at my place can rest assured that the booze isn't watered down and the food is uncompromised. In any big city, both assurances are hard to come by, which is why we're slammed almost every night. Most especially, Fridays and Saturdays.

My boss, Ewan, is on a rampage. I don't waste much time or energy revisiting our brief sexual interlude, but tonight, it seems like maybe the orgasm I gave him was the last one he's had. His otherwise handsome face is pinched in a constant scowl, and he's lambasting the servers every five seconds for things that aren't their fault, like how slow the kitchen is putting out the grub. I suspect the cooks are on downers, everything comes out ten minutes after it should, but Ewan blames the servers.

I hide behind my bar, trying to make margaritas and Alabama Slammers and Slippery Nipple shots and avoid my boss's gaze. Because every time our eyes meet, he shakes his head with regret, and I'm afraid he's going to burst into tears. He doesn't. Instead, he yells at someone who doesn't deserve it.

Ewan is not a bad guy. He's actually pretty cool. He's good-looking and really smart about money, and he's funny in an off-beat kind of way. It's not his fault that I don't want to let him sweep me off my feet and take me away from all this. It's my fault. Because no one can sweep me off my feet. My feet are made of concrete.

I've wanted to tell him this, give him the whole "It's not you, it's me" speech. But he doesn't let me. I've tried. Just last week, at the end of my shift when he was cashing out my register and I was restocking the bar, I said to him, "I really want to talk to you."

And he calmly replied, as he counted out twenties, "Based on my experience, your mouth does much better things than talk."

See? Funny. *Inappropriate*, but funny.

Tonight, we need to have a conversation. Not about our failed attempt at the happily-ever-after, or my unmatched skills at oral. But about the fact that I have to take some time off. Ewan is not going to like that. I'm thirty-three years old, and the bags under my eyes probably look like I lost a fight with a heavyweight champ, and I have a noticeable limp. But my ass is that of a nubile twenty-year-old, and most of our male customers, and a few of our female customers, look forward to seeing this denim-clad offering Wednesdays through Sundays, week after week, month after month. My spectacular talent at mixology and unparalleled cocktails are merely the icing on the cake. My ass is the cake itself.

But I'm going to have to deal with Grace and I can't do that if I'm working. I've already started formulating a plan, and I'm anxious to put it in motion. The sooner I do, the sooner she's out of my life. Hopefully for good this time.

I can't seem to lose myself in the ritual drink making and food service that makes up my duties. My thoughts are elsewhere. I can't stop thinking about the fact that Grace is in my apartment. The idea is completely inconceivable. At this very moment, she could be rifling through my closet, my kitchen, my computer. Not that there's much to find. I live a Spartan life. Minimalist. I don't overindulge on clothes and I don't peruse porn websites. So if she wants to uncover my secrets, she'll be disappointed. The secrets I keep can't be found in my apartment.

But I have a feeling she won't dig. If I had to wager, taking into consideration her OCD and my housekeeping skills, I'd bet money on the fact that she's cleaning. I have no problem with that. Cleaning ladies are expensive.

Mac Riley, one of my newer regulars, sits at the far end of the bar next to the servers' station. He likes to interact with the young servers, but not in a creepy way. Mac is older and gets a lift from eavesdropping on their naive drama. Unrequited love, money problems, and career woes are music to the ears of a man who has survived quadruple bypass, widowerhood, and a son on death row. He listens to the servers complain about their lives, and his lips curl up into a knowing grin. He winks at me occasionally, perhaps because he knows that although I'm closer to the servers' ages than his, my life experiences have made me more *his* peer than theirs.

I top a Long Island Iced Tea with Coke and set it at the servers' station, then glance at Mac. He's staring at me, and when I catch him, he doesn't look away, just smiles.

"You look like a girl with a lot on her mind," he says.

"I think I stopped being a girl when I was six," I reply, and that gets a chuckle out of him.

"Doesn't surprise me." He takes a sip of his scotch.

Mac has a strict two-drink policy, which I respect. A lot of my regulars drink until their eyes cross. Not Mac. He always drinks his first fairly quickly, then takes a good long time with his second. I once saw him nurse his second drink for longer than it took a college boy to down seven beers and two Kamikaze shots. (That did not end well.) Mac comes in Wednesdays, Fridays, and Saturdays, orders two fingers of scotch, neat. Twice. Never more, never less.

"So?" he says. "What gives?"

I pull a drink ticket from the printer and read the order. Margarita. I can make one in my sleep. My bar is full, but no one needs anything at the moment.

"What gives, *what*?" I narrow my eyes at him. "Mac, how long have you been coming here?"

"Oh, let's see, I moved here about, what, four months ago? Took a while to find you. So I guess about three months."

I nod. "You remember the first night you came in?"

"Yes ma'am. I surely do." His kinky hair has more gray than black, and his ebony skin is weathered and sagging. But the twinkle in his eye is that of an eighteen-year-old, and his mind is just as sharp.

"You were asking me all kinds of questions and trying to get to know me, right? And what did I tell you?"

He grins. "You said that one day you might write a memoir, and I could go ahead and buy it and read it, but until then, stick to small talk."

"Good memory. And I appreciate you accommodating me."

He thinks about that for a moment. Takes a short swallow of his scotch, then looks at me intently. "I know more about you than you think."

Unease makes the muscles in my leg spasm. I shift my weight to my right foot and look at Mac. "Really?"

"Well . . . I know about that short dalliance with your minipricked manager."

A laugh escapes me as I assemble the ingredients for the margarita. "I didn't share that with you, Mac. *He* did."

"But you *confirmed* it," he says. He stares at the scuffed mahogany bar, then lifts his glass to his lips. Puts the glass down again, undrunk. "Look, I'm just an old Black man, comes in here three times a week to get my drink on. But I see you, even if you don't want to be seen." He looks up at me, and his eyes lock on to mine. I'm in the middle of making a drink, but I can't break contact with him. The depth of his gaze is hypnotic.

"You're different, Lou." I try to chuff derisively to lighten the mood, but Mac has none of it. He shakes his head curtly then waves a hand in the air and glances around. "You're not like all these other yahoos. You're special."

I reach for the tequila bottle, but my right hand is shaking. I plant it on my hip and try to tell myself that Mac is just spewing booze-inspired compliments. But he doesn't look drunk. Not even tipsy.

He regards me levelly. "Whatever it is you got on your mind, it's all gonna work out all right."

I stare at him for a long moment. If only he knew. Nothing has ever worked out all right with Grace. Nothing ever will.

Giselle, a twenty-one-year-old sociology major at Columbia University, hurriedly rushes to the servers' station and gives me a plaintive look.

"My margarita?"

"Thirty seconds," I tell her. I tear my gaze from Mac and grab the tequila.

FOURTEEN

Melanie

CALIFORNIA—PRESENT

Ray walks straight to the dresser without looking at me. He sets a six-pack of beer next to my dinner tray, unclips his big key ring from his belt loop and slides it next to the six-pack. Then he pulls his wallet out from the back pocket of his jeans and tosses it in the top drawer of the dresser.

I'm not sure what to do. I mean, about the movie. I don't want to pause it—it's getting to the exciting part. But I know it would be rude not to say hi to Ray. I grab the remote and press pause, then wait for Ray to turn around. It takes him a minute. He grabs a beer, twists off the lid, and takes a long swallow. I pull the comforter up, then cross my arms over my chest and wait.

Ray is tall and slender, with dark-brown hair that has some gray in it. More now than when I first came here. He doesn't shave every day, which is actually good for me, not because I care about the hair on his face, but because that means he takes less time in the bathroom. He has muscles, not like Arnold Schwarzenegger or anything, but he's really strong. He kind of looks like the guy from *Justified*. I'm not allowed to watch that old show because it's too violent, according to Delilah. But I've seen pictures of that actor, and that's just who Ray reminds me of.

He looks at himself in the mirror on the dresser, then cocks his head so that he can see me in the reflection.

"Hi, Ray," I say.

He turns around then perches himself on the edge of the dresser and grins.

"Well, look here. Someone's been sleeping in my bed."

"I'm not sleeping," I tell him. "I'm watching a movie."

He glances at the TV, then back to me. "I guess you are." He drinks some more beer, then sets the bottle down.

"I thought you were going out with your buddies."

He shakes his head and frowns. "I was supposed to. But Henry had to get home. Had to deal with a situation with his oldest boy. And Frank felt like he was coming down with something, so he just wanted to crash. That left Andy and me, and I don't really like to spend time with Andy because he's a prick—uh, sorry. He's a dick—um, oops. He's a . . ."

"Jerk?" I supply, and Ray smiles.

"Yup. He's a grade A jerk."

"So, are you banished too?" I ask.

He glances at the door to the bedroom just as a whoop of laughter comes from the living room. "Yes, I am." The idea doesn't please him. He's a little bit angry about the fact that Delilah is good and high, and he's not even a little bit, and he has to hide away in here with his foster daughter who's watching a movie he probably thinks is total bullcrap.

He pushes himself away from the dresser and stretches his arms toward the ceiling. Then he peels his T-shirt off and tosses it into the laundry hamper in the corner.

I gaze at the jagged skull on the round part of his left shoulder. So far as I know, the skull is the only tattoo Ray has. I guess he could have one where the sun doesn't shine, but I wouldn't know, obviously.

"So, what's the movie?" he asks.

"*Hunger Games*," I tell him.

"I liked the book better," he says, and this surprises me. I had no idea Ray read books. He works as a contractor, building things and stuff.

I've never seen him read anything except his stupid blogs. "The movies were kind of disappointing."

I uncross my arms and lean forward, and the comforter falls to my waist. "They're two different medias," I say. "So you can't judge them against each other. You have to judge them as separate entities."

Ray gives up a laugh. "I can't argue with that. How old are you? Twenty-seven?"

"I giggle, then shake my head. "I'm twelve. You know that."

"Yeah, well, you use pretty big words for a twelve-year-old."

He opens the top left drawer of the dresser and pulls out a white T-shirt. That's what he sleeps in. A white T-shirt and his undershorts. If he's getting ready for bed right now, I realize the next thing he's going to do, after putting on the white T-shirt, is take off his jeans.

I turn back to the TV, keeping my gaze firmly on the unmoving screen. "Can I put the movie back on?"

"Oh, yeah, sure," he says. "I'm going to drain the dragon."

The screen comes alive and I focus on the movie as Ray walks over to the door to the bathroom.

This house is small. There's a kitchen and living room, a master bedroom and a smaller room (mine) separated by a bathroom. The bathroom opens into both bedrooms and also into the hall, so that guests can get into it without going through the bedrooms.

As soon as Ray steps into the bathroom, I hear a shrill cry, and then Ray hollers out a curse that would definitely get me detention if I ever said it in school. He steps back into the bedroom, slamming the bathroom door behind him, then leans back against it. I don't want to, but I tear my eyes from the TV screen.

"You okay, Ray?"

He shakes his head solemnly. "I've just seen something I may never recover from. Lori Miller's coochelini."

Lori Miller is one of Delilah's best friends. She's married to Don Miller, the science teacher at my school, and she has two kids she calls "the little assholes." And that's not me cursing, that's just repeating what Lori says. As for the whole "coochelini" thing, I'm glad it wasn't me who saw it.

"Clearly, I'm going to have to hold it for a minute or two," he says.

I don't like having to hold it, even though I do it almost every morning because of him. But I feel kind of sorry for him.

"Why don't you watch some of the movie while you're waiting," I suggest. "Take your mind off of . . . you know."

He glances over at me from his place against the bathroom door, and his lips curl into a smile. A genuine one. Sometimes Ray smiles when he's really pissed off, and that one makes me hide away in my room for as long as I can, because I know something's going to get broken when I see that smile. Like the trash can or one of Delilah's vases or the lamp in the living room. But this smile is good and true. Nothing's going to get broken. I think.

"I'm going to ask you a question, Mel," he says, suddenly serious. "And I want an honest answer." I nod, even though I'm a little afraid of what he's going to ask. "Did Delilah make brownies again?"

I'm not going to lie to him. He could find them in the trash. "Yes, she did."

He thinks about that for a minute. "I thought I could smell them under the . . . uh, well, the aroma was still lingering . . ."

"Is she okay?"

He shrugs, lets out a chuckle. "Oh, she's fine. She just worries too much. Don't let that rub off on you, okay? My mom used to say that worry is like a rocking chair. It keeps you busy but gets you nowhere."

I squint at him. "That's corny."

"Are you trash-talking my mother?"

"No! Maybe?" The toilet flushes in the bathroom, and I grin at Ray. "You're good to go," I say.

He grins back. "I think you might be right."

He waits a short moment, then turns the knob on the door and pushes it open. Looks inside and nods. "Coast is clear." He starts to unbuckle his belt, stops and glances in my direction. He walks to the chair in the corner of the room and grabs a pair of sweats hanging over the back. Then he gives me a quick wink, crosses to the bathroom, and disappears inside.

FIFTEEN

Grace

Good Lord, I'm full. I can't remember the last time I ate pizza. And this one was good, so good that I couldn't stop myself from eating four slices. That's a lot, even for me. But then, I might have missed a few meals on my way to the GWB.

I admit, I had some anxiety waiting for the delivery. I worried that the delivery person would be some kind of axe murderer, or that an axe murderer would sneak in behind the delivery person and swing away, taking out both of us, and the pizza to boot.

But, of course, that didn't happen. The young man who appeared at the door was named Jake. He had tattoos all the way up his arms and over his neck, stopping just under his chin, and he wore a baseball cap backward, which I have never been a fan of. But he was just a nice kid, said please and thank you and all, and because I am a fan of *manners*, I tipped him big from the wad of cash in my fanny pack.

I only have one credit card, strictly for emergencies, so I tend to carry a lot of bills around that I get from the teller at the bank. I don't do those money machines, never have. Always someone watching behind that wonky mirror, plus there's got to be some kind of radiation happening there, which no one talks about.

The boy was really happy with the cash and told me to order again soon. I nodded at him, even though that's never going to happen. Once Lou and I leave this place, I won't be coming back.

I'm sitting on the couch with my hands resting nicely on my stomach, the half-empty box of pizza on the coffee table in front of me. I have harsh words for this city, but I can't deny that it makes the best pizza I ever had the pleasure of eating. I'd like to try a bagel before we go. I hear they're legendary. Maybe Louise and I can grab a half dozen on our way out of town.

I'm fairly content with the cleaning job I did—I couldn't have managed to eat a bite until I got at the grime—although Louise might be pissed off about it. Not just because I used the Nirvana shirt to clean the bathroom, but because I invaded her space. I've already done the job, so that is just spilt milk, and I'm not going to cry over it. Maybe Louise will surprise me and thank me for eradicating the years' worth of dust on the windowsill and the mold under the fridge. Likely, she won't say a word, and that's okay too. My housekeeping efforts don't make up for anything.

She doesn't have a TV, probably watches shows on her computer or her phone. I don't watch the boob tube a great deal myself, but there's not a lot to do here. I could stream something, but I don't want to monkey with her laptop. I still have a few hours to kill before she gets out of work, and if I don't busy my mind with something, I'm going to fall asleep.

I wander over to the stack of shelves on the far wall and peruse the titles of the few books she has lined up there. My heart skips a beat as I recognize the worn jacket of *Stranger in a Strange Land*. Well, would you look at that? I slide it off the shelf and carry it back to the couch. I open the cover to the title page, already knowing what I'm going to see.

This book belongs to Grace Daniels. Don't steal it.

I take a deep breath. The pizza is winding its way to my stomach, loudly. I smooth the Pearl Jam tee across my middle, turn to page one, and start to read.

The book and the T-shirt. If Louise really wanted to eradicate me completely from her life, she would have burned them both a long time ago.

Wouldn't she?

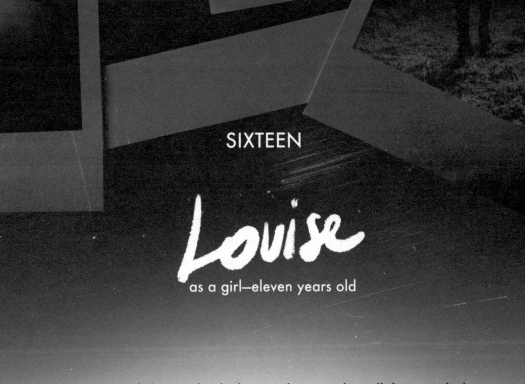

SIXTEEN

Louise

as a girl—eleven years old

Louise is curled up on her bed, pressed against the wall, knees tucked into her chest. This is not an unfamiliar position for her.

Most of the time, she feels safe here. She's been living in this house since the Mexican restaurant incident five years ago. That's what her mother calls it, although they've never spoken about it, even though Louise is old enough now to have that conversation.

She vaguely remembers that day. The police came and took her to the police station and this really nice lady gave her hot cocoa from a machine, and it wasn't very good, but she drank it anyway and thanked the lady over and over again. And after a while, her grandmother showed up and took her home. Louise has been here ever since, and her mom moved in too. She thinks, maybe, Grace didn't have any choice in the matter.

Her grandmother's house is small, and only one story, but Louise has her own bedroom. Her grandma sleeps in the big bedroom, and Grace sleeps on the couch—when she's there. She doesn't complain about it. She has to set up the couch with linens every night and fold them up every morning and stow them in the old antique steamer trunk next to the fireplace. If Louise had to do that every night and every morning, she'd complain all the time, but Grace doesn't. But then, Grace isn't always there. Sometimes Louise comes out early in the morning and sees that the couch has never been made up for sleeping. She doesn't know where her mom goes or where she sleeps when she's not on the couch, but Louise tries not to think about it. She knows what the kids at school think—like Parker McGovern—but Louise doesn't know what's really true and what isn't, and a part of her thinks it's better not knowing.

Her grandma takes good care of her, is always there to make breakfast before school, and always sends a nice, nutritional lunch, and makes dinner every night, and even if Louise doesn't like what her grandma makes, like her Friday-night lima bean casserole, she eats every bite so as not to hurt her grandma's feelings and possibly make *her* want to go away.

But sometimes, like tonight, this house doesn't feel safe. Because her grandma and Grace are arguing. It happens a lot. She knows they're arguing about her, but also about something else that she doesn't understand.

"You can't just run off and leave her alone all the time."

"It's not all the time! And I don't leave her alone. I leave her with you. You left me with your mom sometimes, and I turned out just fine."

Harsh laugh. "Just fine? You're crazier than a shithouse rat." Silence. Then: "Nursing school, Grace. You got all the way through, with me picking up the tab. Took the tests, got your license. And now what? You could get a job anywhere, there's always need. But not when you take off all the time. Employers don't like that much."

"We've been through this before. I can't do that right now, Momma. Someday, maybe, but not now."

"Where is it you go, anyway? And *why*? You take off without a word and come back looking like a damn gutter lump. Never say where you been. Never say a word. And you never ask me for money, either. How is that possible? You wouldn't be . . . serving people's needs in another way—"

"No! How can you even ask me that?"

"Well, I don't know what to think!"

"I've tried to explain it to you. You don't want to hear it."

"Of course not! Because it's nonsense. Utter lunacy, that's what it is! I do not understand why the good lord gave me this challenge."

"I'm not your challenge. I'm your daughter."

"Yes. My *crazy* daughter."

A chill runs down Louise's spine. She wraps her arms around herself and starts to rock back and forth. She knows what's going to happen next. Her mom is going to come in here and say goodbye and tell her she'll be back before she knows it and that she loves her more than all the stars in the universe.

Grace will come back. She always does. But the starry, universal love? Louise isn't so sure about that.

At least she'll say goodbye this time.

SEVENTEEN

Louise

NEW YORK-PRESENT

When I walk through the door at 1:45, I find Grace asleep on the couch with my flea-market fleece blanket pulled tightly around her shoulders, and *Stranger in a Strange Land* splayed out beside her. Her mouth is open slightly, and I hear the wheeze as she draws in a breath. A pizza box sits on my coffee table, and my stomach rumbles in response to the sight of it. I didn't eat at work tonight because I spent my entire break talking to Ewan. It did not go well.

I circle to the coffee table, drop my purse, then lift the lid of the cardboard box to see that there are four slices of pizza left. Nice. But I can't eat before I get the bar grime off me.

My apartment is spick-and-span, thanks to Grace. I could feign ambivalence, but this is the first time in months I've showered in my bathroom without worrying about contracting a fungal infection. I take my time. The one good thing about working into the wee hours is the bounty of hot water at my disposal. I don't interact with the other residents of the building unless absolutely necessary, but I overhear them occasionally, and one of the main complaints I've heard is the lack of hot water at seven in the morning. Twelve am to six am is golden hot-water time.

When I step out of the bathroom, wearing sweats and an oversized tee with the Beatles' *Yellow Submarine* logo emblazoned on the front, I see that Grace is wide awake and waiting for me.

"The pizza's really good," she says. Suddenly, I'm not hungry. "How was work?"

If I answer, "the usual," will she know what that means? The usual is a bunch of drunk people talking total bullshit and a boss who can't decide whether he wants to make love to me or beat the shit out of me. Oh, and a regular patron who's inadvertently messing with my head.

"The usual, huh?" she says.

"You took the words right out of my mouth."

I walk to the couch and sit on the opposite side, as far away from her as I can get without falling to the floor.

"How are you doing, Grace?"

"Your Nirvana T-shirt's in the trash."

I nod, unsurprised. "Okay."

"Have some pizza."

Instead of doing as she says, I hop up from the couch and head to the kitchen. I grab a couple of rocks glasses from the cupboard and a bottle of Jameson, then return to the couch.

"Irish whiskey?"

"I've got vodka, too," I tell her. She doesn't respond.

I pour more than a few fingers of whiskey into each glass, hand one to her, then immediately upend mine. The liquor slides down my throat, leaving a fiery wake. Grace just stares at her glass. I set my empty on the coffee table and reach for my purse. Rifle through it for my smokes, pull one out along with the lighter I keep inside the pack once there's room, and light up.

"Do you have to do that?" Grace asks.

I take a deep drag, then blow it out over my head. Grace winces. "Considering the situation, a little nicotine is the least of what I could require to get me through."

"What did your boss say?" she asks.

"About what?"

She stares at me full on, and I look away. The Jameson is doing its job, forging a path of numbness from my gut all the way up to my brain. Grace doesn't take a sip, just rolls the amber liquid around in her glass for a few seconds before setting it on the coffee table. I know I could lie to her, tell her I didn't talk to Ewan about taking time off. But she'll know better. She can read me like a book.

I take another drag, make smoke rings on the exhale. "Why do I need to take time off, Grace?"

"Because we need to go to her. To Edie."

My stomach flip-flops. I shake my head. "I told you I don't want to hear this."

"She's about to be in a situation, Louise."

"Stop it."

"Listen to me. I know you don't believe me, but it's true." Grace rubs at her left wrist with her right hand, slowly, rhythmically. I recognize the self-soothing technique. She's trying very hard to stay calm. "We need to get to her before the bad thing happens."

I refuse to consider the implications of her words—because I know she's full of shit. This is exactly what my grandmother dealt with, what I swore I would *never* deal with. Delusions, voices, hallucinations, paranoia. Grace has been diagnosed as bipolar, manic depressive, schizophrenic. She denies any of them are true. I've never known exactly what's wrong with her, despite numerous meetings with various psychiatrists. The one thing I *do* know is that she's caused me great heartache.

"She needs us, Lou. I'm telling you—"

I jump to my feet, unable to contain the rage that bubbles up inside of me.

"This is bullshit, Grace! I can't believe this. You show up out of nowhere after six years and tell me we have to find the child I gave up. *I gave her up*, Grace! She's not my problem and she's not *yours*. She's living a good life *because* I gave her up. And this, *this*, is just another one of your fucking delusions. Why couldn't you just stay on your meds?"

"They don't work!" she cries.

"Then stay in the fucking hospital! That's where you belong. You're crazier than a shithouse rat, you know that, right?"

Grace recoils as if struck. When she finally speaks, her voice is a soft monotone. "I'm glad to hear my mother's phrases are alive and well."

I feel sick from my meanness, but I don't apologize. I take a few deep breaths to slow my racing pulse, then grab her undrunk whiskey and down it in one swallow.

"Look," I say. "You can stay here tonight. But that's it. I can't have you in my life, Grace. I just can't. Tomorrow we'll figure out how to get you home."

She gives me a sad, but somehow pitying smile. "I'm not going home, Louise. I'm going to Edie. With or without you."

EIGHTEEN

Melanie

CALIFORNIA-PRESENT

Ray comes back from the bathroom wearing his sweats and his white T-shirt, with his jeans slung over one arm.

I watch my movie but follow his movements out of the corner of my eye. He hangs his jeans in the closet, then goes to the dresser and grabs a second beer. He pops the top and stands there and drinks the whole thing down in, like, less than a minute. When he turns around, I pretend I didn't see him do that. I just keep watching the moving images on the TV screen, even though I've kind of lost track of what's going on. I probably should have read the book first.

Ray pulls another beer from the six-pack, unscrews it, and carries it with him around to the other side of the bed. He sets it on his nightstand, then throws his arms out wide, stretching them toward his back. He rolls his neck, and I hear a couple of cracks above the sound of the movie.

"Wow," I say.

He grins. "Getting old sucks."

"You're not old, Ray," I tell him, though compared to me, he's ancient.

"That's very kind of you to say, Mel." He turns and looks at me and doesn't say anything for a long moment.

I tear my eyes from the TV. "What?" I swipe at my mouth, thinking maybe I have ketchup or mac and cheese goo in the corners.

"You know, Mel, you get prettier every day."

I should probably say thank you, but that just feels weird. "Not as pretty as Delilah," I say instead. Ray scoffs at me. "What? She's the prettiest woman I know."

He considers this for a moment, then shrugs. "Yes. Delilah is very pretty. But if you keep going the way you are, you'll be much more beautiful than her in no time."

I try to swallow, but there's a lump in my throat. I really like the compliment—me, prettier than Delilah? No way. How cool is that? But at the same time, Ray saying this makes me feel funny.

I came to live here when I was nine. Maybe I was more mature than other fourth graders, but still a little girl. I'm three years older now, but I feel totally different. When Ray gave me compliments before, I liked them. Ingrid and Tom hardly ever said nice things to me. If I think about it, Tom didn't really talk to me at all. So, the fact that Ray had conversations with me and asked me about school and seemed like he wanted to hear my opinion on things, even if it was just about Delilah's cooking or if I liked potato chips or corn chips better, made me feel good. But now, him telling me I'm pretty . . . I'm just not sure how to take that.

Gales of feminine laughter swoop in from beyond the bedroom door. Ray scowls at the sound, then lowers himself onto the bed, swings his long legs over and rests them on top of the comforter, crosses them at the ankle and leans back against the headboard. He turns his attention to the TV.

"Okay, so what part are we at?"

I have no idea. "Did you really read the book?"

He nods and grabs his beer, doesn't guzzle it down, which I'm glad about, just takes a small sip. "I read all three."

He looks at me sideways. "What?"

"I thought you just read blogs."

He raises his eyebrows up and down playfully. "There's so much you don't know about me, little girl."

I pause the movie and set the remote down, then lean onto my side to face him. "Like what?"

"Like what, *what*?"

"What don't I know about you, Ray?"

He sets the beer down and smiles to himself. "Oh, Mel. I wouldn't even know where to start. You're too young for a lot of it, by the way."

"Then tell me one thing. Just one. Something appropriate for a girl my age." I make air quotes around the word *appropriate*. Ray glances down at my pj top, then quickly looks away. It's not like he can see anything, the fabric's not see-through.

"One thing, huh?" He leans his head back against the headboard and closes his eyes. He doesn't say anything for so long, I think he might have fallen asleep. I grab the remote and lower the volume, so it won't wake him. I'm about to press play again when he starts to talk.

"I don't know if it's appropriate or not, but I got arrested."

My jaw drops. I can't help it, it's a reflex. And it's not just because I'm pretty sure this is definitely not an appropriate subject, but because I can't imagine Ray doing anything that would get him arrested. I clamp my mouth shut.

"Delilah would kill me if she knew I told you, so let's keep this between you and me, okay?" He opens his eyes and looks at me.

"No, I won't say anything. I promise." Not to Delilah, anyway, but I'm sure going to ask Penny about this. "What . . . um, why did you get arrested?"

"I hurt someone. The details aren't important, not to a kid your age. I did a week at County . . . Jail." He clears his throat. "Longest week of my life, and that's saying something. It's a long time ago, now. Delilah likes to pretend it never happened. Me too. I even manage to forget sometimes. But then, I can't really. Not with this reminder." He gathers up the sleeve of his T-shirt and pulls it over his shoulder, exposing the skull tattoo.

I've asked him about that tattoo before, but he always told me it was just something he did when he was young and stupid.

"You got that in jail?"

He nods. "That's why it looks like crap."

I lean over and inspect the tattoo. Up close, it does look kind of ragged, like the person who did it had a very shaky hand. And the skin underneath is pocked and scarred. My PE teacher has a snake tattoo on her forearm, and the skin underneath is totally smooth. Ray's looks like it hurts. Without thinking, I reach out to touch his shoulder, then realize what I'm about to do and stop myself.

"It feels kind of weird, but you're welcome to touch it."

I inch my index fingertip toward the top of the skull. As soon as it settles on the mottled flesh, I jerk my hand away like it's on fire. Ray flinches.

"What the hell?"

"Sorry, Ray," I say quickly. "I just, I changed my mind. I don't want to touch it."

"That's okay, Mel. It is kind of creepy, huh?" He rolls his sleeve back down. "I'll tell you though, in retrospect, me getting arrested was a good thing. I mean, things came out of it that wouldn't have if I hadn't gone."

"What good things?" I ask, although I'm thinking about the gnarled skin of Ray's shoulder and how strange it felt, and what it must have been like for him in jail.

"You wouldn't be here, for a start," he says. He's got my attention now. I look at him.

"I wouldn't?"

He finishes off his beer, wipes his mouth. "Delilah and I tried to have kids. Um, you know how babies are made, right?" I roll my eyes and nod. He chuckles. "Just checking. So, we couldn't. Not sure why." His words are coming a little more slowly. Maybe from the beer, or maybe this is hard for him to talk about. I can't tell which.

"And then we wanted to adopt, but with my record, well, that was a no-go. We couldn't even adopt a kid nobody in the world wanted. Then this friend of mine from work, he suggested we look into foster care. And here you are." He looks over at me and smiles.

I'm not upset that I'm their last choice for a kid. I'm just glad I have a home and a family, even if it's not perfect.

"I'm sorry, Ray."

He narrows his eyes at me. "What for, Mel?"

"I'm sorry you and Delilah couldn't have babies."

"It hit her worse than me," he says. "She blames herself, which is silly. Sometimes things happen, or don't, and there's no reason. But I think it worked out okay." He grins. "Babies aren't all that interesting. They cry a lot, and eat, and poop in their diapers, they can't talk yet. Older kids are much more interesting."

"And we can do chores."

"That's right, you can."

"I can, and I do."

I suddenly need to pee. I hop off the bed and run to the bathroom. I pause at the door and look at Ray. "Thanks for telling me . . . that thing."

He winks at me. "Our little secret, right?"

"Absolutely."

"Maybe when you're done in there, we can sneak into the kitchen and get ourselves some ice cream. Then find a movie we both want to watch."

"Sounds great, Ray." As much as I don't need dessert, I'd love something sweet right now.

"And, Mel?" He cocks his head to the side and stares at me. "I love those pajamas. That's a really nice color on you."

"Delilah got them for me," I say.

He nods then furrows his brow. "You play soccer? Or, did you? Before you came here?"

I shake my head. "Never. Not even once." He nods slowly. I escape to the bathroom.

NINETEEN

Grace

Despite the way our conversation ended last night, I slept okay. Louise's couch is lumpy, and the odor of cigarettes lingered, but I've slept in much worse places. My daughter had the decency to offer me the twin bed. I don't think she wanted to, but she did anyway, and I declined. It took me a while to turn off my thoughts and to process Louise's resistance, and by the time I did, I was so exhausted, I could have slept on a bed of nails.

I wake before Louise. She's snoring lightly in her sleep, with one arm slung over her eyes. I push from the couch and grab the empty glasses and the bottle of Jameson and carry them into the kitchen. I set the glasses in the sink, and the bottle in the cupboard from where it came. I'd like to make Louise some coffee, just to be nice, but she doesn't have a coffee maker. Makes sense when there's a coffee joint on every corner. Starbucks and Peets and various assorted diners with their blue-and-white cardboard take-out cups.

I take a seat at the tiny kitchen table. That one solitary chair tugs at my heart. How lonely my daughter must be. I grab my fanny pack and zip it open slowly, so as not to make any noise. I reach in and pull out my address book, then check that my keys are still in the outside pocket.

I set the book on the table, then pull out my flip phone. I check the bars of charge and see the battery's full. I tuck it away, then rest my chin in my hand and stare down at the scarred tabletop.

I've got to figure out how to convince Louise about Edie. If I can't, I'll have to make the journey by myself. I'm not sure I can do it without Lou, but I'll have to try. The idea frightens me to my core. The life I've led has taken its toll on me. I'm not sure if I'm strong enough to do what needs to be done.

"Do you really know where Edie is?" I turn to see Louise looking at me from the twin bed.

I straighten in my seat, then nod. I don't know *exactly* where she is, not yet, but I will.

"We got to get to her, Lou."

"How far are we going?" she asks, and I let out a relieved sigh.

"California."

I can see the *Oh, crap* expression on her face from across the room. She stands and stretches, then crosses to me. I note the slight limp from her favoring her left leg. I don't comment.

"So, how are we going to do this? I assume you still have an aversion to planes and trains?"

I want to laugh, but she's not even cracking a grin. Apparently, she doesn't find any of this funny. When I think about the task ahead, I don't either. But she's right. I do not travel by plane or train. I've done it before, but it's never gone well. And it's not about claustrophobia, as I already mentioned. I could get trapped in a closet for three days, and I'd be fine, as long as I was *alone*. Planes and trains trap a whole bunch of souls into a very tight and confined space, and that can have a negative effect upon my person. It probably comes as no surprise that I've never stepped foot into a subway station.

"I brought a car," I tell her mildly.

"What car?"

"My car. Well, if we're being picky, it's your grandma's car, but I guess it's been mine for a while."

"The Camry? Where is it now?"

I flip to the last page of my book where I jotted down the address of the garage. "Sixty-Third. Between Second and Third."

She frowns and shakes her head, and I'm not sure why. Of course, she has plenty of reasons, and it could be just one, or it could be some or all of them combined.

"Let me get this straight," she says. "You drove all the way here from California to get me so that you could drive all the way back to help Edie. That doesn't make any sense! None of this does."

I put up my hands. "I wasn't *in* California, if that helps. I was in Texas."

"What were you doing in Texas? Wait. I don't want to know."

"I need you with me, Louise. You're a part of it. Edie needs you more than me."

"Right. Yeah, okay." Louise still has serious doubts about all this, I can tell, but she decides not to voice them. Instead, she says, "I sure hope you have some clothes in the car."

I let out a *harrumph*. "You think I travel all over the country in my bra and my undershorts?"

She glares at me. "I wouldn't put it past you, Grace." She goes to the sink, pours some water into a fresh glass and drinks it down. "You know, you didn't have to pull that stunt on the George Washington. You could have just called."

I stare at her backside. "Would you have answered?" A beat. "No, you would not have. You would have let my call go to voicemail and then you would have deleted the message without listening to it. No matter how many times I tried. Am I right?"

Her silence is confirmation enough. I watch her shoulders rise and fall.

"I need coffee," she says. "Give me your keys. I'll pick up the car while I'm out."

I get to my feet. "I'll come with you."

"No." She faces me, and her expression speaks volumes. "I'm going to pack. And then I'm going to go down the street to the Star Diner and I'm going to drink a cup of coffee, from start to finish, by myself. I might even grab a bagel. When I'm done, I'll head over to the East Side and pick up the car, then I'll bring it back here and we can get going."

I nod. It's actually good that she goes by herself. I need to do my thing, and I can't have an audience for that. She looks down at her feet, then walks out of the kitchen and heads for the bathroom.

"Think you could get me a bagel too?"

I'm pretty sure she heard me, but she doesn't answer.

TWENTY

Louise

as a girl—twelve years old

Louise sits on the stone wall behind her middle school, clutching the certificate of achievement in her hand. It's already wrinkled in a couple of places, but she doesn't care. Oh, her grandma will make a big fuss about it. Grace would too, if she were around. But outstanding achievement in art is total baloney as far as she's concerned.

She really wanted the citizenship award, but she didn't get it. That went to Lacy DiAmicol, which was no surprise, because Lacy kisses all the teachers' butts and makes a big show of it.

Louise thought her grandma would be at the Friday lunch assembly. Not that she herself knew about the award, but the school always notifies the parents of the recipients in advance, and her grandma is very careful about reading all the stuff that comes home. It was kind of humiliating—yes, Louise knows what that word means, all too well—standing there with the principal smiling down at her and shaking her hand, knowing that there wasn't anyone in the room who cared at all about her getting the award. And after the assembly, all the parents were taking snapshots of their kids with the teachers, and she just stood to the side and watched.

"Hey, honey. Do you need a ride?"

Susie Allen's mom sits behind the wheel of her blue minivan. Louise isn't friends with Susie Allen, but Mrs. Allen volunteers in the library twice a week. After the incident with Parker McGovern, Louise has started spending most of her lunch breaks in the library, so Mrs. Allen has gotten to know her a little. At least, she thinks she has. No one really knows what goes on in Louise's house, but there is a lot of speculation. Hushed whispers through the staff, and all those blatant declarations from the students. Everyone agrees on the simple fact that there is trouble at home.

But Mrs. Allen is nice, and Louise knows she can be trusted, and although she'll have to endure five minutes of Susie staring at her, she thinks that's better than walking home with a backpack that feels like it's full of rocks.

She takes the seat behind Mrs. Allen and next to Susie and tries to busy herself by checking the zippers on her backpack.

Susie surprises her by asking if she can see the certificate.

"Sure. Why not?" Louise answers. "It's just a dumb art award."

"That's not dumb," Susie says. "I wish I could draw. I try, but everything comes out looking like my brother drew it. And he's four."

Louise bites her lip. "I could teach you, maybe," she says, and Susie's face lights up.

"That would be awesome," Susie says. "I could meet you in the library at lunch on Monday."

Louise nods. "Cool. I pretty much go there every day anyway."

The minivan comes to a stop at the next house down from hers. She doesn't understand why until she looks through the front windshield and sees a fire truck blocking her grandma's driveway. There's a sedan parked behind the fire truck with a county emblem on the side and a man and woman standing beside it.

"Oh, dear," Mrs. Allen says. She opens her car door just as Louise grabs the handle for the sliding door in the back. "You girls stay here."

Louise and Susie nod. Louise's brain churns into high gear. It's a fire truck, so her first thought is *Fire!* But then, they had an assembly at school a couple of weeks ago—not an award assembly, but one where the local fire department came to talk to the students about safety. And Louise remembers what they said about not just helping with fires. She can't quite recall what they'd said, but it was like four or five other things. She suddenly wishes she'd paid better attention.

Through the windshield, she watches Mrs. Allen approach the man next to the sedan. He's standing on the sidewalk and he gives her a guarded expression. She says something to him, then points to the minivan. Louise shrinks back against her seat, then turns to see Susie staring at her worriedly.

A couple minutes pass, and Mrs. Allen returns to the minivan. Instead of getting behind the wheel, she comes to the back and slides open the rear door. Her face is a mask of concern. Louise recognizes that expression, she's seen it on the faces of grown-ups many times.

"Honey, I don't know how to tell you this, but your grandma has had a stroke. Do you know what that means?"

Louise has heard the term, but she's not exactly sure what a stroke is, except that it's bad. She knows that sometimes when someone has a stroke, they're never the same as they were before, and sometimes they even die.

Mrs. Allen glances at Susie, then turns back to her.

"They've taken your grandma to the hospital. And they're going to take really good care of her. From what I understand, it was a mild stroke, so that's good news." Mrs. Allen's voice is very high. She's trying to sound chipper, like nothing is wrong. But Louise is not comforted.

"The thing is, the nice people over there need to get in touch with your mom. Do you have any idea where she is?"

She shakes her head from side to side.

"Okay, well. They're going to take you somewhere, because you can't stay here alone. We'd bring you home with us, but . . ." She clears her throat, looks uncomfortable. "Well, we have a softball tournament this weekend, and Mr. Allen has a work thing. I'm so sorry."

Louise nods and gets out of the minivan. "Thanks," she says to Mrs. Allen, then walks toward the man and woman standing next to the sedan.

They take her to a home run by the county. It's safe and clean, but it smells like despair. She's allowed to go to school on Monday—the home provides transportation and everything. Whatever they can do to maintain the status quo for a child in crisis.

Louise waits in the library the entire lunch. Susie Allen never shows up.

TWENTY-ONE

Louise

The plan I started formulating at work took shape in the wee hours of the morning, as I lay in my twin bed listening to my mother's ragged breathing. I'm not sure I can pull it off, but I have to try because it's the right thing to do. Grace didn't seem the least bit suspicious at my sudden change of heart, which is good. I need her to think I'm on board with her mission. I've been told by more professionals than I can count not to play into her delusions, but my plan won't work if I don't. She says we're going to save Edie? Fine. I'll play along. Until I don't have to anymore. I pray that will be sooner rather than later.

As I walk toward Eighth Avenue, I gaze up at the blue sky. I feel the warmth of the sun and a light breeze on my face and realize that today is a beautiful day. This would be the perfect day to head over to Central Park with a blanket and a book and hang out in Sheep Meadow and people watch. Or head down to South Street Seaport and grab a beer and a bowl of chowder on the pier. Or even hop on a train bound for Long Island Beach.

Today is not a great day to trap myself in an enclosed space with my mother for an indeterminate amount of time. Unfortunately, I have no choice.

I reach the corner diner and grab a stool at the far end of the counter and order a coffee regular. As soon as the waitress fills my mug, I pull out my cell phone and peruse my contacts. I find a number I haven't used in many years, then tap the screen. It's early on the West Coast, but hopefully he'll answer. He does.

"Grace is here in New York," I say.

We talk for a few minutes and by the end of the conversation, I feel better. I hang up, ask for a to-go cup for my coffee, then leave a five on the counter.

I don't order a bagel. I don't want to take the time. I have to get this party started.

I walk toward Broadway, sipping at my coffee regular—light with two sugars. The last time I ventured this far east—before my trip to Bellevue—was when I spent the night with Ewan. He lives in Grammercy Park in a fairly swanky two-bedroom. I rarely spend the night away from home. It gives the wrong impression, like I actually want to involve myself in the other person's life, get to know them, see where they live. Ewan is the perfect example. He woke up before me and was so thrilled I was still there, he made me breakfast in bed. I didn't have the heart to tell him that my previous night's tequila-Valium combo practically knocked me out cold. That if it hadn't, I would have left one millisecond after his orgasm.

Ewan doesn't get it, but then, how could he? He doesn't know me. Wants to, yes. But that will never happen. I was known once, a long time ago, by a man I loved with everything I had. Edie's father. After him, I closed up my heart, snapped a padlock on it, tossed the key, and never looked back. Ewan, Jett, the dozens of other men I've slept with, none of them ever stood a chance.

Ewan was furious when I told him about my unexpected and impending sabbatical. Hemmed and hawed about covering my shifts, gave me a lecture on commitment and responsibility and letting people down, which I think had as much to do with our nonrelationship as it did with my job. He said he couldn't promise there would be a job to come back to, but I don't think he meant it. Maybe I'm wrong, and maybe he'll surprise me. Maybe I'll come back and find he's hired a hot blond chick with gargantuan tits to work my shifts. For his sake, I hope he does. For my bank account's sake, I hope he doesn't.

I finish the coffee and toss the spent cup into a trash can, then come to a stop at the corner of Broadway and Forty-First. I realize my left leg is throbbing from my hip to my ankle, and I don't have any ibuprofen on me. I don't want to spend the money, but this walking business is clearly a mistake, especially after my round trip to Bellevue yesterday and my shift at the bar. What was I thinking?

I put my hand in the air and hail a cab.

TWENTY-TWO

Melanie

CALIFORNIA–PRESENT

Delilah's been acting weird all morning. I mean, weirder than usual.

She's talking to herself a lot. At first I thought maybe she was still high from last night, even though I know pot doesn't last that long. But her eyes aren't red, like they can get when she smokes up, and she isn't staring into the refrigerator for, like, five minutes straight, which I've seen her do. And she's not sitting on the couch watching reality TV with a box of Oreos.

No, she's more like the opposite of stoned. She's all over the place. One minute she's scrubbing the bathroom, and the next minute she's up on a ladder replacing the bulb in the hallway that's been out for three weeks, then she's shrieking into the phone to a friend about a sale that's going on at Kohl's and she's got a 30 percent off coupon and they *just have to go!*

Ray had to work today, and I'm kind of bummed about that because it's Saturday, and I was hoping we could go down to the park and shoot some hoops. I'm terrible at basketball, but Ray's really good and it makes him feel good to play—every time he sinks a basket, his whole face lights up.

I feel closer to him this morning because of the secret he shared with me last night, and the fact that we ended up watching one of his all-time favorite movies—*Alien*. At first, I didn't want to because even though I try to act all mature, I'd heard it was really scary. And it was. It scared me so bad, I almost peed my pants, but Ray just put his arm around me and held me close in the scary parts so I wouldn't freak out. And I actually loved it because the story is about this totally ordinary woman who ends up completely kicking alien butt. By the end, I wasn't huddled up next to Ray anymore. I was like, *Go Ripley!* And Ray thought that was funny, and he also thought I was really brave.

I must have fallen asleep at some point, because I remember being smacked on my fanny, and waking up, and seeing Delilah next to the bed. It's fuzzy now, but she looked kind of pale, and her hair was all messy, not like it usually is—perfect. She scooted me off the bed and walked me to my room, then shut my door hard, which she didn't need to do. My bedsheets were cold when I slipped into them, not warm like Ray and Delilah's bed was, but then, it was Ray who was keeping me warm, I guess. I couldn't fall asleep for a while. I thought about pulling out my journal and trying to talk to Penny, but I didn't have the energy to turn on the light, so I just laid there until I drifted off.

This morning I'm just trying to stay out of Delilah's way. She's given me a list of chores to do, but they're easy. Mostly because she doesn't trust me to do a good job on the important stuff. Strip my bed, gather the towels from the bathroom and put them in the hamper, straighten my desk, take out all the trashes, bag up the recyclables, organize my closet, sweep the front porch. When I'm done with my list, the day is mine. I don't have any plans other than to get as far away from D as I possibly can.

She drags the vacuum to the couch. "It's not a thing if you don't *make it* a thing," she says to herself as I grab the broom and head for the porch. "A thing *can* be a thing, but it isn't *necessarily* a thing." There are grooves in her forehead that look painful, like she's thinking so hard it hurts. I want to say something to make her feel better, but I don't know what. "And a thing can be just that, nothing more, and it's okay that it is what it is."

I like Delilah. I won't say *love* because that's too strong. I'm twelve, but I'm old enough to know what love is and the strength that word possesses. I loved Mommy and Daddy—Gladys and John, and I probably loved Pam and Andy a little bit too, because babies and really little kids love a lot easier than older kids and adults. I did not love Ingrid and Tom. They didn't want my love, and having three real kids already, they didn't have any love left over for me.

I like Ray too, although I admit I have stronger feelings for him than D. Not just because of last night, but because he seems so much more, I don't know, I want to say *there*. There for me. Delilah takes me to the salon to get my hair trimmed and she takes me to the family-friendly movies playing at the Cineplex, and she lets me help her in the kitchen when she's *not* making brownies, and sometimes we do our nails together. But most of the time—and I do not mean to put her down—but it feels like she's playing a part. Like, starring in the role of Melanie's mother today—and for the last three years—is Delilah James. It's like she's an understudy, and she knows she is, and she's taking all the right steps and saying all the right lines, but she's not feeling it like the actress that really has the part. Whoever that might be.

But she tries, and I have to give her credit for that, even though she's a little bit kooky.

Ray is much more natural in his part. When he spends time with me—like taking me to the father-daughter dance at school, or to his work on a construction project where he lets me sort nails and screws, or out to watch the elephant seals on the coastline, which we did last summer, it doesn't seem like a chore for him, or something he thinks he has to do. He's normal and natural with me.

"Get it all," Delilah calls to me. "All the dust, Melanie. Dust is one of the top allergenics. Yes, it is. Mold too, but we don't have to worry about mold, thankfully. But dust is a killer. Get it *all* off the porch. Out, out, out, into the street, okay? Don't let any of that dust into the house."

"Right, Delilah. I'll do my best."

"No, not your best." Delilah appears at the front door and looks at me with that furrowed brow. "Promise me you won't let one single speck of dust into this house."

I nod rapidly. "Sure thing, Delilah. Not one speck."

"Good girl," she says, then disappears inside.

I push the broom from side to side. *She's crazier than a shithouse rat*, I think.

My hand stills as a wave of confusion washes over me. Not just because I rarely, if ever, curse. But also, because I've never used that expression before in my life.

TWENTY-THREE

Grace

And we're off.

I'm glad to be in my own clothes. Louise brought my bag up to her apartment before we left so I could change into a pair of khaki pants and a soft long-sleeved shirt. I folded the Pearl Jam tee up into a nice compact ball and stuffed it into my duffel bag without Louise objecting. I'd like to sleep in it on the trip. I think my daughter knows that. I don't consider the shirt a talisman but I do like the energy it still possesses.

Louise is driving, to start. She double-parked when she brought the car to her street, walked into her apartment and grabbed her bag without a word, then stomped back down the stairs. I followed suit and didn't object when she climbed behind the wheel. This is her need for control, and I won't stand in the way of it. I'm goldarn sure she won't be driving the whole way, even if that's her intention. Sooner or later her leg's gonna start buckling up, but there's no need to mention that now.

"H and H," Louise announces as she skillfully weaves through northbound traffic. She claims she's never driven in the city, never had a car here or a need for one, but her prowess in the driver's seat causes me to wonder. Maybe she drove a cab in another life. Anything's possible. I should know.

She continues up Eighth Avenue until it turns into Central Park West. I gaze out the window of my mother's Camry at the great New York City park to my right. A tremor runs through my body, but I do my best to shake it off. A tremor like that always comes before the voices and I cannot afford to be distracted by them right now. Things being what they are, I have to have my priorities in place and adhere to them.

Edie is my priority.

Louise hooks a left at Eighty-Sixth, then another at Columbus, and double parks—again—in front of H&H Bagels. She jumps out of the car and is gone for a good five minutes, during which several drivers make their displeasure at our illegal parking job known, loudly. One man in a Honda CRV violently jerks his middle finger at me. I reply with a peace sign.

Louise returns to the car with a bulging white bag and tosses it to me as she takes her place behind the wheel. Wordlessly, she pulls into traffic.

The bag is warm against my lap, and I can't help but open it and gaze inside at the half-dozen bagels. A couple of everythings, which are my favorite. Two sesames—Louise's choice—and two plains. I pull one of the everythings out of the bag and tear off a piece.

"Thanks for the detour," I say.

She stops for a light and looks at me. "Least I could do. I know you'll never come back to New York."

How right she is. I tuck the piece of bagel into my mouth. The proverbial "they" are correct when it comes to New York City bagels. It's the best bagel I've ever eaten in my life. It melts in my mouth and the various seeds combine to create a cacophony of flavor on my tongue. I'm just a simple girl from Tennessee. But no hush puppies or biscuits or grits ever tasted so good.

"So, we can make it in two days if we drive straight through," Louise says as she winds her way toward the George Washington Bridge. "You haven't given me the specific address, so I can't give you an exact time-line, but Google Maps says forty-three hours to Southern Cal."

"Slow down, girl. You figuring to drive the whole way?"

She glances at me, then nods. "Sorry, Grace, but I don't trust you behind the wheel."

I don't argue. "Whatever," I say.

A quarter of the way over the bridge, I see the spot where the paramedics found me yesterday and I smile to myself.

So far my plan is working out just fine.

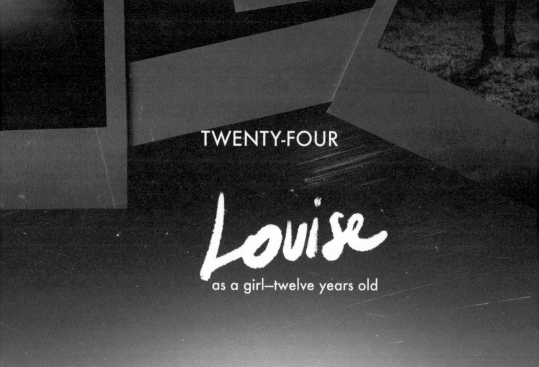

TWENTY-FOUR

Louise

as a girl—twelve years old

The bell echoes throughout the classrooms and hallways, and her heart sinks. Most of her peers hate school, complain about it all the time, can't stand being there, can't wait to get out. But for Louise, school has become a safe haven. Every day, from eight-thirty until two forty-five, she knows exactly where's she's going to be and exactly what to expect. Although she is not in love with all her classes—math is particularly annoying—and even though she doesn't really have any friends, she experiences peace of mind within these walls that disintegrates when sixth period is over.

She could extend her day by going out for one of the after-school sports, but middle school doesn't have that many to choose from. And she would rather die than play soccer again.

Taking her time, she grabs her backpack from the floor and unzips it, then spends a few minutes reorganizing before stowing her notebook and folders inside. She zips the backpack carefully, then stands and slings it over her shoulder. The other students have already fled the classroom by the time she shuffles toward the door.

Her English teacher, Mr. Kramer, watches her from behind his desk. He witnesses this somber retreat every day. He doesn't know exactly what she's going home to, but he always wants to give her a little boost before she leaves.

"Your essay on *Fahrenheit 451* was outstanding, Louise. I really enjoyed reading it."

She pauses and looks at her teacher. "Thank you," she says, and awards him with a closed-lipped smile. "I liked that book. Bradbury never really explained why they started burning the books in the first place. But, you know, that was okay, because sometimes there *is* no explanation for why people do what they do."

She continues to the door.

"Okay, well," he starts but doesn't know how to finish. *Have a great day?* That might sound mean. "See you tomorrow."

"That's the plan," Louise says. "But you never know." She turns and grins at him and he realizes she's joking. She has a sense of humor, despite everything. He hopes she can manage to hold on to it.

The corridor is almost empty. A few stragglers wrestle with their back-packs and lockers, but none of them take notice of her. She walks toward the back of the school, wondering how long she's going to have to wait for her ride. Yesterday she waited for over an hour. But that was okay, because she doesn't like anyone to see her get picked up by the county van.

Three girls, including Susie Allen, are standing on one of the four-square courts. The other two are Macy Lovett and Glenda Smalls. Susie has a ball in her hand. Louise feels their eyes on her as she passes by.

"We need a fourth," Macy Lovett says.

"We could ask *her*," Glenda suggests.

Susie shakes her head.

"Why not?" Glenda asks. "It's not like she's contagious, or anything."

"I have a no-freak policy," Susie says.

Louise stares at her feet as she heads for the stone wall in the back parking lot.

"Just forget it," Susie says. "Let's just the three of us play."

Tears threaten, but she doesn't have long to consider Susie's mean-ness. Up ahead on the street, she sees her grandmother's Camry. And standing beside the Camry is her mom.

No van today, she thinks, then wonders how Grace is going to humiliate and embarrass her this time. She desperately wants to turn around and run in the other direction, but that would be another humiliation, of her own making.

Heart thudding, Louise circles around the stone wall and slowly approaches her mother. Right away, she can tell that Grace is upset. Not crazy, manic upset, but sad. Her face is pale, she has dark circles under her eyes, and she looks like she's been crying.

She knows about the stroke. Of course she does. That's why she's here.

Her mom opens her arms wide, and Louise can't help herself. She doesn't even care if the other girls are watching, which they probably are. She throws herself into her mother's embrace. The two of them break into tears.

Part Two

TWENTY-FIVE

Delilah

CALIFORNIA–PRESENT

I don't know where Melanie has run off to. I think she told me, but I was in such a frenzy with all the cleaning, that I forgot. The park, maybe? That's really the only place she can get to without me giving her a ride, so that's probably where she is. I should go down and check, but I've got a couple of other things on my to-do list. Making brownies is *not* one of them, although I'd like it to be. Because I just *have* to get them right one of these days or I'm going to go nuts. But that would be three times this week, and if Ray catches me at it again, he's going to go ballistic.

Anyway, I'm sure Melanie is fine. She's twelve, after all, and can take pretty good care of herself, which is a good thing since she's had to a couple of times. When she first came to us, she was nine, and I wasn't prepared for her. Not that I didn't have everything in place as per DCFS regulations. What I mean is, I didn't know what to expect from a nine-year-old. I knew she wouldn't drink from a sippy cup, obviously, but I worried about other things. Like what kind of books and TV shows were appropriate? Could she be left alone at all? Did she know how to make food? Could she brush through her own hair? Was it safe to let her walk home from school by herself? I guess if you have a baby, or adopt a baby at birth, and you're with them the whole time raising them up, you get a feel for what's right for them. But I didn't have that time with her, so I worried I'd mess up.

It went pretty smooth, though, mostly because Melanie is grown-up for her age, which makes sense. She's been through a lot. I cook most of her dinners and make her lunches, even though I know she could do both, and probably better than I do. But it makes me feel more like a mom. I know that's stupid. I'm not her mom, and I never will be. She'll never *think* of me that way. Maybe if she'd come when she was five or six, but nine's too old for that kind of connection. I read it in a book, I think, or maybe in a parenting magazine at Eileen's.

Speaking of which, I need to get in to see Eileen to get rid of all these gray roots. I add that to my to-do list, though I probably won't be able to fit it in today.

I feel much better than I did a few hours ago. I don't know what came over me. It was like I was wired for sound. Maybe it was from smoking so much pot last night. That must be it. I went way over-board. The evening is pretty much a blur. I vaguely recall finding Mel asleep next to Ray, and I had this notion that something was going on there. But I know that's ridiculous. For God's sake, she's twelve. But I was really stoned.

I guess I passed out after that, but when I woke up this morning, all these crazy ideas popped into my head. Ideas about Ray and what's going on with him. He's been a little distant lately. Longer than that, actually. I used to know exactly what he was thinking at any given moment, or how he felt about things. I'd say something, and he'd go, "I was just thinking that." We've always been connected, from the very beginning. But now, not so much. And I don't know why. I thought maybe there's another woman, or another man, which—again—is ridiculous because Ray is as straight as they come. He once broke a guy's finger when the guy tried to poke him in the butt, just as a joke. So, is it another woman? Or other *women*?

And then I started wondering if maybe Ray isn't really Ray, like the man sleeping next to me is an alien body snatcher who kidnapped the real Ray and is taking his place with me on earth while Ray zooms around the galaxy, or whatever. See? This is what I'm talking about. Crazy ideas. It has to be the pot. Lori brought it over and she warned me it was really potent, but I didn't expect this kind of hangover.

So I went on my cleaning jag to take my mind off things and to hopefully push the weed through my system faster. I talk to myself a lot when I'm alone. It keeps me company. But I was doing it this morning, just letting everything that was going through my mind come out of my mouth, which was probably not a good idea considering Melanie was here. Thank God Ray went to work.

I swear, I am *never* getting high again.

It's almost noon, and the house is spick-and-span. I don't want to mess up my beautiful kitchen with lunch prep. If I were allowing myself to make brownies today, I would, but I'm not. I made that decision and I'm sticking to it. Melanie will probably be home soon and hungry— she didn't eat breakfast—and I don't want *her* messing up my kitchen. I decide to run out and grab some burgers.

I grab my cell from the counter and try calling Mel. Her voicemail picks up on the first ring, which is not unusual for her. That girl isn't like the rest of her generation, she's not glued to her phone. She lets the battery run out all the time and forgets to take it with her. It's probably in her room. I end the call and dash off a quick text, then leave a note just to cover my bases. I grab my purse and my keys from the kitchen table and head for the front door. A quiet voice in the back of my mind tells me I should probably find Melanie and see what she's up to. I ignore it. I'm sure she's fine.

She always is.

TWENTY-SIX

Melanie

CALIFORNIA—PRESENT

The park is only a block from the house. Not even really a whole block. It's at the end of our street, so, like, seven houses down. Behind the houses is all wilderness and trees and stuff that stretches for acres and acres. There's a stream down there that leads to the river, and it gets way overgrown sometimes. A kid got lost there last year, and the park rangers and sheriff's department had to search half a day to find him.

The park is long and grassy and has a concrete path that runs through it where people can walk their dogs or jog or push strollers. There's a jungle gym for little kids and a basketball court and a handball court. The blacktop under the courts is kind of uneven and cracked, and weeds grow up through it in places. Ray says the city ought to come out and repave the courts, that they're a safety hazard, but they haven't done it since I've been here.

Way past the jungle gym and off to the side is a dirt path that cuts back behind the houses and into the woods. The path ends pretty soon, but then there's a trail that leads down the bank toward the stream. Across the stream is a little hut made of wooden boards. I don't think very many people know about it. It might have been a hunting fort a long time ago, but hunting's not allowed anymore. Maybe some teenagers go in at night to make out, or whatever, and probably some homeless guys have spent the night there. I've found candy wrappers and empty water bottles, and there's graffiti on the walls, like hearts with initials inside them, and a couple of phrases that I can't—and wouldn't want to—say out loud. But I've never seen anyone else when I've been there. I can get to the hut from the back of my house, like as a shortcut, but the brush is thick and scratches my arms, so I mostly just go around the park.

The fort has become my sacred place, my haven. I don't feel unsafe with Delilah and Ray, never have. But inside these walls, I'm free to be who I am without anyone watching me. I can talk to Penny here and not worry that D or Ray will catch me.

When I finished my chores, I told Delilah I was going to the park. I don't think she heard me. I mean, she *heard* me, but I don't think she was paying much attention.

I have a feeling, when she stops acting all crazy, she's going to wonder where I am. Maybe she'll remember. But even if she doesn't, she probably won't worry too much. Delilah worries about a lot of things, but I'm not one of them. Because I don't need to be worried about. I do what's expected of me. I go to school and get good grades and finish my chores in a timely manner. I can make my own lunches, and even dinners, too, if I need to. I don't act out in school or at home. I don't hang out with "undesirables," or *anyone* for that matter. I don't do social media, so there's no need for Ray and D to worry about "negative influences."

I carry my journal in a rucksack that Ray gave me, and when I push through the door of the fort, I see that I have the place to myself. There's a platform on the far side with stairs that lead up to it. On the wall of the platform is a hatch that opens and closes so you can see out, I guess, although it's always closed when I come, and I've never tried to open it because the hinges look rusted.

I go to my spot in the far corner, next to the platform but below it. It's kind of like a cave, and I like the idea of hibernating, away from the rest of the world. Some of the wooden slats of the perimeter walls don't quite meet each other, and sunlight streams through the cracks and creates stripes of gold across the dusty floor. If Ray built this hut, there wouldn't be any cracks. I know how mindful he is when he builds a thing. But I'm kind of glad he didn't build this, because if there weren't space between the slats, it would be dark as night, even midday, and that would be a little spooky. I have enough spooky in my life, don't need any more.

I pull my little fleece blanket out of the rucksack. I shake it out and set it on the floor, then lower myself down onto it, crossing my knees and tucking my feet under my butt. Then I pull my journal out of the sack.

For a minute, I just sit. Sometimes, in the summer, it gets really hot in here, but today, the temperature is perfect. Not too hot and not chilly. I think, if I laid down on my fleece blanket, I could fall asleep. I'm still a little tired from last night. But I'm not here to take a nap, and I know that. I open the journal and pull out the pen. And wait.

It never takes long, not when I'm in the fort. Whoever or whatever Penny is, her radar picks me up real quick when I'm here. I feel that familiar tingle, and the hair on the back of my neck stands up straight. I clutch the pen in my left hand and set it on the open page of the journal, then close my eyes.

My hand seems to move for a very long time. Usually when Penny first comes, she starts out with a short greeting, like *Hiya.* Or *What's up, buttercup?* or *What's shakin', bacon?* But not today. I want to open my eyes and read what she's telling me, but I learned a long time ago that if I do, I'll somehow break the connection. So, I let my left hand do its thing, let Penny control it, and try to be patient. It's hard, though.

After what feels like a long time but is probably only a minute, my hand stops moving. I give it a few seconds, because sometimes Penny takes a break, then starts up again. But she doesn't this time. I open my eyes and look down at the page.

You need to be careful. Some things are not what you think they are. Peer through the cracks. Watch your back. Be ready. I'll help if I can, but it's on you.

I read Penny's words once, then again. A chill creeps up my spine. I trust her, I do. But I have no idea what she's talking about.

"What do you mean, Penny?" I ask aloud. My words bounce off the walls of the wooden hut and echo back to me. I close my eyes and grip the pen. Nothing happens. I try again. "I don't understand. Who are you talking about? Why do I have to watch my back? Why do I have to be on guard?"

I realize she's not going to answer me. She's gone.

I open my eyes and look around. A shadow falls across the floor of the fort, erasing the stripes of sunlight. Someone's standing outside the door.

TWENTY-SEVEN

Louise

Despite the detour to H&H Bagels, we've made good time. We've been on Interstate 80 heading west for about four hours, and we're already halfway through Pennsylvania.

Grace has been very subdued since we left New York. The whole way over the GWB, she was singing "Jeremy" but went quiet as soon as we reached Jersey. She hasn't said a word for the last hour, just gazes out the passenger window and watches the countryside slide past.

When I was young, during rare periods of normalcy between her episodes, my mother and I took the occasional road trip. What I remember most about those trips was her running commentary on everything that came into view. "Oh, my, look at those cows! Peaceful as can be. They've got no idea they're about to be someone's dinner." "Wow, two-for-one burgers, Louise! I wonder if they grill up the onions or just set 'em up on the patty raw. We should check them out." "Poker, black-jack, jai alai. You'd think we were in Vegas, Lou, with all of those choices. I could clean that casino out, if I had a mind to. But that wouldn't be sporting, now would it?"

On and on she went, as if her words somehow made the journey more interesting. And if I had to be honest, they did. She helped me find wonder in the mundane, awe in the mediocre. I got excited about blackjack, even though I didn't know what it was. Her play-by-play of the sights and sounds around us kept a little girl entertained.

Which is why I'm disturbed by her silence.

"Look, Grace," I say, pointing to the side of the road. "Buy one crate of strawberries, get the second one free." The hand-painted sign promises a strawberry stand half a mile off the next exit.

"Stop and get some, if you want," she says.

I like strawberries, but I don't want to take the time. "No. That's okay."

I feel her turn and look at me. "Lou, I know you've got it in your mind to drive straight through to California. But that just isn't going to happen."

"I thought you said we needed to get there."

She nods. "We do. But Edie's okay right now."

I suppress the urge to give voice to all the thoughts battering through my brain. *If Edie's okay, what the fuck am I doing in this car? This whole thing is a shit show. You are crazy, end of story. You want to get back with me, to reconnect, make up for lost time, beg my forgiveness—all the things you should do because of what you've put me through—and now you're using the daughter I gave up to do that? Fuckety fuck. And fuck you, Grace!*

I take a breath, remind myself of my plan, and stare straight ahead at the endless highway.

"I won't be able to sit in this car for more than eight hours at a stretch, Louise. And I have a pretty good idea that you won't either. That leg of yours must be giving you some strong objections already."

She's right. The dull ache I felt on my way to the East Side this morning has morphed into stabbing needles of pain. Sitting prone in the car will make it worse. I need a good long stretch, which I can't do if I'm driving.

I glance over at her. She's rifling through her black book. Comes to a particular page and reads the entry. "There's a place we can stop for the night," she says. "About two hours from here. Can you last that long?"

I don't know if I can, but I'll be damned if I'll show weakness. "Two hours. Sure. What's the place? Motel 6? Quality Inn? You're paying, right?"

"I already have."

"Because I'm taking time off work, so funds are a little tight—wait. What do you mean you already have?"

"I'll give you a head's up when the exit's coming," she says, avoiding my question. She turns to stare out her window again. A few minutes pass in silence. I don't want to ask, but I can't help myself.

"What is it, Grace? You're so quiet."

"Just taking it in," she says.

For the last time, I think. I don't know where the thought comes from. Despite all the reasons I hate my mother, I don't like that thought at all.

TWENTY-EIGHT

Grace

OHIO–PRESENT

We reach the exit about two and a half hours later. We'd have made it sooner if we hadn't gotten stuck behind a limping semi on a stretch of construction-narrowed highway. All's well, though. My bladder has held up, which is a relief. And we'll be to our destination soon enough.

"Hudson, Ohio?"

It sounds like a question, so I nod. "Take Route 8."

Louise does as she's told and swings the Camry onto the southbound highway. A few minutes later, I tell her to take the exit to the surface street. She eases onto the road, first yielding to a pickup truck with a houseful of furniture in its bed and a Harley Davidson, which reminds me of Louise's daddy. A Budget Inn comes into view ahead on the left and Louise starts to slow the Camry, clicks on her turn signal.

"No, Lou. We're not staying there. Another mile up the road, then make a right, okay?"

Without a word, she turns off her blinker and accelerates to the speed limit. I point when the road comes up and she makes the turn.

"Go slow, now, so we don't miss it," I tell her.

Huge trees obscure what's left of the day's sunlight, and the road is bathed in shadows. This residential neighborhood is almost more rural than suburban, enormous lots of land with unseen houses set back from the street. Mailboxes line the gravel berm. I scan each box as we cruise past, reading the names and numbers. I feel Lou's questioning stare, can almost hear her thoughts, which I'm certain contain harsh language directed at me. But she keeps them to herself and waits for me to do or say something to direct her.

Six mailboxes in, bingo. "This is it, Lou. Make a left."

She glances at the name on the box. "Palmer. Who are the Palmers? Grace, what are we doing?"

"Just trust me."

She scoffs at that. I don't blame her. Still, she makes the left and slowly drives down the long winding path.

The house is large, a two-story with gray clapboard siding and a wraparound porch with an overhang. The grounds are lush and green with thick trees and tall grass and an assortment of flora and probably fauna, too. It doesn't look professionally landscaped, more likely tended to by the owner's hand.

A silver Subaru SUV and a yellow Chevy pickup truck are parked side by side next to the house. Louise pulls the Camry to a stop behind them.

"Well?" she asks. "Are you going to tell me what we're doing here?"

Before I can answer, the front door of the house opens and a middle-aged woman in a floral dress steps out on the porch and squints down at us. Her graying hair is tied in a loose, messy knot on top of her head, and tendrils fall next to her ears.

I grab the door handle and push my door open, then heave myself out of the Camry. When I reach the bottom of the porch, the woman's expression shifts from wariness to recognition. Her mouth spreads into a huge smile and she rushes down the steps. She throws her arms around me and embraces me tightly, and I respond in kind.

"Grace! Oh, Grace. I am so happy to see you." She steps back and looks at me, and I see that, despite the deepening lines around her eyes, she is as beautiful as she was when I first met her. She shakes her head. "I'll tell you, Grace, I've had a feeling all day, just something in the back of my mind. Now I know why!" She hugs me again, then releases me as Louise wanders over.

My daughter's expression is a mix of suspicion and incredulity that almost makes me laugh.

"Oh, this is my daughter, Louise," I say. "Louise, this is Mary."

Louise makes to put out her hand, but Mary steps forward and pulls her into a hug. Louise doesn't know how to respond, just stands there awkwardly, arms at her sides, tense as a jackrabbit under a wolf's voracious gaze.

"I'm so very happy to meet you, Louise," Mary says, releasing her. "Come in, come in. Jared's going to be so pleased to see you. I made a huge Crock-Pot of chili. Thought I'd have to freeze some, but here you are!"

Mary ushers Louise and me into the house. The interior is warm and cozy, farmhouse-style, with large comfy furniture, hardwood floors, and handmade rugs. The aroma of chili permeates the air, and I realize I haven't eaten since the bagel this morning. My stomach rumbles.

I follow Mary through the downstairs to the kitchen, Lou right behind me.

"Randall's away at college. He'll be back in two weeks. Oh, he'll be sorry he missed you. But Will's home. I mean, not right now. He's studying at a friend's, but he'll be home for supper."

The kitchen is a large open space with a solid wood dining table that almost runs the length of the room. A counter island bisects the cooking area from the dining area. The appliances are not new, but they're spotless, and I can tell they've been kept in good order. The fridge is stainless steel and covered with photos, some in plastic cases, some simply tacked to the doors with magnets.

Mary stops at the counter. She glances at me, then her eyes dart to Louise who is checking out the table. Quick as a wink, Mary scurries to the fridge, grabs one of the photographs, and tucks it into a side drawer.

I recognize the picture, but I don't say a word. Mary returns to the counter and smiles brightly.

"The guest room has a queen bed. Y'all can share. I'd put Will on the couch and let one of you stay in his room, but being that he's sixteen, I'm not sure you'd feel comfortable in there, what with all his dirty socks and so forth."

"Guest room's wonderful, Mary. Thank you."

"Excuse me," Louise says, and Mary and I turn to look at her. She's bent over, massaging her left leg. She takes a sharp intake of breath.

"Yes, honey? Oh no, do you need some ibuprofen? I have some in the drawer here."

Louise shakes her head curtly, then stands up straight and regards us. "No, thank you. I have plenty." She looks down at her feet, then back up again. "I was just wondering . . . Mary. If you didn't know we were coming, how do you know we need a place to stay?"

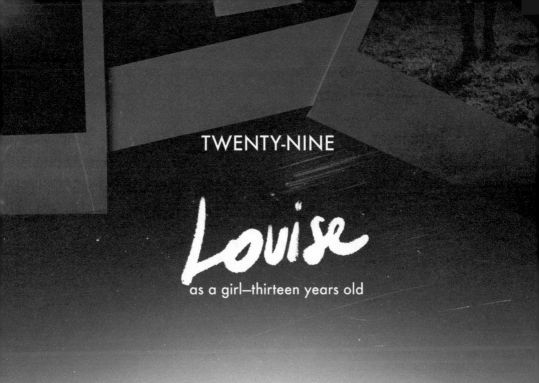

TWENTY-NINE

Louise

as a girl—thirteen years old

Louise sits in class, trying to concentrate on Mrs. Walton's instructions. She's a straight-A student, but math is not her best subject and she finds geometry particularly challenging. She really needs to pay attention but she's starting to feel worse.

At first, she thought it was hunger. Her grandmother's doing better, she's back at home, but she can't do the things she did before yet, like make meals and drive. Grace has been helping out more, which is good, but when Louise got up this morning, she discovered her mom was gone again. Big surprise. So after getting her grandma situated, Louise didn't have time to eat anything. When the gnawing pain started in her gut in second period, she figured it was from skipping breakfast.

The pain has morphed into really bad nausea. And along with the nausea, she's starting to feel a cramp on the right side of her stomach. She's a little bit clammy, too. If anyone were looking at her, they might say she looked pale, although no one is looking at her. But she doesn't want to miss the lesson, and she doesn't want to make a fuss, and she certainly doesn't want to go to the nurse's office, where she'll have to listen to Ms. Semple try to get a hold of her mom.

Louise stares at the board. Mrs. Walton is explaining the difference between acute and obtuse triangles but she might as well be speaking in a foreign language. Louise's heart has started to race, and sweat runs down her back under her blouse.

"Are you okay?" Olivia Gomez asks. Olivia sits next to her, and while she isn't a friend, she's always friendly. Louise doesn't know whether Olivia talks about her behind her back, but she thinks maybe not. "You kind of look like you're going to barf."

And suddenly Louise realizes that's exactly what she's going to do. She jerks her hand into the air to get Mrs. Walton's attention, but the teacher is busy drawing on the board, with her back to the class.

She springs out of her seat and races for the door. Sensing movement behind her, Mrs. Walton turns to see her student flee from the room.

"Hey! Where do you think you're going?"

"I think she's gonna barf," she hears Olivia say just before the classroom door bangs shut.

Louise races for the girls' room. Feeling the bile rise up from her stomach and into her throat, she's afraid she's not going to make it. She grips her hand over her mouth and pushes through the door of the restroom, then hurls herself into a stall and wretches violently into the toilet. Some of last night's dinner explodes out of her, but it's mostly liquid. Her stomach spasms painfully. She heaves until there's nothing left and still, she continues to heave. Tears stream down her cheeks, mixing with the snot pouring out of her nose. She has never felt so horrifically awful in her entire life, and she wonders if she's going to die, right here in the girls' bathroom of her middle school.

Finally, thankfully, the spasms ease and she lays her head on the toilet seat, forgetting, for the moment, all of the terrible germs that live there. She reaches out to the lever with a shaking hand and flushes the foulness down, then continues to rest, her heartbeat slowly returning to normal. After a moment, she tears some toilet paper off the roll and wipes at her mouth as best she can. She pushes herself to her feet and presses her palm against the wall of the stall to steady herself. She feels dizzy, but more than that. An exquisite pain has begun to throb in her lower abdomen.

When she feels like she can walk without collapsing, she leaves the stall and shuffles to the sink. She cups her hand beneath the open faucet and drinks. Nausea sweeps through her again, and the throb in her abdomen becomes a roar, radiating through her entire body.

I'm going to die, she thinks. *I'm going to die in this bathroom.*

"Where is she? Where is my baby?"

The familiar voice echoes through the halls on the other side of the bathroom door. Louise finds the strength to move to the entrance, but the door is so heavy, so darn heavy, she can hardly pull it open a crack. She musters the will to yank it open, then practically falls into the hallway.

She looks to her left, toward the administration offices, and sees Grace barreling toward her. The school secretary, Ms. Roach, chases after her.

"Ma'am, you need a visitor's pass! You can't roam through the school without a visitor's pass!"

"To heck with that!" Grace shrieks, then sees Louise by the bathroom door. Relief and concern dance in a do-si-do across her mother's face as she races toward her.

Classroom doors open up and down the hallway, and curious faces peer out at the commotion. But Louise doesn't care. Her knees go weak, but before she falls to the floor, her mother is there, sweeping the girl into her strong embrace.

"Oh, my baby. I'm here. I've got you. You're going to be all right."

Louise looks up at her mom. "I thought you left," she croaks.

"I did, honey. But I came back because you're more important than the others."

She doesn't quite understand her mother's words, but she gets the big idea just before the blackness takes her.

I'm more important than the others.

THIRTY

Melanie

CALIFORNIA—PRESENT

Outside the hut the shadow moves suddenly, and the stripes of sunlight fall back upon the wooden floor. My breath hitches in my throat. I don't know why I feel afraid, except for the words Penny wrote in my journal. I close the book and stow it in the rucksack, then jump to my feet. Wood creaks from the platform above my head, and I scurry away from the sound, dragging the rucksack and blanket with me. I press myself into the far corner of the hut, away from the platform, and try not to make a sound. I know I'm being a baby but I can't get Penny's warning out of my head.

"Who's in there?" The demanding voice sounds vaguely familiar, but I can't place it. It's a boy, for sure. Someone I know from school? "I'm going to take the fort, so whoever's in there better watch out! I'm going to storm the place."

Recognition slams into me. It's Reuben Meserve from my Core class, the kid who's reading Warriors too. I'm relieved because I know him. He's not just some random dude who might be a serial killer. I mean, I guess he *could* be a serial killer, but from what I understand, serial killers don't start murdering until they're adults, so Reuben's probably still at the animal-torturing stage.

That is not a happy thought, and I don't know where it came from. It wasn't Penny. It was me. I might be a little twisted sometimes. But I guess when a girl has an entire person living in her left hand, thinking creepy serial-killer thoughts is not much of a stretch.

The door to the hut swings open and bangs against the wall, and Reuben Meserve looms in the doorway. I jump from the sound, but then stand up straight and puff out my chest.

"You can't just take the fort, you know," I say.

Reuben spreads his mouth wide, showing me teeth that look like Tic Tacs. "I can if I want to," he replies mildly. And he probably could. He's half a foot taller than me and outweighs me by at least thirty pounds.

"I was here first," I tell him.

He cocks his head to the side and thinks about this. Reuben has a face that kind of looks like the moon, all round and stuff, with a really high forehead. I try not to listen when kids at school are being mean, especially because a lot of the time they're being mean about me. But sometimes, I can't help it. Sometimes a story is repeated so many times, at some point you're going to hear it.

According to the legend, Reuben got hit in the head with a baseball bat when he was five. It was an accident, supposedly, in T-ball. A kid was at bat, swinging at the ball on top of the rubber tee, and Reuben ran in front of him at just the wrong moment. He was in the hospital for the rest of the year, which is why he had to repeat kindergarten.

Some kids say he's not the same as he used to be, that the baseball bat knocked something loose, and now his brain is a little bit scrambled. I didn't know him before, so I don't know the difference.

The weird thing is, I've been coming to the fort for, like, six months now, ever since my twelfth birthday when Delilah decided it was okay for me to come to the park alone. And I've never seen Reuben here. Yesterday, when I commented on the Warriors book, was the first time I've ever spoken to him. I get that tingly feeling on the back of my neck, but obviously, I can't pull out my journal and talk to Penny with him standing there.

"It's you," he says. He jabs his index finger in my direction. "You're that freak foster kid."

I shake my head. "Foster kid, yes. Freak? No." Okay, maybe I am a freak, but he doesn't know that.

Reuben steps inside the hut, and even though he's only thirteen, his presence is huge.

"Get out, freak," he snaps. "I'm taking the fort."

My body goes all tense, but I don't want to back down. I think about Penny's journal entry, and for a split second, I wonder if I should just hightail it out of here. But this is my special place. *Mine.*

"I will not get out," I tell him, and I'm glad my voice doesn't crack because I'm feeling kind of nervous. "You can come in if you want, and I'll share the fort." I don't want to share with Reuben, not even a little bit. The tingly feeling is stronger than ever, and my hands are shaking. The fort is public property, so if Reuben wants to come in, I can't stop him. But I'm not going to leave just because he says so.

He takes another step toward me, and I see the backpack in his hand. It's bigger than my rucksack but doesn't have a lot of stuff in it. I can tell because the outer pockets fold in on themselves, and it's kind of flat.

Reuben glares at me, and I glare back.

We do this for a long moment, and finally, he hangs his head.

"Well, fine then," he says. He looks around, then walks to the opposite corner of the hut. "I'll take this side."

"Fine," I say. I pick up my blanket and shake it out, then lower it to the floor. I sit down and watch Reuben get himself comfortable. He doesn't have a blanket, just sets himself down on the wooden floor, obviously not caring about the dust that's going to decorate his shorts. He pulls his backpack to his chest, unzips the outside pocket, and takes out a candy bar. Unwraps it and takes an enthusiastic bite. He chews with his mouth open, and makes funny noises, like a dog, and drools a little chocolate onto his chin.

I'm not sure what I'm still doing here. I mean, I didn't want to back down to Reuben, but I can't really talk to Penny with him around, can I? What am I supposed to do? Just watch him eat and drool? *Gross.*

He sets the candy bar down and looks at me. "You're just a girl," he says.

I don't get offended easily. I've sort of had to roll with certain insults. But, no, I can't let that slide. "*Just* a girl?"

"Yup. Just a girl." He wipes at his mouth with his arm. "I'm a boy. Boys are stronger than girls."

"Physically, yes," I say. "But not psychologically and emotionally."

"Huh?"

"Never mind." Why waste the effort?

"You're a girl, and I'm a boy," he says, and I simply nod. I guess the rumors are true. This kid has issues.

"I'm stronger. I could hurt you if I wanted to."

The fear comes back like a whirlwind.

"I could hurt you," he repeats. "I could kill you, too, you know."

His eyes are kind of blazing, and I notice that his pupils are really small, and his green irises are huge. I know from science class that in the low light of the fort, his pupils should be dilated, but they're not. They're like pinpricks. This is more than concerning. This is downright scary as crap.

I suck in a breath and quickly gather my things. "Yes, Reuben, you could," I say as I hoist my rucksack over my shoulder. "But why bother? Middle school sucks, but I think prison is much worse."

He looks confused, like he's not sure what he said or why I said what I did. "Huh?"

I don't take the time to explain. "See you," I say, then I'm out the door.

THIRTY-ONE

Louise

OHIO-PRESENT

Dinner is a feast, from my perspective, anyway. I don't spend a lot of time or energy on meals, don't put a lot of effort into food in general. I eat when I'm hungry, satiating my appetite with microwavable dinners, granola bars, cheese and crackers—whatever is readily available or at hand.

The cooks at my bar and grill provide family meals for every shift, but I rarely partake. Instead, I use my free time to restock bottles or squeeze oranges or slice garnishes or wash glasses. Partaking of the family meal involves socializing with my fellow employees, making small talk and gossiping. So, yeah, *no*. Not my thing.

But tonight, I have no choice in terms of the "family meal." Mary made cornbread and caramelized brussels sprouts to go with the turkey chili. We're seated around the large wooden dining table—me; Grace; Mary; her husband, Jared; and their son, Will. The chili, the cornbread and the brussels sprouts sit in the center of the table, waiting to be violated by our gluttony. My stomach growls, but apparently, no one eats until a prayer is said. Jared's blessing stirs up a memory.

What do we always do before we start eating?

We say your name!

I crush the memory and keep my expression neutral as Jared thanks God for his copious blessings and for bringing Grace and me to them that they might partially repay the gift that was given to them. I don't know what he means and I'm trying not to care—forcing myself not to care or question or think about it too much. I'll have time for that later. The truth is, I haven't had a sit-down, solid meal for a hound's age. And the chili smells better than a pizza pie from John's in the village, which is saying a lot.

Jared is all country. He's an engineer whose smarts contributed to streamlining milk production from dairy cows. But he comes from a long line of farmers, and the soil is in his blood. He's humble and quiet but occasionally comes out with a gem of knowledge or social commentary that makes me chuckle. He doesn't like the current administration, but thinks politics is all a game anyway, so why get your knickers in a twist?

Will is a sweetheart. I don't come in contact with many sixteen-year-olds, so I don't have much basis for comparison, but this kid is as cool as they come. Polite to strangers—i.e. Grace and me—and deferential to his parents. And not in a disingenuous way. He really seems to look to them for guidance and affirmation. But the thing about him that affects me most is his reaction to Grace. He looks at her like she's a god damned movie star, like she's the coolest person on the face of the planet. He makes a point of serving her chili and cornbread, then carefully spoons the brussels sprouts onto her side dish, asking if she wants more, then blushing crimson when she tells him he's the best server she's had the pleasure of being served by.

Something's going on here, of which I am not a part. Everyone at this table seems to be bound by a secret, but none of them are letting me in on it. Mary never answered me when I asked her how she knew we needed a place to stay. She and Grace exchanged a look, then she made a lame excuse about having to check on the chickens.

I want to know what's going on, but then, a part of me doesn't. A part of me wants to just enjoy the chili, which is delicious, and the cornbread, and the fabulous brussels sprouts, and listen to Jared and Mary talk about life in this Ohio suburb. A part of me wants to fall asleep with a full belly and forget for seven hours that I'm on a road trip with my mother . . . and what I have planned for the end of it.

"Grace tells us you tend bar in New York City," Mary says.

I nod.

"That must be pretty darn interesting," Jared says, as if my profession rivals his, which, even on a good day, doesn't come close. "I imagine you have to deal with all kinds of personalities."

"Well, I've had a lot of practice with that," I say. Grace clears her throat but says nothing.

"I might tend bar," Will says around a mouthful of cornbread.

"Will!" his mother admonishes.

He swallows hard and grins. "Sorry." He takes a sip of milk, then clears his throat. "I'm going to college in two years. I'm hoping to get into UCLA, and there's lots of restaurants in Westwood, so I thought I could get a job, you know? To help my parents with tuition."

He'd do well, too, with his piercing blue eyes and thick, wavy sandy-blond hair and dimpled, shit-eating grin. The university girls would go apeshit over him. I don't say as much.

"Maybe you could give me a few pointers," Will says.

I smile. "Just pretend you know what you're doing," I tell him. "That's the secret. If someone orders something and you don't know what it is, just fake it. With confidence. Nine times out of ten, they'll just drink it and tip you big."

Will smiles at me, dimples flaring. "I'm so glad you guys came. I've heard so much about Grace, but I didn't know if I'd ever get to meet her in person—"

"Will," Jared says, interrupting the boy.

I look at Grace. Her eyes are shimmering. What the hell is going on?

"Sorry," the boy says again.

I pounce. "For what?" I stare at Will. "Why are you apologizing?"

He shrugs. "I know I'm not supposed to say too much."

Grace reaches out and pats his hand. "It's okay, Will. You didn't do anything wrong."

My self-control and forced ambivalence evaporate. I stand up and plant my hands on my hips. "Will someone please tell me what's happening? Grace? What are we doing here? How do you know these people?"

My mother looks at me with that commanding maternal stare, the one mothers all over the globe use to regain control over their wayward offspring. The *Do as I say, or else* look.

"Sit down, Louise. Those are questions for another time." Her gaze softens. "And I'll answer them, I promise. But for now, just enjoy the meal with our lovely hosts."

My impulse is to run from this room and from this lovely family. But then, that's always been my default. Run. Run away from anything that makes me feel uncomfortable or makes me feel out of control or makes me *feel* anything at all. Which is why I've never had an intimate relationship with a man that lasted more than a month, and why I wasn't with my grandmother—who practically raised me—at the very end.

I sit down hard in my seat. A weighty silence takes the table, but Mary breaks it quickly.

"More brussels sprouts, Louise?" she asks.

I nod. "Yes, thank you. They're amazing."

"I'll give you the recipe." She winks and smiles kindly at me. "They're easy as pie."

A dozen snarky comments cross my mind, starting with the fact that I'd likely burn down my apartment building if I tried her recipe. I keep my sarcasm to myself and try to relax back into the meal. Which only works if I don't look at my mother.

THIRTY-TWO

Grace

OHIO-PRESENT

I find her out front by the Camry, smoking one of those goldarn cancer sticks, talking on her cell phone. When she sees me, she hangs up quickly, tucks her phone into her pocket, and averts her eyes.

There's still plenty of light in the sky, and I can see the look on her face, plain as day. As my fifth-grade teacher, Mr. Begley, would say, Louise is not a happy camper. Funny, the things we remember. She doesn't look at me as I approach, keeps her eyes on the car, on her feet, on the landscape around her. Everywhere but on me.

"I sure wish you'd quit that awful habit," I tell her.

"Yeah, well. If wishes were fishes, and cattle were kings . . ."

"The world would be full of wonderful things," I finish.

She takes an inordinately long drag off the cigarette, likely to spite me, then enthusiastically blows out a plume of smoke.

"Who were you talking to?" I ask.

Her eyes dart to the left. "A girl from work."

Maybe she's telling the truth. Probably not.

"The Palmers," she says. "Nice people."

I nod. "Salt of the earth. That Will . . ." I can't help but smile thinking about the boy. "He's going to rule the world, huh? Those dimples . . ."

"And you know them how?"

She waits for a response, but I don't give her one. "Because, I mean, you said you'd answer my questions, right? Isn't that what you said in there? That you'd tell me what the fuck is going on?"

"Language, Lou."

She throws down the butt and stomps on it. "Oh my god, Grace! Seriously? No bullshit. What the fuck is going on?"

I move in close to her and force her to make eye contact. "I was kind of wondering the same thing, missy."

"What?"

"What the, uh, *heck* is going on here?"

She gives me a nervous look and takes a reflexive step back. "I don't know what you mean."

Maybe she does and maybe she doesn't, but it's been gnawing at me all day.

"Well, now, it seems like you did a pretty quick one-eighty on this whole trip to help Edie. Last night you were done with me, ready to send me packing with a fare-thee-well and good riddance, and now here you are, behind the wheel, barreling us toward California. Why?"

She sucks in a breath, then presses her palms against her eyes and shakes her head.

"Well?" I prod.

"Oh, for fuck's sake! Why do you think? The George Washington Bridge stunt? I was worried about what else you might have in your crazy bag of tricks if I didn't come with you. Impale yourself on Lady Liberty's crown maybe?" She laughs without humor, then reaches for her cigarettes. Her hand shakes as she lights another one. "I don't want you in my life, Grace. But I don't want any harm to come to you. Especially not because of me. I'm going to get you home, where you belong." She takes a long draw off the smoke. "Then I can be done."

That's not the whole of it, I can tell. I nod anyway. No matter her reasons or my reasons, we're in this together, at least until we hit the West Coast. Then, the you-know-what is likely to hit the proverbial fan. But I'm not going to think about that right now.

"Thank you for being honest, Lou." She flinches but I pretend not to notice.

"And the Palmers?" she asks, using her cigarette to gesture toward the house.

"It's not the big deal that you're making it," I say. "I helped them out, a long time ago."

Louise narrows her eyes at me. "Helped them out? How?"

I think of how to say it. "I gave them back something that might have been taken away." I know I'm not making sense to my daughter. "They were in need, Lou." I shrug. "And I showed up."

"You're not going to be more specific, are you?" she asks.

"Do I need to be?"

"This is just . . . this is so typical of you." Louise looks up at the house, then throws back her head and laughs without humor. "Thirty-six hours ago, I was having sex with a musician named Jett in my nice little apartment in Hell's Kitchen."

"He wasn't very good though, was he?" I say, and her eyes go wide at that. "I'd be willing to bet you enjoyed Mary's brussels sprouts more than you enjoyed Jett. Am I right?"

The corners of her mouth twitch like she's trying to suppress a grin. "They were good brussels sprouts."

"Yes," I agree. "Darn good brussels sprouts."

The front door bangs open and Will bounds out of the house. He stops at the railing that surrounds the porch and looks at us. Louise quickly tosses her cigarette down and crushes it in the gravel.

"Mom told me to come get you guys," he calls. "She's putting out dessert. Chocolate chiffon cake. You really don't want to miss it. It's like, wow. So good."

Louise smiles at Will. "Better than the brussels sprouts?"

"Oh." He shakes his head. "Blows the brussels sprouts completely out of the water."

"I'm in," she says. As she walks toward the house, she glances at me then quickly averts her eyes.

Oh yes, she's hiding something. I hope I see it before it's too late.

THIRTY-THREE

Melanie

CALIFORNIA-PRESENT

I'm out of breath by the time I reach my street. I didn't want Reuben to think I was afraid of him, so I kind of fast-walked to the trail and up to the path until I was sure he couldn't see me anymore. As soon as I hit the park, I broke into a run and didn't look back, didn't stop until I saw the familiar house at the end of my block with the cracked blue paint and rusty bicycles laying on the front lawn.

My heart is pounding, even though I know I'm safe. But the thing is, I don't *feel* safe. I feel like if I turned around, Reuben would be standing right there, his chin covered with chocolate goo, licking his lips and reaching out to me with a claw hand, ready to choke the life out of me. He said he could, and he wasn't lying. That boy could kill me twice without even trying.

Sudden relief washes through me when I see Ray's truck pull to the curb in front of the blue house. He rolls down his window and waves to me from the driver's seat.

"Hey!" he calls. "What'cha doing?"

I walk slowly to the truck, taking time to catch my breath so he doesn't see that I'm upset. That's my job. To not make waves. Be calm, be cool, be easy. Be *normal* so I don't get sent away again.

"Hey," I say, my voice all steady and *normal*.

"Want a ride home?" he asks.

I scrunch my face up at him. "It's only, like, a thousand yards."

Ray shrugs good-naturedly. "Suit yourself." He makes a show of putting the truck in gear.

"Wait!" I yell, and he grins. I circle to the passenger side, open the door and climb up to the seat. "Are you done with work?"

He nods.

"That's great, Ray. You shouldn't have to work at all on Saturdays. I mean, I don't have to go to school on Saturdays, so, really, it's like a governmental day off." I'm babbling, mostly because I'm happy to be in Ray's truck and not in a hut with a crazy kid who wants to murder me.

Ray sighs. "Well, I have to go to work when there's work to be done."

"I guess that makes sense."

"It's not all bad," he says. "I work mostly outside, you know. I get to look up and see a big blue sky. Clouds, too, occasionally. The sky's beautiful. Kids today have their heads down all the time. They miss a lot."

"Like the sky?"

He gives me a funny look, like a glare, but I know he's not really mad. "Are you making fun of me?"

"No. I'm just glad you're done for the day."

"Me too, and now, I'm looking forward to a nap."

I look at my lap, trying to hide my disappointment. I was hoping Ray would want to do something with me.

He chucks me on the shoulder. "I'm beat from our movie fest last night," he says. "But maybe after my nap, we could play a round of gin rummy or build a card house. Or we could bring the basketball to the park."

"Not the park," I say quickly, and he cocks his head to the side. "I mean, I've already been there today."

"Everything okay, Mel?" he asks. I feel his eyes on me and try to keep my face *normal*.

"Totally," I say. "Too much fresh air isn't good for kids. Stunts their growth."

He laughs out loud at that, then shifts into drive and eases down the street. We reach the house in thirty seconds. The driveway is empty.

"D's out?" he asks.

I shrug. "She was home when I left."

Ray nods and pulls into the driveway, puts the truck in park. Instead of getting out, he stares through the windshield at the garage door. I'm not sure what to do, so I just sit there, waiting for him to do something. He spreads his fingers over the steering wheel and I hear him breathe in deep. His fingers are long and lean, but strong too. I stare at them.

"Are *you* okay, Ray?" I ask.

He takes another breath and sighs. "Life's funny, Mel. You never know what's going to come your way. I guess you'd know that better than anyone."

I don't respond.

"Are you happy?" he asks, still staring at the garage.

I'm not sure how to respond, like maybe this is a trick question. I could tell him what I think he wants to hear, and that's probably what I *should* do. But in the end, I decide to tell the truth. My twelve-year-old truth, at least.

"I don't really know what *happy* means, Ray."

He turns to me and looks at me, then grins. "What are you, thirty-five?"

I smile, glad to fall back on our usual banter, glad that he's not upset by my answer. "You know how old I am."

He opens his door and jumps out of the truck, and I do the same. We walk side by side to the house, then I follow him in.

"Wow," he says. "She cleaned."

"She was like a whirling dervish," I tell him, and he squints at me. "*Sound of Music.*"

"You're not going to make me watch that, are you?"

I smile at Ray. "I was thinking, maybe, *Aliens*?"

"I'll consider it," he says. "Right now, sleep is calling."

He walks down the hallway toward his bedroom, and I suddenly feel small and alone.

"I'm going to take a nap, too."

"Good idea," he says. "We'll meet out here in two hours and build the biggest card house you can imagine. We'll have to call the Guinness Book of Records to come by and measure it."

He disappears into his bedroom. I wander into my own room, set my rucksack down on the floor, and go to my bed. I lay down on top of the covers and try to relax. I'm tired, for sure, but I don't think I can sleep. Because, when I close my eyes, I see Reuben Meserve glaring at me with his pinprick pupils. I grab Chauncy the Dolphin and hold him close, but my stuffed animal doesn't make me feel better.

After a few minutes, I hear Ray's soft, comforting snore resonate through the hallway. I listen to it for a little while, measuring my own breathing by his inhalations and exhalations. My eyes feel grainy and my eyelids heavy, but sleep doesn't take me.

I suddenly remember that Reuben knows where I live, just like I know where he lives. I jump out of bed and hurry to the front of the house, then look out the living room window at the street. An older man who lives around the corner—I don't know his name, but he's always friendly—is walking his fluffy white dog and a couple of kids are riding their skateboards, trying to do tricks off the curb. There's no sign of Reuben, but that doesn't mean he isn't out there. I go to the front door and see that we left it unlocked. I quickly turn the bolt. It's not that I really believe Reuben is going to bust in here while I'm napping and strangle me in my sleep. Better safe than sorry, though.

I still feel uneasy, even with the door locked. I consider pulling out my journal so I can ask Penny to tell me more. But I'm too tired for a conversation. Talking to Penny takes a lot of energy, and when I'm this tired, she doesn't show up. I wander to the bathroom and do my business. But instead of going back to my room, I go to the door that leads to Ray and Delilah's room. I crack it open and peer inside. Ray is fast asleep on top of the comforter. He looks so peaceful, like a little kid, and for some reason, that makes me love him a little bit. I think of last night, how he shared that secret with me, and how he kept me from being afraid during the movie, and how he held me with his strong arms, and I felt safer than I've ever felt before. I want to feel that way right now.

I tiptoe into the bedroom and, as quietly as I can, climb onto the bed. I shimmy over toward Ray. I'm careful not to wake him, but I want to feel his warmth and comfort.

He stirs in his sleep and throws an arm across my waist. I freeze for a moment, then relax against the pillow. The weight of his arm is like a shield of armor.

When I close my eyes, I don't see Reuben Meserve. I see a big blue sky with clouds sailing past.

THIRTY-FOUR

Delilah

CALIFORNIA–PRESENT

I'm late. I don't know what came over me. I went out to grab lunch for Melanie, and now I'm coming home with three enormous bags from Kohl's. The burgers are definitely cold.

Ray is going to have a shit-fit when he sees the credit card statement. I have a Kohl's card, it's one of the only credit cards I have because I'm not a good risk. I've applied for several cards, but my . . . what's it called?— my fical score, or whatever, is mediocre. Okay, mediocre is stretching it.

But this guy at Sully's—that's a bar me and Ray used to go to, only now, Ray doesn't go there because he says they water down the drinks, but I go every once in a while. Anyway, this guy I was talking to one afternoon, he told me that to get a better credit score, you've got to use the credit cards you have and pay two-thirds of them, but keep a balance on them, or some shit like that. I don't really understand the whole thing, but I took what I needed from the conversation and boiled it down to the fact that I'm supposed to *use* the card in my wallet instead of just letting it sit there.

Kohl's was having this big sale, and we needed some things, God knows. The rug in the bathroom is nearly worn through, and the shower curtain is torn and practically falling off the rod. I rationalized that if

DCFS came by to make a random inspection, we better have a fresh shower curtain.

Of course, there's no rationalization for the red suede pumps, which I'm sure I'll never have a chance to wear, or the six brassieres, or the leather miniskirt that I had to get in a larger size than my usual. It still looks good, I mean, you know, they don't make leather minis for fat chicks, but I admit, I almost broke down in tears when I had to go the next size up. Still, I bought it because it made me feel good to do that, and I haven't felt really good about anything for a really long time.

And this voice in the back of my head kept telling me to put things in my cart, things that Ray might like, and it might help get us back on track in the sack. That's what my friend, Audrey, says. Marriages have to be "on track in the sack." We haven't been for a while, Ray and me. It was never a problem before. We were always "A-okay in the hay." I'm not sure what changed. Maybe it's just the natural course of marriage. But I don't like it at all.

It's tougher now, with Melanie in the house. She was just a little girl when she got here, but she's growing up. She's started getting boobs and hips, and more than that, she's *aware*. They did the whole sex talk in school last year. I had to sign a permission slip so she could learn the lesson, so she knows all about it. Which makes it difficult to get into it with Ray. We used to make all kinds of noise and move from room to room. Now we have to wait until we're sure Melanie's asleep, and then we have to keep it down, so we don't wake her. Sometimes, we can do it while she's at school, but with Ray's work schedule, that doesn't happen very often.

I still find him attractive, though, and that's a good thing. I think he still finds me attractive too.

While I was in the fitting room at Kohl's, this voice—not the one that was telling me to buy stuff, but a different one—whispered in my brain that Ray's *girlfriend* probably doesn't shop at Kohl's, but shops at the adult store in town and teases him with strawberry-flavored undies he can eat and rubber rings that fit around his thing and make him howl in ecstasy. I told *that* voice to shut the hell up, and I think I scared another shopper, because I said that out loud. At least I was in my try-on room, so I could pretend I was on my cell phone.

I don't *really* think Ray has a girlfriend. Although I guess anything's possible. My friend Jennifer? Her first husband, Scott, cheated on her with Kitty Bartholomew, the waitress at Spooner's, the best diner in town. They were doing it three times a week in Jennifer's own bed, and she never had a clue about it until one of the busboys—Ernesto—made a pass at her and told her, well, if your hubby can do it with a waitress, why can't you do it with a busboy? Jennifer went all crazy for a while, but once she got rid of Scott, she found Russell, who happens to be a purveyor of weed, and I've never seen her happier. That makes sense, right?

But Ray? No. Even with those whispered voices, I just can't believe he'd cheat on me. He's got integrity. That's what drew me to him in the first place. He's made mistakes, sure, but he learned from them and came out a better person. He takes pride in everything he does, and marriage is one of them. I don't see him as the kind of guy who would shtoop a diner waitress in my bed. If he wanted to, I think he'd tell me first, end the marriage, save me the heartache. But then, you never know, do you?

Ray's truck is in the driveway, which I didn't expect. I got plenty of food—cold as it is—so he won't go hungry, and I can toss it in the microwave, even though the microwave will make the hamburger buns kind of spongy and the fries kind of chewy. But Ray won't care. When he's hungry, I could give him a plate of rocks with sauce, and he'd down them without question. And Mel . . . Well, Mel never makes a fuss about anything. That's just the way she is.

But I better leave the Kohl's bags in the car and sneak them in later. Just to be safe.

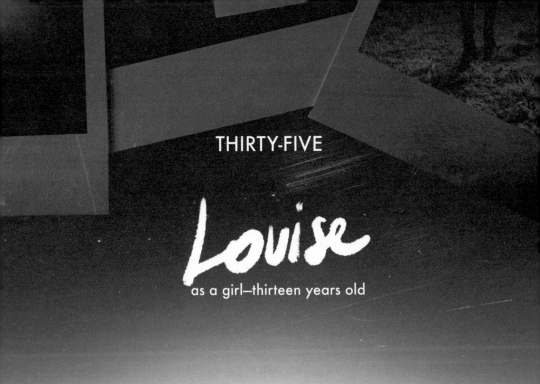

THIRTY-FIVE

Louise

as a girl—thirteen years old

A motorcycle roars down the street, waking her. Louise rubs her eyes and looks at her bedside clock. 5:45 a.m. Her alarm isn't set to go off until seven, and she groans. She was up late the night before, working on a project for science, and she really needs the extra hour. But she has a feeling she won't be able to get back to sleep. Still, she tries. The sun hasn't risen yet, so it's mostly dark in her room, although there is a faint lavender light creeping through the curtains. She closes her eyes and wills herself to relax into her pillow. Another motorcycle blows past, its engine screaming, and Louise groans again.

Her grandmother lives in a pretty good neighborhood. The houses are smallish, mostly single story, but nice enough. The only bad thing is that she lives on a very long street that dumps out on both sides to the main highway. Cars and motorcycles barrel down the street like they're in a race.

Just as she suspected, she can't fall back asleep. She keeps waiting for the roar of another motorcycle. *Donorcycles*, her mother calls them. Her mother is a nurse. Well, sort of. She doesn't have a job right now.

Louise lays in bed and stares at the ceiling. She drifts for a few minutes. But then, a new sound floats to her from the street. The low hum of an engine. The sound doesn't increase or decrease, just stays the same. She gets out of bed and goes to the window, and when she pushes aside the curtain, she sees an ambulance parked at the curb next to the driveway.

Her chest tightens, and she suddenly can't breathe. She thinks of her grandmother and the stroke that made her talk funny and not able to drive, but also robbed the older woman of something intangible, something Louise can only describe as an essence, a life-force, like in Star Wars. She doesn't care that her grandmother isn't the same as before, as long as she's here, because she's the only person Louise can rely on, the only person who is always there for her.

Terror clutches her heart as she races out of her room and rushes down the hall toward the living room. She stops at the archway, and her terror turns to confusion. Her mother is there, and her grandmother too. And also two men wearing white uniforms. They stand on either side of Grace, each holding one of her arms. Her mom is glaring at her grandmother and struggling against the paramedics.

Another man, a little younger than Grace, stands next to her grandmother, speaking in low tones. He wears a suit and tie, and he's handsome, if a little on the thin side.

"No, please. Please don't. This is wrong, and you know it. Please, Momma, don't do this." Grace is trying to keep her voice down, and Louise realizes that she doesn't want to wake her up. But here she is, already awake, and watching this terrible scene that feels like a movie or a TV show, but it's actually happening.

"You don't know what's good for you, Grace," her grandmother hisses.

Louise makes a strangled sound in her throat and all eyes turn to her.

"We need to go," the thin man says to the paramedics. The EMTs nod and tighten their grip on Grace.

"Mom?" Louise says, and even though she's a teenager now, her voice sounds like that of a little girl.

Her grandmother sucks in a breath. "You get back to your room, Louise, and wait for me to come in there, understand?"

Louise doesn't understand. She shakes her head. "What are they doing to my mom?"

"It's okay, honey," the thin man says. His voice is soothing, but Louise is not soothed. "Your mom just needs to come with us for a little while so she can feel better."

"I feel fine, you sons of bitches!" Grace cries. "Let go of me. Momma, don't do this. Don't let them take me. I'm begging you. Please don't let him take me. I'll be better. I won't run off. I swear. Please, Momma!"

Louise's grandmother glares at Grace. "Take her," the older woman says, and the men start to drag Grace to the front door. She doesn't go easily. She kicks and twists and writhes to keep them from taking her.

When they reach the door, her mother grasps the doorframe and turns back to her.

"I love you, baby. I'm so sorry about this. This has nothing to do with you. Whatever your grandma or that man tells you, don't believe it all, okay? Just know I love you."

The EMTs haul her out of the house, and as soon as they reach the walkway, Grace gives over to them and allows them to put her into the back of the ambulance. Louise turns to her grandmother, her mouth open and ready to ask a question. But her grandmother shakes her head, and the question dies in her throat.

"It's for the best," her grandmother says, then looks at the thin man. "Tell her, Dr. Brenner."

But Louise doesn't give him the chance. She turns away and runs back to her room. She slams the door shut and presses herself against it. Her heart races and she feels like she might have a panic attack. She forces herself to breathe.

She runs to the window and watches the ambulance pull from the curb, taking Grace away with it. Tears slide down her cheeks, and she doesn't really understand them. Louise is mad at her mother most of the time. Resentful of how she is treated at school because of Grace's behavior. Ashamed of her. But this, this removal of her mother from her life by the thin man and the white-smocked paramedics and her grandmother seems wrong somehow.

Louise knows she needs to calm down. Her eyes search her room for something to comfort her. Her gaze lands on the sketchbook on her desk. She retrieves the book and a pencil and sits upon her bed.

A couple minutes later, when her grandmother knocks on her door, Louise doesn't answer.

THIRTY-SIX

Louise

OHIO–PRESENT

I can't fall asleep. The bed is comfortable, the mattress firm, just as I like it. The twin bed in my studio isn't very big, but I can bounce a quarter off it. I haven't slept beside Grace for a couple of decades. Even when I was a kid, I didn't do it often. The couch bed was lumpy, and I was always worried I'd wake up alone, and that possibility haunted me.

But Grace doesn't stir much, and she's not snoring right now, so that's a plus. My stomach is comfortably full—the chocolate cake was better than the brussels sprouts, as promised. And I'm exhausted from the trip. But sleep eludes me.

I took several ibuprofens to shut off the dull throb in my leg, and it's doing its job. But I can't shut off my thoughts.

I don't know what my daughter's name is now. I won't admit it to Grace, but I think of her as Edie too. I haven't seen her for twelve-plus years, but I still remember the feel of her chubby little fingers in mine. The nurses let me hold her for thirty minutes before they took her from me. That was one of my conditions. I was an adult and entered into the contract fully aware of what I was doing, what I was giving up, and the reasons I was doing so. But I wanted that little piece of time with her before I let her go. Those thirty minutes were the best of my life.

For that half hour, I was completely and utterly connected to another human being. I was whole. I needed and *was* needed, and both of our needs were met by the other.

I've done an okay job at burying the memory, like so many other memories, but it comes to me occasionally. I don't cry, won't let myself, and I certainly don't regret what I did. It was the right decision. But I do have quiet moments of longing. They hit me from out of the blue. I long to feel that completeness again. I've tried to re-create it with sex, but not even the most noteworthy lovemaking can fill that void. If I allowed myself to love another person, the sex might come close, but again, I won't let myself. Loving someone always leads to emptiness. I loved my mother. Look where that got me.

Even though this whole *finding Edie* thing is bullshit, a delusion created by my mother's diseased mind, it has stirred up the idea of seeing her. Over the last decade, I've occasionally entertained thoughts of seeking her out, but always dismissed them as quickly as they arose. What would be the point? And to what end? Going down that path would only introduce more heartache into both our lives.

I think she's okay. I mean, if that maternal intuition thing is real, I've felt it. Maybe I'm trying to make myself feel better or assuage my own guilt about giving her up. But there have been times where I've had a sharp stab of worry, or gasped at a phantom fright, or laughed out loud over nothing, and I suspect they came from my daughter. Now I sound as crazy as Grace, I know, but it's true. Overall, though, when I think about my daughter, which is rarely, I feel she's fine. Of course she is. She's not with me.

Are you sure she's fine, Louise?

I force the question from my mind.

As I lie next to my mother in the Palmers' guest room, struggling for slumber, I try to imagine what it would be like to see her. I don't know what she looks like, so it's difficult to envision. Does she look like me, or does she favor her father? Just the thought of him hurts. This whole line of thinking hurts. And it's moot anyway, so why am I torturing myself?

In a few days, Grace will be dealt with, and I can put thoughts of

Edie back where they belong. On a dusty shelf in the back of my mind. And I can get back to my life. It's not much, but it's mine.

I roll onto my side. The digital clock glares red and I watch the display for an entire minute.

"Heavens, child, turn down your thoughts," Grace murmurs. I jerk at the sound of her voice, then roll over to find her gazing at me through half-closed lids.

"It's late," she says. "We have a long day ahead of us. You should try and get some sleep."

"I *am* trying."

"Okay, then don't try so hard." She smiles, then closes her eyes. I watch her drift back to sleep, and something about the hypnotic rise and fall of her chest soothes me. Before long, I drift away with her.

THIRTY-SEVEN

Melanie

CALIFORNIA—PRESENT

Dinner was a nightmare. And not just because Delilah made burger casserole, my absolute least favorite dinner she makes. She always overcooks the noodles—they're like mush—and the meat tasted like it was leftovers from a fast-food meal that she just kind of chopped up and threw in. But it was more than that. Something's going on between her and Ray. Weirdness. That's the only word I can come up with to describe it.

When I lived with Ingrid and Tom, I was younger, but I still noticed things. Like the fact that the two of them hardly talked to each other at all. The only conversations I ever saw or heard between them were about the kids and the household stuff. Like, "Can you pick up Trey from baseball?" and "If you go to Target, I need some shaving cream." At dinner, they mostly stayed quiet and looked at their phones. Sometimes they'd ask the kids about their days. *Their* kids, I should say. Not me. They never asked me about my day. I sat between Holly and Mitchell and basically never said a word because no one ever talked to me.

Ingrid and Tom never showed any affection for each other either. They never touched each other or held hands or looked at each other with secret smiles. Come to think of it, they didn't ever look at each other at all. Which I didn't think anything of back then because I was just a little kid. But now, I realize that not even looking at your husband or wife is kind of strange.

Maybe that's because of Ray and Delilah. When I came to live with them, I was struck by the way they were with each other. I have fuzzy memories of my first parents, and when I think of them, I feel warm and cozy, so they probably liked each other and showed it. But I don't remember specifics. Same with Pam and Andy. I don't know how they were together. My time with them was pretty short because Penny showed up and got me out of there pretty quick. But with Ray and Delilah, it's different. I was nine when I came here, so my memories are clear. When I came here, I could tell that they liked each other. That they . . . what's the word my social studies teacher says? They . . . *related* to each other. They were affectionate in a way I'd never seen before, or, at least, remembered I'd seen, because I think my first parents held hands and kissed each other, but I can't trust those memories.

But Ray and Delilah were crazy about each other, and anyone around them could see it and feel it. And I was glad to be sent to a home where the foster parents actually got along and liked each other. I mean, they fight sometimes, and Ray can get really steamed. When he does, he kicks stuff or throws stuff, and it's kind of scary, how mad he gets, like maybe he's going to totally explode. But he never hits Delilah and he never hits me, which is a good thing. And even though I'd never admit this to anyone else, sometimes when he gets mad at Delilah, I kind of agree with him. She does stupid stuff. Not that she's a dummy, or anything, but she doesn't think things through sometimes, like when she gave all of Ray's baseball gear to the Goodwill, or when she bought a new recliner and had the delivery guys take away Ray's favorite easy chair, the chair he called Svetlana—not sure why, but I'm pretty sure if someone names a piece of furniture it's because he really, really likes it and doesn't want it being hauled off to the dump.

And yes, sometimes he gets mad about silly stuff, like when his football team lost the Super Bowl and he was totally depressed for a whole week and snapped at Delilah and me for every little thing. He apologized later, though, and took us out for ice cream to make it up to us.

Anyway, they always got along for the most part. They'd wink at each other and make googly eyes, and they'd kiss real long and slow, and I'd pretend not to notice, because—*gross*. They'd sit on the couch really close together when we watched movies and feed each other popcorn and M and M's and laugh when they missed each other's mouths.

But lately it feels like they're not getting along so well. I haven't seen them kiss in months, and they hardly ever make googly eyes anymore. And when we sit down to watch a movie, Ray has me sit next to him and makes Delilah sit on the recliner she bought. And Ray feeds me popcorn, but not like he did with Delilah. More like, he tosses the kernels to me and I try to catch them in my mouth, and when I do, he high-fives me. Delilah complains that she wants to sit on the couch, and Ray tells her that if she wanted to sit on the couch, she shouldn't have brought that damned recliner into the house.

Tonight at dinner Ray just pushed the food around on his plate and Delilah stared at him with this anxious expression on her face. I ate all my casserole, like the good little foster kid I am. I learned from Ingrid and Tom to clean my plate, because if I didn't, I had to sit at the dinner table all night and into the next day, and if I still couldn't stomach it— and sometimes I could not, even when it started out delicious—I got treated to a paddling, right before school, which made it difficult to sit through class with bruises blooming on my butt.

It's late now. After eleven. I was going to watch TV for a while, but Delilah sent me to my room like she was mad at me. I don't know what I did, but I didn't argue with her. I never do. I just nodded my head, thanked her for (that awful) dinner, and escaped into my bedroom.

I'm playing a game on my iPad but I can hear low voices from the living room. It's Ray and Delilah, for sure, not the TV. I can tell when it's the TV, because the TV's right against the wall, and it vibrates through my room when the volume's up high enough for them to hear. I can't make out what they're saying, and I'm pretty glad about that. Deep down inside, I'm always worried that my foster parents will fight about me.

Maybe because that's already happened a couple of times.

I don't want her in this house, Tom.

Yeah, I know, she's weird.

Weird? She talks to her fucking hand!

But she's not dangerous, or anything.

How do you know? How do you know she's not going to have some kind of, I don't know, psychotic break, and kill us all in our sleep?

You watch too much Forensic Files, *Ingrid.*

It happens. That's all I'm saying.

What about the check? That girl pays for your hair appointments and your fancy nails and your vodka.

So we'll get another kid. A normal kid.

But I can't make out the conversation in the living room, and that's good because that means they're not fighting. When Ray and Delilah fight, they are not quiet about it. Maybe they're making googly eyes at each other. Maybe they're going to have sex. The thought makes me cringe, but them having sex is much better than the alternative.

I shut down the iPad and grab my rucksack, then pull out my journal. An image of Reuben Meserve floats across my brain, and I push it away. I open the journal and grab my pen, then close my eyes and wait. The hum of conversation continues on the other side of the wall. I do my best to block it out.

"Where are you, Penny?" I whisper. "I need you."

A long moment passes. Then another. Just when I think she isn't coming, my skin starts to tingle, and my left hand starts to move. When it stops, several minutes later, I look down to see what she wrote:

I can't see it, not yet. But it's close. I'm trying, I promise I am. Be vigilant. Keep your eyes open and your head clear. Do not let down your guard.

A chill runs through me and I slam the journal shut and push it away. What is Penny telling me? Why is she trying to scare me?

I don't like this at all.

THIRTY-EIGHT

Grace

OHIO–PRESENT

I wake at the first crack of light through the guest room blinds.

Louise snores softly beside me, and I'm glad for the sound. I have the strongest urge to scoot up next to her and wrap my arms around her and snuggle with her the way a mother and daughter do. But I won't. She'd just push me away, and anyway, what she needs is sleep. Without it, she'll likely spend the day brooding. A brooding Louise is not someone with whom I want to spend twelve hours in a car.

Doesn't matter. I've got to do my thing anyway and can't have her breathing down my neck while I do.

Carefully, so as not to disturb her, I get out of bed. My bag is on the chair where I left it, and I quickly trade the Pearl Jam shirt for a pair of jeans and a sweatshirt. I slip my feet into my loafers, grab my address book from my fanny pack and tuck it into my back pocket, then leave the room.

The aroma of strong coffee permeates the whole downstairs, and when I reach the kitchen, I find Mary already up.

"Good morning," she says. "Did you sleep okay?"

"Best night I've had in a long while," I tell her.

"That's good." She smiles warmly. "Louise. You found her, Grace."

"I did."

"I'm so glad," Mary says. "I like her. She's a strong woman. But vulnerable too. Just isn't willing to admit it, is all."

"She's a pain in my hind parts."

Mary chuckles, then turns serious. "She doesn't know about you, does she?"

I consider my answer. "She knows a lot of things about me, Mary. Just not that one thing."

"Well . . ." She opens the cupboard next to her and pulls out two mugs. "That one thing is pretty important, don't you think?" She shakes her head. "I'm sorry. It's not my place."

"Don't be sorry. I appreciate your counsel." She smiles, relieved. "Will is a terrific young man."

Mary beams. "He is, isn't he? We're so proud of him. And his brother too, of course. But Will, he's a miracle, right? Sometimes I think about what might have been and . . . well, I can't even imagine." She starts to tear up, and I have a feeling she's about to launch into a long, emotionally charged monologue of gratitude. It's not that I don't appreciate her gratitude, I just don't have the time for it right now. I change the subject.

"You're going to have to beat off the girls with a stick."

"Already do. You should see it when I drop him at school. They practically flock to him. Oh, he's not interested in any of that yet. I mean, he does like this one girl, Lily, but it's nothing serious at this point. He wants to concentrate on school and track."

"He's a runner?" I ask.

She nods. "And long jump. You just cannot believe how far he can go. It's like he can fly."

"That must be quite a sight." I remember Louise in high school, and it's my turn to think of what might have been.

Mary holds up a mug. "Coffee?"

"Not just yet."

Her eyes go wide. "Oh, that's right. You have to do your . . . thing." She glances at the kitchen door. "The porch is lovely this time of year. The sun hits it as it comes up, warms it nicely. Might be the perfect spot."

I nod. "Sounds wonderful."

She points to the chair at the end of the kitchen table, at the blanket folded over it. "Take that with you. It's still a bit chilly."

"Thank you."

I grab the thick wool blanket and carry it with me to the back porch. The sun is just rising, and the far horizon blazes pink. A couple of large wooden chairs with overstuffed canvas cushions line the porch. The day will be warm, but Mary's right. It's still cool out here. I wrap the blanket around my shoulders, then pull my address book out of my back pocket and sit on one of the chairs. The cushion exhales beneath my weight.

I open the book, then settle my fingers upon the pages. I stare at the horizon for a long moment, then close my eyes and take a deep breath.

Nothing happens for a few minutes. Then it starts. Voices and images roll through my mind as I slowly turn the pages. Voices and images. Words and places and faces, some familiar, some unknown to me, a symphony of sights and sounds and feelings and thoughts. On this page, they're louder or more vivid, on the next softer, fuzzier or opaque. Before the middle of my book, the symphony strikes a booming chord. I open my eyes and glance down at the page and read the name upon it. My breathing is suddenly shallow, and I force myself to take a few long inhalations. I mentally flag the page—I haven't dog-eared a book since I was six and got a world of whoop-ass from my momma—then close my eyes and continue.

I'm almost to the end when I hear the back door creak open. I know it's Louise before I open my eyes. Mary would never interrupt me. The symphony stops abruptly. The sudden cessation of images and voices leaves my brain scrambling for thoughts.

"What the hell are you doing, Grace?"

I turn and see my daughter glaring at me, arms crossed. My heart skips a couple beats, and I fumble to close my address book. I'm still reeling, but I manage a smile.

"Just greeting the day with a little meditation," I tell her. She glances at the book, then cocks her head to the side.

"Where did you learn to meditate?"

I stand and stretch, grab the blanket before it falls to the floor, then give Louise a pointed look. "The nuthouse."

I walk past her and escape to the warmth and safety of the kitchen.

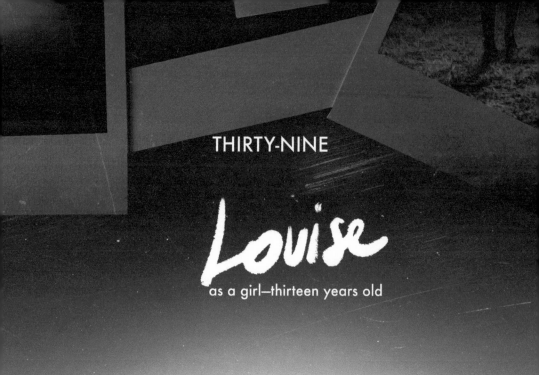

THIRTY-NINE

Louise

as a girl—thirteen years old

Louise sits in her room listening to music. She glances around for her sketchbook and remembers she left it in the living room last night. She gets up and walks out of her room, then heads for the coffee table, but the sketchbook isn't there. Strange. She could have sworn she set it there. She'd been sitting on the couch, working on a drawing, then put the book down when one of her favorite shows came on.

She looks at the living room around her. Since the stroke, her grandmother hasn't been big on cleaning. Louise does most of those chores herself, vacuuming, dusting, and the like. But her grandmother has always been staunch about avoiding clutter, and that hasn't changed. There are no magazines on the coffee table, no piles of detritus on any surface. If her grandmother found her sketchbook on the coffee table this morning, she would have stowed it away somewhere. But where?

Her grandmother is out at the neighborhood garage sales with a friend from the senior center, so Louise can't ask her. She wanders to the bookshelf on the far wall, thinking it might be tucked in with some books. She doesn't see it. She moves to the breakfront and opens the wooden doors, then the drawers, but again, comes up empty.

She turns in a circle, scanning the room for another possible location. Her gaze lands on the steamer trunk in the corner next to the fireplace. Louise doubts her sketchbook is there. But then, her grandmother's faculties have been slightly compromised. Not too much, just the occasional forgetfulness or confusion with how to operate an appliance, or she'll search for a certain word, an easy word like *lamp* or *waffles* and come up empty. Nothing out of the ordinary, the doctors say.

Louise walks to the trunk and runs her fingers across the smooth dark wood. She pops open the latches on either end, lifts the lid, and looks inside. And there it is, resting atop her mother's bed linens. The sight of those sheets and blankets, folded neatly, and unused for many months now, fills her with sadness.

She picks up her sketchbook and begins to close the lid. Something catches her eye from beneath the pile of linens. It appears to be the corner of a manila envelope. Louise reaches down and tugs at it, pulls it free.

The envelope is large, 9×12, and puffy at the bottom. She considers that the envelope doesn't belong to her, that perhaps she shouldn't look inside, that the contents are someone else's private possessions. But curiosity gets the better of her. She sets her sketchbook aside, then sits on the floor next to the trunk. She carefully opens the flap and peers into the envelope.

Photos. More than twenty, perhaps even more than fifty photographs, some 4×6, some 5×7, some wallet-sized. Louise reaches in and pulls one out and gazes at the face of a toddler, maybe two or three, her strawberry-blond hair in curly pigtails, her cheeks smattered with freckles, her smile wide and gleeful. Louise has no idea who she is.

She pulls out another photo, this one a 5×7 and faded. A high school baseball team, from the looks of it, nine strapping young men, standing tall, smiling proudly, the two in the middle holding an enormous trophy. All strangers to her.

She doesn't understand what she is seeing, but she has no time to contemplate her find. She hears the slam of a car door outside and knows that her grandmother has returned. Quickly, hands shaking, she drops the photos back into the envelope with the rest, then tucks the envelope beneath the linens. She closes the lid of the trunk just as a key turns in the lock of the front door.

Louise grabs her sketchbook, jumps to her feet, and takes a step toward the couch. Her grandmother walks in and regards her suspiciously. But then, perhaps not suspiciously. Perhaps Louise is projecting her own feelings of guilt onto the older woman.

"Well, hello," her grandmother says. "Is everything all right? You look upset, child."

Louise blinks rapidly. "I was just looking for my sketchpad."

"You found it, I see."

She nods. "Grams?"

"Yes, child?" The older woman starts for the kitchen. "Are you hungry? I'm starved. I'll make us some sandwiches. Peanut butter and jelly okay?"

"When is my mom coming back?" Louise asks. Her grandmother stops moving but doesn't turn and doesn't answer.

"Let me know when you're ready for lunch," she says.

Louise raises her voice. "When is my mom coming back?"

Her grandmother turns around and looks at her sternly. "Is that a tone I hear in your voice?"

Louder still. "Are you going to answer me? I have a right to know. When is my mom coming back?"

She isn't sure why she's making such a fuss. Her grandmother will certainly take away the TV, and probably dessert for a week. But suddenly, it's *very important* for her to know what's going on. She smacks the sketchbook down onto the coffee table.

"Why is she in a hospital? What's wrong with her? Why won't you tell me?"

Her grandmother explodes. "Because she's insane, girl! And you better hope you don't have that in you, too! She hears voices, all different voices. Demons is what they are. Demons born of her mental illness. And they tell her to do things, and she does them, without thought or question. Leaves you and me and races all over the damn place doing their bidding! She's psychotic. Are you happy now? To know your mother is certifiable?"

Louise swallows hard. "Can that doctor help her?"

The older woman glares at her. "I do not know, but I hope to God he can. For your sake."

A cold chill runs through Louise, and she's gripped with the irrational fear that something terrible has happened to her mother. "I want to go see her."

"No."

"Why not?"

"Because she doesn't want to see you!" her grandmother cries. "Okay? She doesn't want to see you, so just leave it alone!"

Louise stumbles backward as though she's been slapped. She rushes for the front door, yanks it open, and escapes into blinding sunshine, her sketchbook momentarily forgotten.

FORTY

Delilah

CALIFORNIA–PRESENT

Ray and me made love last night. It wasn't totally amazing like it's been in the past. We had to keep it down because we knew Melanie was still awake. And the couch is not the best place to do it. Ray wanted to go into the bedroom, but I just couldn't. Not after I walked in yesterday afternoon to find him and Melanie napping together. I mean, at first I thought it was kind of sweet to see them that way. They looked just like a regular dad and his little girl. But I was also jealous because Ray hasn't spooned with me in a very long time. And then I got to looking closer at them and realized that Melanie is not so much of a little girl anymore, and that made me feel really uncomfortable.

I walked out of the room and went to the front door and opened it and slammed it shut as loud as I could, and sure enough, Melanie came walking out of my bedroom, rubbing her eyes and smiling up at me, and saying, "Hey, D, you're back!" like she was happy to see me. And then I felt bad because the whole time I was at Kohl's, not once did I even think about buying something for her, and that's not a sign of a very good mother, now is it? I could go back to Kohl's and buy something nice for her, but then, I think maybe I maxed out my card, so that might have to wait until I can pay it down a little.

Anyway, it was good to be intimate with Ray last night, even if it wasn't the best sex we've had. He seemed distracted and kept his eyes shut, which he never does, and when he finished, it was almost like I wasn't even there. But I'm not going to complain, because I *was* there, and I finished too, and I felt like maybe this was the start of us getting back on track in the sack.

This morning, I'm in a much better mood than I was yesterday. I don't have the urge to clean and even if I did, there's nothing left to do. The house is practically sparkling. Melanie's still sleeping, or at least she's still in her bedroom and being quiet. Ray got up a while ago to go for his run. It's funny, because he doesn't eat too healthy, but he never misses his Sunday-morning run. When he gets back, he always reeks, but he's also kind of sexy, slick with sweat, his cheeks all red and his eyes really bright. And he's always in a good mood after he runs because of the endorphins.

Early on in our relationship, he explained about endorphins, how good, hard exercise releases this happy-making hormone. He tried to get me to run with him, and I tried once, but I never got that happy feeling. Instead, I got a charley horse in my calf and thought I was going to have a heart attack before I even went a mile, and I was pretty much cranky and useless for the rest of the day. He never bugged me about going with him again.

I made a pot of coffee. Ray likes to come home and shower, then he gulps down a huge bottle of water, and when he's through with that, he likes to sit at the kitchen table and drink a cup of coffee and read the news on his iPad. Sometimes I sit with him, and sometimes Mel does too, like we're a real family. Mel does crosswords or sudoku or plays games on her iPad, and I flip through my magazines, like I'm doing right now, and we talk about what we're going to do together that day.

I take a sip of coffee and thumb through the first few pages of *People* magazine, which I bought on impulse at the market a few days ago. I know it's expensive. There's other magazines that have all the Hollywood stars in them that are a lot cheaper, but *People* is the best. I love looking at pictures of actors and actresses that I see on the TV or in the movies.

I like reading about their real lives and their challenges and heartbreaks. It makes them more . . . I don't know . . . connected to me, I guess, like they could be friends of mine.

I flip to the next page and gaze down at the image of a famous actress who was in a movie I saw last month that I absolutely loved. I've read a lot about her and I know she's roughly my age—thirty-eight, give or take. In the picture, her head is thrown back with laughter and her arms encircle her enormous belly. She's very pregnant, and her gorgeous husband, another actor who she starred with a couple movies ago, stands just behind her and looks down at her with a kind of reverence.

My tears are sudden and fierce. They spill down my cheeks before I even know they're coming.

I wanted a baby, more than anything. From the time I was a little girl, I always wanted to be a mom. My friends wanted to be princesses and airline pilots and rock stars and marine biologists, but whenever anyone asked me what I wanted to be, I always said I want to be a mom. And I got a lot of funny looks. And Maureen Applegate, who was my best friend when I was a kid, well, her mom heard me say this and she said, "You can be a mom *and* be something else, you know. We are not living in the Dark Ages."

I didn't know what the Dark Ages were at the time, but I just shook my head at her. "I don't want to be anything else but a mom."

"Well, Delilah," she said. "That's very noble of you."

I didn't know what that meant either. Maureen's mom said it with kind of a sneer on her face, like she wasn't being completely honest with me. But I didn't care, because I knew what I wanted.

We tried, as soon as we were settled and Ray had a steady job. That took a while, but it felt good to wait until we were ready. I went off my birth control pills, and he threw away his condoms and we screwed like rabbits. Every chance we got. It was fun and kind of exciting, because we knew what we were trying to do, which was to make a life, part him and part me, and we laughed about how God was pretty darn cool to make the hugely important, and very serious task of creating a human being so damn fun.

But then, we didn't. And we didn't, and it kept not happening. At first, when my period came, we'd kind of brush it off and say, "Okay, so, there's always next month." But then the next month came, and same thing. After a year, I got to the point where I'd see blood in my underwear and just completely fall apart.

We looked into fertility treatments, but I couldn't handle the daily injections because I hate needles more than I can say. I think Ray was relieved. IVF costs as much as a house. So we kept trying naturally. By the end of the second year, I was practically suicidal. A year after that, we decided to give up and look into adoption. That did not go well either. Because of Ray's record.

I hear the front door slam open and I quickly wipe my eyes and close the magazine. A moment later, Ray appears at the kitchen threshold. I can tell immediately that I'm in trouble.

"Are you fucking kidding me?"

He's sweaty and flushed, as I expected. What I didn't expect was him holding the three Kohl's bags in his hands.

I meant to bring them in from the car last night after he fell asleep, but after our lovemaking, I guess I forgot.

Shit, shit, shit!

FORTY-ONE

Louise

OHIO-PRESENT

I'm starting to feel guilty about what I have planned for Grace. Not just because of how the Palmers treated her, like she was an angel from heaven, which is totally inexplicable to me but no less true. But also because I'm ambushing her, and I'm not sure what that might do to her long term. I decide to give her an opportunity to come clean with me so that I can do the same.

"You've been jerking me around, right, Grace? This whole road trip is just a lame excuse for you and me to reconnect."

We're back on Interstate 80 heading west. We got a late start because Mary Palmer had to feed us a gargantuan breakfast, of which I had seconds. Grace sits in the passenger seat, a strange smile playing about her lips.

"I don't much like that expression, Lou," she says. "But I can understand you thinking what you're thinking."

She holds a brown paper sack on her lap, given to us by the illustrious Mary. It's full of muffins made with freshly procured eggs from the chicken coop and blueberries picked from the garden behind the house. They smell fucking fantastic, but after two helpings of spinach frittata and pork belly, I couldn't eat another bite.

"How's your leg?" Grace asks, not so subtly changing the subject.

I don't answer. My leg is the same as always. Throbbing. It's funny, because I know I could get a job behind a desk. I have the education. But I choose to work behind a bar, which is punishing, even for people without prior life-altering injuries that make standing for eight straight hours absolute hell. I made a conscious decision to take that job, not just because the lifestyle suits me, but because, in some small way, it's penance for my own sins. Sins which I pretend not to remember, but which occasionally crawl out from under their figurative rocks to remind me that I'm not without them.

Paper crinkles, and I look over to see Grace clutching the sack, her knuckles white. Her face is pale, and I notice the dark circles under her eyes. I don't know if they were there before—I haven't looked too closely at her this morning, or I've made a point *not* to look at her after I found her on the back porch "meditating."

"Are you okay?" I ask.

She forces a smile and nods. "I'm fine. But I wonder if you might just pull off at the next exit? I could use a ladies' room."

We haven't been on the road forty-five minutes, and Grace visited the bathroom several times before she got into the car.

"You sure you're okay?"

She heaves a sigh. "For goodness sake, Louise, I just need the loo, that's all. It'll give you a chance to smoke one of your cigarettes."

I see a sign for gas, food, and lodging at the next exit and engage my blinker, then check the sideview mirror. As I start to ease into the right lane, Grace thrusts out her hand and shrieks, "Watch out!" A millisecond later, a box truck rockets past on the right. Reflexively, I swerve to the left and almost get clipped by a Mercedes doing ninety.

"Jesus Christ!" My heart is galloping at triple speed. I pull my foot off the accelerator, and the driver in the car behind me leans on his horn. I couldn't give a shit. I check my sideview again, then my blind spot, and ease into the exit lane, this time without incident. As we cruise down the offramp, I take long slow breaths to keep myself from hyperventilating.

"The Gas 'n Go will do," Grace says evenly.

I head for the red-and-yellow sign up ahead, turn into the drive, then wind around toward the far side of the building. I park in an empty spot in front of the bathrooms and glance at the entrance to the minimart. "Want anything?"

Grace shakes her head then gets out of the car and makes her way to the ladies' room on the left. The little turn-dial above the door handle shows green for vacancy. She pushes the door open and disappears inside. I watch the turn-dial shift to red.

I grab my Marlboro Lights from my purse and get out of the Camry. My hands shake, and it takes me a couple of tries to light my cigarette. I suck in a long drag and feel the smoke burn its way to my lungs. It doesn't feel great, I admit, but it reminds me I'm alive, and the ritual calms me in that sick and dysfunctional way that bad habits do.

I can't help wondering what would have happened if Grace hadn't stopped me from changing lanes. She would not be in that bathroom, and I would not be out here increasing my chances of lung cancer. Grace would likely be dead, and I would probably be on my way to intensive care. I've been there before and the memory of that time makes me shudder.

But she did stop me. I don't know how she knew. She wasn't looking in the sideview mirror. She was looking down at the bag of muffins, concentrating on it, or perhaps concentrating on not showing me what was actually going on with her, but she did not *see* that box truck with her eyes.

That's not possible.

I finish my smoke and grind it into the pavement, then lean into the Camry and pull my cell phone from the bay between the seats. A message light flashes up at me, and I swipe the screen to read it. It's from the man I called yesterday morning, which seems like a lifetime ago. My stomach tightens as I read.

Let me know when you know your final destination. If you don't know until you get there, contact me as soon as you do. My team and I can be anywhere in California within three hours. Call if you'd like to discuss further. Brenner.

I close the phone and toss it back into the car.

Grace is still in the bathroom. It's been ten minutes. I consider going over and banging on the door and asking her if she's all right. Instead, I light another cigarette.

And try not to think about the god damn box truck.

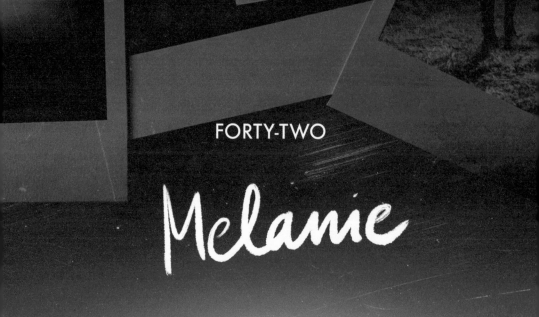

FORTY-TWO

Melanie

CALIFORNIA-PRESENT

Delilah is up a creek. I know that because as quiet as they were last night is as loud as they are this morning.

I woke up early, before six, but then I kind of fell back asleep. I had this really strange dream. I can't remember it all the way because it was all over the place like some dreams are. But there was this woman, and at first, I thought it was Delilah, but it turned out not to be. It was someone I've never seen before, but I felt like I knew her, and she was singing to me some weird song about butterflies. And in the dream, the butterflies were important, but then I woke up and everything faded away, even the woman's face. I tried to bring the picture of her back into my brain, but I couldn't.

Anyway, I came out of the dream kind of slow. I was in my bed and I needed to pee. So I got up and went to the bathroom, but while I was in there, on the toilet, I felt the hair on the back of my neck stand up, and my heart started beating real fast in my chest.

I didn't flush. I don't know why not, I always do, even though they tell us at school that the best way to save water is not to flush after every pee, but I do it because I don't want Ray or Delilah to see the yellow in the toilet bowl. But I didn't this time. I went back to my room and grabbed my journal and sat on my bed. Then I heard the yelling from the other room, and that made me freeze.

It's not like I've never heard yelling before. Delilah and Ray fight sometimes. Pam and Andy used to go at it pretty good. Ingrid and Tom didn't yell. They just kind of frowned at each other when the other wasn't looking. And I don't remember my first parents enough to know if they fought.

But Ray is pissed. Delilah spent a lot of money at Kohl's—that much I heard through the wall. And I know that money is tight. What they get from the state for having me here doesn't amount to much. (I got that little tidbit from my caseworker, Pearl, not from the fight that's going on in the living room.)

"I'll get a job," I hear Delilah say.

"Oh yeah?" Ray says. "What kind of job? Seriously, Delilah, what kind of job are you going to get? What the hell are you qualified to do?"

I think that's kind of a mean question for Ray to ask, but I wonder the same thing. What could Delilah do? She can't work at the salon because she doesn't know how to do hair. The two haircuts she tried to give me were disastrous. She'd make a terrible waitress because she wouldn't be able to keep orders straight. I know that sounds as mean as what Ray said, but it's the truth. I guess she could work at the ThriftMart. She's much smarter than the cashiers down there. Some of them seem like they're special needs, and Delilah is smart in a lot of ways, and she'd be good with customers because when she smiles, a person can't help but smile back.

"I have a degree," Delilah cries. "I have a bachelor's from UC Davis, for crying out loud."

"In what?" Ray says.

She doesn't answer. It's quiet for a minute, and I realize I'm holding my breath.

"I'm sorry, Ray," I hear her tell him. "I don't know what happened." Her voice is high and squeaky. "I just couldn't help myself. I kept putting things in my cart. But they were all for you, just look! In the bags. They're all things I thought you'd like. I love you, Ray!"

Another silence.

"I love you too, D."

I get a funny feeling in my stomach when I hear this. I'm glad they love each other, because that's what parents are supposed to do. But no one has ever said that to me in my entire life. Maybe my first parents did. But I don't have any clear memory of it, so it doesn't count. I realize, as I eavesdrop on Ray and Delilah, that I would give anything for someone to say that to me. *I love you, Mel.*

"I love you," Ray repeats, "but this is not okay. You're going to have to take all this shit back, you hear me? You'll take it back today."

"But—"

"No fucking buts, Delilah."

"I thought we were going to have family day," she says. Family day happens on Sundays, and we go to the mall or the arcade, or the swap meet. It's mostly stupid, but I smile and play my part and help them pretend we're a family.

"I'm too pissed off to have family day with you. You go to Kohl's. I'll figure something out with Mel."

Delilah doesn't answer. A moment later, there's a knock on my door, then it opens, and Ray stands there.

"Hey, sunshine," he says. "How fast can you get ready?"

I give him my automatic response. "Faster than you."

He grins. "We'll see about that." I watch as he moves through my room and goes into the adjoining bathroom. As soon as I hear the shower blasting, I grab my journal and open it to the first blank page. Pencil in my left hand, I close my eyes and wait. I feel my left hand twitch then move. Not for long, though. When it stops, I look down.

Soon. It's happening soon. Be careful. Watch out!

I reread the passage and shiver. I'm scared of what Penny is telling me, but also, maybe because I'm older now, I'm seeing things a little bit differently. Maybe Penny is a liar. Maybe she isn't real. Maybe I shouldn't listen to her. She's the one who told me not everyone is who I think they are. Maybe she isn't either.

But she's never steered me wrong before.

Still, I'm about to spend the day with *Ray*. He won't let anything bad happen to me. He'll keep me safe.

"I'll be okay, Penny," I say aloud.

The hair on the back of neck stands up. The journal calls to me.

I ignore them both and hurry to get myself ready.

FORTY-THREE

Grace

OHIO-PRESENT

The bathroom is disgusting, much as I expected, but it's a single stall and I'm grateful for that. I turn the lock then press my forehead against the door. I can practically feel the germs from the door crawling into my pores, so I push away quickly and head for the sink.

A single fluorescent strip hangs above the mirror. I glance at my reflection and gasp at what I see. I closely resemble a dead prizefighter. It's possible the fluorescent light is adding to the horror, but the dark circles that bleed well past my lower lids make me look like I have two black eyes, and the rest of my face is ghostly pale.

I bend over and cup some water in my hands, then splash my cheeks. Damn, but don't I feel just awful. My heart thuds a slow but painful beat, and the pain spreads through my chest. It stops at my shoulder and that's a good sign. If it were going all the way down my left arm, I'd probably have to take a long hard look at my mortality right about now. But my arm feels fine, for the moment, at least.

There's no paper towels in here, just one of those blower machines, so I use my shirt to dry my face and my hands. My momma would pitch a fit if she saw me do that. But she isn't here, so I couldn't give a goldarn. I might be seeing her sooner rather than later, though. I genuflect reflexively.

I press the first two fingers of my right hand against my left wrist and count to thirty. My pulse is weak and thready, and I know what that means. It's been a long time since I formally practiced nursing, and that didn't last long. But I remember all my learning.

I'm not surprised by this. I just didn't know when to expect it. I thought I had more time, and the realization that I might not makes me furious, and my fury brings my blood pressure up a little, so I let it flow.

Dizziness sweeps through me, and I collapse against the edge of the stained porcelain sink. I grip the sides with shaking hands and suck in a few deep breaths. A low hum fills my head, and as the moments tick by, the volume rises steadily until it's a deafening roar. I want to scream to drown out the sound, but Louise is just beyond the bathroom door and her hearing my screams would just prove what she already suspects about me.

"More time," I whisper. My voice bounces off the tile walls and my words reverberate through my skull, mixing with the cacophony already playing. My fury returns, reinvigorated.

I'll be damned if I am going to die in this filthy bathroom. Forgive me for cursing, Lord, but I'll be damned if I am going to kick before Louise and I get to Edie!

My brain goes quiet, just like that, and the sudden silence makes me swoon. I let go of the sink and slowly straighten up. The pain in my chest has receded and my heartbeat is almost back to normal. In the mirror I see that color has returned to my cheeks, minimizing the intensity of the dark circles beneath my eyes. I don't look fabulous, God knows, but I look a whole heck of a lot better than I did a few minutes ago.

I glance over at the toilet in the corner of the room. I don't really need to pee, but I might as well since I'm here. As I'm doing my business, there's a knock on the door.

I start to respond, but my voice cracks before I can get a word out. I clear my throat and try again. "Occupied."

"No shit." Louise. "Are you okay in there?"

I keep my pace leisurely as I wipe and flush and cross to the sink to wash my hands. Nice and easy, so as not to enrage my blood pumper. I take one more look at my reflection—not too terrible—then move to the door and unlock it. Louise stands there, arms crossed, doing her best at ambivalence, but I can see the worry etched into her features.

I force a scowl. "Good lord! A woman can't even have a bowel movement in peace." I shake my head, then brush past her and head for the car.

I'm pretty sure she knows I'm full of horse pucky.

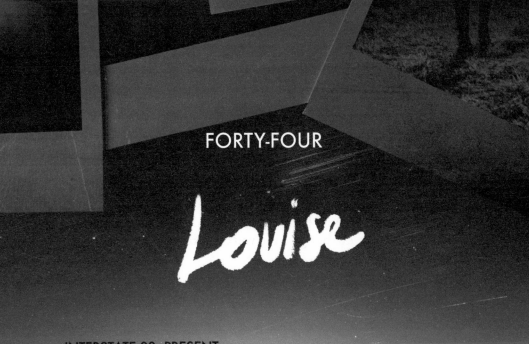

FORTY-FOUR

Louise

We've logged a hundred and fifty miles since we left the Gas 'n Go, and Grace seems pretty much okay. Her color is much better, and she's livelier than before, even launching into commentary about things we pass on I-80. Maybe she really did have to take a shit. Personally, I get very cranky when I don't have my morning constitutional. I smile to myself at the thought. That was my grandma's phrase. Morning constitutional. *I'll make your breakfast as soon as I take my morning constitutional.* When I was a kid, I had no idea what Grams was talking about, but I got the gist of it after a while.

Anyway, maybe that's what was going on with Grace. Ten minutes in the bathroom did wonders for her. But I think I might be kidding myself. She did not look like a woman who needed to poop. She looked like a woman about to keel over.

Not to be insensitive, but the last thing I need on this trip is a dead mother.

"Oh, look at that, Lou," she says.

She points at a passing SUV with a motorized wheelchair attached to the back. It looks pretty slick too, not that I know anything about wheelchairs. One of my customers at the bar and grill—Ollie

McClintock—rides one, but his is a piece of crap. It's always breaking down, and his wife ends up having to push him out of the place manually, and by then he's good and drunk and more than a little cantankerous and hurls the most terrible insults at her.

"I think I'd like to get me one of those someday."

I grin. "I can't ever imagine you riding around on one of those, Grace."

"Well, why not? A lot less effort than a bicycle, cheaper than a car 'cause you don't have to buy gas. And you can mow down all those idiots waiting for samples at Costco."

"That would be a plus," I agree.

"I could have used one on the George Washington, that's for sure." I glance over at her. "I saw a couple of people riding them, and I'll tell you, the cyclists and the pedestrians parted for them like they were Moses."

"I'm guessing those people were handicapped, Grace. You're not. You don't need a wheelchair, motorized or not."

She turns to me. "I'm glad to hear you say that."

"What?"

"That I'm not handicapped."

I chuckle. "Being physically handicapped and mentally incompetent are two different things."

"So, you're saying I'm a nut but I'm in good shape."

I shake my head but keep my eyes on the road. "I'm saying, you don't need a motorized wheelchair."

"I guess not," she concedes. "Not yet, anyway."

We settle into an amicable silence. I realize that Grace and I just had the longest conversation I can remember that wasn't fraught with conflict, hostility, or derision—at least since I've been an adult. I don't want to feel good about it—I don't want to feel *anything* about it, but I do. *I just had a nice and somewhat humorous conversation with my mother.* It's not a miracle on the same level as the parting of the Red Sea, but it's something.

Thirty minutes later, Grace's mood plummets. I glance over to see that her hands are clutched tightly against her chest, and she's subtly shaking her head left to right and back again. Her expression is pinched.

"What is it, Grace?"

"We need to stop."

"Why? Are you feeling okay?"

She ignores the question.

"Grace!" I say with more volume than I intended. "What is it?"

She turns to me. Her face is slack, as though she's forcing herself to appear calm, neutral. It's not working. She looks like a wax dummy.

"I'm hungry, Louise. And we have to do something. Find a fast-food joint."

We stop at the next McDonald's we come to. I pull into a free parking space, switch off the engine, and turn to look at her.

"What gives? What do we need to do?"

Again, she ignores me. She opens the glove compartment and pulls out the Thomas Guide, then starts mumbling to herself.

"I don't know if we can do both, but we have to, that's all there is to it. I *know* that!"

She rifles through the guide, tracing her finger along the map. I'm not sure what to do. I know I'm not supposed to point out her mania. That would be a mistake. But I can't just sit here and watch her talk to herself.

"Thompson Guide, huh?" I say. "Welcome to the Dark Ages."

She looks up at me, confused.

"What are you looking for?" I ask. "Just use my phone. Google Maps."

She rolls her eyes. "You know that smartphones give people tumors, right? Big fat carcinomas bulging out from the sides of their heads."

"Yeah, right."

"It's true," she insists. "Believe me or don't."

"I don't," I tell her.

"That's fine. Think what you want. But one thing's for certain. Good old paper never killed anyone."

"Except trees."

She squints at me for a few seconds, then bursts out laughing. I'm relieved by her laughter. I can't deny that. So much so, that I join in with her.

"That's a good one," she says, wiping the giddy tears from her eyes. "You're quick, Lou." She sobers instantly and returns her attention to the Thomas Guide. I try to see what she's looking at, but she's hunched over the map. Suddenly, she jerks her head sharply to the right and looks up at the ceiling.

"What?" she shrieks.

"What, what?" I ask, but she's not talking to me.

"I *know*! I heard you! That's what I'm trying to do!"

Her eyes are wide, her pupils dilated. She shakes her head from side to side. "No! I will not! I can't!"

I suck in a breath as I watch Grace spiral. I've seen this before. It's more than unsettling. It's downright fucking terrifying.

"Grace," I say quietly. "Grace?"

She snaps her head toward me but she seems to be looking right through me. The muscles in her face are taut with tension, like a mirror about to shatter. A tremor courses through me.

Then suddenly, her features relax and her gaze focuses on me.

"That phone gets the internet, right?"

For a long moment I'm speechless, but I force myself to recover. "You mean the phone that's giving me carcinomas?"

"That very one."

"Yes," I say. "Why?"

"I need you to use it. I need you to book us a flight to California."

My shoulders spasm reflexively. Grace doesn't fly. She can't handle it. Now she wants to get on a plane.

"I'll give you the credit card. Des Moines Airport to Ontario International. We got to get there by tomorrow morning. Understand?"

"No. I don't! Why Des Moines? We're closer to O'Hare."

She shakes her head. "Des Moines. Trust me."

"Trust you?" I chuff derisively. "That's fucking hilarious."

"Just do it, Louise," she says.

"What are we going to do with the car?"

"Who gives a goldarn? We'll leave it in Des Moines, come back for it when all this is over and done with."

I give her a pointed look. "Grace. What about your aerophobia?" Based on the last two minutes, fear of flying is the least of her problems, but it's something I can focus on.

The vein in her left temple pulses. She begins to rub her left wrist with her right hand. "That's for me to deal with."

"No. I'll have to deal with it too. What's happening?"

"If you don't want to come with me, that's fine," she says. "But I'm going, so book me the darn flight."

I take a deep breath to settle my nerves. *Okay. Think, think.*

I remember my conversation with Dr. Brenner last night, after dinner with the Palmers. Whatever is going on with Grace is clearly escalating, just as he said it would. Getting to California sooner is a good idea. And Grace has never said exactly where we're going, which has presented logistical problems for my plan. This will work out much better.

I grab my phone from the dash and swipe it open, then open my Google app.

"Des Moines to Ontario?"

Grace nods.

Within minutes, I find several flights to choose from. "We can go tonight, but they have layovers and plane changes, and the flights are long," I tell her.

"No," she says adamantly. "Like I said, just got to get there by morning."

"First one out gets there by 9:41 a.m. One stop, no plane change."

She purses her lips and hands me a credit card from her fanny pack. Her face is pale.

"Do it."

"Fine." I complete the transaction quickly. "Okay, done. Should I book us a motel for tonight? I can find us something close to DSM."

"Don't bother. We'll find something when we get there, I think."

I shrug and hand her credit card back. She tucks it into her fanny pack, releases a sigh, and manages to smile. "Thanks, Louise. I guess those tumor-causing contraptions are good for something." Once again, her mood has shifted. She seems more at peace. Which freaks me out more than anything. "Let's go get us some fries and milkshakes. Afternoon snack. My treat."

Everything has been her treat. "Maybe we should do the drive-through. We're going to have to log some miles if we want to get to Des Moines by tonight."

"It'll only take a few minutes, give you time to stretch your leg."

I shrug. "Whatever you say, Grace." *This is your shit show.*

She nods, then gets out of the car and heads for the restaurant. I watch her through the rearview mirror until she's inside, then I look at my cell phone. If I had any doubts about my plan, they evaporated the second she started hearing voices. I copy the flight information, then paste it into an email, type in Brenner's address, and touch Send.

While Grace gets the grub, I walk around the McDonald's parking lot, pausing occasionally to stretch my calf, my hamstring, my Achilles tendon. The sun is shining, but in the distance, I see clouds gathering, and my leg tells me we're likely to get some rain. Weathermen are right maybe 50 percent of the time, but my leg is never wrong. The ibuprofen is taking the edge off but doesn't reach all the way down to the bone where the genesis of the pain lives. Even stretching doesn't really help, just allows me to pretend I'm doing something proactive. I'd give anything for a Percocet, or four, but I've been down that road before and it's not a happy place to go even if it does kill the pain. Actually, that's not true. Nothing kills the pain. But Percocet *separates* me from the pain, like I'm in a movie theater and the pain is on the screen, so I'm watching it and aware that it's happening, but not intrinsically affected by it. I don't know if that makes any sense, but it's the best way I can describe it.

Vicodin's pretty good too. But I left my scrip at home. Dumb.

My phone pings with an incoming email. I pull it from my pocket and swipe it open, then read the message from Dr. Brenner. I tap on the attachment he sent. An electronic document with a place for me to sign.

I quickly scrawl my signature on the screen, then look up to see Grace coming out of the restaurant. She carries a greasy, bulging white sack in one hand and a cardboard tray holding two milkshakes in the other. As she strides toward me, I slip the phone into my pocket.

"What?" Grace asks when she reaches me.

"What *what*?" I counter.

"You've got a funny look on your face just now."

"It's probably from using my smartphone."

She cracks a grin, then hands me the bag and the tray.

"I'm going to drive for a spell, Lou. Give me the keys."

"No, Grace. I'll drive." I don't like the idea of relinquishing the wheel to my mother. She's insane, for God's sake. I know she made it across the country without incident, and as far as I know, she's never had her license suspended—while she wasn't in the hospital, that is—or been involved in any accidents. But fifteen minutes ago, she was talking to invisible people—*arguing* with invisible people. Not to mention the fact she looked like she was on the verge of a coronary this morning. Wouldn't that just be the icing on the fucking cake? Grace has a heart attack behind the wheel, runs the Camry into an oncoming vehicle, killing us both.

But she saved us both before with the box truck.

Shut up!

"I can see your brain working overtime, missy." She lays a hand on my shoulder, and I do my best not to recoil. A few seconds pass, and I realize the feel of her touch isn't horrible.

"I'm good to drive, Lou. I promise."

She looks directly into my eyes, and something in her expression tells me I can believe her. And, God help me, I do.

"You can sit in the back if you want," she says. "Stretch out your leg, maybe get a little rest. I know you didn't sleep too well last night."

I hate that she's right. I hate this whole business. I remind myself that twenty-four hours from now, this will all be over.

"Okay," I say, and hand over the keys. "But just for a little while."

She nods but averts her gaze. "Just for a little while."

FORTY-FIVE

Melanie

CALIFORNIA–PRESENT

Ray takes me to the Starry Starry Night Diner for a late breakfast. I know—it's a stupid name for a restaurant, but that doesn't matter because they make the best pancakes in town. There's, like, forty different kinds of pancakes, and they serve them all day, which is a good thing because we don't get there till after eleven.

That's totally my fault. At first I couldn't get Penny and her words out of my head. And she kept calling to me, but I didn't want to take the time with the journal, and I was afraid Ray would come in and catch me. And also, for the first time ever, I really didn't want to know what she was going to say. I might be a little worried that she's warning me about Ray, and, well . . . crap. She couldn't be. Ray's *Ray*. He's the only person in my life I can count on. So I forced myself to *not* think about Penny, and that made her mad. She kept clenching and unclenching my left hand, which she's never done before, and the hair on the back of my neck, which usually just stands up straight, felt like it was on fire. I had to recite the preamble to the Constitution twice before she let up.

Then, it took me a while to pick the right outfit. I wanted to look cute but also be comfy since we're going to the movies later. And then there was that whole thing about me needing to be on the lookout for danger, or whatever, and maybe be ready to run, which I was trying to forget about, but couldn't all the way. Ray was out of the shower by then, and he kept knocking on my door and telling me to hurry the heck up and asking what's taking me so long. But when I finally walked out of my bedroom in my pink jeans and my maroon tank with my flannel shirt unbuttoned, and my high-top sneakers, he smiled and said didn't I look so good it was worth the wait.

At the diner, we take a booth by the front window. A few minutes later the waitress comes over carrying a mug and a carafe of coffee. Her name is Roberta, and she's super nice. She's a little bit older than Ray. Her skin is the color of milk chocolate and she's got a bunch of wrinkles at the corners of her eyes that make her look like she's always smiling.

"Well, good morning, starshine," she says to me, then looks at Ray. "Morning, sugar."

As she sets the mug in front of him, she gives Ray a grin, and I recognize it from school. It's the same grin I see on some of the girls' faces when they're looking at boys they think are cute. I've noticed that Ray gets that grin a lot from a lot of women, but the funny thing is, he doesn't seem to notice. Either that, or he pretends not to, which is pretty cool, if you ask me. A lot of the cute boys at school act like they're better than everybody just because of their looks, but Ray never acts that way. In fact, he acts kind of the opposite, like everybody else is better than him, or at least better than they really are.

He glances at the mug and smiles warmly at her. "God bless you. You are a mind reader. And may I say how stunning you look today."

She shakes her head, but her eyes are brighter than they were before. "Flattery will get you everywhere, mister."

"Don't I wish," Ray says. "Except for the part about your husband beating the crap out of me."

"Maybe I'll leave him one day. Try some white meat for a change."

They share a look, and I guess it's kind of a jokey, sexual look. I roll my eyes and focus on the menu. When Roberta finally looks at me, I order my favorite, number thirty-two. Ray orders some coffee and a ham-and-pepper-jack omelet.

"Bacon on the side?" Roberta asks him, and he shakes his head.

"Not today," Ray tells her. She winks at him, then at me, then walks to the counter to put our order in.

Ray's still kind of upset about Delilah, but he's trying not to show it. He gazes out the window of the diner and watches the cars pass on the street, the pedestrians walk by on the sidewalk. I wish I could make him feel better.

"You should get the pancakes when you come here, Ray. It's their specialty." I know this is a stupid thing to say since Roberta is long gone, but it's all I can come up with.

He shifts his focus from the street to me. "You're right. Pancakes are their thing. I'm just not in the mood for anything sweet."

"The omelets are good too. I mean, I've never had one. I always get the pancakes, but they look delicious."

Ray nods. "They are." He clasps his hands together and lays them on the table in front of him. "Listen, Mel . . ."

Before he can finish, Roberta comes over. "So sorry, but we're out of pepper jack. You mind Swiss?"

"Swiss is fine."

"You got it, sugar." She walks away slowly, and I swear she's swinging her (kind of big) hips back and forth with extra enthusiasm. But when I glance at Ray, he's not even looking at her, he's looking out the window again.

"Sorry about this morning," he says. "With D and me."

I shrug. "You don't have to apologize, Ray. I understand."

"You do?" He raises his eyebrows. "Then maybe you can explain it to me. How one person can spend four hundred bucks on clothes and such in one damn trip."

"I didn't mean that," I tell him, because I have no idea how that might feel. I've never been on a shopping spree in my entire life. Delilah gets me things I need when I need them, and she's got fashion sense so they're always fine, and some are pretty cute.

Ingrid used to take me to Walmart, where I'd watch her throw piles and piles of clothes into her cart for her *real* kids. She'd ask me if I thought Mitchell or Holly or Trey would like this or that. And I'd have to nod my head and say things like, *Oh, yes, that would be perfect for Mitchell*, or, *Wow, Holly will absolutely love that!* or *That color will look great on Trey*. Ingrid never bought anything for me unless I totally needed it, like when both my knees showed through the holes in my jeans, or my shirts got so trashed my teacher actually commented on them.

"I meant that I understand married people fighting sometimes."

"Yeah, well, it's not right for us to do it in front of you like that."

"You didn't, Ray," I say. "You were on the other side of the wall from me. What were you supposed to do, take it out onto the sidewalk to keep from upsetting me?"

Ray chuckles. "Mrs. Fitzpatrick would have had a field day with that."

Mrs. Fitzpatrick lives across the street from us in a one-story turquoise house that has, like, a thousand gnomes in the front yard. There's probably a thousand more around back, but I've never seen her backyard and probably never will.

Mrs. Fitzpatrick lost her husband a few years back, before I came to live with Ray and Delilah. Apparently, since he died, she likes finding out everything about everyone and then reporting what she knows to anyone who'll listen. Ray calls her the neighborhood busybody, and Delilah tells him not to talk mean about her because she's older and a widow, and she also makes amazing homemade baked goods, and D's hoping to get all the recipes from her at some point.

"Fighting's okay, Ray. It's normal even, I think. And it's good to get stuff out instead of letting it brew inside you where it ends up getting worse."

He narrows his eyes at me. "I think that's funny coming from you," he says.

"Why?"

"Because *you* never fight with anyone, Mel. You've been with us for over three years and you've never raised your voice to either one of us. That's unusual."

I swallow hard. "I guess I never had a reason . . . to fight."

He contemplates that, then shakes his head back and forth. "I don't think that's it. I think it's something else." His face gets all thoughtful. "You know what I wish, Mel?"

My pulse races just a tiny bit. I lean forward, pressing my stomach against the table.

"What, Ray?" I ask. "What do you wish?"

"I wish—"

"Here we are, the number thirty-two!" Roberta announces as she sets an enormous plate of pancakes in front of me. "And the ham-and-Swiss omelet."

"Oh, boy, that looks good," Ray tells her. "Thanks, Roberta."

She flashes her bright white teeth at him, then walks away. I wait a few seconds for him to finish what he was going to say. When he doesn't, I try to get him back to the subject.

"What do you wish, Ray? You were just about to tell me."

He stares at me for so long, it starts to make me feel uncomfortable, but I don't look away, I won't let myself. Finally, he shakes his head.

"Doesn't matter. Let's eat. Then we can decide what movie we're going to see."

"Are we going to pick up Delilah to come see it with us."

"Nope. Just you and me, kid. You don't mind being seen with an old guy like me, right?"

"I don't mind at all, Ray."

"And?" He makes a face.

"And?" I think for a moment, then realize. "Oh! And, you're not *that* old."

"Thank you very much. Took you long enough." He grins then digs into his omelet.

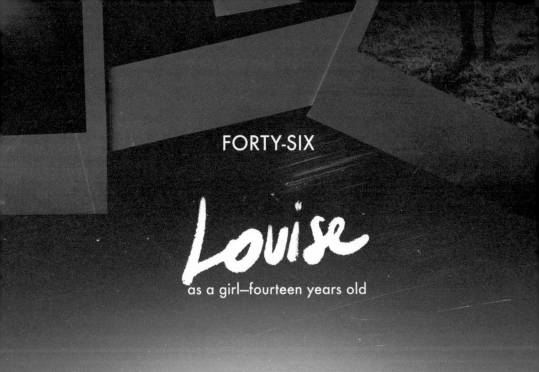

FORTY-SIX

Louise

as a girl—fourteen years old

Louise can't sleep. Tomorrow is her first day of high school and she has high hopes that things will be different. There will be a lot more kids so it will be easier for her to not stand out. And she made the junior varsity track-and-field team, which will be great because she gets to stay late after school every day and postpone going home for a couple of hours.

She hasn't participated in organized sports since she played soccer, and she wasn't sure how her body would heal after the thing with her appendix, but once she felt well enough, she took up running and it was the best thing she's ever done. She knows she can run well. Like the wind, actually. She can sprint and do long distances without getting tired, and when she runs, she experiences the same feeling as when she sketches. Total escape. When she runs, everything bad in her life falls away.

Grace is gone again. She got out of the hospital almost a month ago and she was okay for a few weeks. Took her meds faithfully, although they made her sleep most of the time. Then she went off them. Started singing Pearl Jam again. Started fighting with Louise's grandmother again. A couple days later, she left. She didn't say goodbye, but she did leave some cash for Louise to get school supplies and a few new clothes, so Louise took the bus to the mall. She likes the bus. She sits in the back, staring out the window, and imagines she's headed into a new life, away from her mother. *Someday*, she thinks. *Getting closer every day.*

The clock reads four after twelve. She pushes back her covers and turns on her bedside light, then reaches for the sketchbook she keeps in her nightstand.

She scans her drawings as she thumbs through the book to find a clean page. Some of the drawings she remembers doing, others she doesn't. Sometimes, when she's sketching, she loses all sense of time and awareness of the world around her. But she recognizes all the images. She's improved over the last year, at least to her own eye. She's never shown her drawings to anyone except her mom and her grandmother. Maybe she will someday.

There are still plenty of blank pages left in the book. It's thick, the *industrial size*, Grace had said when she'd given it to her. Lots of drawings left to be done before she'll need another.

Louise grabs a charcoal pencil from the drawer, checks the tip for sharpness, then, as she always does, notes the date and time in the top left corner of the page. She takes a deep breath and starts slowly, not certain what she's going to draw. It will come to her at some point, either somewhere in the middle or after she's finished. Dark lines appear on the blank page, and within moments, her right hand is a blur of movement. Moments pass, minutes, then tens of minutes.

She doesn't remember falling asleep, but the next thing she knows, she is being awakened by her grandmother and light streams through the window.

"Wake up, sleepyhead. You don't want to be late for your first day of high school."

The older woman smiles down at Louise, then her attention is drawn to the sketchbook on the bed.

"What's this?"

Louise glances at the sketchbook, then looks up to see the puzzled expression on her grandmother's face. She pulls the sketchbook toward her and gazes down at the image she created. She narrows her eyes at the detailed image on the page.

The countryside at night. The moon hangs in the upper right corner of the page, flanked by threatening gray clouds, illuminating long rows of wheat that seem to stretch on forever. But the main focus of the drawing is a passenger train, the front several cars derailed and lying askew in the field, its mangled wreckage bleeding smoke up into the sky.

"That's kind of dark, huh? Sorry, Grams." Louise shrugs. "I couldn't sleep."

"It's very good, child. You have a lot of talent."

"Thanks, Grams."

The older woman stares at Louise. "But I think you should concentrate on lighter subject matter, don't you?"

Louise smiles wryly. She knows why she drew what she did. Subconsciously, she views her own life as a train wreck, at least up until now. She doesn't tell her grandmother that. Instead, she says, "I'll try."

FORTY-SEVEN

Grace

Despite what's just ahead of us, I'm feeling pretty okay now, no baloney. That business back in the bathroom at the Gas 'n Go feels like something that happened to someone else, or like a dream I had. I know it didn't, and I know it's not, but I'm okay to drive, okay to get us where we need to go. I would never have gotten behind the wheel if I thought I'd put my daughter in jeopardy. I know that sounds funny, coming from me. It seems like maybe I've put her in jeopardy many times over the course of her life with my absences. But if I thought, for one instant, that I'd drive my mother's trusted Camry off the road, or into oncoming traffic, I wouldn't have demanded the keys.

I know Louise is upset about what happened in the McDonald's parking lot, though. I didn't mean for her to see it, but I can't control it. Never have been able to, which is part of the challenge. When they come, they come on strong. She's seen it before, God bless her. Didn't know how to handle it then, and doesn't now, which is not her fault. She doesn't have all the information.

She's grumbling from the back seat, telling me to slow down, or speed up, basically taking issue with every single move I make. That's okay with me. It means she's present and involved. She's also tired.

Weary. Not just from her fitful night of sleep, but from her life as a whole. Louise is unhappy. She's unfulfilled. She doesn't trust anyone and she doesn't trust herself, and that's darn exhausting. I know from personal experience.

For a time, when I was younger, maybe right about the time I fell in love with Louise's father, Niko—who was the spitting image of Eddie Vedder and sang just as sweet—I wanted out. I thought of my gifts as a curse and rejected them out of hand. I wanted a normal life, so I denied who I was. A more miserable person there never was. I was so darn tired from the denial that I wanted to die. I ended up driving Niko away and came a hair's breadth from killing myself.

I was living in an apartment, just finished nursing school. So I should have known that a bottle of aspirin wouldn't do the trick. Something deep inside me understood that I was playing a greater part in the world, that I was an instrument, that what I did, before I tried to deny it, was good, important, necessary, not just to others, but to me. Which is why denying those gifts was a kind of death too.

My momma found me. She stopped by out of chance, had picked up some paper towels for me at Walmart—I was always running out and she kept me stocked. I don't remember much, except her crying and hollering and asking what on earth she was going to do with me. She took me to emergency and demanded a psychiatrist. That was the first time I had the pleasure of meeting Dr. Brenner. Of course, not the last.

The hospital had no trouble pumping the aspirin out of my stomach. The ER nurses told me it was a miracle that my baby survived. My *baby*. The minute they said it, I knew she was a girl and that I'd name her Louise.

"Grace," Louise calls to me from the back seat, pulling me back to the present.

"I'm here."

"Obviously," she says, and I allow a grin. She's a sarcastic little peach.

A moment of silence passes. "Did you want to say something?"

Another pause. "I just wanted to make sure you're all right." Her voice sounds small, like that of a little girl.

"I'm just fine, missy. Don't you worry about me. You just get yourself some rest."

"What happened back there?" she asks and tries to stifle a yawn.

"At the Gas 'n Go? Nothing you need to worry about," I say, reassuring myself as much as her. "I'm of a certain age, you know. Peculiar things happen to the body. But they pass." Most of the time, anyway.

"No, Grace. In the car. At McDonald's. When you were . . . I don't know . . . talking to yourself?"

I don't answer. I have a strong sense she's going to find out soon enough for herself.

I hear her yawn again, and when she speaks, it sounds like she's already asleep. "Ewan doesn't have that small of a penis. It's actually pretty nice."

I, myself, haven't confronted an actual penis for a longish time. But that's okay. I understand the concept.

"It's going to rain," she says. "You sure you're okay to drive?"

"Absolutely."

I won't relinquish driving duty to her. She wouldn't take us where we need to go. Exactly where that is, I'm not sure quite yet, but I know I'm heading in the right direction.

A few moments pass. Louise says something completely unintelligible, then starts to snore softy. I glance at the open Thomas Guide on the passenger seat, then focus on the highway ahead.

Something's about to happen. And we're getting closer, I can feel it.

FORTY-EIGHT

Louise

IOWA—PRESENT

I jerk awake at the sound of the revving engine and pounding rain. My surprise at actually falling asleep during the day is overtaken by the realization that the car is going fast, very fast, *too* fast, and Grace, behind the wheel, is talking to herself—again.

I pull myself up to seated and glance out the window at the countryside rolling past. I have no fucking clue where we are. The sky is a mass of charcoal and black clouds and rain is coming down in sheets.

"Grace."

"Why?" she wails. "Why is it always this way? Why can't you give me some goldarn notice?"

"Grace," I say more forcefully. She doesn't respond. The dashboard clock reads 6:45 p.m.

"What if I don't get there in time? What if I don't make it?"

"Grace!"

"I don't *always* make it, and you know that!"

The car swerves suddenly as Grace makes a wide turn off the highway and onto a double-lane road. I sail across the back seat and plow into the car door. My shoulder takes most of the hit. Pain radiates down my arm, but I hardly register it because we're fishtailing, the car careening toward the berth.

"Grace, what the fuck!"

She either doesn't hear me or she's ignoring me, but whichever it is, she manages to lean into the turn with the kind of skill I'm not sure even I possess. A moment later, I feel the tires regain purchase on the road beneath us.

"I'm going as fast as I can!"

I rub at my shoulder, grab the two front seats and shove myself forward.

"What the fuck are you doing, Grace?"

Her hands white knuckle the steering wheel. She jerks her head back and forth, but her eyes never leave the road. The windshield wipers slam across the windshield at triple speed.

"Storm. Water's rising. Got to get there."

"Where, Grace? Where are we? Where are we going?"

"Hush!" she cries, but I don't think she's talking to me. She makes another turn, and the tires shriek, and suddenly I'm transported back seventeen years to another time and another car. The phantom screech of brakes echoes through my head. The blinding headlights sear my retinas, the explosion of impact reverberates through my body.

"GRACE!"

My heart slams against my ribcage and for a split second, I think I might come apart at the seams.

"Almost there." Her voice is calm and natural, surreally so, and pulls me back to the present. The Camry skids to a halt, and Grace is out the door before my brain can process that we've stopped. I grip the door handle and yank, push the door open, and haul myself out of the car. Through the blanket of rain, I see what looks like a cabin that more closely resembles a shack, its porch light offering minimal illumination in the steadily darkening day. I don't have time to wonder who lives here or why we've come because Grace is barreling around the side of the cabin. She disappears from view before I can catch up to her.

My leg screams at me to slow down, but I can't, because I have no idea what the holy fuck is going on. Around the back of the cabin I go, running faster than I have since before the accident, pushing my muscles to obey, even though my left leg is thirty-eight inches of fiery agony.

I catch a glimpse of Grace's backside and follow her through a wooded path. A clap of thunder explodes all around me. I cringe, my ears ringing, but I push forward.

"Grace!"

Over the whoosh of the rain comes the unmistakable rush of water and a hoarse, urgent barking. I move closer to the sounds, and seconds later, the woods clear and I stand on the edge of a swollen river.

Grace is down at the rocky edge, arms flailing, feet trying to gain purchase as she moves closer to the churning water. Another bark. I turn to see a hound dog standing sentinel, nose pointing down at the river, chuffing madly.

"Lou!" Grace yells. "I need you! Hurry!"

I pick my way toward her as quickly as I can, but the going is rough, the rocks slick and uneven, and I can barely see. I slip and land on my left hip, and a jagged spear of pain blasts all the way to my toes. I'm drenched and shivering, but I pick myself up and head for Grace. She is crouched low and reaching down to the river, clawing at something. I scrabble over to her, look down, and see a bearded man just below her. One of his hands is clutching at the branch of a fallen tree. The rest of him is about to be consumed by the raging current.

"I can't pull him out myself, Lou!"

Instinct takes over. My leg is forgotten. I climb down to an outcropping of rocks just above the man. I reach for his forearm with both my hands as Grace grabs for his midsection.

"Pull!" I scream.

The man coughs and with great effort turns his face upward. "My shoe," he sputters. "Caught."

The voice. Something about the voice. I push the thought away and crawl toward his feet. One of them kicks at the water, but the other is hidden below the surface. I reach down and feel along the rocks, run my hands over his left foot, which is twisted oddly and buried under a large stone. With all my strength, I grapple with the stone until it finally pulls free. I hurry back to Grace and grab his arms once more.

"Now, Grace!"

Side by side, in perfect unison, we heave the man from the river.

He rolls over and wretches, spewing river water from his mouth, then collapses onto the rocks. His chest rises and falls spasmodically. The hound dog scampers over, lets out a howl of relief, and starts licking him furiously.

I sit, breathing hard, watching him. Grace, beside me, does the same. The rain continues to fall. After a minute or two, the man pushes himself onto his elbow and peers at my mother and me. He starts to say something, sputters. Coughs up more water, then wipes his mouth.

"Hi, Lou. Hi, Grace. It's damn good to see you both."

I gasp at the sight of him.

Holy fuck, this cannot be happening.

FORTY-NINE

CALIFORNIA-PRESENT

I sit on the couch for the longest time, just staring at the three Kohl's bags. I know I have to take all the stuff back—except for the rug and the shower curtain—and that makes me want to cry. Those beautiful bras, and the lingerie, and that leather miniskirt, and all the rest. I had a 30 percent off coupon, so it was way cheaper than it would have been if I didn't.

Still, I understand why Ray's so mad. We can't afford for me to go off and spend a ton of money on stuff I don't need. He works really hard and never complains about having to pay all the bills, and I respect him for that. I should get a job. And I could, too. I'm not stupid. I do have a degree, although not one that could do much good for me around here. But I could wait tables or tend bar or walk dogs—but no, I'd have to pick up all the poop, and that's not appealing to me at all. But I could get something, anything that would take the whole burden off Ray and also give me a little spending money to use at Kohl's or wherever.

My friend Audrey got her Realtor's license last year, so maybe I could talk to her about that, although I know she had to study really hard and take tests, and I haven't done that since college, and college seems like a very long time ago. But I'm still okay-looking and could clean up nice, and I bet Audrey would help me. We could even start a little realty business together . . .

But I'm getting ahead of myself. I'm not going to get a job today. It's Sunday, and I doubt any restaurants or markets are doing any hiring. Audrey and her husband, Mike, are on a little getaway to Temecula to taste wine, so I can't bother with the Realtor license thing. And, anyway, I have to go to Kohl's to return all of these beautiful things.

My phone chimes at the same moment there's a knock at the front door. I grab my cell from the coffee table and see a text from Ray. He's taking Melanie to a matinee of the new Pixar movie at the Palm.

I wonder if they'll hold hands in the theater.

I don't know where the thought comes from, but it makes me squirm. That's a totally ridiculous notion, and I know it.

Is it really?

The knock sounds again, and I drop my phone onto the couch, then push myself up. I walk to the front door and pull it open. A kid stands on the other side, looking up at me. I'm not good with ages, but he looks a little bit older than Mel. He's got a big round face, and he's kind of beefy too. Not fat, but really solid. His eyes are farther apart than they should be, which makes his gaze seem distorted.

"You selling magazines or something?" I ask. "Because we don't want any."

He looks confused. I see that he's not carrying a folder or notepad or envelope to collect money, so I'm probably wrong about the magazine thing.

"What's up, guy?"

He clears his throat. "Is Melanie home?"

"Nope." *She's on a date with her daddy.* Jesus Christ. *Stop it!*

The boy flinches and I realize I said that last part out loud. "Sorry. She's not here. Who are you?"

"Reuben?" He says it like a question. "Melanie and I have Core together."

What the hell is Core? "Is that so?"

"She's in the gifted half," he says. "I'm not. My mom thinks they shouldn't put the gifted kids and the . . . uh . . . not gifted kids in the same class. But I don't mind."

Melanie is gifted? News to me. I mean, she's smart, that's for sure. Talks like an adult. But I don't really have a point of reference since I haven't spent much time around kids other than her. So Melanie being how she is at twelve, well, I just assumed all twelve-year-olds were the same. *Gifted.*

Huh.

"Are you a friend of hers?" I ask, mostly because I've never met a single friend of my foster daughter's. She never asks to go to anyone's house after school—except that one time when she was doing a science project with a classmate—and never wants to invite anyone back here. When I was a kid, I was always hanging out with other kids, and my house seemed to have a revolving door for all of my brother's and my friends to wander through.

He shrugs. "When will she be back?"

I shrug back. "I don't know, Reuben. But I'll tell her you stopped by."

"No!" He shakes his head. "Don't tell her."

I grin down at the kid. He has a crush on Melanie. She could do better, even I know that, because this guy seems like he's not the brightest watt in the bulb. But it's kind of sweet.

"You're pretty," he says suddenly. I feel my cheeks flame and want to kick myself a thousand times for my reaction. But, honestly, I haven't heard those words from a member of the opposite sex in a very long time, so even though they're coming from a pipsqueak with weird eyes and possibly an overactive thyroid, I can't help but be pleased.

"Melanie's pretty too," he adds.

"I guess." I don't want to think about that, but it's true. I feel a stab of jealousy at the thought of how beautiful Mel is becoming. She'll be much prettier than me before too long. The idea of that makes me a little frightened, though I'm not sure why.

"You're both pretty," he says. "But different. That's because you're not related."

This kid is as sharp as a tack. "That's right."

We stand there for a moment. Finally, I heave a sigh. "Okay, well, it was nice meeting you, Reuben, but I've got to get moving. I will *not* tell Melanie you came by."

He stares at me but says nothing. A shiver crawls over my skin. "Bye now."

I close the door on him, then stand unmoving and wait. After a minute, I hear his sneakers slap against the porch as he walks away.

I go to the living room and grab my phone and the Kohl's bags, then march back to the front door. Might as well get this done. My hands are full, so I fumble with the knob, but finally get it closed behind me. I take the bags to the car and toss them in the back seat, then get behind the wheel and turn the key in the ignition. The engine revs to life, and I back out of the driveway.

When I reach the street, I see Reuben standing on the curb, staring up at the house.

Odd boy, I think. Then absently wonder if I locked the front door.

FIFTY

Melanie

CALIFORNIA-PRESENT

Ray and I decided on the latest Pixar movie, but there were only a few seats left in the front row. The Palm Theater has bargain matinees, even on Sundays, so the place is what Ray likes to call "pig-pile." I've never been on a farm, so I don't know what that means literally, but figuratively it means that the theater is crowded as crap.

Neither of us wants to sit in the front row. Ray says his neck will get all torqued and he'll have to see the chiropractor, which he really doesn't want to do. The last time I sat in the front row, I got sick to my stomach. We go back and forth for a few minutes, and the cashier in the box office is getting kind of annoyed, but we ignore her. Finally, we pick another movie that neither of us knows anything about except that it's PG-13 and has gotten good reviews.

"You're thirty-two, right?" Ray jokes as he hands the cashier some cash.

"You know how old I am," I say. It makes me feel kind of excited that Ray thinks I'm mature enough for PG-13.

"Yes, I do," he replies. "I also know that you're a hell of a lot more mature than most adults I've come in contact with."

"Thanks."

He chucks me under the chin. "Let's get some popcorn and Milk Duds. Wait. Unless you're too full after that stack of pancakes."

"I'm never too full for popcorn and Milk Duds," I assure him, and he shakes his head and laughs.

"Oh, to have the metabolism of a tween."

We get our snacks and head into the theater. This movie has been out for a while, so there's plenty of seats to choose from. We make our way to the middle section and get situated. As soon as I sit down, I hear a sarcastic giggle from behind us. I turn and see Missy Lambert, Chloe Paulson, Dylan Lundquist, and Jeff Patterson staring at me from a couple rows back. Missy points at me and whispers something to the others, and whatever she says cracks them up good.

Ray follows my gaze, and his eyes narrow at them.

"Something funny?" he asks, and my whole body goes tense.

"Ray, don't."

He glances at me.

"Please." I grasp his hand and squeeze. His expression softens. He kisses the back of my hand and lowers it to his lap.

"I hate assholes," he says. "Um, sorry."

"It's okay. I hate a-holes too."

"A lot of them in the world, Mel."

Don't I know it.

"You can't let them get to you."

"I know, Ray."

"I'd like to slap the hell out of them."

"I know that too, Ray."

"I won't though. Not unless you want me to."

I smile and feel myself relax. "Not now. Maybe later."

"You just give me the word, okay, Mel?"

I nod as the lights in the theater dim. I don't let go of Ray's hand.

Not until a while later, and I don't let go of him so much as he lets go of me.

It turns out this movie is about a guy who gets arrested for a crime he didn't commit and then gets sent to jail.

Oops.

I can tell it's the kind of movie where everything's going to turn out all right in the end, and the guy is going to get revenge on the bad guys who set him up. But when the cell door of the county jail clangs shut on the screen, I feel Ray go all stiff. He yanks his hand from mine and sits up real straight in his seat. I remember what he told me Friday night, and I suddenly feel so awful for him, I could cry.

"We can leave," I whisper to him.

"It's okay," he says. "I'm fine. I just have to use the bathroom. You'll be okay for a few minutes, right?"

As soon as I nod, he's on his feet and scooting down the row to the aisle. I watch him until he disappears through the double doors, then I turn back to the screen.

Less than a minute later, I feel the first kernel of popcorn hit the back of my head.

FIFTY-ONE

Louise

Oh my god, it's *Danny*. Danny, the man I haven't seen in almost thirteen years, the only man I've ever loved, the man I abandoned when I found out I was pregnant. The father of the daughter I gave up because my mother was crazy, and I was afraid I'd end up crazy too. Or worse, my daughter would be crazy, and I wouldn't know how to deal with her, wouldn't know how to navigate between two lunatic bookends.

Danny.

He stares at me, grinning, raindrops sliding down his cheeks. "Your timing always was pretty good."

Thoughts and emotions ricochet through me as the rain pelts down on the three of us. Well, *four of us,* including the dog. I feel my mouth open and close, but nothing comes out. No sound, no words, as though the circuitry in my brain has overloaded and I can't seem to produce a rational line of thinking. My stomach flip-flops and I have the sudden urge to throw up. I swallow down the bile that rises in my throat and finally manage three coherent words.

"What. The. Fuck."

"Language, Lou." My mother's voice is barely a croak. I turn to her, and the snide, reflexive comeback dies on my lips. Even in the darkness of the late afternoon, I can see that her face is ghostly pale—like it was at the Gas 'n Go—and her whole body is trembling.

Danny follows my gaze. "We need to get inside."

I nod and push myself to my feet. "Can you walk?"

"I think I can manage it," he says.

I make my way to Grace and put my hand out to her. "Are you okay?"

"Please don't fuss. I'm fine." She bats my hand away and slowly stands up. Brushes debris off her thighs and butt and tries to hold the tremors in. Unsuccessfully.

The dog shakes to dry himself—spraying water in every direction, then lets loose a couple of raspy barks.

"Come on, Buck, heel," Danny says, and the hound trots to his master and falls in step beside him.

Danny leads us away from the river, limping slightly. The canopy of trees diffuses the downpour, but large droplets splatter down on us as we make our way to the cabin. Grace moves like an old woman, gingerly and glacier-paced, but refuses to take my help.

I don't know what just happened. I don't know how Grace and I came to be here. How we just, obviously, saved Danny's life. But I won't allow myself to think about it. *Can't* allow myself. All I can do is put one foot in front of the other and follow Danny and Buck through the woods. Because I have the strong suspicion that my world is about to career off its axis and I'm not prepared. Not even slightly.

We reach the clearing off the back of the cabin. Buck scampers ahead and scratches at the back door.

"We're coming, boy," Danny assures him. "Just take it easy." He turns to me. "There are towels just inside the door, in the cupboard on the right. Take as many as you need. I'll get a fire going." He glances at Grace. "Got to get her warm and dry."

Grace chuffs. "I would appreciate it if you wouldn't refer to me as though I'm not here."

Danny pulls open the door and ushers Grace inside. I follow her but stop at the threshold.

"You have booze?" I ask.

He smiles. "Of course."

"Good. I hope you have a lot."

FIFTY-TWO

Grace

I've stopped shaking, but I feel chilled to the bone. There's a host of things I could worry about, pneumonia being at the top of the list, but I've got a more pressing issue at the moment. Louise. That girl is about to lose her mind.

She's hiding it pretty goldarn well. Went right into get-it-done mode the second we left the river. Get Grace to the cabin, wrap her in towels, get dry clothes from the car, get her undressed, redressed, get her to the couch, suffocate her with blankets. She hasn't said more than two words to Danny or me this whole time. And now she's in the bathroom cleaning herself up and likely trying to stave off a nervous breakdown.

I pull the blankets tightly around me and look around the room. The cabin is smallish but warm and cozy. The living room is at the front and the kitchen at the back, and from what I can tell, there's only the bathroom, but no bedroom to speak of. I sense that Danny sleeps in here, on this very couch, pulls it out at night and puts it away in the morning. The kitchen table only has one chair, and for a moment, I'm struck by the similarity between Danny's living space and Louise's. Solitary lives forged by a happenstance almost thirteen years ago. At least Danny has Buck. My daughter has no one.

Danny walks into the living room with the hound at his heels, carrying two short glasses of bourbon.

"I don't normally drink much," I say, and he smiles down at me.

"I don't either."

"I'm drinking today."

He hands me one of the glasses and takes one for himself. "Me too."

FIFTY-THREE

Melanie

CALIFORNIA-PRESENT

It's them, those stupid jerks behind me. The popcorn kernels keep coming. Some hit me in the back of the head and get stuck in my hair, and some fly past me and land on the floor. I'm trying to ignore them, but it's hard. If I turn around and say something or yell at them to stop, they'll know they got to me and they'll just keep doing it. I learned that lesson a long time ago. But I *do* want to yell at them. Because they're being so awful and for no reason whatsoever. I never did *anything* to them. I'm just me, a foster kid who pretty much keeps to herself and maybe is a little different from everyone else. And *that's* what I did. I trespassed upon their airspace, or whatever, with my *different*-ness. Pearl says that people fear what they don't understand, and that fear makes them lash out. It should make me feel better that those a-holes fear me, but it doesn't. It just makes me feel more alone.

I wish Ray would come back. They were only whispering when he was here and didn't start with the popcorn until he left. I bet they'll stop the minute he sits down. He hasn't been gone very long, though, so he probably won't be back for a little while, especially if he really did have to go to the bathroom. But I don't think he did.

I've lost track of what's going on in the movie, but the main guy is still in jail, so it's better that Ray's gone. Better for him, anyway, not for me.

"I didn't know Freakshow had a boyfriend," I hear Dylan say, not very quietly.

"He's so totally old," Missy says.

"I know," Chloe agrees. "Like, yuck!"

I have to be honest. I'm a little bit disappointed in Chloe. I mean, Missy is a conceited princess, and Dylan and Jeff are just mean, but I thought Chloe was different. She and I were assigned a science project together a couple of months ago where we had to build a roller coaster. We worked on it every day after school for two weeks. She insisted we work at her house, and I thought she was being stuck up about it, but it turns out her dad has this really cool workshop in the garage and he had all the materials we needed. Chloe wasn't very good at the science part, but she was great with the decorations and the flair, and we got along okay. She was nice to me, even showed me her room and invited me for dinner a few nights when we went late. I thought maybe I finally made a friend.

"Well, she's yuck, too, right?" Missy says.

"So, they're perfect for each other!" Chloe says.

I guess I was wrong about the friend thing. At least we got an A.

"Here, use this," Jeff whispers.

A split second later, something hard hits me in the back of the head that is so not popcorn. It clatters to the floor behind me.

I flinch and gasp in surprise. A man a couple of rows in front of me jerks his head around and gives me a sharp look. I clamp my mouth shut and shrink down in my seat. More giggles from the jerk brigade. I see movement at the aisle to my right and turn to see if it's Ray, but it's just some random woman making her way to her row.

Another hard something hits me behind my ear, and this hurts. Tears sting my eyes, but I will not cry. *I will not cry.* I look down at the floor and see a gumball roll past my feet.

"Maybe he's not her boyfriend," Dylan fake whispers. "Maybe he's her pimp."

"What's a pimp?" Chloe asks, and the boys snicker.

"Oh my god, Chloe, grow up," Missy says. "Like, she's a prostitute and he's the one who passes her around to all the customers."

"I hear foster kids give good bjs," Jeff says.

"I know what a bj is," Chloe says smugly.

"Last one."

"Wait, Dylan, that one's too big—"

"Fire in the hole!"

"I wanted to eat that—"

I start to get up, but before I can get away, one of those giant jawbreakers—the ones that are the size of a baseball—thwacks me right on my cheekbone. Sharp pain erupts in my cheek and the tears come, and I can't stop them. I press my hand against the side of my face as I scoot down the row. I reach the aisle and scramble for the exit.

"It's a hit!" Dylan cries.

Their laughter echoes in my ears as I push through the theater doors.

I see Ray across the lobby, standing next to a unisex restroom, gazing down at his phone. He looks up as I run over to him.

"Mel? What is it? What's the matter?"

I collapse against him and start to sob uncontrollably.

FIFTY-FOUR

Delilah

CALIFORNIA–PRESENT

Kohl's wasn't as bad as I thought it would be. I mean, I didn't want to return everything, but the cashier was very sweet. She said that people return stuff every day, and half the time, they wear the clothes and then bring them back, basically used. I can't believe people do that kind of thing, it's just so wrong. She also said that a lot of the stuff I bought will be on clearance in two weeks, so I should come back then. Surely my husband wouldn't be upset if I cut my bill in half.

Ray probably still wouldn't be happy unless I get a job by then. Kohl's could be my reward for becoming gainfully employed. I don't know if I can get a job in two weeks, but it's a goal. And it's good to have goals. I can't remember the last time I had a real goal. Well, that's not true. My last real goal was getting pregnant and starting a family, but I don't want to think about that.

The return takes no time at all. When I get back to my car, empty-handed this time, I feel a little bit sad. And lonely, too. I think maybe I'd like to see Ray and Mel. My family. *My family.* Even after three years, I keep having to remind myself that a family is what we are.

My parents got divorced when I was little, and I spent every other weekend with my dad. He was a great guy, and I didn't understand why my mom wanted out of the marriage until much later. But I remember Sunday mornings with him in his tiny apartment. He'd read the paper and make me eggs over easy and ask me about school and my dreams and what I planned to do with my life. I had no idea, obviously—I was only nine—and we'd laugh and try to come up with the craziest careers we could think of, like clown-makeup organizer or discarded-fingernail collector. Occasionally he would get all serious and try to give me life lessons, which mostly went over my head. But one of them stuck with me, even though I don't practice it as much as I should.

"D, my love, you gotta come at everything from a place of gratitude. You always have to be thankful for what you got before you complain about what you *don't* got."

I think about his words as I sit in my car in the parking lot, with my engine running and shoppers scurrying in and out of the store. Okay, so I *don't got* lacy bras or a leather mini or various and assorted clothes and shoes that made me feel pretty, at least they did in the fitting room. But I *do got* a family. We're not a traditional one, god knows. Mel isn't from my egg or Ray's sperm. She came to us already formed. But that's okay, right?

I've had some strange thoughts these past few days about Ray and Mel. I don't know where they've come from. Maybe it's a hormonal thing. Maybe I've got some kind of nutritional imbalance, like lack of iron or magnesium. I don't know. But I'm embarrassed by the thoughts I've been thinking. But that's okay, too, I guess. Because I recognize those thoughts as silly and based on nothing.

I grab my phone from my purse and reread Ray's text. The Palm Theater is only a couple miles from where I am. I can buy a ticket to the Pixar movie and surprise them. I've probably missed half of it, but that doesn't matter. I'm not going there for the movie. I'm going there to be with Ray and Mel. Ray is probably still miffed at me, but he'll appreciate me making the effort to be with them, even though I know he's miffed. He'll give me that sideways grin of his, and then he'll put out his hand, and I'll take it, and we'll sit there, holding hands, with Mel on the other side of us. And anyone who walked by who happened to look at us would think, *Oh, there's a nice family.*

I hit several red lights, so it takes me ten minutes to get to the theater. The Palm has a parking lot in back, but it's completely full. Sunday matinees are very popular around here. I don't want to try and find a meter on the street, so I just circle the lot, waiting, hoping someone will come out of the theater and leave.

After about five minutes, it happens. A couple of teenagers walk to an old Mustang, holding hands. The girl is curvy and has long blond hair like Melanie's that bounces with her when she walks, and the boy is dark and handsome and fit. They stop at the back of the car and the boy grabs the girl and moves her against the trunk, then kisses her long and slow. I feel creepy for watching, but I can't take my eyes off them. He grabs her ass, and she throws her arms around his neck, pulling him closer. He wedges himself between her legs, moves his hands up to her head, and grasps her hair.

I feel something inside me stir at the sight of them. Ray and I made love last night, but even though he was inside of me, pushing himself in and out as I wrapped my legs around him and squeezed him tight, there wasn't any passion between us, not like the passion I see between these two kids dry humping on the back of a Mustang.

The boy finally pulls away from the girl and I let out a breath I didn't even know I was holding. Both of them are smiling dazedly, almost like the rest of the world doesn't exist. I remember that feeling. It's addictive, like the best and worst drug. I want to honk my horn to get them moving because I'm suddenly anxious to see Ray and Mel. But I'm afraid that if I do, they'll take their sweet time, maybe out of spite. They'll resume their kissing, draw it out even longer just to annoy the fast-approaching middle-aged woman waiting for their space.

Slowly, lazily, they get in the Mustang and leave, and I pull into their parking spot. I'm so distracted, I almost hit the car parked in front of me, but stamp on the brakes just in time.

I get out of my car and fast walk around the side of the theater. I can't explain why I'm in such a hurry since I've already missed the beginning of the movie.

When I reach the box office, I glance up at the digitized display above the cubicle that shows the movies and times. Movement from inside the theater grabs my attention, and I gaze through the glass doors to see Ray and Mel in the lobby, standing by the far wall next to the bathroom. Melanie is groping Ray, her arms clenched tightly around him. His hands grasp both sides of her face, and I watch, with dawning horror, as he leans down and kisses her tenderly on the cheek.

He lowers his hands, then takes one of hers. Intertwines his fingers with her fingers. He says something, and she shakes her head. Then he opens the door to the bathroom and pulls her inside.

I turn and run.

FIFTY-FIVE

Louise

as a girl—fifteen years old

Louise is ecstatic. At today's meet against her high school's rival, she won first place in the middle distance and the long distance and was instrumental in her team winning the relay. They were behind, but she easily made up the time with her long, measured strides.

She pins the three blue ribbons to her corkboard and smiles with pride.

It's so easy for her. Her teammates don't understand. Running is work for them, even for those who are really good and fast. For her, it's a breeze. She's going to join the local Roadrunner's Club so she can train for a marathon with the 5Ks and 10Ks and half marathons they regularly put on. Louise thinks that running for 26.2 miles would be sheer heaven.

The best part of today was winning those ribbons. The second-best part was that there was a scout in the bleachers from Stanford who waited to talk to her. Stanford is still in California, not as far away from Grace as she'd like, but it's a good start. From Stanford, she could go anywhere.

The third-best part of today (and maybe, secretly, she thinks it's the best) is that her teammates invited her to a party. This is the first time that's happened, and Louise knows why. They have come to value her. Freshman year was awkward. She made the JV team because of her speed, but everyone else was older. As usual, she was the odd person out. But this year, she's a sophomore, which carries a little more cred, and she's also on the varsity team, and the other girls are more concerned with winning than with social standing. They don't care if her mother is crazy or that she lives with her grandma. They care about her contribution to the team. Because Louise is fast and brings in wins, she has attained some status. She's never had status before. At least not *positive* status. She relishes it.

She strips off her uniform and tosses it into her hamper, then goes to the bathroom and showers. When she's finished, she dons her terry-cloth bathrobe and returns to her room, then checks the clock. Her teammate, Tessa, who's a senior, said she'd pick her up at seven. It's just before six. Plenty of time.

She sits at her desk and stares out the window, reliving the events of the day again. Her hand absently moves across the cover of her sketch-book, her fingers stroking the brown cardstock. She feels the urge to draw and reaches into her desk drawer for a charcoal pencil.

Louise closes her eyes and sees the clay-colored dirt of the track, the yellow tape of the finish line, the people in the bleachers. She notes the date and time on the first blank page, then begins to sketch, and, like always, loses herself in the drawing. She isn't aware of time passing until she hears a knock on her bedroom door. She snaps to the present. The clock reads 6:46. *Crap.* Without even glancing at the sketch, Louise snaps the sketchbook closed, jumps to her feet, and tears off her bathrobe.

"Can I come in?" Grace calls.

"No," she says, annoyed. "I'm not dressed."

She wished her mother had stayed away longer this time, but no, there she was at the meet this afternoon, hollering and whooping like the whack job she is. Luckily, Louise has learned to ignore her.

The door opens and Grace steps inside.

"I told you I wasn't dressed."

"I've seen you naked a hundred-thousand times, missy."

Louise quickly puts on her clothes, irritated by her mother's lack of boundaries. She's fifteen. Her body is more woman than girl. She doesn't need an audience.

"I'm so proud of you," Grace says. "I've never seen a person literally run like the wind, but you do."

Louise stares at herself in the mirror, trying to decide what earrings to wear. "Thanks," she says absently.

"Why are you getting all gussied up?" Grace asks.

"I'm going to a party with the track-and-field team," she replies.

"I thought we were going to celebrate here. I ordered two pizzas."

Louise sighs. "I don't eat pizza anymore. Geez."

"I ordered a big salad, too. Surely, you still eat salads."

"I'm going to a party," Louise repeats. She slings her purse strap over her shoulder and checks her reflection. She wishes she had more time to apply some makeup—*Shouldn't have started sketching*, she thinks—but decides a little lip gloss will be enough.

"No," her mother replies, her voice firm. "We're going to celebrate your amazing victories *here*. Together. You and me and your grandmother."

"That is so lame. Like I want to be with you and Grams?" Louise tsks derisively. "I'm going with my friends. I finally *have* some friends, no thanks to you."

She glances at Grace in the mirror, and the expression on her mother's face defies description. Her face is tilted upward toward the ceiling, and she looks as though she's hearing something, but there's nothing to be heard. Grace shakes her head violently, and her eyes go wide.

"No," she says. But not to Louise. She's talking to someone Louise can't see.

"What the fuck?" Louise says, and is surprised that her mother doesn't reprimand her. Language is big to Grace, but apparently, her attention is elsewhere.

This is the craziness, she thinks. *This is what Grams was talking about.*

She's never seen it firsthand, and it's more than a little disturbing. But she refuses to put up with it. Not now. Not when her teammate will be here any minute.

"Okay, I'm going," Louise says.

Grace jerks violently then shakes her head back and forth. "I don't understand!" she cries. Then her eyes fly open and her gaze narrows on Louise. "You're not going anywhere. I won't allow it."

"Really? You 'won't allow it?' Like you can really tell me what to do? Um, sorry, *Mother*. God, I can't even call you that with a straight face."

"I don't care what you call me," Grace says. "You're not going to that party."

A car horn sounds from out front. Louise turns on her heel and heads to the living room. Her mother grabs her arm before she reaches the front door. Louise shoves her off.

"Get away from me!"

Grace stares at her. "I know things," she says, then corrects herself. "No, that's not right. I'm privy to information that is relevant."

Louise rolls her eyes. "What does that even mean?"

"I'll tell you if you'll listen."

"No. I won't listen. Because you are a nutcase, like Grams says. You've already fucked up my life enough."

Grace looks stricken. "Language!"

"Language? Fuck you. I'm going to hang with my friends, and there's nothing you can do about it."

Her mother presses herself against the door even as she turns the knob. "If you go, something bad is going to happen to you."

Louise pushes her mother out of the way. "Something bad already happened to me! Getting *you* for a mother. I'm not listening to you. I hate you. You've ruined my life. Up till now. I'm not going to let you ruin the rest of it."

The car horn sounds again. Louise opens the door and races down the porch, then climbs into the back of Tessa's parents' Lexus.

FIFTY-SIX

Louise

IOWA–PRESENT

The rain has stopped, but the storm in my head still rages. I've been trying to piece things together, make sense of the past hour, and the sheer enormity of what might be going on is pushing me to the brink of a panic attack. I stand in the bathroom for a full ten minutes, splashing water on my face and alternately gazing at my haggard reflection and mentally screaming at myself to keep my shit together.

When I finally pull open the bathroom door, I see that Grace has gotten herself situated on the couch. She looks very small under the thick layer of blankets. Her color's better, and she's not shaking anymore, but she doesn't exactly look like the picture of health. Danny crosses to her, carrying two short glasses of bourbon.

"I don't normally drink much," I hear her say.

"Me neither," Danny replies. He hands her one of the bourbons.

"I'm drinking today," she says.

"Me too."

He starts to raise his glass but before he can take a sip, I barrel toward the two of them.

"I normally drink a shit ton," I say, and snatch his glass away from him. I down his shot in one long swallow. "And today will be no exception." I hold the glass out to him. "Another? Please? And then my mother is going to tell me what the fuck just happened."

Danny quickly complies, grabs the bottle of Maker's Mark and a third glass from the kitchen table, pours a shot in both, and hands me back my glass.

"Lou—" Grace starts to say, but I stop her with a look. I move around the couch, shoot the second bourbon, then set the empty glass on the coffee table and lower myself onto the couch. I turn and look at my mother.

"Grace?"

Danny stands unmoving, bottle in one hand, glass in the other. His gaze shifts back and forth between Grace and me. "I should give you some privacy."

"That's all right, Danny," Grace says. "Nothing's going to be said that you shouldn't hear. Now, get off that ankle."

After a brief hesitation, Danny sets the Maker's bottle next to my glass and retreats to the easy chair in the corner of the living room. Buck follows him and collapses at his feet with a low moan. Grace and I stare at each other and for a long moment, the only sound is the crackling of the logs in the fire. My heart beats a staccato rhythm, my pulse throbs in my temples, and I recognize that as much as I want to know the truth, a part of me is terrified for it to be unleashed. I take a deep breath and slowly exhale. Take another breath, then another.

When I try to speak, my voice catches. I clear my throat and try again. "How did you know, Grace?" I ask. "How did you know Danny was in trouble?" Now that I've started, I can't stop. The words tumble out of my mouth, my volume increasing with each syllable until I'm practically screaming. "I mean, you just saved his life, right? That's what fucking happened, right? Somehow you knew, somehow . . . Somehow you knew that he was going in the river, you knew that he would get stuck, his foot would get stuck, that the river would swallow him if no one got to him in time. You saved his life!"

"We," Grace says quietly. "We saved his life."

"But HOW DID YOU KNOW?"

Buck raises his head and gives a shrill bark. I press the heels of my hands against my eyes, then drop my hands in my lap, clench them into fists.

Danny clears his throat. I turn to see him stroking Buck thoughtfully. "I was kind of wondering the same thing. Not that I mind you showing up. Clearly. Still, it's a good question."

I turn back to Grace. "How did you know?"

Grace smiles at me sadly then reaches out and places her hands over mine.

"I'm guessing you've already worked out the answer, Louise."

I yank my hands away from hers and spring to my feet. "No. I don't believe it. It's not possible."

"You not believing doesn't change it."

"No! It's bullshit! Fucking bullshit!" I start to pace. A bark of panicked laughter escapes me. "So, you, what? You have ESP? Mental telepathy? Fucking what, Grace?"

"Something like that."

I shake my head with such force, my temples throb.

This cannot be true. Cannot. Be. True.

"What the fuck." Suddenly, I'm breathing too fast, I'm breathing too hard. My heart pounds at triple speed. My vision tunnels, my stomach roils. I'm going to pass out or vomit or both. I hear Grace call to Danny, but her voice sounds very far away.

"Danny, get a paper sack. Now."

I feel my mother grasp my shoulders, gently but firmly. "Lou. Look at me. You've got to take it easy."

But I can't take it easy. I can't do anything. I can't think, can't see, can't breathe. *Oh, Jesus, who am? I what have I done? Edie, oh, Jesus, help me* . . . Darkness is swallowing me, I'm going away—

"Lou!" Vaguely, I hear a sharp sound like the crack of a whip, then something is shoved into my face. "Breathe, Lou, now, goldarn it!"

Sack. Paper sack. I understand. I claw at the bag and press it to my mouth. I force my thoughts away and concentrate on filling the bag and emptying the bag. Expand, contract. Breathe in, breathe out. Again. Again.

Finally, the world swims back into focus. I lower the bag and stare at my mother. She stands before me, her hands still planted on my shoulder. Her concerned expression shifts to one of relief.

"Why?" My voice is a raspy whisper. "Why didn't you tell me?"

Grace sighs. "Oh, honey, I tried."

"No. You didn't."

"I tried to explain everything the night you . . ." She glances at my leg. "The night of the accident."

I jerk away from her, and her arms fall to her sides. "I don't remember."

Grace nods. "I'm not surprised."

I run my hands through my hair, then press them against my skull, as though I can squeeze all the turbulent thoughts from my brain.

"When you were young," Grace says quietly, "I couldn't explain it to you in a way that would have made sense. As you got older, well, your grandma, she didn't want me to tell you at all. She threatened to throw me out if I did, if I put any crazy ideas into your head. And I knew she would, too. Because she didn't understand it and refused to acknowledge it. By that time, she had conservatorship of me. And she had enough ammunition to get sole custody of you, and I couldn't let her do that, Lou. I would have died not being able to see you.

"I couldn't lose you," she says. "So, I kept it to myself. But then, you were a teenager, so grown-up, and I could see things were happening with you. And that night I knew I had to tell you, get it all out so you could understand and maybe forgive me a little . . ."

My fingernails dig into my scalp. "But I didn't give you the chance to explain."

"Oh, honey, you were fifteen, with a crazy mother, hormones raging, just starting to make friends, make your way in the world. I didn't blame you then. I don't blame you now. Not for anything."

With great effort, I relax my hands, then lower them and cross my arms over my chest. I hug myself tightly and meet Grace's eyes. "But you're not crazy, are you?"

"Not in a clinical sense. But I'll tell you, sometimes I do feel a little bit nuts."

"But you're not. Crazy."

Grace slowly shakes her head. And that's all, folks. My knees buckle, then my legs go out from under me, and I am falling, down down down to the couch, yes, but also all the way down the rabbit hole. Moving images, like a film montage, career through my mind, memories of Grace, Grace and me, Grace and my grandmother, memories now slanted, skewed, distorted, as though I'm seeing them reflected through a funhouse mirror. And now I see Edie, the infant I held in my arms, gazing up at me, sucking on my finger, clutching at my breast, and the woman from the agency pulling her from my arms and disappearing though the hospital door.

The wrenching, uncontrollable sobs take me, and I give over to them.

A moment later, I feel Grace ease in beside me. She reaches for my hands, and I let her take them.

"I gave her up," I moan. "Edie. I gave her up because I thought you were crazy and that meant I'd end up crazy, too. I didn't want to do that to her. I didn't want her to have a crazy mother, because that would have been too awful." I'm railing like a lunatic, but I don't care. I gulp in air, hiccup. The tears are an endless river. Grace tightens her grip. "Grams said . . . She said you were . . . that you heard voices and they told you things . . . they told you to *do* things . . . and she was worried, she said it was hereditary and that I was probably crazy too . . . and I knew I . . . I just knew I had to end the cycle." I look at Grace.

"Those are your grandmother's words," she says.

I nod, and she reaches up and pushes a strand of hair behind my ear.

"She said it wouldn't be fair to the baby. To bring her into our world of insanity. I didn't know what to do." I swing my gaze to Danny, and an exquisite new pain explodes inside me. "I pushed you away, Danny. I denied you. You loved me and I abandoned you. I stole a life from you."

Danny sits forward on his recliner, his features blanched. He blinks rapidly. "I thought . . . you said you were going to have . . . an abortion."

"I couldn't go through with it," I cry. I suddenly think of the cubicle in the clinic, the fluorescent lights, the acrid smell of antiseptic in the air. How frightened I'd been. How lonely I felt. How I'd escaped before the nurse came back.

"But then, I couldn't keep her. I just, I couldn't." I turn back to Grace. "You were so excited about it when I told you. When I told you I decided to have the baby. You said it was a girl and we should call her Edie. You said you'd help, you said you'd be there for me, and then all of a sudden, you were gone. And you didn't come back and you kept not coming back and I didn't know where you were and Grams wouldn't tell me, said she didn't know . . . and I didn't . . . I just didn't know what to do!"

"Your grandmother lied, Lou. She knew exactly where I was. She sent me back to the hospital. I'm guessing she planned the timing so I wouldn't be there to stop you from giving Edie up."

"But *why?*"

Grace takes a deep breath. Nods her head at me, and I take a deep breath with her. We exhale together.

"Your grandma was afraid," she says. "Afraid of me. Afraid *for* you. And for Edie. People who operate from a place of fear tend to make the wrong decisions."

A fresh batch of tears spills down my cheeks. I swipe at them. "I thought it was the *right* decision."

"I know, honey."

"I thought I was protecting Edie."

"I know."

"What do I do now?"

"The only thing you can do," she says. "Get there. Get to her."

"To Edie."

She nods. "To Edie. Or whatever her name is now."

FIFTY-SEVEN

Melanie

CALIFORNIA–PRESENT

Ray and I enter the house to the aroma of chocolate. We look at each other because we both know what it means. Delilah is making brownies again. Which also means that Delilah is off the rails.

Ray introduced me to that phrase, and I kind of like it—maybe because *I* feel off the rails more than I don't.

Anyway, Ray got me some ice at the theater, so my cheek is okay. He was so cute about it, too. He took me into the bathroom and got some paper towels and put them under the cold water and pressed them against my cheek. But he realized they weren't going to be enough to keep my cheek from swelling, so he went to the concession stand and fought with the theater employee to get a bag of ice. I think he might have threatened to sue the theater if they didn't do something to help my situation. But he got the bag, and we spent a few minutes in that smelly bathroom, with me pressing the ice bag against my cheek, and Ray trying to make jokes to make me feel better. It worked, too. I kind of forgot all about Missy and Chloe and Dylan and Jeff and all their awfulness.

We decided not to go back into the theater. Not because of the movie itself. Ray said he was okay to watch it. But I didn't want to go back in. And it wasn't just because of those horrible kids, though Ray was pretty steamed about them and kind of wanted to tell them off. But I didn't want to put Ray through more heartache.

Of course, the heartbreak I was trying to save him from showed up at home.

"Go to your room," Ray says quietly. I nod, but I don't go right away. Instead, I watch him walk into the kitchen. I shuffle to my right to get a better angle through the archway. There's Delilah, sitting in a kitchen chair she pulled up next to the oven. She stares at that oven with all her might, as if it's going to start talking to her and tell her the secrets of life.

Ray moves in next to her and kneels beside her. "Hey, D," I hear him say. "What's up?"

He says it all casually, but I can see the look on his face, and it's anything but casual.

He jerks his head in my direction and catches my eyes. He gives me a curt, serious nod, and I know what that means. He sent me to my room, and I didn't go, and he needs me to obey him. I don't want to. I want to see if Delilah's okay and how he deals with her. Not because I'm worried he'll be mean. He's not that way, most of the time. But I want to make sure he doesn't fly off the handle because I know he's fed up with her. Still, I have to do what he says or face the consequences. I back up into the hallway, then go to my room. I leave the door open a crack, just in case anyone needs me.

My cheek still feels a little sore, but at least the marble-sized bump has gone away.

I can't decide whether to play games on my iPad, read my Warriors book, or try to talk to Penny. None of my choices excites me at all.

I walk over to my bed and stop suddenly. Perched against my pillow is a folded-up piece of paper with a red heart drawn on the front. I recognize the paper—it came from the notepad that sits on my desk. My own heart, the one inside my chest, starts pounding. I don't want to touch that note, but I know I will because my curiosity is too strong to resist.

I reach out and grab it from my pillow. I'm almost surprised the note doesn't burn my fingers. But no, it's just paper. Of course it won't burn me.

The heart is perfectly symmetrical, its border black, like from a thin Sharpie, and filled in with thick red Sharpie, maybe. I glance over at my desk and see both of those markers sitting in my pen cup. My hands start to shake.

I unfold the note and read what's written inside.

Sorry I scared you. I didn't mean to do that. I would never hurt you, Mel. I promise. Maybe we can try again. -R.

I know, without even a bit of doubt, that Reuben Meserve wrote this. But how did he get in here? The idea of him being in my house, being in my *room*, makes me totally creeped out. Reuben touched my stuff. He touched my notepad and my pens. I glance around my room and wonder what else he touched. Did he hold Mr. Chinchilla or Chauncy the Dolphin?

This is D's fault. She must have let Reuben in. But why would she do that?

Because she's off the rails.

Still, that is *not* okay.

My hands feel sweaty and slick, and the note scratches against my palm. I want so bad to go out there and ask Delilah about this, but at the same time, I'm the kid who never makes a problem, who never yells, who never causes *conflict*. But how can I let this go? Delilah let some freaky kid who threatened to kill me into my private place. What would my caseworker Pearl say about this?

I stomp to my bedroom door and open it wide, then walk down the hallway. When I reach the living room, I hear Ray and Delilah arguing from the kitchen.

"This is a problem, D."

Delilah cackles. Not a pleasant sound. It grates against my eardrums.

"No, Ray. This is not the problem. We have one, but this is *not* it."

I press myself against the wall of the hallway so they won't see me. But I can see them. They're both on their feet, and Ray is trying to get at the oven. Delilah tries to block him.

"What are you doing?"

He shoves her aside. "I'm getting the goddamn brownies."

"No!" she cries. "They're not ready."

"They're never fucking ready, Delilah! You've got to stop this."

"You've got to stop, too." Her voice is a screech. "You think I don't know what's going on?"

"What the fuck are you talking about?"

"Don't you open that oven," Delilah says. "Don't you dare. You do, and I swear . . ." To my horror, Delilah grabs a knife from the butcher's block and waves it in the air.

I don't know what to do. A part of me thinks I should dial 911. But another part of me knows this is how Ray and Delilah operate. *High drama*, Ingrid called it. It's what she said when Holly got all bent out shape about not getting the lead in the middle-school play, or Trey struck out in his championship baseball game and totally sulked for a whole week, or Mitchell was devastated when he got an A instead of an A+ on his science test. *High drama*. Still, D never waved a knife before, not the I know of.

On tiptoes I backtrack to my room, and this time, I shut my door tight. I go into the bathroom, crumple Reuben's note in my hand, and toss it into the trash. I carefully wash my face then brush my teeth. It's only late afternoon, but I have a real strong feeling that I'm not going to get dinner tonight. It doesn't matter. I'm not hungry.

I go to my bed and grab my journal from my nightstand. I wonder if Reuben read my journal while he was here. The thought makes me seriously sick to my stomach. I sit cross-legged on the floor next to my bed, open the journal, and stick the gel pen in my left hand.

"What's going on, Penny?" I ask, then close my eyes.

Nothing happens for a few minutes. Then my left hand starts moving and doesn't stop until my fingers are cramped and clawlike. I look down and start to read—*Melanie, make sure you don't*—but another word halfway down the page steals my attention, written in bold letters—*Ray*. Before I can read what it's about, my bedroom door flies open and Ray himself appears in the doorway. I slam my journal closed and shove it under my bed. Ray doesn't seem to notice. His face is red and his eyes are wild.

"Get your shoes on. We're out of here. Come on, quick!"

"Where are we going?" My heart races. I have to read what Penny told me, but I can't with Ray standing right there.

"I don't know. But I can't be around her right now. I'm afraid of what I might do. And I can't leave you with her while she's like this. Hurry up, Mel. Let's go."

"Can I pee first?"

"God damn it, Mel! You can pee when we get where we're going."

I flinch, then quickly jump to my feet and grab my sneakers from my closet. I glance back at my bed, see the corner of my journal peeking out from under the edge of my comforter, then follow Ray into the hall.

FIFTY-EIGHT

Louise

IOWA-PRESENT

Okay, so my whole world has turned upside down. I think I'm handling it pretty well, considering. I've chain-smoked six cigarettes on the back porch of Danny's shack and I've thrown back a few more shots of Maker's Mark. Unfortunately, the bourbon doesn't seem to be having any effect on me. Danny took the Camry to gas it up and Grace is making some sandwiches for the road. I asked what I could do to help, and she told me the best thing I can do is to get myself together and calm the fuck down. She didn't say "fuck." That's my addition.

She pokes her head out the back door.

"You okay, Lou?"

I nod.

"Okay. I'm almost done. We got to get going soon. Sure you're okay?"

"Sure."

She ducks back into the kitchen.

"Sure," I repeat. "I'm fine and dandy. Just as right as rain."

Buck lays next to me, his trunk pressed against my left thigh. He seems to sense my distress. Every few minutes, he glances up at me worriedly then licks my bare arm with his enormous tongue as if to comfort me. In truth, his attention is worth more than a thousand therapists.

The rain is gone, taking the clouds with it and leaving a shimmering panoply of stars in their wake. I haven't seen a sky like this since I've lived in NYC. But I can't appreciate it.

I'm not sure how to deal with this revelation. I think a part of me—deep in my subconscious—has always suspected Grace isn't crazy. Which is terrible and horrible because I've based huge life decisions on the fact that she's insane. But now I know for sure. She's not. And I'm starting to remember, starting to allow myself to think about those occasions when she was there for me, despite being previously gone or unavailable. When my appendix ruptured, for example, or when Grams had her stroke. Grace showed up because she knew I needed her. And the accident. She tried to warn me, but I didn't listen, *wouldn't* listen because I'd already assigned the insanity label to her as a way for me to cope.

I'm trying not to blame myself, trying not to let the shitstorm of regret rain down on me. Because I was a kid. Psychic abilities were intangibles. They still are. Most people don't believe in them, not really. I mean, sure, we watch reality TV and *oooh* and *ahhh* over purported psychics and nod our heads at their proclamations of communing with dead people. But we don't *really* believe any of it. If a friend or an acquaintance or a customer came up to us and said, "Hey, I'm psychic," we might nod to be polite, but then we'd roll our eyes and snicker and secretly call them a nutjob.

I've always been militant in my rejection of anything paranormal or otherworldly or extrasensory. Because I was forced to be a realist at a very early age. But now, something niggles at me. Something long buried in my subconscious. I can't put my finger on it, exactly. The more I work at the thought, the more it eludes me.

Let it go, Louise. At least for now. Get back to the big idea.

Grace is not crazy. Grace is psychic. That's the big idea right now, isn't it?

"Louise," my mother calls from the door. "Danny's back. Time to go."

I nod, calm, casual, totally in control. That's me. "Okay." I gesture to my cigarettes. "Can I have one more? It's a long drive to DSM."

"If you must. Five minutes won't make a difference. Make sure you use the loo before we leave." She tries for a smile, looks up at the sky.

"Turned out to be a nice evening, huh?" She levels her gaze at me. "A good storm always leaves everything clean."

When I'm sure Grace is gone, I pull out my cell phone. I've tried to reach Dr. Brenner several times in the last half hour. To call him off. He hasn't responded, and why should he? I gave him all the pertinent information—that which I *thought* was pertinent. Funny how a perspective can change in an instant.

I realize *perspective* was part of the problem. Because I never stepped outside myself and looked at the situation from my mother's side. I can forgive myself for my childhood. Kids are egocentric—they're supposed to be. But as an adult, I always viewed Grace from the safety of my righteousness, never taking into consideration her challenges or her pain. Furthermore, whether she was crazy or not (and I now know she was *not*) shouldn't have mattered. I should have allowed myself to empathize, to consider her, to be compassionate, to accommodate. But I never did. I never asked questions. I never sought the truth from her because my own truth was my armor.

Dr. Brenner is going to be there, waiting for us at the end of this journey. Because of me. Ready and able to take Grace. To put her away, possibly for good. Because of me. Because of what I've told him, that biased and prejudiced judgment from a suspicious and totally self-preserving mindset.

I check my phone for a response to the numerous texts and emails I've sent.

> All is well

Followed by another text,

> Grace is fine. No need to take her in. I can handle her.

No response means Dr. Brenner doesn't believe me. Or he thinks my cell phone, and/or I, have been compromised. That Grace is on the other end of the line, trying to feed him bullshit to avoid the inevitable.

Whatever he suspects, it's not good. I light my seventh cigarette and suck in a huge drag, blow the smoke up away from Buck.

I have no way of stopping Brenner from executing the plan I set into motion because I gave him the right to take her. I signed away my mother's freedom on that god damn e-document.

What have I done?

Danny appears at the door, comes out, and sits on the step next to me. Buck repositions himself between us, lays his head down with a snort. Danny nods to my cigarette. I hand it to him and watch him take a long pull. Damn him, he looks the same as he did thirteen years ago. Maybe a few grays in his dark wavy hair and a few more wrinkles around his ocean-blue eyes, but still gorgeous.

"God, I miss smoking," he says.

"That's why I don't quit. So I don't have to miss it."

He chuckles, takes another drag. "What a night, huh? Helluva lot to process. Your mother is a bona fide clairvoyant, and I have a daughter."

I don't know what to say, have no idea how to express how deeply I regret what I did to him. I don't expect his forgiveness, don't deserve it.

"I'm sorry, Danny. So very sorry."

He takes one last hit, then relinquishes the butt. Stares out at the darkness.

"I know, Louise. We were young. We both made mistakes."

"You didn't do anything wrong. I didn't give you a choice. I pushed you away. I said horrible things to you, lied to you. I banished you from my life. And hers. It wasn't fair."

He looks at me. "No, it wasn't. But I let you. Because a part of me was terrified. I was afraid of being a dad, of having my life derailed. I was stupid. I'll always regret not fighting for you."

I swallow the lump in my throat and change the subject before the tears take me again. "You never got married?"

"I did," he replies, and although it's ridiculous, I feel a tinge of jealousy. "It didn't stick, though. She pretty much raked me over the coals. Not unlike you."

"Is that why you live out here like the Unabomber?"

He laughs, and the sound stirs up a host of memories that warm me.

"This isn't the wilderness, Lou. I can get a pizza delivered in fifteen minutes. Anyway, I had an apartment in town, just came out here on weekends and holidays. But my ex got it in the divorce. I like it here. My writing's never been better. I can crank out two novels a year."

"Wow. You're a writer. Impressive."

"It's commercial fiction. I'm not changing the world."

"But you're happy?" I ask.

"Reasonably. You?"

"Not even a little."

"I'm sorry," he says quietly. He puts his arm around my shoulders and gently pulls me to him. I lay my head against his chest and feel his strong heartbeat against my cheek.

"I loved you, Danny. I know it doesn't mean anything now. Doesn't make up for anything. But I really did love you."

He's quiet for a moment. Then, "I loved you too."

"I'm scared." So hard for me to admit, but undeniable. "I'm scared for Edie. For Grace. For me."

"I know," he says. "But you'll be okay. You always have been."

I start to protest, but then realize he's right. As much of a hot mess as I am at this moment, as fucked up as I feel, I'm still okay. Maybe someday I'll be better than okay. Maybe someday, I'll be good, or fantastic, or, god-willing, *happy*. But for now, I'll take okay.

It's all I've got, and I have to hold on to it. To get to Edie.

I push myself to my feet. "Let's go."

FIFTY-NINE

Grace

The Camry hums along the highway with Danny at the wheel and Lou and me sitting side by side in the back seat. At this hour, the road is mostly ours. We've got several hours of drive time before we reach Des Moines. Lucky for all of us Danny turned his left ankle not his right, otherwise Lou or I would have to drive, and we wouldn't be able to do what we're doing now. Which is having a conversation we should have had long ago. But that's just water under the goldarn bridge, right?

"Grams said they were demons born from your mental illness," Louise says.

"Yes, your grandma had a way with words."

"Can you explain it to me? How it works?"

I take a deep breath. Blow it out. "I can try. I call 'em Peepers. That's from an old book. You'd call 'em voices." I allow a chuckle. "The docs called 'em *auditory hallucinations*. Sometimes there's just one of them, and sometimes there's a thousand, just depends. Everyone in the whole wide world has some form of ESP, Lou. It's like when the phone rings and you know who's on the other end of the line before you pick it up. Or when you got a song in your head, and you turn on the radio and that very song is playing. Some people are tuned in better than others,

I guess. Some people, not too many I think, hear them so well, they might go crazy after all.

"It took a while to figure out what they were, exactly, and what they wanted. When I was a little girl, they were like imaginary friends. Your grandma didn't like it—me talking to myself and whatnot. She'd always say, 'Grace, you got to get rid of all those imaginary friends of yours so you can make some *real* ones.' But they were real. As real to me as my baby brother, as my momma and daddy.

"I was about ten the first time they sent me out. By then I was hiding it from everyone. I was in the middle of doing my chores—feeding the chickens—and the voices started jabbering to me about little Mary Ellen McClusky who lived a mile or so down the road. They said something bad was gonna happen to her, but I could stop it.

"Well, I dropped my feed and headed for the gate. Momma came out of the house and asked me what in tarnation I was doing. I told her I'd be right back, was just gonna take a little walk. She was livid. 'You are not allowed to leave this property until you finish your chores,' she said.

"I begged her to let me go, almost told her what the voices said, but I was afraid to say too much. She already had it in her mind that I was different. And she didn't let me go. Wasn't an hour later, we heard the sirens. Mary Ellen fell under her daddy's tractor. She died."

Louise sucks in a breath.

"I didn't know Mary Ellen well. Her family was new to Chattanooga, and she was a few years younger than me. So, I wasn't sad or grieving, exactly. But I felt a world of guilt. I could have stopped a senseless death. I don't know how. Guess I would have known once I got there. 'Course, I *didn't* get there. And I was so angry at your grandma. I never spoke of it. But I made a promise to myself that when the voices sent me, I was going to go, and there was nothing anyone—not even your grandma— could do to stop me."

A moment of quiet passes, each of us lost in our thoughts. Mine revolve around a seven-year-old girl with tight blond ringlets wearing a dress very similar to Dorothy's in *The Wizard of Oz*. A girl I could have saved. Ah, but there were so many others after Mary Ellen. Those I *did* save.

"That's why you became a nurse?" Louise asks.

I reach for the seatback pocket, where I stashed the manila envelope before we left Danny's. Up till then it's been in my duffel bag, but I knew I'd need it.

"My training has come in handy on more than a few occasions, I admit."

I pull the tattered envelope out and lay it on the seat next to me.

"Like with the Palmers?" She looks at the manila envelope, and her eyes narrow with recognition.

"Danny, would it be okay if I turned the light on back here? Just for a little while?"

"Sure, Grace. Won't bother me a bit."

I click on the rear interior light, then open the envelope and spill the contents onto the car seat. Photographs cover the entire space between my daughter and me.

"Mary was going to give birth in the wrong place at the wrong time," I say, searching through the photos. "I was able to intervene."

"You saved Will."

My fingers close around the familiar 4×6 photo of the dimpled blond infant with the radiant smile. I hand it to Louise. She looks at it. Then her gaze falls across the car seat, at the hundreds of other pictures laying there.

"I found these," she says. "A long time ago. I found the envelope in the steamer trunk." She shakes her head with awed disbelief. "All of them? You saved all of these people?"

"Yes, I did. But I also missed your very first track meet."

"You came to other meets," she says as she shuffles through the photographs. She picks up one, stares at it, sets it down and picks up another. My heart beats hard in my chest. Finally, finally, I can share this with her. For all the bad I've done to her, I've done some good too. I know it doesn't make up for anything, but I'm glad she can see the other side of who I was. Of who I am.

She holds up an old 8×10 photo of a group of laughing teenagers standing on a beach, arms draped around each other, their expressions gleefully goofy.

"That was the day of the Mexican restaurant," I say.

Louise looks at me, then studies the photo.

I let out a sigh, then square my shoulders. "Looking back on that, I'm conflicted. What I did to you—totally inexcusable, unforgivable even. It's right that we went to live with your grandma. She cared for you better than I could. But you have to understand. When I get set on a task, there is no conflict, no reservations, no thought other than getting where I need to be and doing what needs to be done. Sometimes it takes hours, sometimes weeks. That day, the task involved that whole group of kids. I didn't have time to find a phone, call your grandma, take you to the neighbors, talk to the hostess. To be honest, I didn't even think about any of that. I just had to stop the bad thing before eight teenagers got killed."

"And you did."

I nod. "But no matter how many situations I helped or people I saved, I still regret all the ways I failed you as a mother."

"I wish you'd told me, Grace," she says quietly.

"Me too. I wish I'd found a way."

"The . . . Peepers?" She says the word uncertainly. "They told you about Edie?"

"They have been communicating with me regularly about her for a while now."

"We're going to get to her in time, right?"

"Yes," I say, because that's what I know to be true, at this moment. But I also know that truth is fluid and the Peepers occasionally withhold pertinent information, like the exact whereabouts of my granddaughter. General location, yes. Street address, not yet. I have to trust they'll tell me by the time I need to know it. I'm going to try not to think about that right now, and I'm certainly not going to worry Louise about it either.

"We'll get to her."

She nods thoughtfully, then continues sifting through the photographs.

I glance out the window. Beyond the highway is only darkness.

SIXTY

Delilah

CALIFORNIA–PRESENT

I'm thinking maybe the job search is going to have to wait. I'm thinking maybe I need to find a doctor. A *headshrinker*, my dad would have said.

My hands are shaking so badly, I can hardly open the bottle of wine. But I definitely need a drink. I manage to get the cork out and pour some of the cheap red into a tall water glass. A wine glass would be a bad idea right now. I'd knock it over for sure.

Ray said I'm losing it. I should have just told him what I saw at the movie theater and let him explain it to me. Because there has to be a rational explanation, right? The things I'm thinking cannot be true, can they? No, they can't. *Can they?* But I didn't say anything because I couldn't find the words, and maybe a small (or big) part of me was worried that he might confirm my crazy suspicions. And then what?

I chug the wine and drain the glass, then refill it. I carry it with me to the living room and sit on the couch. The house around me is eerily quiet. I don't know where Ray took Mel. He was so upset, the look on his face, I thought he was going to hurt me. Which is ironic, considering I was the one waving the knife around. I choke back a laugh that sounds a lot like a sob.

I have no idea what got into me. Ray and me can go at it pretty good, though much less since Melanie came to us. But still, in all the years before her, I never pulled a knife on him. And now, sitting here staring at the blank TV screen, I can hardly even remember doing it, even though it just happened.

I swallow down some wine. Then some more. It's pretty shitty, but I don't care. I'm not drinking it for the taste. I want the numbness. I want to forget all about the fight and the knife and the brownies. Oh, god, the brownies!

I jump up and race to the kitchen. I grab the oven door and yank it open. The brownies are perfectly cooked, not burned to a crisp like they should be. I see that the knob's been turned to off. Ray must have done that at some point, but I can't recall it. Good thing he did, otherwise I might have set the house on fire. I reach for the brownies before I think to grab an oven mitt, and recoil at the bright burst of pain in my fingertips.

"Damn it!"

I grab a mitt, then pull the pan from the center rack and place it on the counter next to the stove. They are beautiful, a work of art. At least on the outside. But I know they'll taste like shit. They always do.

The tips of the fingers on my left hand have started to throb. I toss the mitt next to the pan and head for the bathroom. I stumble a bit in the hallway and have to slap my good palm against the wall to keep from falling over. I continue to the bathroom, brushing my hand against the wall as I go.

My fingertips are bright red, but I know they'd be a lot worse—blistering by now probably—if Ray hadn't shut off the oven. I run cold water over them, then carefully dry them on the hand towel and grab some ointment and Band-Aids from the medicine cabinet.

It takes longer than it should. The wine has slowed my motor skills, and I waste two Band-Aids before I manage to cover the three affected fingers. I gather the wrappers and take them to the trash bin in the corner.

As I toss the wrappers, I see a crumpled-up note resting on top of some discarded Kleenex. I rescue the note from the trash and slowly smooth it out. The paper is from one of Melanie's notepads. I follow the creases of the paper to return it to its intended shape. On the cover is a perfect bloodred heart. I unfold it and read the message.

> Sorry I scared you. I didn't mean to do that. I would never hurt you, Mel. I promise. Maybe we can try again. —r.

I crumple the note in my right hand and squeeze my fist as tight as I can. An image of Melanie and Ray in the movie theater blazes across my brain, wedging itself into my thoughts where it will not budge. I glance through the open doorway into Melanie's room and catch sight of something poking out from under her bed. As I move closer, I see that it's a book. I bend over and a wave of dizziness takes hold. I rest my hand on the bed to steady myself and take a few breaths. I reach for the book and slide it out from where it's resting under the edge of the comforter.

It's a journal. *Melanie's* journal.

I lower myself to the floor and open the book to the first page.

I know what I'm doing is wrong, a betrayal, but I don't care. I feel the love note crumpled up in my right hand. My heart pounds. My thoughts race.

I start to read.

SIXTY-ONE

Melanie

CALIFORNIA—PRESENT

Ray takes me to a place called Kid City. It's like Boomers, only a little cheaper and a little dirtier. It's still fun, though. There's lots of stuff to do, especially when the weather's good, like tonight. They have go-carts and a really big pool they call the Lagoon with bumper boats that have pressurized hoses on the front that pull water from the pool and shoot it out toward anybody who's in the way. There's a Ferris wheel, too, only that's really for the little kids. A miniature golf course spreads out at the far end of Kid City, right next to an empty lot. The lot is overgrown with weeds and littered with beer bottles and other things I can't identify. Inside the building is a restaurant and a huge arcade with all different kinds of video games and other games too, like the basketball toss and Skee-Ball and air hockey.

Ray and I start with golf while there's still daylight. I win the first round and I know Ray's letting me win. I tell him so when we get to the final hole.

"I don't want you to lose on purpose, Ray."

He gives me his trademark grin. But under that grin is a totally stressed-out expression. He's been wearing it since we left the house and can't hide it even though I know he's trying.

"What's that supposed to mean?" he asks. "I'm not letting you win. I would never allow a girl to beat me on purpose."

I don't crack a smile like he wants me to. "Do you really think losing a round of miniature golf to my foster dad would be that big a deal to a kid like me?"

His grin fades.

"It feels a little patronizing."

I watch his Adam's apple bob up and down as he swallows. He clears his throat. "I just thought that's what grown-ups were supposed to do, you know, to boost their kid's self-confidence. But I keep forgetting you're not a kid. Not really." He reaches out and lightly taps his index finger against my forehead. "Not in here, anyway. I'm sorry, Mel. Sincerely."

I shrug, uncomfortable with his apology. Ray has never apologized to me before because I've never called him out on anything. It feels good, but also weird, to speak up for myself without worrying about the consequences.

"It's okay, Ray."

"How about another round, Miss Thing. I will show you no mercy and you'll beg me to go easy on you."

I laugh and nod my head. "Sounds good."

The next round is close at the beginning, but by the sixth hole, Ray is totally killing me. He's pretending to be all macho about it, too, saying things like "I told you so" and "Careful what you wish for." But I don't think he's having much fun. When he thinks I'm not looking, he strips the happy mask off his face and lets the stress show. It must be exhausting. I should know. I wear a mask all the time.

We do the bumper boats next. There's a lot of people out on this Sunday night, and all the boats are full, so Ray and I have to share one. We sit side by side, our legs pressed together in the cramped space. For a while, he lets me control the water shooter, but then takes over to get revenge on a couple teenagers who totally soaked us. Another boat comes at us from the side, and I duck behind Ray for protection. His whole upper body is tense. I can feel his back muscles against my cheek.

"I'm gonna get you little bastards," he says. His tone is hostile and sort of, I don't know, brutal. I've heard him get angry and frustrated before. I've heard him pop his cork, as he jokingly refers to it after he calms down. But I've never heard his voice sound this way and it makes me nervous.

"Ray," I call to him over the whoosh of the water shooter. "I want to go back. I'm totally soaked."

"Got to get them first, Mel!" he shrieks. "Got to make them pay!"

The teenagers are retreating as fast as they can, and the boat on the other side, driven by two Asian adults, is moving away.

"You won, Ray," I say as loud as I can. "Come on. Let's go back."

He looks down at me, and for a split second, it's almost like he forgets who I am. He blinks hard, then tries to smile.

"Yeah. Okay."

The Lagoon has towels for people to dry themselves. Ray and I do the best we can, but it's pretty much useless. We were planning to do the go-karts after the boats, but we decide to get some food and let our clothes dry out a little.

We walk past the arcade and into the restaurant. The hostess smiles at us like we're long-lost friends.

"Do you want a kids' menu?" she asks in a high breathy voice.

Ray leans in like he's telling her a secret. "She looks like a kid but she's really forty-three. Just the regular menus will be fine."

As soon as she seats us, Ray orders a pitcher of beer.

"My date will have a Coca-Cola," he says, and winks at me.

"I'll let your server know," she says, giving Ray a last look before she walks away.

My date. As Ray looks over the menu, I think about what it would be like to be his girlfriend, or his wife. Then I get creeped out for wondering that.

"Penny for your thoughts," Ray says. "No, wait. That was when I was young. Inflation and so forth. A quarter? A buck?"

I'm not going to tell him what I was thinking, even if he offers me a twenty. "Are you going to drink that whole pitcher of beer?"

He narrows his eyes at me. "Why? You want some?"

I don't answer.

"I'm kidding, Mel, obviously. What is it? Are you afraid I'll get drunk and won't be able to drive?" I shrug. He shakes his head, annoyed. "Don't worry about me, Mel. If I were you, I'd be more worried about myself."

I almost pee my pants at this. It wouldn't make much difference since my jeans and undies are already soaked. "Why, Ray?"

"Nothing. I didn't mean it."

But he *did* mean it. I'm suddenly desperate to see what Penny wrote in my journal.

"Look," Ray says, running a hand through his hair. "It's cheaper to buy a pitcher than two bottles of beer. I'm already spending a lot of money tonight that I didn't plan on, what with breakfast and the movie . . ."

I lower my head. "Okay, Ray."

"I won't drink the whole thing. I promise I'll get us home safe."

"Okay, Ray."

He says nothing for a few seconds, then he slams his palms down on the table. "You know what? Enough of the whole *okay, Ray* thing." His voice is loud enough to draw the attention of the people at the tables around us. I try not to feel embarrassed.

"You have every right to question me about the beer, Mel. You tiptoe around D and me all the time, never saying boo about anything. And *that's* not *okay*. You're going to be a grown-up really soon. You don't want to be the kind of person who just flattens out and lets people walk all over them. Do you?" I shake my head. He cups his hand to his ear. "I can't hear you."

"No," I say quietly.

"What was that? Huh, Mel? You want to let people walk all over you?"

"No, I don't."

"Say it louder."

"No, I don't!" I shout, and it feels kind of good. The waitress scurries over with the pitcher of beer and a coke.

"Everything okay here?"

Ray gives her a genuine smile. "Everything's just peachy keen." She nods and moves to another table but keeps an eye on us. Ray looks at me. "Okay, I'm glad you feel that way. The next step is for you to be real with me."

I have no idea what he's talking about. I shrug.

He leans toward me and lowers his voice. "Like you were with the miniature golf. Telling me not to let you win. That was good, Mel. A good start. Now, I want you to tell me two things you don't like about me."

I feel my cheeks get hot. "I like everything about you, Ray."

"Bullcrap. Two things. I know you can think of a lot more than that. Right now. Tell me."

I squirm in my seat. Be real, huh? I don't know how to do that. I've been pretending too long.

"I'm waiting . . ."

"I don't like how long you take in the bathroom," I say before I can stop myself. "In the morning."

Ray looks surprised, then bursts out laughing. "All right then. I will have a talk with my bowels about that."

He's not mad. It's incredible. I just told him something negative and he's not going to punish me or hit me or humiliate me or turn it around and make it my fault.

"What else?"

I look down at my lap. This one's hard, and I probably shouldn't say it. "I don't like how you sometimes throw things or kick things when you get mad."

He blinks a couple of times, and I think maybe I went too far. But then he lowers his head and nods. "I don't really like that about myself, either, Mel. I'm working on it though. Sometimes feelings inside me bubble up and I get to the point where I can't keep them down anymore or I'll explode. When that happens, I feel like I have no control, can't stop myself from doing what I'm doing. It doesn't happen too often though, does it?"

"No," I agree. "It doesn't." I think about what he said before, and what he said just now. "Ray, what did you mean about me needing to worry about myself?"

"Sorry about that. I don't know why I said it. It doesn't mean anything."

Maybe he's sorry, but I don't feel any better. Because even if he doesn't know why he said it, it *does* mean something.

All of a sudden, my left hand starts clenching and unclenching, like it did this morning. Ray notices and cocks his head to the side.

"What's with that, Mel?" He makes a fist and swings it through the air with a grin. "You planning to pop me one?"

I force a smile, then grab my left hand with my right and put them both in my lap. "Not at all, Ray. I'd never do that."

Stop it, Penny!

"That's good to know." He winks. "Look, I gotta hit the head. When the waitress comes back, order me a cheeseburger, medium, and fries. Got that?"

I nod. The fingers of my left hand are still opening and closing, straining, clawing, relaxing, tensing, untensing.

"I got it, Ray."

He jumps out of the booth and disappears down the hall. I suck in a breath and look down at my spasming left hand.

"What are you doing, Penny?" I whisper.

The waitress approaches. I shove my left hand under my butt and I force a smile.

"Could I have a kids' menu, please," I ask through gritted teeth.

She nods and reaches into her apron, pulls out a tightly folded piece of paper and three-pack of crayons. She sets them down on the table. "I'll give you a couple minutes?"

I nod. When she leaves, I unfold the menu and tear open the crayons. I put the red crayon in my left hand. As soon as I lower the tip to the paper menu, my left hand jerks all the way across the table leaving a thick red line in its path.

What the heck?

I try again, placing my left hand on the menu. Again, my hand goes flying out of the booth, this time with enough force to pull me along. I stumble to my feet, almost fall over, then right myself at the last second.

I look around, the place is filling up, but nobody notices me. My left hand twitches around the crayon, my index finger points toward the arcade. I don't know what's happening. Penny has never done this before. I grab the menu with my right hand, then head for the arcade, my left hand seeming to pull me in that direction.

Bells, whistles, alarms, horns, sirens, a cacophony of sounds assaults me as I move through the various video games, but I hardly hear them. It's like I'm in a trance or something, like I'm underwater. The people around me seem to be moving in slow motion, or maybe I am. I don't know, but I keep moving forward, going in the direction my left index finger is pointing. I pass shooting games and driving games, a dance simulator, a virtual roller coaster.

And now her voice echoes through my head, Penny's voice. I recognize it immediately, even though she's only ever communicated to me through the written word. She's singing, one of her old-timey songs. *Come fly with me, come fly, come fly away with me.* Her voice is warm and sweet and warbles a little bit at the end of each line. I like her voice. It makes me feel safe and loved.

Once I get you up there where the air is rarified, we'll just glide, starry eyed. Once I get you up there, I'll be holding you so near, you may hear angels cheer 'cause we're together.

When I reach an enclosed capsule called Flight 57, with a picture of a huge airliner on the outside, my left hand immediately goes still and the voice in my head goes silent.

I gaze at the capsule, run my fingers over the smooth surface of the plastic perimeter. Then I crouch down and tuck myself inside, scoot onto the seat in front of the faux airplane control panel. On the screen before me is a digital simulation of a runway.

I have no money, and Ray has our game cards, but I'm not surprised when the game launches. The seat jolts as the plane begins its journey down the runway.

My left hand twitches and my whole body breaks out in goose-flesh. I set the menu on the seat beside me and lower my hand. Instead of closing my eyes, I watch the digital screen, feel the simulated plane gain speed, see the runway fall away as the airplane lurches into the sky.

Penny's talking to me, telling me something, my hand is moving, slowly, very slowly, and I smell the waxy scent of the crayon as it grinds against the menu—

Something slams against the outside of the capsule.

"Mel? Jesus Christ!"

It's Ray. And he's upset.

And Penny's gone.

"I'm here," I call to him. I grab the menu and ease out of the capsule. I look up at him and see the worried expression on his face.

"What the hell? I leave you alone for five minutes and when I come back, you're gone." He runs his hand through his hair. "Shit, Mel. I mean, *shoot*."

"Sorry," I say. My voice is a hoarse whisper.

"You almost gave me a heart attack. Places like this, a pretty girl like you . . . bad sh—uh, bad *stuff* can happen."

"I'm fine, Ray."

He blows out a sigh. I watch him gather himself. "Okay." He looks at the capsule, takes in the concept. "This does look like a pretty decent game. You can play it after we eat." He narrows his eyes at me. "You did order, right?"

I cringe and shake my head.

"Well, crap," he says. "Come on. I hope you're not starving 'cause it's getting pretty crowded in there."

"Nope, Ray. I'm good," I tell him. So much for being real.

Side by side, we walk through the arcade. Before we get to the restaurant, I sneak a glance at the kids' menu. Two words are scrawled across the word search puzzle in thick red crayon: *Say good*

Huh? Not much help there. I wad up the menu, toss it into the nearest trash can, and follow Ray to our booth.

We spend another hour and a half at Kid City. I can't wait to leave, to get back to the house so I can read my journal, especially what Penny said about Ray. And I'm hoping maybe that entry will give me a clue about what *Say good* means, too.

I keep yawning exaggeratedly, hoping he'll get the hint, but he doesn't. It's like he wants to stay out forever. We do the go-karts then go to the arcade. Ray plays the zombie-shooting game over and over again, almost like he's in a trance. I use most of my tokens on the dancing and driving games, but I stay away from Flight 57. I'm waiting for Penny to show up again, waiting for my left hand to start twitching. It doesn't and she doesn't either.

After a while I can hardly keep my eyes open. Finally, Ray runs out of tokens and notices me slumped against the fake bucket seat of Nascar-Zoom. He apologizes and scoops me up.

Ray keeps his word and gets me home safe. But I fall asleep long before we get there.

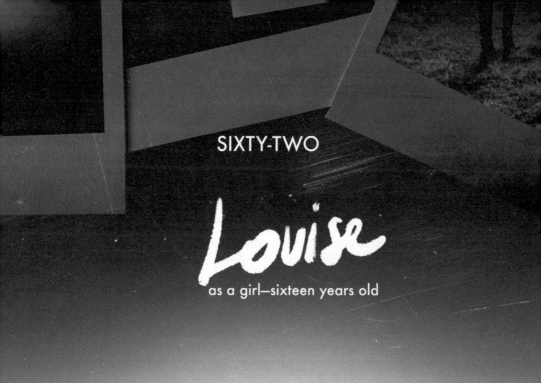

SIXTY-TWO

Louise

as a girl—sixteen years old

The alarm sounds from Louise's watch. She switches it off, then hoists herself up from the lunch table and grabs for her crutches. She secures the padded ends under her arms, checks their integrity, then slowly ambles toward the front of the school. School policy forbids her from carrying her own medication, so twice a day she hobbles to the nurse's office where Miss Fields administers three lovely little white pills that help her stay ahead of the pain.

She could have asked for a wheelchair. Insurance would have covered it. But she didn't. Not only would a wheelchair have brought more attention to her, she thinks it might also have caused her to become complacent. She needs to recover. Sitting prone for most of the day would not help. So the girl pushes herself. Her life, now, is concentrated on one thing. Getting better in order to get away. No more track and field, obviously, no more friends, no more sketching stupid pictures. She threw her sketchbook away as soon as she got out of the hospital. She doesn't speak to her mother, barely speaks to her grandmother. All her energy goes toward planning her escape.

Almost a year has passed since the accident that ruined her life. No, wait, Grace ruined her life long before that, but the accident was the finishing touch. Stanford is a dream she once had.

Today, the nurse's office is locked and dark and the rest of the administration offices are eerily quiet. Louise remembers that today is the staff appreciation luncheon, thrown by the seniors in the gymnasium, and the admin staff is likely there.

Panicked, she limps down the hall. Surely *someone* has stayed behind to man the office. She needs her meds. Already, the ever-present ache has begun to magnify. Soon it will take flame and scorch her from the inside out.

A phone rings but goes unanswered.

"Hey there," comes a voice from behind her.

Louise turns and is relieved to see Mr. Pascual, one of the guidance counselors. He smiles at her and she manages to smile back.

"Hi," she says as she exhales. "I need my . . . meds."

"Of course. I'm sorry. Miss Fields must have forgotten, what with the luncheon. Come on."

He moves past her, then slows his gait to stay beside her, and they move toward the nurse's office.

Louise likes Mr. Pascual. He is younger than the rest of the staff and relates to the students more than most. He wanders the quad, fist-bumping and high-fiving, rapping with the kids, getting to know them.

He is nice to her, too, treats her like a person. He doesn't look at her like she's less than, doesn't give her a wide berth. He talks to her about the accident and her injuries and her recovery, not with pity or false empathy, but with genuine interest. He even flirts with her a little, tells her how pretty she is. She's never been told that before by someone of the opposite sex, and even though he's a counselor, his flattery makes her feel good. Sometimes when she looks in the mirror, she sees what he's talking about. Louise has even practiced flirting on him, because he is safe, or so she thinks.

"How come you're not at the luncheon?" she asks. "Shouldn't you be appreciated too?"

He grins down at her. "Darn right, I should. But I drew the short stick."

"I'm sorry."

"I'm not," he says. His grin fades, but he continues to stare at her.

They reach the door of the nurse's office. Mr. Pascual glances around the outer offices, down the hall, then uses his passkey to unlock the door. He allows Louise to step inside before him, then closes the door behind her. She doesn't notice him reengage the lock.

"Lights?" Louise asks when he fails to flip the switch.

"I don't need them. Do you?"

Louise shifts, suddenly uncomfortable, and a stab of pain radiates through her leg.

"You are so lovely, Louise. You know that, don't you?"

"Mr. Pascual, I really need my meds."

"I know you do. We'll get them. In a minute."

He moves toward her. She backs up clumsily, her crutches catching against the carpet, causing her to hop on her right foot. She feels the counter and sink behind her. Nowhere left to go. He reaches a hand up and lightly caresses her cheek. Her heart pounds as a wash of conflicting emotions courses through her. His fingertips on her skin feel good, and yet she knows it's wrong, all wrong. He's a grown-up, and at the same time, she can't deny that she has fantasized about him touching her, caressing her, kissing her.

"So lovely," he breathes.

He leans over and brushes his lips against hers. And the feel of his lips, the *reality* of his lips on hers, ends the conflict within her. This is wrong. *Wrong.*

Louise knows that she brought this upon herself, flirting with him and allowing him to flirt with her. And now she is trapped, with no chance of escaping him and no possible way to overpower him. The embers of pain in her leg are glowing red, ready to ignite. Any movement will lead to combustion. Louise can't even struggle against the inevitable. To struggle would be torturous.

"I don't want to do this," she whimpers.

"I promise I won't hurt you," Mr. Pascual says. He lowers his hands to her breasts, cupping them tenderly. Her stomach turns even as her body reflexively shivers.

"I'll make it nice for you. I know it's your first time."

Tears slide down her cheeks. She suddenly wishes the car crash killed her instead of leaving her this sniveling, weak, crippled victim. She hates feeling this way and vows that when this is over—and hopefully it will be quick—she will never allow herself to be vulnerable again.

Mr. Pascual's hands slide down to her waist. She closes her eyes, knowing she will submit. What choice does she have?

The squawk of the PA system engaging blares through the speaker on the ceiling. Mr. Pascual jerks with surprise and takes a step back. The lilting but insistent voice of Mrs. Gilbreath, the ASB director, booms into the nurse's office.

"Mr. Pascual. Mr. Pascual, you are needed in the ASB student store ASAP. I repeat, Mr. Pascual, you are needed in the ASB student store, ASAP."

He gives Louise a strange, disbelieving look, as though he isn't sure how he got where he is. Then his expression darkens with remorse. "I'm so sorry."

He backs away from her. When he reaches the door, he quickly unlocks it and leaves.

Louise breathes deeply until her heartbeat settles. Then she hobbles across the room, out the door, and out of the admin building. She didn't get her meds. But she knows the pain will be a small price to pay.

SIXTY-THREE

Louise

IOWA-PRESENT

In the past two hours, so much has been revealed, the truth uncovered, sins forgiven, resentments laid to rest at last. And yet I still haven't been able to bring myself to tell Grace what's waiting for us at the other end of our flight. I need to tell her, but I just don't know how.

As Danny logs mile after mile, bringing us closer to DSM, we look at the photographs. Grace remembers every name, every situation in which she intervened. It's incredible, to have had such a catastrophic impact on so many lives. I am humbled. At great sacrifice, she used her gifts to help people. I think of the Palmers and how different Mary's and Jared's lives would be had Grace not been there for them. I don't know any of the others, but I see the gratitude in their eyes, and the affection Grace has for each of them is evident in her own. We don't get through all of the pictures—that would take too long, and it's not fair to Danny. He says it's okay, but I know the rear light is a distraction. Finally, we tuck them back into the envelope.

"Just under an hour to go," Danny says.

"You need a break?" I ask, and he shakes his head. "The ibuprofen and the caffeine are both working. Don't worry about me."

We decided he should keep the Camry with him until Grace and I can get back for it. I like the idea of having a plan to see Danny again. Not that I'm still in love with him or think we have a future. Too much water under the bridge. But I'm glad for the excuse to maintain contact with him. I plan to do that from time to time, from now on.

Grace lays her head back against the seat and closes her eyes. I covertly check my phone for texts or emails. There are none.

I put the phone away and gaze at my mother. I have an understanding of her life that I've never had before, and I am overwhelmed by all the emotions coursing through me, and also humbled by the power of them.

"I know you still have a lot of questions," she says.

And also, yes. I have *lots* of questions.

"I don't know how many of them I can answer, so you best prioritize them."

I smile to myself as Grace opens her eyes and looks at me.

"Well? What are you waiting for?"

"Okay. It seems like the Peepers are pretty clear about what's going on and what needs doing."

"That's mostly true," Grace replies.

"But not with Edie. I mean, you don't really know what's going on with her. Not specifically. Just that she's in trouble. First you said it was urgent, but tonight you said she's okay. I don't understand."

"I don't either, Lou. Sometimes they're specific from the get-go, and other times, they're only specific when they need to be. I once stood on a train platform for seven hours waiting for whatever was going to happen to happen. I had no idea what it was till a couple of seconds before. That was kind of scary. But there's a cosmic timing to it, I guess. Lessons learned, truths discovered in the moment I intervene. I don't know. Maybe I'm just making it up. The only time everything really went to hell in a handcart was the night of your accident . . ."

My shoulders tense. Grace reaches out and caresses my cheek. Her eyes well with tears. "I didn't know the what, the where, or the when. They didn't tell me. I could only see your face, twisted in pain. I stole your grandma's keys, drove around for hours looking for you. Didn't find you." A tear slides across her temple and drips onto her lap. "I was beside myself. I cursed the Peepers. Told them I was done with them. Told them if they wouldn't help me save my little girl, why should I help them save anyone else? My resolve didn't last too long, though. Because the next time it happened, their timing was better. Not great, but better. With that goldarn guidance counselor of yours. Mr. Pascual?"

"You knew about that?"

"The Peepers came through just in time."

The realization hits me. "It was *you*. You got him called to the student store."

"Phew, that was a close one. Too damn close. Had to think up a harebrained story about the ASB treasurer embezzling funds. Still can't believe that Mrs. Gilbreath bought it."

"I sometimes wonder what happened to him," I say.

She glances out the window. "Oh, well, he got what was coming to him. Don't you worry about that."

I never saw Mr. Pascual after the almost-assault. A few weeks later I heard he got a better job at another school.

"Did you get him fired?"

She smiles knowingly. "No. I did not get him fired. Let's just say I was instrumental in the ruination of his life, by way of maneuvering his wife to catch him doing something immoral, unethical, and illegal."

"Wow," I say, impressed, and also grateful. I always felt guilty about the other girls he might have hurt because I didn't speak out.

We're both quiet for a moment. Then I grab her hand and hold it in mine. It's time.

"Grace, there's something I have to tell you. About today. About when we land in Ontario."

She shakes her head. "You don't have to say anything, Louise. I already know."

Of course she does. "The Peepers?"

"No, honey. I looked in your phone. Back at Danny's while you were having a little nervous breakdown in the bathroom."

I want to be upset, but how can I, considering what *I've* done? "Are you mad at me?"

"Louise," she says. "How can I be mad at you? You only did what you thought needed doing."

"Just like you always did."

"I guess we're more the same than we're not, huh?"

I consider that for a moment. "I guess we are." She doesn't respond, but I sense a weight lifting off her.

"What are we going to do?" I ask. "About Dr. Brenner?"

"We'll figure something out. The important thing is getting to Edie."

"But how are we—"

"Hush, now, Louise. Close your eyes now and rest a spell. We're going to need our strength." She gives my fingers a squeeze, then releases them and lays her head back once more.

"Um, Grace. There is one other thing we really need to discuss."

She sighs heavily. "What now?"

"You can't fly."

SIXTY-FOUR

Grace

IOWA–PRESENT

Louise is right. I can't fly. But darn it, I'm going to have to.

We're just outside of Des Moines. The closer we get to the airport, the more I start to panic.

"Jesus, Grace," Louise says. "If you don't calm down, *I'm* going to have a stroke."

"I'm okay," I lie. "Right as rain."

"Sure you are."

We have some semblance of a plan, just for the flying part though. The rest we haven't figured out yet. Danny gave me his noise-canceling headphones along with his vintage portable disc player, which he swore he never uses anymore. He tucked a CD I am well-acquainted with into the player, and I stowed the whole contraption in my fanny pack. Louise is going to buy a package of Advil PM at the airport. I don't like pills—God knows I've been forced to take more than my fair share in my lifetime. But I'd be lying if I didn't admit how much I wish I had some lithium right about now. But the Advil PM might take the edge off.

I'm not completely confident this is going to work.

We reach the airport by 3:49 a.m., two hours before our flight, as instructed by the airline. At this time of day, there's not a lot of commotion, which I'm thankful for. Danny pulls the Camry to the curb in the loading zone in front of our airline, pops the trunk, then gets out to grab our bags.

Louise and I get out too, but instead of going to the curb, I tuck myself behind the wheel and sit there for a long moment. I gaze around at the interior of the Camry, then run my hand along the dashboard, let it linger there. I allow myself to feel love for my mother for the first time in a long while. If Louise can forgive me, maybe I can forgive her.

"Goodbye, Momma," I say. Then I step out into the early morning.

Danny and Louise are exchanging cell phone numbers. Our bags rest on the concrete.

"Let me know you got there safe," Danny says, handing Louise back her phone. "And that she's okay."

Louise nods solemnly. "I don't know when we'll be back for the car. Shouldn't be too long, though."

"It'll be here." He kisses the top of her head. "Really good to see you, Lou."

"Give Buck a kiss for me," she says.

Danny moves to me and grabs my hands. "Thank you. For saving my life. I'll see you soon."

I don't answer. He gives me a questioning look, but says nothing.

"You take good care of yourself, Danny."

"I will, Grace. You too."

He walks around the Camry and gets in. Without a backward glance, he pulls away.

Louise blinks rapidly a couple of times, then turns her attention to me. Her mouth is a tight white line.

"Are you ready?"

"Not even a little bit."

She cracks a grin. "Okay, then. Let's do this."

At check-in, we upgrade to business class. I hand over my one credit card, and request priority seating so we can board first. I don't give a second thought to what it all costs. The airline employee could have asked for my left arm and I would have hacked it off, right there in front of her.

The airport is rapidly filling with travelers. I'm still okay because the airport itself is not the problem. The *airplane* is the problem.

We make it through security easily enough, although I do not like removing my sneakers and traipsing through the metal detector in socks. I think of all the millions of people that have passed through— shoeless—before me, heading for countless destinations, vacations, job opportunities, weddings, funerals, family reunions. Journeymen and women, some filled with anxious expectation, hope, delight, others with grief or dread. I also think of all the germs and bacteria and foot fungus they've left behind that I'm walking over. Although I'm pretty sure the airport staff runs a floor cleaner over the place regularly, I tiptoe just the same, and make short work of getting my shoes back on my feet.

When we reach our gate, I find a secluded seat in the corner of the waiting area and Louise heads for the nearby shop to get the Advil PM. She comes back with a plastic bag full to brimming.

I eye the bag. "How much Advil PM do plan to give me?"

Sporting a guilty grin, she withdraws her bounty, item by item, and hands it to me. A couple magazines, a baseball cap with *Des Moines* embroidered on the face, two bottles of water, a bag of peanut M and M's.

"I always buy a bag when I fly. Superstition."

"So, if you skip the M and M's, the plane goes down?" I ask.

"I've never skipped, so I don't know. I thought it best not to tempt fate."

How right she is, although I'm tempting fate just by getting on a plane.

She pulls out the last item—a small bright-yellow stuffed animal—and holds it up. Her smile evaporates and her expression turns thoughtful.

"It's a goldfinch," she says, staring somberly at the bird. "Iowa's state animal, apparently. I got it for Edie . . . I don't know why. She's too old for stuffed animals, right?" Her eyes fill but she doesn't let the tears flow. "I gave her a stuffed animal, right before I gave her up. It was a dolphin. Named Chauncy. The woman from the agency, Earline McInerny . . ." A melancholy smile plays at her lips. "She was nice, I guess. I gave the dolphin to her, and she told me she'd make sure it went with Edie."

I want to reach out and take hold of Louise, but I don't want to intrude on her memory or the emotions it brings. After a moment, she takes a breath, lets it out on a sigh. "Who knows. It probably went into the dumpster behind the hospital."

"Or not," I say gently. Louise looks at me and I smile. She nods, then shrugs.

"Or not," she says. She stuffs the goldfinch back in the bag, then grabs the other things from me and stows them with the bird.

"Let me contribute." I unzip my fanny pack to grab some bills, but Louise rests her hand on mine to still me.

"I got this one, Grace."

My fingers brush against my black book and a shiver runs through me. I have to do my morning thing. Lord knows I won't be able to on the plane, so I might as well try here. It probably won't work. I'm used to being alone, not surrounded by harsh lights and people scurrying past, and the aroma of cinnamon buns battling with fried potatoes, and squawking flight announcements.

"Go ahead." Louise says. "You can do it here. Your *meditation*? I have to book us a rental car." She nods to the nearby corridor. "I'll just stand over there."

I smile at her. "No need to leave me alone. I'd kind of rather have you close."

We sit side by side. She pulls out her phone as I withdraw my book. I never realized how noisy airports are, even at this hour. I close my eyes and try to block out all the sounds. It doesn't work. I open my eyes and see Louise pointing to my fanny pack.

"Try the headphones."

Why didn't I think of that?

Because you have a lot on your mind. Yes, indeed I do.

I put the headphones on, and sweet silence envelops me. I close my eyes again and draw in some deep breaths. My fingers move slowly through the pages of my book. But I feel nothing, not even the slightest whisper from the Peepers.

Toward the end of the book, I feel a jolt. Not from inside my head, but from next to me. I open my eyes to find Louise giving me a laser stare, her expression suspicious and angry. I remove the headphones and she jabs a finger at the open page of my book.

"Why do you have him in there? What is he doing in your book?"

I know who she's referring to. I don't bother making excuses. "He helped me find you, Louise."

"I don't understand."

"Every person I ever . . . did a service for is in this book. All those photographs? They're all in here, names, addresses, phone numbers. And every single one of them has a picture of you. I gave it to them, or I sent it after the fact. So they could be on the lookout for you. Mary Palmer has one on her fridge. She tucked it away before you could see it. It's an old photo, but you haven't changed much. The only reason I keep this goldarn flip phone is on the off chance one of these good people saw you and got in touch."

I look down and read the name in the R section of my book. Dear, sweet Mac Riley, one of Louise's best customers at her bar and grill. Two years ago, on a busy street in Cleveland, I kept the massive coronary from taking him.

"I wasn't really surprised when he called. Not that I had any plans to come see you. I didn't want to disrupt your life. Again. But I sure did like knowing where you were, that you were safe. Then the whole business with Edie came up, and I had to come get you."

Her suspicion shifts to confusion. "I just assumed the Peepers told you where I was."

I chuckle. "Why would you have thought that when you didn't even believe in them till last night?"

She shrugs and shakes her head. "I don't know. I don't know what I thought."

"Louise, you've been blocking me out for years. Like that little green fella in *Star Wars* said, 'the Force is strong with you.' The Peepers couldn't get into that head of yours for anything."

Louise narrows her eyes at me. "What the hell are you talking about?"

I don't have time to explain, because at that moment, they call our flight. And the panic I've managed to keep at bay takes over.

Part Three

SIXTY-FIVE

Melanie

CALIFORNIA-PRESENT

I wake up in a frenzy.

My clock reads 7:15. I must have slept, like twelve hours, which is unbelievable. I have a vague recollection of Ray carrying me from the truck to my bed last night. I think he kissed my forehead and ran his fingers across my cheek, but that's all I remember. As Ray would say, I crashed like a tree.

And now, I'm late, late, late, but that's not why I'm upset. I wanted to read my journal the second we got home—all I could think about for the last half of our night at Kid City was getting home and reading what Penny wrote. But I slept instead. *Overslept*, now.

I climb out of bed and hunch down on the floor. I reach under the comforter to where I left my journal, but it's not there. My heart thuds. I lay on my stomach, pressing my cheek against the carpet, and peer under the bed. I see the fuzzy slipper I've been looking for, and the stuffed flamingo Ray won for me at the carnival last summer. But no journal. My whole body goes cold, I actually feel it happen. It's like a chill that starts at my toes and zips all the way up to the top of my head.

I scramble to my feet, then turn to my nightstand. Maybe I put it in there and just forgot. I grab the handle of the drawer and yank so hard the whole drawer comes flying out and crashes to the floor, banging me in the shin on the way down. I'm in such a panic, I barely feel it. I look through the drawer, but it's not there. I go to my desk, then to my bookshelf—no luck.

I dig through my closet, my heart pounding and sinking at the same time, which is a very weird feeling. I know the journal isn't there, but I search anyway.

I close the closet to hide the mess, then turn in a slow circle, spying every corner, crevice, and cubicle. I feel myself start to panic.

My journal is gone.

I race to the living room. Ray comes out from the kitchen, a mug of coffee in his hand.

"Hey, Mel. What'cha doing? You need to get ready for school."

"I lost something," I tell him. "I need to find it. It's important."

"What is it? Homework assignment? I'll help."

I look at him. His face has that same expression from last night. Stress, and maybe tiredness mixed in.

"It's not homework," I snap, and I don't even care that I used a bad tone. "It's my journal."

He steps into the room and looks at me questioningly. "I didn't know you had a journal."

"Well, I do. Miss Pearl told me I should keep one, so I do." This is sort of a lie. Pearl did suggest I keep notes about my home life. She did *not* tell me to have conversations with the girl who lives in my hand. "But it's gone. It was in my room, but now it's not."

He goes right for the cabinet by the front door which is a catchall for mail and circulars and other crap. "Okay, now, Mel, settle down. We'll find it."

Even as he says the words, I know he's wrong. I can feel it, almost like Penny is telling me, but in my head instead of on paper. I feel sick with dread.

"Where's D?" I croak. "Is she still asleep?"

Ray shakes his head as he rifles through the piles of crap on top of the cabinet.

"She was gone before I got up. I don't think she ever came to bed last night. She was passed out on the couch when we got home. I didn't wake her." He pauses his search and turns to me. "You sure that journal isn't in your room?"

Totally sure.

I try to breathe normally, which is hard to do. "I might have left it at school."

"Okay, well, why don't you get dressed. If you skip your shower, we can get you there early, so you have time to look for it."

I nod, then clear my throat. "Did D text you or leave you a note? Tell you where she was going?"

"No, she did not. I texted her, but she hasn't gotten back to me yet. I'm sure she's fine, if a little hungover. Hey, maybe she went to look for a job." He winks at me.

Normally, I would chuckle with him. Not today. Today might be my last day here. If D read the journal . . .

Oh crap. She'll show it to Ray, and then Miss Pearl, and good old DCFS will be around pretty quick to scoop me up.

I swallow hard. "I'm going to go get dressed."

Ray's got a funny look on his face, but I don't know what it means, and I don't really care. I turn and walk to my room, but I feel his eyes on me the whole way.

Twenty minutes later, he pulls to the curb in front of my school. Hardly anybody else is here yet, which is good, because I am going to go straight to the girls' bathroom and throw up. I've held it in for as long as I can.

I climb down from the passenger seat without saying goodbye. Ray rolls down the window and calls to me before I can step away.

"Hey, Mel. Are you all right?"

I force myself to give him a big, bright smile, using my teeth and everything. "I'm fine, Ray. Thanks for the ride."

"That was good, you and me last night, right?" he says, and I have no idea what he's talking about. I don't respond. "You and me at Kid City? Being real with each other? I like it when you speak up, Mel. I like us being honest with each other. We gotta keep doing that."

"Sure, Ray," I say.

He narrows his eyes at me, and the look on his face is kind of intense, almost to the point of creepy. I think about his name written in bold in Penny's message last night. The message Delilah must have read by now.

"You know you can tell me anything, right, Mel? No matter what it is."

I wish that were true. But, anyway, Ray'll find out about me soon enough.

"I know," I say, then wave him off and head for the school entrance.

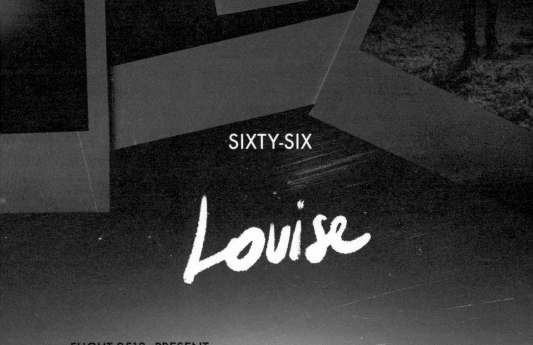

SIXTY-SIX

Louise

Priority boarding is worth every penny Grace spent. Same with business class. The seats are wide with plenty of legroom and the overhead bins are open and empty. I set our bags on the aisle seat, then grab for Grace's duffel to stow it.

"Wait," she says, stilling me with her hand. "I've got something for you."

Her face is taut with tension, but she attempts a smile. She unzips her bag, then digs through her clothes and pulls out a large paper tablet. A jolt of recognition slams through me as I recognize my old sketchbook.

"I threw that away," I say. "After the accident."

"Yes, well, I rescued it."

"Obviously."

Grace holds the book out, but I don't take it. She waits for a moment, then shrugs and slides it into the seatback pouch. Without another word, she shimmies over to the window seat, slams the blind closed, and connects her seat belt. She dons her sunglasses and the noise-canceling headphones, pulls her jacket tightly to her chest, and visibly folds in on herself.

I gaze at the edge of the sketchbook peeking out from the pouch, mesmerized. Slowly, I reach for it.

"Blankets," Grace whispers. "Lots of blankets."

I clench my fingers into fists and resist the urge to grab the book.

"On it," I tell her. I situate our bags in the overhead bin, then glance toward the front of the plane where a flight attendant stands sentinel. She's tall and blond and mean looking. I wave at her, and she promptly paints on a fake smile and makes her way to us.

Her name tag reads *Tammi*, and I think *God*. I know it's wrong, but I can't help but hate her based on the *i* alone. Tammy should be spelled with a *y*. Only pretentious fuckheads spell their names with an *i*.

"We need blankets," I say. "A lot of blankets."

Tammi glances at Grace, furrows her brow.

"My mother is a fearful flyer," I explain. "Blankets are comforting for her, so as many as possible. Please."

The flight attendant restores her smile and gives me a curt nod.

Three minutes later, I have Grace wrapped in four airline blankets, burrito style. I press Play on the Discman, and although I can't hear the song playing in her ears, I note the slight relaxation of her features.

As the plane starts to fill, I take my seat. I place a gentle hand on her knee, just to let her know I'm there. She doesn't flinch or respond in any way, and I take that as a good sign. I pray the cocoon we've created for her lasts.

Unfortunately, it doesn't.

We've been in the air for two hours. Grace hasn't moved or made a sound, not even when the airplane rocketed into the sky. If it weren't for the barely perceptible rise and fall of her chest, I'd think she was dead.

The thought makes me shudder.

The Discman is on autoplay, Danny's Pearl Jam CD on an endless loop. Pearl Jam is Grace's favorite band, always has been. When I was young, and Grace was home for long stretches, I could always count on hearing that band playing from the stereo in the living room. "Better Man," "Jeremy," "Alive," "Even Flow." Drove Grandma nuts. Occasionally, she peppered in Frank Sinatra, probably for Grams's sake, but mostly it was Pearl Jam. Even now, it's hard to reconcile that my mother, who is in her late fifties, still has an affinity for them. Their strident tunes don't strike me as calming. But she loves them, and that's what matters. She had a huge thing for Eddie Vedder too, back in her youth. I remember her telling me that she loved my father but she *adored* Eddie. Said Eddie was her soulmate, even if he would never know it.

Pearl Jam and Eddie Vedder are the reason we think of my daughter as Edie.

I always preferred Nirvana. But there isn't a feminine take on Kurt.

Grace twitches and mumbles something. Sounds like "22B." I look over and see that her eyes are rolling back and forth beneath her lids. I don't know whether she's in REM or getting information from *them*.

It is strange to think of the Peepers as real. At the same time, I have no problem accepting it, which is odd. Me, the pragmatist, so quickly believing in ESP and telepathy and spirits that communicate things to my mother that no one else is privy to. I consider the possibility that I've been drawn into Grace's delusion. Dr. Brenner would say that. But no. I was there at the river with Danny. He's alive because of her, I have no doubt. And the photographs. All proof positive.

Grace jerks in her seat. She tears off her sunglasses, flicking them away from her as though they're on fire. She yanks off the headphones then grabs my hand, and the force of her grip is painful.

"There's a man," she says. Tremors run through her, and her eyes are wild. "There's a man on this plane."

My first thought is terrorist. 9-11 is a long time ago, now, but the ripples will disrupt the proverbial pond for ages to come.

"He's going to leave his wife."

I take a quick breath. Okay, no shoe bombs or box cutters or buildings falling to the ground. Thank God. Just a guy who probably wants to screw his secretary. But Grace's agitation is no less intense than if a crazed man stood up and pointed an AK-47 at all of us. "It's okay, Grace," I say as soothingly as possible.

"No, it's not!" she shrieks. Tammi, who is handing out cookies to a young couple a few rows ahead, looks sharply in our direction.

"I shut them out, Lou. It worked. I shut them out. But they're too strong. They don't like it when I don't listen. They get angry. And *loud*. There's a man on this flight . . ."

"Grace," I whisper. "You have to calm down."

She ignores me. "If he leaves his wife, it will all fall apart. He doesn't think she loves him, but she does. Her name is Nicole. His name is Nicholas. They knew they were destined to be together because of their names. But now he thinks she's bored, unfulfilled, angry. She's not. She wants to make him happy but doesn't know how."

Tammi hurries in our direction.

"He can't leave her, Lou. He *can't!* "

"I need to ask you to lower your voice," the flight attendant says. She stands over me, trying to use her considerable height as an advantage. Grace ignores her.

"His daughter? Her name's Frances." My mother speaks quickly, her sentences rolling over one another. "She hates it, makes people call her Frankie. She's tender. Fourteen. She gets bullied because she's so smart."

The other people in business class have taken notice. They furtively watch us as they chomp on their complimentary cookies. Apparently, we are more entertaining than the in-flight programming.

"Excuse me," Tammi says with a sneer. "You are disturbing the other passengers. I will have to ask you to calm down."

I can't contain myself. "Or what? You'll have us removed? Nowhere to go at thirty-thousand feet. Now, back the fuck off, Tammi-with-an-*i*, so I can help my mother through this."

The young woman's eyes are round as dinner plates. She says nothing but retreats as though she's been struck. I turn to Grace.

"22B," she says again. "Frankie, his daughter. If he leaves, that girl is going to kill herself. She will wrap a belt around her neck and hang herself in her closet. Nicole will find her, blue and bloated with her swollen tongue hanging out of her mouth."

"Oh my God," the woman in the seat in front of me remarks loudly. I couldn't give a fuck what anyone else thinks. I know what's happening. Grace needs to get to 22B to talk to this Nicholas.

I put my hands on Grace's shoulders and squeeze them as hard as I can. She flinches, but then her eyes focus.

"I hear you, Grace," I tell her. "And I know what you need to do."
She nods, listening. "But if you don't calm down, it can't happen."

Her eyes brim with tears. "It's hard, Louise. So very hard."

"I know. But you have to hold it together. I'll get you to 22B. Just take a few deep breaths for me, okay? *With* me. We'll take them together."

She nods again, and simultaneously, we draw in oxygen and blow it back into the cabin. Once, twice, three times. Our eyes are locked.

"22B," she says.

I return the noise-canceling headphones to Grace's ears. She smiles with gratitude, then closes her eyes.

I stand up and glance toward the cockpit. Tammi glares at me from the galley. I give her my best patronizing smile—the one I reserve for customers at the bar who don't know when to cut themselves off. Then I turn and push through the curtain that separates business class from economy.

I count the rows, which start at ten. Fourteen rows down, I spot him. Nicholas sits in the middle seat on the right side of the airplane. The window seat is occupied by a very large older woman. The aisle seat next to Nicholas is empty.

I return to my mother in business class. I tap her lightly on the arm. Her eyes fly open and she looks at me. I nod to her, then take her hand and lead her out of her seat. Down the aisle, Tammi takes a menacing step toward us. I cast her a withering glare, and she freezes.

Good little Tammi. Get a real fucking name.

I push aside the curtain and gesture toward Nicholas. Grace hardly acknowledges me. She pushes past me and heads down the aisle. When she reaches 22B, Nicholas looks up at her questioningly. She says something to him, and even from where I stand, I know she's pouring on the Tennessee charm. A moment later, Nicholas gestures for Grace to sit in the empty aisle seat.

For the next several minutes, I watch with awe and wonder as my mother saves a marriage, not to mention another life.

SIXTY-SEVEN

Grace

FLIGHT 2513–PRESENT

Nicholas Beecham in 22B is a nice man, a good man. He hasn't saved as many lives as I have, but he's saved a few. Growing up in a Southern Baptist environment, with an evangelical father and a mother who religiously collected game pieces from the local supermarket in order to win a Chrysler minivan, screwed him up pretty good, but he's trying to move past his upbringing.

He's slight but strong. His blond hair is thinning on top, and I know he's self-conscious about it, worries that Nicole finds his receding hairline unattractive. She doesn't, just FYI.

He stares at the reading app on his tablet, but I can tell he's not reading. I come up beside him and ask him if he doesn't mind me taking the seat next to him for a spell. He nods distractedly. He couldn't care less one way or the other. He's got a lot on his mind. I can relate.

Information is flooding my brain. If this were a game show, and I was the contestant, and the host asked me to name something private about every single person on this plane, I could do it. For instance, the young gal across the aisle from Nicholas is a kleptomaniac. She only steals laxatives. Because she's bulimic and doesn't want anyone to know. And the older woman beside ex-lax girl has been married for thirty-five years but is still in love with a tap dancer she knew in college.

Two rows back, in 24C, sits a man named Paulo who is struggling with the fact that he needs to come out of the closet in order to find happiness with Benjamin, his personal trainer, who has been sending signals for six months now but is starting to lose hope.

I get all of this, and it is exhausting. Enough to drive me completely mental. This is why I don't travel by plane or train. Too much information coming at me all at once. *TMI*, the young folks call it. I might have opened the emergency hatch midair if it weren't for Lou. Or keeled over dead.

The woman sitting in the window seat looks a lot like I did a while ago. She's covered with blankets and wears headphones and an eye mask and has generally checked out of the present for the duration of the flight. She's a fearful flyer, like me. Well, not like me, because she doesn't have a thousand voices jawing at her incessantly. She simply has visions of twisted metal and charred corpses spread out along a smoky landscape running through her mind. I'd make her feel better if I could. But my focus needs to be on Nicholas Beecham. He's the one at risk. The old woman will get off the plane safely in Southern Cal and be greeted by her daughter and grandkids and spend a luxurious week at a cottage on the coast. She doesn't need me. Nicholas does.

I turn to him and smile. Then start with my pitch.

"I wonder if you wouldn't mind doing me a favor," I say. He glances over, clearly irritated. Then he smooths his features to appear more welcoming.

"Sure," he says.

"I'm afraid to fly," I tell him, which is the God's honest truth, although not in the way he assumes. "Do you think you might hold my hand?"

He squints at me. "Excuse me?"

"Just for a minute," I assure him. "I'm trying to keep from jumping out of my skin, because I know if I do, they'll reroute this plane to Utah or something so they can get the crazy woman off the plane." Nicholas frowns at this, as I knew he would. Nobody likes a travel delay. "I just need a little human connection and I think I'll be fine. Could you? Just hold my hand for a minute?"

I watch him struggle with himself. He isn't a germaphobe, but I am a complete stranger. And the only hands he's held for the past sixteen years are his wife's and his daughter's. Rerouting to Utah, however, would be a pain in the backside.

"Just for a minute, okay? I'm in the middle of a good book, and I'd like to get back to it."

"Sure thing, Nicholas." I put out my hand and he takes it. He doesn't realize I called him by his name until I entwine my fingers with his. Before he can call me out or pull his hand away, something happens. The thing that *always* happens. My energy flows through to him, and his flows back to me. He opens his mouth to say something, then closes it. He looks at me, *really* looks at me, for the first time.

"Who are you?" he asks.

"My name is Grace. And I have some things I need to talk to you about. But you're going to have to be open to them."

"How did you know my name?" His question comes out calmly, easily.

"I know a lot of things about you. And I want to help you. You and your family. But, like I said, you're going to have to open your mind and open your heart to what I'm going to say. You're going to have to cast off all the doubts and preconceptions that living as a realist in this world has built up in you. Can you do that, Nicholas?"

A few seconds pass, with him just staring at me, and me holding his eyes so he knows I'm serious and not trying to mess with him. Then he nods, very slowly.

We talk for a while, Nicholas and me, with Louise looking on. Then we cry a little bit together.

And finally, forty-five minutes later, he releases my hand.

I return to business class spent, but content. Tammi keeps her distance as Louise escorts me to my window seat. Lou doesn't say a word about Nicholas. No questions, no comments, nothing. But she looks at me as though I'm a superhero. Because she knows what I've done.

To see that look on my daughter's face . . . well, words can't describe how that makes me feel. My head is still buzzing, though. The Peepers have more intel for me, but I don't think I can handle their communication right now.

"Distract me, Lou," I tell my daughter.

She doesn't ask how, just grabs her sketchbook from the seatback in front of her as though she's been waiting for a reason. She runs her hand across the cover but doesn't open it.

"Perfect," I tell her. "Go ahead."

As if in slow motion, she peels the cover back, and within seconds, the Peepers fade, and I'm swept away by her sketches.

Drawing and running were her gifts. She gave up both. One because tragedy forced her to. The other because she thought she needed to. But darn if she wasn't talented. In more ways than one.

As Louise turns page after page, her images imprint themselves upon my retinas and my gray matter. Each sketch has the date and time noted in the top right corner. A hummingbird midflight, a volleyball match, a rocky cove with waves crashing upon the sand, a fire burning across barren hills. The carnage of a train wreck sprawled in a field beneath a full moon. The wreck reminds me of what I have in my fanny pack, what I've held on to for almost two decades. I won't show it to her yet. I don't think she's ready. She's taken a lot in over the past twelve hours.

A satisfied sigh escapes her as she gazes down at her drawings, as though a part of her that was missing has been returned. She starts to turn the pages more quickly, and I feel myself tense up because I know what's coming. I have to stop her before she gets to that particular sketch. I grab the book from her and slam it shut. She jerks with surprise.

"Oh my, Lou, but you need to get me to the ladies and quick!"

I'd rather be anywhere on earth than in an airplane bathroom, but desperate measures, and all. I shove the sketchbook into the seatback and grip Louise's shoulder.

"Okay, Grace, take it easy." She looks at me worriedly, then unbuckles her seat belt and pushes out of her seat.

"You got to be there with me, Lou."

"In the bathroom, Grace? There's no room."

"Stay just outside. You gotta promise you won't leave me, Lou. Promise."

She takes my hand and gives me a smile. "I promise, Grace. I won't leave you."

And she doesn't leave me. Not yet, anyway.

SIXTY-EIGHT

CALIFORNIA–PRESENT

Reuben Meserve is stalking me.

I kind of forgot all about the note he left in my house—*on my bed*. I know, hard to forget, but with everything else going on, maybe not hard at all. The human brain has to prioritize what to focus on. But as soon as I saw Reuben, I remembered. He was waiting for me at the front of the school when Ray dropped me off. He didn't say anything when I passed him, but I could feel him close behind me all the way to the bathroom. Then, after first period, he was hanging out across the hall when I came out of class, and he followed me to my row of lockers.

Like I don't have enough on my mind, what with Delilah taking my journal, and me not being able to read what Penny wrote, which I think might be pretty important. And not knowing what Penny said about Ray which could also be *very* important. And the fact that foster children who keep getting bounced around tend to be labeled as troublesome, and thirteen-year-olds who still have imaginary friends might be considered *more* than troublesome. They might be considered psychotic or delusional or crazy.

Am I? Am I crazy?

All of these thoughts are bouncing around in my stupid head and

I can't make sense of them and I can't talk to Penny because I'm in the middle of English class.

The teacher is making us write haikus. I couldn't care less about haikus, but I don't want to get a zero. I look around and see all my classmates hunched over their desks, scribbling out their poems on their wide-ruled lined paper. All except Reuben Meserve. He's staring at me, hard. He gives me a creepy grin and a chill goes through me. I turn away from him and look down at my own blank paper.

The fingers of my left hand twitch. *Penny?* Real or not, I carefully place my pencil in my left hand and press the lead tip against the top line of the page. I close my eyes and take a deep breath and pray that no one is watching me. I mean, I know Reuben is, but he's behind me so he can't see my face.

I feel my hand move. When it comes to rest, I look down and see a perfectly formed haiku.

> *Furtive peril prowls*
> *Shadows hide in broad daylight*
> *Fear not the stranger*

I look up to see Mrs. Rogers standing beside my desk.

"Are you finished, Melanie?" she asks, and I nod self-consciously and try to hide the poem with my arm. "Would you like to share your haiku with the class?"

That would be a definite *no way*.

"Come on, Melanie. It seems like the rest of the class is having some difficulty with this assignment. Perhaps you can inspire them?"

"It's not very good," I say.

Mrs. Rogers smiles at me. "I'm sure it's excellent. Would you like me to read it for you?"

She doesn't wait for an answer, just pulls the paper out from under my hand and lifts it away from me. She scans the poem and her smile fades.

"This is very good," she says quietly. "Although the subject matter is a little worrisome."

"I watched *Alien* over the weekend. It's kind of about that." Quick thinker. That's me.

Mrs. Rogers lets out a relieved breath. "Ah. That makes sense. All right, friends," she calls to the class. "This is Melanie's haiku, and the inspiration for it is a very scary movie." She clears her throat then reads the haiku. All the students look bored, but my heart is pounding. When she finishes, she looks around proudly, as though she wrote it herself. Which is funny because *I* didn't even write it. But I can't feel the humor right now. I can only feel dread. Because something bad is going to happen. Soon.

SIXTY-NINE

Louise

CALIFORNIA–PRESENT

The stopover in Phoenix was mercifully short and painless, but once we got back in the air, Grace started to get agitated again. She stayed under her blankets, but her legs were bouncing up and down, and her hands were fidgeting so badly I had to hold them to keep them still. And she kept repeating the mantra, *Get there, get there, get there.*

Now that we've landed in Ontario, she's better. She keeps the noise-canceling headphones on and her eyes closed while the rest of the passengers deplane. I sit beside her, watching her lips move. She's no longer saying her mantra. Instead, she silently sings along to the song playing in her ears. I recognize it. "Better Man." I hum along with her until the plane is nearly empty.

I stand and stretch my left leg, wincing at the thousand needles of pain that accompany my movement. Just as I reach for the overhead bin, Nicholas Beecham appears next to us. Grace seems to sense his presence. She removes the headphones, opens her eyes, and looks up at him. Neither says a word, but a knowing smile passes between them. Then Nicholas continues to the exit.

A sense of peace blossoms inside me as I watch him walk away. He will be all right. His daughter is going to be all right, too. Because of

Grace. I turn to my mother to tell her what I feel, but the words die before I can voice them. Her smile has vanished, and she suddenly looks pale and shriveled, as though she's going to disappear beneath the cheap airline blankets. She jerks her head toward the ceiling. Nods her head. Squeezes her eyes shut.

"It's about goldarn time, you bastards."

"Grace?"

"I'm okay. Get our bags, Lou."

She peels off the blankets, unzips her fanny pack, and pulls out her black book and a pen. Scribbles something in the book, returns it to her pack, then struggles to push herself to standing. She wobbles, and I grab her arm to steady her. She looks at me.

"You have a plan?" she asks. I nod. "Good. 'Cause I know where you're going."

"Where *we're* going."

She rolls her eyes impatiently. "Yes, yes, that's what I said. Now get moving. Time's running short."

She holds on to the seatback for support as I grab our bags from the overhead and stow my sketchbook into my duffel. In my peripheral vision, I see Tammi going about cleaning up the cabin while giving us a wide berth. I don't hold any ill will toward the flight attendant—she was just doing her job—but I'm glad she's keeping her distance.

I root into the plastic bag from the Des Moines Airport gift shop and withdraw the baseball cap, then hand it to Grace.

"He's not allowed through to the gate. I told him we'd meet him at baggage claim." She dons the cap, tucking her hair into it. Only the graying roots above her ears show. "I'll meet him, try to distract him. You go straight to the car rental and get our car. It's under your credit card. Okay?"

"Then what?"

"Then you drive around the airport until you hear from me. Is your phone on?"

She unzips her fanny pack and checks the flip phone. "It's on."

"Okay. It's going to be fine." I try to sound confident, but this ranks up there as one of the worst plans of all time.

"Edie needs us. Got to get there." Her color is only slightly better.

"Let's go." I start to move toward the exit, then feel Grace's hand on my shoulder. I stop and look back at her.

"Whatever happens to me, Lou—"

"No, Grace. Do not do that." I really don't want to hear what she has to say.

"I just want to tell you that I'm glad we found each other again. I can't erase the past. Don't know that I would. But these past few days with you have been the best of my life."

My throat closes and I bite the inside of my cheek to keep the tears at bay. Because I feel the same way. I can't give in to the emotion, though. We don't have time.

"Grace, we have to go."

She nods solemnly, squeezes my shoulder, then releases her hold. She looks about a hundred years old.

We separate as soon as we reach the gate. I carry both bags, leaving Grace to walk unencumbered. I follow the signs for the baggage claim, and she peels off in the direction of ground transportation. I keep glancing back at her until she is out of view. When I lose sight of her, my heart seizes in my chest and I almost retrace my steps and go after her. But I know I need to move forward and try to make this work.

I step onto the escalator that leads down to baggage claim. Other travelers push past me, in a hurry to wait for luggage that may or may not appear. I linger, wishing I could slow the damn machine down. As I descend, I think about all the times I've seen Dr. Brenner before this day. On each of those occasions, my perspective was that my mother was certifiable. Today my perspective has radically shifted. Today, Dr. Brenner is the bad guy.

The escalator finally deposits me to the ground floor of the terminal. Ontario is a small airport in comparison to many, but the area still bustles with activity. I scan through the throngs of people waiting for the carousels to start turning or begin spewing baggage. I wonder where Grace is, then put that question out of my mind.

I spot him almost immediately, standing next to the wall behind carousel three. He is thin, as always, with a severe widow's peak and a correlating pointy chin. He wears glasses now, wire-rimmed, and his hair has gone mostly gray. I force myself to move toward him and I don't smile, because me smiling would make him suspicious. I attempt a neutral and weary expression. The neutral bit is a challenge. The weary bit comes naturally.

As I draw closer, the corners of his lips pull up into a small smile, the same smile he always wears, but today it's a sneer, at least in my mind. He narrows his eyes and looks past me, searching for Grace.

"Louise," he says with his soft, deep voice. "You look well. How was your trip?"

"You can probably guess," I say. "A complete nightmare. I can't wait to get back to New York. To my *life*."

"Hhhmmm, yes." He looks around again. "And where is your mother?"

"Where do you think?" I ask with mock consternation. "She's in the ladies' room. She refused to use the bathroom on the flight, said demons live in the commode." I roll my eyes for effect. "She'll be right along."

"Are you certain?" he asks. "I was concerned about the numerous communications I received from you. 'All is well,' 'Grace is fine,' etcetera. I thought perhaps she coerced you to alter the plan."

I set the bags down at our feet. "Yeah, well. She played me pretty well. I thought, you know, she's delusional but not dangerous." I feel sick to my stomach about what I'm saying. My words feel like a betrayal, but my reasons are pure. "I assume since you're here, you got my last message from this morning?"

He nods, his eyes darting left and right. "Baggage claim three. Keep with the plan. Something like that?"

"So, where is your car?" My pulse races. I can feel it throb in my neck. I pray Dr. Brenner doesn't notice.

"Where is your mother, Louise?"

"I told you, she's in the can. Jesus. Can't wait to get her back to the hospital, can you, Dr. Brenner? So you can start billing her insurance?"

He cocks his head to the side. "What's this nonsense?"

"Oh, listen, I don't give a shit. Grace needs to get put away, right?" I start babbling to give Grace more time. If I can distract this asshole long enough, she might make it to the car rental before he starts looking for her. "Still, it's all a racket. I mean, I know there are a lot of sick people that really need psychiatric care and benefit from it. But, um, I've had a few therapists in my life. Only the first one after the accident did me any good. But the rest?" I start to giggle nervously because as I'm talking the realizations hit me. "The rest were just soaking me. Now that I think about it, they actually created problems I didn't have, just to keep me in therapy. Abandonment issues, those were correct. But isolation issues, antisocial behavior, sociopathic behavior, misanthropic tendencies, misogynistic tendencies—that's a laugh—god damn frigidity? Ka-ching. Ka-ching. You psychiatrists love your money, don't you? I can tell *you* do, Dr. Brenner." I reach out and stroke the lapel of his suit. He reflexively steps back.

"This is ridiculous," he says, and shakes his head with disdain. "Your current behavior suggests that all of your therapists were correct."

I jab a finger at him. "Let me ask you something, Doc." He flinches at the Bugs Bunny term. "You've put my mother in the hospital three times—"

"At your grandmother's request, I might remind you. And now at *your* request."

"No, I know that. My question is, if Grace is so ill, why do you keep letting her out?"

He leans toward me, so close I can smell the Listerine on his breath. "It was your grandmother who rescued her on each of the occasions of which you speak. Had it been up to me, your mother would never have been released."

His eyes blaze, betraying the kind of rage unfit for a psychiatrist, and suddenly I realize why.

"You know about Grace, don't you? That she has a gift."

"You *have* been drawn into her delusion," he chuffs, but I can tell he's bluffing.

"What did she tell you? What does *she* know about *you*? Must be something pretty bad for you to hate her so much."

For a split second, Brenner looks scared. Then he sneers at me. "No one hates her more than you, Louise, isn't that right? You'd have to hate her to sign that paperwork. Your grandmother is gone. No one to save her. Grace is my ward now. And I have no intention of failing her this time."

My blood runs cold in my veins. I start to back away from him, but he grabs my arm and pulls me in close. "Now tell me where she is."

Terror and fury grip me. "Let go of me or I'll start screaming bloody murder."

Just then, *Grace* starts screaming.

SEVENTY

Grace

CALIFORNIA—PRESENT

As soon as Lou and I part ways at the gate, I go to the bathroom to wash my hands and splash my face with cold water. I don't take but a minute, don't even use the toilet—we can find a rest stop once we're on the road—but the brief visit gives me enough time to see my reflection in the warped airport mirror. I don't look good.

I hustle out of there, thankful my daughter took my bag because I'm so exhausted I think my bag might topple me over if I had to lug it. I get my bearings and follow the signs for ground transportation, which is right next to baggage claim. Close. Too goldarn close. My hands are clammy, and I've broken out in a cold sweat, but I keep moving forward toward the sliding glass doors that lead to the outside. If I can just get out there and board one of the shuttles that'll take me to the rental car, we'll be okay.

About twenty feet from the exit, I glance toward baggage claim and I see them, Louise and that snake Brenner, talking heatedly. I didn't tell Louise what I know about him. I haven't told anyone. I consider it psychic/psychiatrist confidentiality. But maybe I should have. He's a bad man in more ways than one. I see him jab a finger at Louise and my heart nearly leaps from my chest with the desire to protect my daughter.

But I know I need to stick with the plan. I hunker down under my cap and make a beeline for the doors.

Just before I cross the threshold, I get a message, loud and clear.

Do NOT *go outside.*

But it's too late. I'm already through.

Get there.

A shuttle idles at the curb to my right, its hydraulic door just starting to slide closed. I holler and race for it, waving my hands in the air. *Like a crazy person.* In that instant, I realize my mistake. I've given myself away.

Strong hands grab my arms on either side and yank me away from the shuttle. I look left and right and see two men in white scrubs, one tall and lean, the other squat and muscular. They don't bother with pleasantries or calming words, just start hauling me farther down the sidewalk toward a waiting ambulance.

"What are you doing?" I cry, but my voice is barely above a whisper. I summon whatever strength I've got left and try to yank myself from their clutches. "Let me go! I said, get your everloving hands off me!"

They ignore my entreaties, as they've been instructed to. They don't know me or who I am. But I know *them* immediately, and I can't help but think what an inopportune moment the Peepers have chosen, because neither of these orderlies will listen to the seven ways I can help them.

The people around us gawk and scurry to get out of our way. A kid with a huge hiking pack on his back points his cell phone in our direction but makes no move to intervene.

I struggle as hard as I can, but the men don't seem to notice. I try to make myself dead weight, but these two are strong. They lift me off the ground like I weigh no more than a pomegranate.

Panic takes hold. I jerk my head to the right and see Louise and Brenner through the glass. He's in her face, scowling that scowl of his, telling her off by the looks of it. I wait a second until I see the glass doors of baggage claim slide open. Then I start hollering at the top of my lungs.

The men tighten their grips, and I yelp at the way their fingers dig into my flesh. Louise rushes through the glass doors with Dr. Brenner close behind her. She sees us and her face goes crimson with rage.

"Get the fuck off her!"

Quick as a wink, she jumps at the man on my right. He bats her away, but she scrambles back at him, clawing at his sleeve. Brenner comes up next to her and yanks at her hand.

"Calm down, Louise. I know this is upsetting, but this is the way it must be."

Louise pulls away from him and tries for the orderly again.

"Police!" Dr. Brenner shouts.

Suddenly, a lightning bolt of pain rips through me. Every muscle in my body spasms, then my insides loosen and I go completely slack. I guess I am truly dead weight now, because the orderlies stop moving.

"Let her go," Louise commands, and this time, they do.

I feel myself hurtling toward the sidewalk, but it feels like slow motion. The Des Moines cap flies from my head and lands on the asphalt in front of the cab kiosk, and I absently wonder if someone will find that cap, and who that person might be, and I realize that I'll never know, and that's okay, that's just fine. But still, I am falling. Louise catches me before my head can smash against the concrete.

"This is a tactic," Brenner says snidely. "I've seen this before."

"How dare you?" Louise spits at him. "Look at her!"

"Why don't you come along, too, Louise. The hospital might do you some good."

"I'll fucking kill you!" She lunges for him.

Brenner nods at the orderlies, and they close in on Louise.

I watch all of this as though it's a dream, yet I'm aware of the cold concrete beneath my shirt, the stink of exhaust from the cars and cabs circling the airport drive, the whoosh of airplanes overhead, the kid with the camera, filming, filming, the airport security guards running toward us, and the desperate shrieks of my daughter as the orderlies grab her.

The pain is still there, fiery and fierce. It starts at my center and radiates outward. I'm still conscious enough to hear the Peepers. They're talking to me, telling me what to do, but their words are getting softer, and I understand that I'm running out of time.

"What the hell is going on here?" comes a familiar voice.

I feel rather than see Nicholas Beecham kneel down next to me. He takes my hand and looks closely at me. "You'll be okay."

I crack a smile. My limbs feel hot and numb at the same time. "I might not, but you will be."

Nicholas looks up at Brenner and the orderlies. "This woman is in cardiac arrest, you idiots. Let go of her daughter and do your jobs."

The next second, Louise is beside me. "Grace. Grace!" Tears stream down her cheeks, and I want to reach up and wipe them away, but I don't have the strength.

"Did I tell you 22B was a doctor?" My voice is paper thin. My thoughts start to scatter. "Furtive peril prowls," I say, although I don't know exactly why.

"Grace. I'm so sorry. This is my fault."

I shake my head. It takes tremendous effort. I reach for one of her hands. That takes even more. I place her hand on my fanny pack and attempt a squeeze.

"Take it and go."

"No, Grace. I'm not going anywhere."

"For once in your life, do as I say, Louise," I croak. "Get outta here. You have to find Edie. The address is on the last page of my book. Get there."

"These morons don't know CPR," Nicholas says, his voice shaking. "Let me in." He looks at Lou, reaches out, gently squeezes her arm. "I'll take care of her."

Louise's face is pinched with turmoil. She nods at him then bends down and kisses me on the forehead. Her eyes find mine.

"Don't you leave me, Mom," she whispers. "You hear me? Don't you dare leave me now."

She unclips my fanny pack and gains her feet, then grabs our bags from the sidewalk. Before anyone can stop her, she rushes to the curb and climbs into the back of a cab.

Get there, Lou. For both of us.

My vision is fading. The noises around me sound like they're coming from down the length of a long tunnel. The Peepers have gone silent. I'm vaguely aware of 22B pounding on my chest. Darkness seeps in, slowly at first, then faster. I slip into the darkness with one last thought, a thought that fills me with joy and erases any fear I might have of my current destination.

My daughter finally called me Mom.

SEVENTY-ONE

Melanie

CALIFORNIA-PRESENT

By the time lunch comes, I'm good and freaked out. I keep thinking about Penny's haiku—*furtive peril prowls*—and Ray and Delilah and Reuben Meserve and my journal and DCFS. I could barely sit still in fourth period.

As soon as I go to the cafeteria, I feel his eyes on me. I turn and see him standing on the far side of the metal picnic-style tables. He's watching me, for sure. It's not like I'm being paranoid.

Normally on Mondays, I bring my lunch, and I usually take it into Mrs. Clarke's classroom. She's the social skills teacher, and even though I don't have her for any classes, I go in there because it's a safe space for all the losers and mentally challenged kids—which the other students call retarded—and the socially awkward kids. Everybody keeps pretty much to themselves. They eat and draw and sometimes go on the computer and watch a video or two. I don't talk to anyone, and no one talks to me. No one makes fun of me either.

Today, Delilah didn't pack my lunch, so I have to buy. The line is long. I stand in my place, moving forward as slow as a snail, and I think about Delilah and wonder where she was this morning.

Someone bumps me on the arm. I look over to see Reuben standing beside me. My shoulders shoot up to my ears.

"No cuts," I tell him, and my voice doesn't sound wimpy or weak.

He turns and glares at the kid behind me. The kid steps back and lets Reuben in. Stupid jerk. I turn toward the lunch counter and try to ignore Reuben, but he comes up right behind me and talks into my ear.

"Did you get my note?"

I whirl around on him. "'Course I did! It was on my bed. You totally broke into my house. I could report you to the police!"

Reuben's moon face shows no expression at all.

"You wouldn't," he says.

"Oh yeah? Why wouldn't I?"

"You know why," he whispers, then he chuckles, but still with that blank expression, and that makes the chuckle totally creepy and like out of a horror movie.

I leave my place in line and head for Mrs. Clarke's room across the quad. I don't know where else to go. She has composition books, so maybe I can try to talk to Penny.

I push into her classroom, but there's only a few other kids there and no Mrs. Clarke, just an aide. The aide is super skinny and wears bright, patterned leggings and enormous hoop earrings.

"Hi there," she says brightly from behind Mrs. Clarke's desk. "Are you eating with us today?" I nod. "And where's your lunch?"

"I'm not hungry," I tell her, then make a beeline for the back table where Mrs. Clarke keeps all the school supplies.

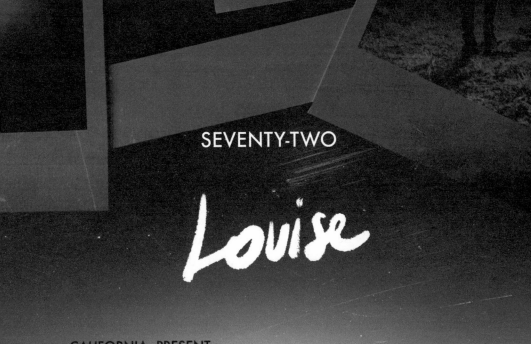

SEVENTY-TWO

Louise

CALIFORNIA—PRESENT

According to the GPS on my phone, Edie's house is an hour and three minutes inland from the Ontario Airport. Grace's wad of cash would cover it three times over.

The cab driver, a stout middle eastern man with a booming baritone, almost threw me out of his car when I gave him the address. I showed him a trio of Benjamins, and he zipped his lip and laid on the gas and hasn't said a word since.

I'm still in shock. I abandoned Grace, left her to die. I know she wanted me to go. And my leaving wasn't going to have any effect on her outcome, but I'm sick with guilt.

More than that, Grace should be here. No. *Mom.* Mom should be here, sitting beside me in the back of this spotlessly clean cab. Finding Edie was as much her mission as mine. *More* hers, because she set the wheels in motion. I could kill myself a dozen times in a dozen different ways for reaching out to Brenner. I didn't know then what I know now. But that doesn't make me feel better.

My tears have dried. My cheeks feel crusty and chafed. My eyelids are so swollen, I can barely see through them. The harsh sunlight bears down on the highway and the landscape around me. I don't have my sunglasses. Grace—*Mom*—must have accidentally left them on the plane. I imagine them tucked between the seats, Tammi finding them and smiling meanly and keeping them for herself.

I've been sitting rigidly, leaning forward, all my muscles taut. My left leg twitches, and the pain which has been muted by more important matters returns full blast. I rummage through my purse for my ibuprofen, shake out three gel caps, and swallow them down with water from the bottle I bought at the gift shop. I think about Grace in the baseball hat, how it flew from her head when she crumpled to the sidewalk. I almost tell the driver to turn around and go back, but I don't. I force myself to lean back against the seat. There's nothing I can do for Grace right now except get to Edie. And I can't make the cab go any faster. The driver is already pushing seventy-five. I have to sit tight and relax. Ha. Right.

What will happen when I see her? What will I say to her? I have no idea what kind of situation she's in that she needs to be rescued from, nor what the circumstances of our reunion will involve. I will be a stranger to her. I'd like to imagine some kind of idealistic scenario in which Edie will recognize me immediately, but I know that won't happen.

I think of what my mother would say. She'd say, "Just get there and help her and then deal with the rest of it as it comes."

She'd be right. That's all I can do.

I pull out my phone and check the time. Twenty-five minutes have passed. I swipe the screen and see that I have a new text. I suck in a breath, wondering if it's from Brenner. But it's not. It's from Ewan. And it's lengthy.

> Hi, Lou. We miss you around here. I miss you. Donna is absolute shite behind the bar, and your regulars are regularly chanting your name. I'm sorry about how I was the other night. I know if you ask for time off it must be important, so I hope whatever you have going on is going okay. Your job is safe, Lou. And I know you might

not want to hear this, but, no matter
what's happened between us, I do care
about you, and I'm here for you if you need
me. You think you're the grand bitch of all
time, but you're not. I know that even if
you don't. E.

I hate that I want to cry over a stupid text from a twerp of a guy who gets overly attached way too fast and who gets off on bossing the waitstaff around. But the truth is, he's not a twerp and he's fair with his employees, and if I were *really* being honest, I know he doesn't have attachment issues, he has genuine feelings for me. He's wrong about the bitch part. Because if I weren't such a bitch, I would have let him in and allowed him to get to know me.

But I never wanted him to get to know me. Because I've always thought I was broken. And broken people tend to break those close to them.

I shut my phone down and set it on the seat beside me. Then I grab my mother's fanny pack. I pull out the Discman and slip the headphones over my ears. I press play and Eddie Vedder's voice fills my head.

Even flow
thoughts arrive like butterflies . . .

I grab the little black address book and start flipping through it, slowly this time. So many names in this book. So many people she helped. So many lives she touched. I feel their life-force spring from the pages.

At the letter N, I discover the newest entry. Nicholas Beecham. My heart thuds. Here is his cell number and home address and email address, which is classic because Mom doesn't have the ability to email anyone. I could call his cell. I could call and ask how my mother is. But then, he might tell me something I don't want to hear, even if a part of me already knows what he'll say. I gaze at the page. A rush of emotion courses through me.

I reach the end of the book, where Edie's address is written, and I see a folded piece of newspaper tucked into the back flap. The sight of it fills me with dread, though I have no idea why. I turn off the Discman and yank the headphones from my ears and set them aside. With shaking hands, I pull out the newspaper clipping, slowly unfold it, then gasp so loudly, the driver swerves.

"You okay?" he barks.

"Yes, I'm fine," I tell him. But I'm not fine, not remotely. I stare down at the clipping and read the article Grace saved, the headline which screams TRAIN WRECK RAVAGES NEVADA COUNTRYSIDE. The picture below the caption is the spitting image of the sketch I drew when I was, what, fifteen? With shaking hands, I retrieve my sketchbook from my duffel and tear through the pages until I reach the train crash. I check the date, then scan the newspaper. My heart jackhammers in my chest.

I drew the wreck *twelve hours before it happened.*

Impossible.

Not *impossible.*

I flip through the book until I reach the last sketch, the one I didn't get to on the plane. The one Grace kept me from looking at with her bathroom emergency. I feel light-headed, like I might pass out, but I force myself to look at the page. And there it is. The accident. Unmistakable. Tessa's parents' Lexus, smashed to bits, with an ambulance just behind it.

Drawn three hours before the event.

I lean back against the seat and stare at the countryside outside the window, breathing in and out until my heart rate returns to normal. I consider the drawings—my sketches that, as it turns out, were premonitions. Not Peepers exactly, but extrasensory, without a doubt. I realize I'm not surprised, not freaked out. In fact, I'm overcome by a profound sense of completion, as though I've finally come full circle.

For a while I sit in stillness, allowing my thoughts to drift. I'm not used to stillness. After the accident that crushed my leg, I knew nothing *but* stillness because I had no choice. I think I've been fighting against it since, as though I'm a shark who needs to move in order to stay alive. Stillness equals death.

The cab roars down the road, bringing me closer to Edie with every rotation of its tires.

I run my fingertips over the image of Tessa's Lexus. Then I slip the pencil out from the spiral wire at the top of the pad.

My right hand starts to tingle. I flip to the next blank page and for the first time in seventeen years, I give myself over to the sketch.

SEVENTY-THREE

Melanie

CALIFORNIA–PRESENT

I can't reach Penny.

The other kids in Mrs. Clarke's room are playing Pictionary with the smartboard. They didn't ask me to join in, but I wouldn't have anyway. I sit in the back corner of the room, watching them but not really paying attention.

I have a composition book open to a blank page and a pen in my left hand, but I don't feel the slightest tingle.

I see movement at the door. Reuben Meserve stares into the room through the glass panel. I jump up, glance at the aide to make sure she isn't looking, then sneak through the back door. I hurry through the adjoining classroom, which is empty with no teacher, and if I get caught in here, I'll be in trouble. I make it to the back hallway. One end leads to the janitor's storage room and the gymnasium. The other end leads out to the quad. There's no one else here and it's eerily quiet, like the quiet in the horror movie right before the monster jumps out with razor claws and starts slashing guts.

The squeak of a shoe echoes through the hallway and I flinch with alarm. I turn to see Reuben at the mouth of the corridor, blocking access to the quad.

"I just want to talk to you, freak," he says.

"Leave me alone, Reuben!" I yell, but my voice is shrill.

I turn and race for the gymnasium. I hear the slap of his sneakers behind me. My heart pounds and my throat starts to close, making it hard for me to breathe. I rush past the bleachers just as Reuben pulls open the gym door. He's big and fat and slow, so if I keep going, if I can just keep sucking in air, I know he won't catch me.

"I . . . said . . . I just . . . want . . . to talk to you . . ." he says between gasps. "Why are you . . . running . . . away from me?"

I don't stop. I think of the shack in the woods and how he told me how easily he could kill me and how I ran away from him. He didn't follow me on Saturday.

Because it's happening today.

I almost stop dead at the thought. But I know if I hesitate for even one second, Reuben will get me. I close in on the exit doors and burst through them into the sunshine and nearly cry with relief at the sight of the administration building.

I go straight to the glass door, open it, and step into the air-conditioned office. My breath comes in ragged wheezes. The school attendant, Ms. Blizzard, looks up at me from behind the long counter.

"Oh, dear. Melissa, isn't it? No, sorry, Melanie. What's the matter?"

"Asthma," I whisper, then cough for full effect.

She ushers me around the counter and into the nurse's office where I collapse across the vinyl chair.

"The nurse won't be in today," Ms. Blizzard says. "Do you have medication stored here?" I shake my head.

She gives me a worried look. "Okay, well, I'm going to have to call your fos—your parents."

I want to tell her not to do that, that I'll be fine, but she's gone before I can get the words out.

I've never been in the nurse's office before. I've hardly ever been in the administration building because I never get in trouble. D and Ray and me had a meeting with the principal when I first came here. Mr. Hall went on about how happy he was to have me as a student, and how

the school was a fine institution and there was a zero-tolerance bully-
ing policy and blah blah blah and that if I ever needed a safe place, I
could come to him. Penny told me things about Mr. Hall—not creepy
child-molester stuff, just stuff about his wife and how he treats his kids—
that made me think I would never go to him if I needed a safe place.

As I look around, an awful sense of déjà vu washes over me, like
something bad happened here. But *not* here. Not in this bright, cheer-
ful room with the smiling cartoon thermometer taped to the medical
supply cabinet and the mural of a beach during sunset painted on the
far wall. Another nurse's office in another school, maybe. As quickly as
it comes, the feeling vanishes.

Ms. Blizzard pokes her head in and smiles at me. "How are you
feeling?"

"Better," I say, which is true. I can actually breathe again, and my
heart has slowed back to normal. "I think I can stay and go to the rest
of my classes."

She shakes her head. "School policy," she says. "One of your parents
will be here shortly."

Shortly turns out to be fifteen minutes later. Ray's truck rolls up to
the curb in front of the administration building. I walk outside with
Ms. Blizzard watching closely from behind her counter. Ray gets out
and comes around to the passenger side. His expression is hard to read.
Anger? Annoyance? Disdain? Has he talked to D? Did she show him
my journal yet?

"What happened, Mel?" he asks. "You okay?"

So, no, probably he doesn't know about the journal yet. If he did,
he probably couldn't care less how I am.

"I had an asthma attack, I guess."

"You guess? You ever had one before?"

"Not that I remember."

"Nothing like that's in your file."

I shake my head.

No, there wouldn't be . . .

He opens the door for me and helps me into the passenger seat, then jogs around the truck and gets behind the wheel. As he pulls away from the curb, I catch sight of Reuben, standing by the bike racks, his arms crossed over his chest, staring at me. I hunch down in my seat and turn toward Ray.

"I thought Delilah would come get me."

"School couldn't reach her."

"Where is she?"

Ray glances at me. He shrugs casually, but his jaw is tight. "I have no idea."

I do. She's gone down to the Department of Child and Family Services, Ray. Took my journal with her. Not the kind of reading material Miss Pearl is used to.

Well, at least when they send me away, I won't have to deal with Reuben Meserve anymore.

There's that.

I watch Ray watch the road and try not to think about anything.

Doesn't work.

SEVENTY-FOUR

Louise

CALIFORNIA–PRESENT

We hit a traffic jam ten minutes outside of town. My driver speaks for the first time since I gasped at the newspaper clipping.

"Must be an accident."

My GPS confirms his suspicions.

"Is there any way to go around this?" I ask. "A back way?"

He shakes his head curtly. "Only way is this one."

I try to stay calm. I take deep breaths in through my nose and out through my mouth. Doesn't help. I try closing my eyes and picturing my reunion with my daughter. That makes my anxiety rise.

If I thought I could get out of this cab and run there faster, I'd do it, bad leg and all. I'd cripple myself to get to her. Because I know that whatever bad thing is going to happen to Edie, the event Mom and I have been trying to prevent, it's almost here. It's almost time.

The Peepers aren't telling me anything. I've never heard them, and I never will. They belonged to my mother. But *her* voice is in my head, loud and clear.

Get there. Get there. Get there, get there, get there get there . . .

SEVENTY-FIVE

Melanie

CALIFORNIA-PRESENT

I don't know what I was expecting to find when we got home. But it was definitely not what we found.

Delilah's car is in the driveway, and even though Ray's been pretending he's not worried about her, he lets out a relieved sigh when he sees the Saturn.

"She's home," I say.

"Looks that way," Ray replies.

We get out of the truck and walk toward the house. I take slow, measured steps. The last thing I want to do is go inside. I don't want to know what's waiting for me.

Neither Ray nor I say anything, but I know we're both wondering what kind of mood D's going to be in. Me especially, because of my journal. But Ray, too, because of how Delilah's been lately.

Ray reaches the front door. I want to stop him from going in, make him sit down on the front steps with me, and tell him all about Penny. I'm sure he won't understand. Who would? But he wants us to have an honest and truthful relationship. And if DCFS is here or is going to show up any minute because of what Delilah probably told them, I want him to hear my side first.

But I don't say anything, just follow him into the house.

The smell of chocolate brownies hits me. *Uh oh.* Ray and I exchange a look.

Delilah comes out of the kitchen and sees us. Her mouth opens in delight. She's dressed in jeans and a Rolling Stones T-shirt and she looks totally normal.

"Well, look at you two," she says. "What are you doing home?"

"Mel had an asthma attack," Ray tells her. He looks at her suspiciously, like maybe she's an alien and the real Delilah has been abducted and taken to the mother ship.

"Oh no," she says and crosses to me. She lays a hand on my forehead. "Are you all right, Mel?"

"The school called," Ray says before I can answer. "They tried you first. Couldn't get ahold of you."

She shakes her head and gives him an embarrassed grin. "My cell battery died. Just completely. It won't take a charge."

"Where were you this morning, D? We got up and you were nowhere to be found."

"I know!" she cries. "I'm sorry if I worried you. But it's actually really great. You'll see." She takes Ray and me by the hand and leads us to the couch. "Sit. I have a surprise for you." She practically pushes us down onto the cushions, then goes to the kitchen, talking as she does.

"I know I've been acting a little strange lately. I'm sorry about that. I might be going through the change early." I hear the clank of a metal pan. "My mom went through it early. But that's no excuse. You guys must think I've gone crazy."

She comes back into the living room carrying two glasses of milk. She sets them down in front of us and smiles. I smile back, relieved. I was expecting her to lay into me about my journal, tell me to pack my things. I thought she'd be totally upset and weirded out. But she's not. She's being her old, kind of goofy, happy self, like maybe she didn't even read it.

Don't be fooled. Shadows hide in broad daylight.

"So, last night," she says, "I was lonely without the two of you here, so I went over to Mrs. Fitzpatrick's house, and I told her I needed her chocolate brownie recipe because I wanted to make it up to you guys for being such a complete nutcase these past few days."

She goes back to the kitchen.

"She seems good," I say. Ray nods, but his jaw is tight.

"And you know what?" Delilah calls. "She gave me the recipe. And you know what else? It came out perfect!"

Delilah practically dances out into the living room with a tray of brownies.

"I got up early and went to the market to get the ingredients."

She sets the tray on the coffee table and beams with pride. And I have to admit, the brownies look totally scrumptious. Delilah crosses her arms over her chest and stares at us.

"Well? Aren't you going to try them?"

"Um, sure," I say, and reach for one of the gooey chocolate squares. Ray does the same.

I take a bite. Delilah's right. The brownies are perfect. Moist but not runny, and the chocolate flavor is perfect.

"Wow," I say around my mouthful. "These are so good."

"Don't talk with your mouth full," she tells me, and I mumble an apology.

"Damn, D," Ray says. "This might be the best brownie I've ever had."

"I knew it!" she cries. Ray and I keep eating, and D starts talking again. "I just, you know, I've been having all these thoughts that are just tumbling around in my head. About the two of you."

Ray stops chewing and looks up at her. "What kind of thoughts?"

She gives him a harsh look. "What did I just tell Melanie?"

He swallows down his bite of brownie, takes a sip of milk. "What kind of thoughts, D?"

I get that tingly feeling all of a sudden. My mouth goes dry. I grab my glass from the coffee table and take a couple gulps of milk.

"Oh, just nonsense thoughts," Delilah says, but her eyes seem different. I don't know, clouded. "Anyway, I don't want to talk about it right now. I just want to enjoy the two of you enjoying my brownies."

The milk is cold and wet on my tongue and quenches the dryness. I drink most of it before Delilah reprimands me.

"Not too fast," she says. "You'll get a stomachache."

"Why don't you sit down with us," Ray suggests. "The three of us can talk. Mel and I, well, we've been working on something together."

"I bet you have," Delilah snaps, then realizes how she sounded. She smiles, but I can tell she's forcing it. The tingly feeling has gotten bigger. My skin prickles with goosebumps and I rub at my arms.

"I just meant the two of you have been thick as thieves lately."

"D, sit," Ray says sternly. "The three of us need to have a conversation. Mel and I, we've decided that it's best if we're all honest with each other about what's going on with us."

Delilah doesn't sit. She wanders to the back of the couch. I scoot my butt around so I can keep an eye on her. Something's telling me I should run out the door. It's not Penny. I would recognize her. It's something else, or someone else. But I think I should listen. Only I can't seem to get myself up.

"Honest, huh?" she says. "Honest is good."

Out of nowhere, my mouth stretches open in a yawn so wide my jaw pops. I rub at my eyes, then look at Ray. He sets his milk on the coffee table, then makes like he's going to stand. Before he can get to his feet, the brass lamp smashes into the back of his head. I look up to see Delilah holding the base. Her expression is completely blank.

Oh, crap. Holy shitting crap!

Ray lets out a strangled yelp, then collapses against the coffee table. I struggle to get off the couch, but my legs have turned to lead.

"What are you doing, D?" I scream, but my mouth feels funny too, like it's full of cotton.

She drops the lamp and looks down at me. "It's okay, Mel. Don't worry."

I need to call 911. Ray's head is bleeding like crazy. He could die. He could never wake up. He could spin the bottle and dance the jig. Wait, what? No. 911 . . . my thoughts are scrambling.

"I'm going to take care of you," Delilah says in a weird sing-song voice. She bends over the arm of the couch and looks in my eyes. I can't focus on her. I'm terrified, but at the same time, I can't feel the fear. "Won't be long now. Don't try to get up. I don't want you twisting your ankle."

"What did you do, D?" I think the question, but I'm not sure if I said it out loud. Everything around me is gray.

And then the gray turns black.

SEVENTY-SIX

CALIFORNIA—PRESENT

I feel so bad about Ray. That was not on the agenda. Of course it wasn't. He's my husband and I love him, despite what's going on with Mel. The whole thing is her fault. She's almost a teenager, with her adolescent hips just starting to curve and her boobs budding and her pretending to be all innocent and Goody Two-shoes, but then sliding into bed next to my man. He's weak, that's all, like most men, like my dad was. He's not evil. Not like her.

But then, when he started talking about how they've been making plans and decisions together, and he said the three of us had to talk, well I just lost it. I thought if I don't hit something, I'm going to explode. I didn't mean for that something to be Ray's head. But the voice inside *my* head started screaming at me to grab the lamp and swing, and that's what I did.

The voice told me what to do with the milk, too, and told me about Ray and Mel. Told me to buy all the stuff at Kohl's. It got a LOT louder after I read Mel's journal, and now it just won't shut up. A part of me thinks I shouldn't be listening to that voice, but I can't help it, and also, the voice makes so much sense. About everything. Maybe I didn't hit Ray as hard as I think. He went down like a ton of bricks, for sure, but that might have been more about the drug than the lamp. I hope so, even if he didn't drink much milk.

Anyhow, I can't think about that, not while I'm in the middle of what I'm doing. I have to concentrate, because I'm getting all torn up. I'll figure out how to deal with Ray later. He didn't actually see me hit him, so he doesn't know it was me.

Tell him it was an intruder. The voice again. *That's what you tell him.*

For that to work, I'll have to do some kind of harm to myself.

Wouldn't be the first time.

No, I won't think about that either. It's been a long time since I've done that. But I can do it again, sure.

Mel saw me hit Ray, but that won't make any difference in a little while. And Ray will believe me, and he'll feel so bad when he sees my own wounds from the intruder, so guilty that he didn't protect me, he'll probably get down on his knees and beg my forgiveness and vow to be the best husband in the world. And then we'll make love and we won't have to worry about making noise or getting crazy like we used to and everything will go back to normal.

If he isn't dead.

Stop that!

I just have to put one foot in front of the other, which is not as easy as it sounds. Mel's moving pretty well, especially for someone with Rohypnol in her system. But I'm bearing most of her weight.

I still can't believe how easy it was for me to get the drugs. Two different kinds, and both illegal. I just went into a chatroom on AskGreg.com last night, and within a minute, I had a meeting with a guy early this morning in Los Angeles. If Ray knew how much I spent, he'd have an absolute conniption, but it's not like Kohl's. I can't take this stuff back.

Mel's rucksack gets caught on a branch, and I have to yank at it. Mel almost falls out of my grasp, but I hold tight to her. She starts to moan, and I know I have to hurry.

We're almost there. We're going to make it.

My plan was to tell Ray that Mel ran away. *Because* of him. Because

310 of what he'd done with her. That won't work now, not after I bashed his brains in.

of what he'd done with her. That won't work now, not after I bashed his brains in.

"Verregone . . ." Mel mumbles.

The voice solved my problem. Told me just what I needed to do. So that's what I'm doing.

SEVENTY-SEVEN

CALIFORNIA–PRESENT

My driver is trying to make up for lost time. He doesn't have ESP, but he wouldn't need psychic abilities to sense my tension. It comes off me in waves and fills the cab with so much energy, if I lit a match, I'd blow us to kingdom come.

We passed the accident ten minutes ago, and I shuddered at the sight of the sedan with its crumpled side and the pickup truck with its accordioned front end. Memories.

The town is spread out, like most of these suburbs. We sail past the mall, a movie theater called the Palm, several fast-food joints, a Sizzler. I didn't even know Sizzlers were still around.

We pass a sprawling, dusty trailer park, then hitch a right into a neighborhood of small, one-story houses with postage-stamp yards. Not a lot of money here, but the residents do their best to keep their places neat and tidy. We're getting close, I can feel it with every beat of my heart, with every breath.

Please, God, don't let anything happen to her. Please let me get there first.

Ninety seconds later—I'm keeping track on my phone—we pull to the curb in front of a small, clapboard-sided house, painted light coral. The lawn is a dried-out brown with intermittent patches of green. I double-check the address in Grace's book. This is the place. This is where my daughter lives.

I hand the driver the three hundred-dollar bills, then add a fifty for good measure. He turns and smiles at me. "May Allah smile upon you."

"I hope he does."

Bags in hand, I jump out of the cab and rush to the front door. I drop the bags then knock, softly at first. No answer. I knock with more force. Still no answer.

Too late, too late, too late . . .

I try the knob on the front door. Locked. I glance to my right. A bougainvillea bush grows against the side of the house, under the large front window. The curtains inside are open halfway. I step down from the front porch, press myself against the stucco wall, and shimmy between the house and bush. Sharp thorns attack me, puncturing my back, but I keep going until I reach the window. I steeple my hands together against the glass and peer into the house. I see a living room with tired wallpaper and worn carpet. A couch in the center. And beyond the couch—is that a person? Yes! There's a man slumped over the coffee table. Looks like back of his head is bleeding.

A jolt of fear runs through me. I pound against the glass.

"Hey!" I shriek. "Hey!"

Forgetting the thorns, I tear through the bush to the side of the house. The gate is unlocked. I push through it and head to the backyard. A fence separates this plot from the neighbors on both sides, but there is no perimeter fence at the end of the property. The yard leads into a wooded area, thick with trees and brush as far as I can see.

At the back of the house, a sliding glass door yawns open. Without hesitation, I run inside.

The kitchen is eerily familiar. It looks just like my grandmother's kitchen. I move through it to the living room. I don't consider the fact that I'm breaking and entering and could go to jail for this. *Well, I didn't break, only entered*, I think, and I have to stifle a bubble of hysterical laughter.

I reach the living room. There he is. The man I saw through the window. I kneel beside him but I don't know what to do. I wish my mother were here. She would know.

Grace, help me. Mom, *help me.*

I shove my hands under his armpits and slowly ease him to the floor, then I push the coffee table toward the fireplace to give us room. He moans, and I consider this a good sign. He's alive. I press my fingers against his neck and feel for his pulse. I've never done anything like this before, but I must have beginner's luck, because I feel it, throbbing beneath my fingertips. Strong and steady. Another good sign.

I get up and go back to the kitchen, to the fridge, and pull an ice pack from the freezer drawer. I am compelled by another force. I recognize that these are things I wouldn't have thought of—the pulse, the ice pack—without external guidance. Grace—*Mom*—is with me.

I return to the man, kneel beside him, and gently lift his head and place the ice pack beneath it. The coffee table and the floor around it is covered with blood.

Head wounds bleed like a stuck pig. It doesn't mean the worst.

"It's okay," I say to this stranger on the floor beside me. He looks to be in his early forties, handsome, too. He reminds me of that actor in that old series, *Justified.* After a few minutes of ice, he stirs. His eyes open and he looks up at me, confused. His confusion accelerates to agitation in a split second.

"Whatha—"

"Shhh," I tell him. "You have a serious head lac." *What the fuck's a head lac?* "I'm going to call 911. I just wanted to make sure you were . . ." *Alive . . .* "Stable."

His eyes rove from side to side. "We'i'see?" he slurs, his words running together.

"You need to keep still. You've lost a lot of blood."

He grasps at my shirt and tries to focus on me. "Mel," he whispers. "Where's Mel?"

My heart skips a beat. "Mel?"

"Me-lan-ie," he says slowly, overenunciating each syllable. "Fost'dahta. Whe-where?"

Melanie. That's Edie's name now. Melanie. I like it.

You don't have time to like it. Get there.

"I don't know where she is. I thought she was here."

Oh no, oh no, something bad, something awful, get there, Lou . . .

The man's eyes go wide, and he struggles to get up. "Delilah."

I push him back down. "You can't move. Just relax. I'm going to call for help."

"Delilah . . . crazy," he says.

I gain my feet and go to the front door, unlock it, and yank it open. I grab my bags from the porch and haul them inside. By the time I return to the living room, the man is trying to pull himself to a seated position. The back of his head is a jumbled mass of matted hair and drying blood.

"Be still," I say, but he is determined. He gets his butt beneath himself, then slumps against the couch as though the effort is too great.

I grab my cell from my purse and dial 911, then kneel beside him.

"Gott'fine the," he mumbles.

The ringing of the call sounds in my ears. A click. Then, "911, what is your emergency?"

A thought comes to me. I set the phone down on the coffee table. The 911 operator continues to ask questions, which I don't answer. She'll find him, I know. She'll triangulate the call and send someone to its source.

I reach for my duffel bag, unzip it with shaking fingers, and pull out my sketchpad. I hurriedly flip the pages to the end, to the drawing I made in the cab. I crabwalk to the man and hold the sketch pad before him.

"Do you recognize this?" I ask.

He can't seem to focus. I grab his hand and squeeze it, then shove the sketch pad into his lap. The man sags against me and closes his eyes.

"Please, I need you to tell me. Do you know where this is?"

"*I* do," comes a voice from behind me. Startled, I jerk my head around to see a beefy, moonfaced kid standing a few feet inside the door.

"This is 911," says the operator. "We're sending someone to your location."

"You know where this is?" I ask the kid.

"It's Melanie, right? She's in trouble?" His voice is as flat as his expression, but his eyes are alive.

"Yes, Melanie's in trouble. Where is this place?"

The kid steps toward me. "I'll take you there."

SEVENTY-EIGHT

CALIFORNIA—PRESENT

As soon as I come to, I know where I am. This is my place and it's as familiar to me as my room in my house. Well, Ray and Delilah's house.

I'm in the fort.

I lay on my side with my cheek pressed against the floor. For a few minutes, or a few hours, or years, or eons—I can't tell, because I feel sort of woozy and totally out of it—the walls of the shack seem to be breathing. I recognize, as I watch the splintered wood pulsate, that this is not a normal feeling and probably is not really happening

My head pounds. D must have put something in the milk. Or maybe even the brownies, but I don't think so because poisoning brownies would be sacrilegious. I never realized how sacrilegious and sacrifice sound alike even when I'm just saying them in my head. Sacramento, not so much. Whoa. This must be what it's like to take drugs. I'm so glad I don't. Breathing walls and sacrilegious brownies.

I close my eyes and wait for my thoughts to get less fuzzy, then I open my eyes again.

I don't see D, but I know she's here. I can feel her and her madness close by. It's real dark in the hut. Still daylight outside, but there must be clouds or something. Unless it's already dusk, but I don't think so. I hope not. I don't think that much real time has passed. But I can't really trust myself to know anything right now.

Ray. Oh no! I suddenly remember what happened, the lamp smashing down on the back of his skull, the wet smacking sound, the skin bursting, the blood pouring from the gash. Him slumping over onto the coffee table.

If Ray's dead, it's all my fault.

Please let someone find him.

My hands and feet are tied together with something soft, a couple of D's scarves, maybe. Not so tight that it hurts, but tight enough that I for sure can't get free. I try to shimmy myself up into a seated position, lose my balance, and fall face-first against the floor. I turn my head just in time to keep from breaking my nose, but my cheek takes the hit pretty hard. Pain shoots through my whole head and my teeth rattle. The only good thing is that my thoughts get clear really quick and the image of Ray's crushed skull goes away.

I try to get up again, and this time I succeed, end up on my butt with my back against the wall.

"D?" I whisper. She must be up on the platform. "D, are you there?"

"She's awake," Delilah says. "I thought she might sleep for a while longer." Her voice floats down to me. She sounds just like she always does, but there's an edge to her tone, a hollowness, maybe, that kind of freaks me out. Like me being drugged and brought to the hut in the woods and tied up wasn't enough to freak me out.

I wonder what Penny wrote in my journal yesterday. Did she warn me about Delilah? Is that why Delilah went bonkers, or did Delilah go bonkers before and finding the journal just sent her over the edge? Chicken or egg, it doesn't matter now.

"D, are you okay?" I don't know what else to say.

The floorboards above my head creak, then she hops down to my level. She grabs her shoulder bag from the corner of the hut and slowly walks over to me. I can only see her outline and the shadow of her, which is probably a good thing, because I'm pretty sure the look on her face is not going to make me feel better.

"I always wanted a daughter," she says, then lowers herself to the ground. She sits a few feet away from me. "Ray and I tried for years to have a baby. Did you know that? Then we were going to adopt. That didn't work out either."

So, they turned to the system. Ray told me that. A lot of people foster for the right reasons, and a lot of people do it for the money. Ray and Delilah did it because they really wanted a kid. I am like the worst consolation prize ever.

Nothing I say will help, so I keep my mouth shut.

"I should have known about you, Melanie. I should have seen it. All my friends warned me about taking in a foster kid. They said you never know what you're going to get and most of the time fosters are trouble. But you were the perfect kid. 'Yes, please' and 'No, thank you,' and you never make a fuss and you always get good grades. Not even real biological kids are that perfect."

She leans forward, and she's close enough now that I *can* see her. Her eyes. There's a blankness I've never seen before. The hair on the back of my neck stands up, but not in the *Penny* way. More like in the *D-is-going-to-murder-me* way.

"D, I'm not perfect, I swear."

She lets out a harsh bark of laughter, "Oh, I know you're not. I know all about you."

"You read my journal."

"What do you mean, *your* journal?" D shakes her head. "I may not be a great mother, but I do recognize your handwriting, and that wasn't yours. How nice for you to have a friend, Melanie, although I will say, she's kind of a bitch. Thinks she knows so much . . . But she's just like you. A liar and a pretender. But I know what to do about you. Because I have *friends* too, and they tell me things just like *your* friend does."

My heart starts to bang against my ribs and I'm scared half out of my mind. Because that bad thing, it's happening now. *Penny, help me. Tell me what to do.* But Penny doesn't answer, and I know I have to figure something out. D wouldn't drug me and bring me here if she didn't have a very specific plan. I'm not used to being this afraid. My body aches with fear.

She slings a bag from her shoulder—my rucksack—and drops it to the ground with a thud, then kneels down and rummages through it. *Why does she have my rucksack?* She pulls out a lumpy shape and throws it at me. I wince, but the thing doesn't hurt, just bounces off me. I realize it's my stuffed animal, Chauncy the Dolphin. Suddenly, I want to cry. I fight the tears with everything I have and watch as D withdraws a large glass bottle from my sack.

"This was my dad's favorite," she says, then sighs. I think maybe she's going to smash it against my head, like she did with Ray. But she doesn't.

"There are so many things I wanted to do with my daughter." Her voice has gone kind of dreamy. I'm trying to listen to her, but also testing the scarves to see if I can wriggle free. I feel the skin on my wrists chafing.

"Firsts, you know? Like baking a cake together and shopping for prom dresses. I remember the first time I ever had an actual alcoholic drink with my mom. I was sixteen. Long time ago, now, but I remember it so clearly." She peers at me like I'm a bug. "You never wanted to bake a cake, did you, Mel?" She chuckles, but there's no humor in it. "And we both know you were never going to go to the prom. But we can do that other first, Mel. We can have that drink together. Like my mom and me did."

She uncaps the bottle and takes a swallow. Then she holds it up to my mouth.

"No, D. I don't want to."

"This is a first for us, Mel," she says, almost tenderly. My stomach rolls over. "Our *last* first. If I have to force you, I will. But I'd rather not."

I shake my head, and quick as lightning, she grabs me by the neck and shoves the end of the bottle into my mouth and upends it. The taste is foul, like the worst medicine ever mixed with something that spoiled. I cough and wheeze and try to writhe away from D, but she holds fast. If I don't swallow, I'm going to choke, like, *really* choke, so I do it. A wave of fire burns down my throat, all the way to my stomach. Delilah releases me and I cough and spew and try to suck in air. Spit dribbles down my chin, mixing with the tears streaming down my cheeks.

"You don't have to do this," I sob. "You can just send me away."

"I'm not doing anything. It's what *you're* doing." Now her voice sounds completely different. Monotone, no emotion at all, like she's reading lines. "It's what you've already done, Mel. It'll probably make the papers. Troubled foster kid, sent from home to home. Finally goes crazy and attacks her foster parents. Then runs away. When they find her, weeks later, dead in a hut in the woods, surrounded by her precious belongings . . . overdosed on pills and booze . . . We'll all be sad. Ray especially. But I'll take care of him."

Reuben Meserve comes to mind. He's the one who's going to find me. I can feel it. Knowing him, he'll probably play with my corpse for a while before he goes to the police. I almost laugh out loud. Instead, I wet myself. I can't help it. Hot urine pours out of me, down my legs, and onto the floor of the hut. Delilah doesn't notice.

"Are you ready for another sip?" she asks brightly.

"D, no. Please."

"After this one, you're going to swallow down some pills, Mel. They'll go easy enough, I promise. And it won't hurt. In fact, I think you're going to like the way it feels. Until you don't."

She presses the bottle against my lips. I jerk backward against the wall and she tumbles forward. I scramble to my knees as D comes at me.

"Damn it, Mel, don't make me force you again!" She grabs the back of my head and yanks it toward her, pulling at my hair hard enough to make me yelp. I crouch, ignoring the pain, and drive myself forward with as much force as I can. My head smashes into her chest and the air whooshes out of her. She coughs, then grabs for me again, shoves me down against the wooden floor. She presses on my neck with one hand and reaches for the bottle with the other.

Just then, the door to the hut flies open and bangs against the inside wall. My first thought is Reuben, but it's not him. It's a woman I don't recognize.

Fear not the stranger.

Delilah looks up just as the woman grabs her and hauls her off me. D goes reeling across the hut, but immediately rushes back at the woman. She swings the bottle like she did the lamp, but the woman grabs D's wrist and twists until D drops it. It crashes against the floor of the hut but doesn't break. Delilah goes for the woman's throat, but the woman slaps Delilah hard across the face then grips both her shoulders and pushes her against the wall to still her.

"I'm here for Melanie," the woman says, and her voice reminds me of someone, but I don't know who.

D shrinks away from the woman and presses herself against the corner of the hut.

"What?" she cries, but she's not asking me or the woman. She glances toward the ceiling, then drops her head to her chest, then straightens, all within the space of a few seconds. "I don't know," she says, as though she's answering a question. "No, I don't. What do I do?" She looks back and forth between the walls of the hut, as though someone else is here, or a couple of someone elses. Then she crumples to the floor and starts to shake.

"Reuben?" the woman calls. "Go back to the house and get some help. The responders should be there by now."

I look over at the open door and see big, old, creepy Reuben staring in at me.

"You okay, freak?" he asks, but he looks really upset.

I nod. "Thanks, Reuben."

The woman glances at Delilah then comes to me. She limps slightly, and when she kneels down, she exhales sharply, like something hurts. Even in the low light of the hut, I can see that she's beautiful. And achingly familiar. She doesn't flinch at the pungent smell of my pee and immediately goes to work on my wrists.

"Are you all right?" she asks.

"I feel kind of sick," I tell her, which is like the understatement of the decade, because I feel nauseous and dizzy and lightheaded and my whole body is shaking uncontrollably.

"Ray?" I ask, even though I'm afraid of the answer.

"I think he's going to be okay," the woman says as she frees my ankles. I exhale, relieved. My breath is sour.

The woman notices that I'm trembling and wraps her arms around me. "I'm here."

I relax into her, this stranger who I think maybe I've known all my life. We sit like that and watch Delilah. She hasn't moved from where she's curled up in the far corner of the hut. It's like she's forgotten we're there. Which is totally fine with me.

"What's wrong with her?" I whisper to the woman.

"Your mom is having some kind of breakdown."

"She's not my mom," I tell the woman. "You got here just in time." She pulls away and looks at me. "Penny told me you were coming."

The woman's eyes flick with recognition. "Penny?"

"She's the girl who lives in my left hand," I say. This is the first time I've ever said those words out loud. The woman doesn't seem surprised or suspicious. She simply nods.

"Penny is my mother's middle name," she says.

"Can I have my dolphin?" I ask, reaching toward my stuffed animal on the floor a few feet away.

She grabs the dolphin and studies him for a moment. A smile spreads across her face. She presses him against her cheek. "Chauncy," she says. I should be surprised that she knows his name. But for some reason, I'm not. She hands him to me, and I clutch him to my chest.

"Thanks," I say.

"You're welcome," the woman replies.

She holds me tighter.

We stay that way, watching D wrestle with her demons, until help arrives.

SEVENTY-NINE

Louise

CALIFORNIA–PRESENT

I stand outside my daughter's hospital room. She's going to be okay.

Melanie. I like her name. I'm comfortable with it. It suits her more than Edie did.

She is a brave girl. Strong and sensitive and resilient.

Just like me.

I haven't acknowledged those traits in myself, but they exist despite my denial.

We are both going to be okay.

My mother passed away on the concrete sidewalk of the Ontario Airport, with Nicholas Beecham by her side. His presence gives me comfort because he knew her. In their short interaction, they formed a bond, and he cared for her, like Mary Palmer did, and countless others over the past five decades.

I will have to reach out to them, to all the people whose names are carefully written in my mother's address book, whose photographs fill the manila envelope she carried with her when she came to find me. I don't relish that task, but I will perform it, as it is my duty . . . as it is my privilege.

I called Ewan. My job is still mine. So is his heart. I might just test that theory. We'll see.

I didn't get to say goodbye to Grace. I didn't get to tell her I love her. But she knows. Somehow, she does. Because the truth is what it is. We fetter it with our preconceptions, and rail against it when it doesn't suit us, and redefine it if it serves our needs.

But the truth is what it is. I know that now. I will live by it. And try to make my mother proud by using the gifts she gave me.

EIGHTY

A FEW DAYS AFTER

Melanie and Louise stand side by side in front of Grace's grave. The Southern California day is unseasonably cool, with clouds overhead obscuring the sun.

Ray stands off to the side, giving them privacy. His injury has healed for the most part, although he still has a headache, and likely will for a while.

Melanie and Louise don't talk much. They've been talking nonstop for over a week, filling in blanks, catching up, getting to know one another. But right now, words are unnecessary.

Delilah is in a facility. There is, as of yet, no official diagnosis, but the doctors feel strongly that she can be helped. With the help of medication, she might even return to society, although she will not be married anymore and will never be responsible for a minor again. But she might achieve contentment in some form.

Melanie will stay with Ray for the time being, although their situation is under review with DCFS. She and Louise bore witness on his behalf, and Melanie feels safe with him. But things may transition soon, depending on how all three of them navigate the coming months and the decisions they make.

Louise leaves tomorrow. She's going to see Mel's biological father, Danny, and get her grandmother's car, then she'll return to New York. Melanie wants to meet her father, and she will. She wants to visit Louise in New York, and she'll do that too. They've discussed making that happen over summer vacation.

None of them knows what the future looks like. Mel could probably see into it, if she wanted to, even though the girl who lived in her left hand is gone. Louise might be able to sketch the possibilities. But they have all agreed to try and take things one day at a time.

Louise kneels down and brushes some leaves from Grace's headstone. "I found her, Mom," she whispers. "I got to her. I *got there.*"

Melanie watches her mother kiss her fingertips, then brush them along the headstone. She stands up and the two of them stare down at the epitaph.

THE TRUTH FINDS US, SO WE, TOO, FIND EACH OTHER.
DAUGHTER, MOTHER, GRANDMOTHER, RESCUER
GRACE PENNY DANIELS

Acknowledgments

I have recently been thinking about my career, the goals I set for myself, the aspirations and dreams I nurtured alone against my pillow in the dark of night. But the idea of success today is subjective and often contested. So, to measure my own accomplishments, I must revert to my inspiration for writing in the first place: to tell the best story I can. If a reader is moved, touched, entertained, if he or she laughs or cries or has an aha moment, if they are changed in some small way, I have achieved success, because that is what this is all about for me. To give readers an escape in which they can think, question, believe, love, laugh, cry, look within, look without, and in the end, become friends with my characters, that they might learn alongside them, as I am learning alongside them, every day.

Thank you, reader, for choosing to spend your precious time with Grace, Louise, and Melanie.

I have been blessed with extraordinary people who have brought this book to life. To my truly gifted agent, Wendy Sherman, thank you for your knowledge, your trust, and for always believing in me, no matter how long I take. Thank you, Megan Wahrenbrock, Josie Woodbridge, Ciera Cox, Hannah Ohlmann, Ananda Finwall, Alenka Linaschke (your cover rocks!), and the rest of the Blackstone team for giving *Finding Grace* such a fantastic home. Much thanks to my developmental editor, the incredibly talented Sara O'Keeffe, for your wisdom and thoughtful input. You made this a better book.

I could not navigate my writer's journey without my family, friends, and loved ones. Sharilyn Nicargi, Linda Fields, Hilary Murphy, Michael Steven Gregory, Maddie Margarita, Penny Thiedemann, and Mark Thomas, thank for your unfailing support, your wise counsel, your insight, all the laughter and love, and for helping me remember how I want to show up in the world. There are so many more of you, too numerous to name, and I am grateful for every one of you.

To my writerly tribe, the Southern California Writers Conference and the Southern California Writers Association, my beta readers, my partner in crime Ara Grigorian, thank you for keeping me sane.

In the movie *City Slickers*, Jack Palance tells Billy Crystal that life is about *one thing*, that one important thing that is different for everyone. Alex, AJ, and Elle Hamlin—for me, *you* are that *one thing*. Thank you for being you and for letting me be me. Thank you for your daily hugs, for still telling me you love me, and for understanding that when I'm talking to myself, it's *usually* for a story. Love you with all my heart.

About the Author

Janis Thomas is the author of bestselling domestic suspense novels *What Remains True* and *All That's Left of Me*, as well as three critically acclaimed humorous women's fiction novels, *Something New, Sweet Nothings*, and *Say Never*. Janis is a popular workshop leader and speaker and a passionate writing advocate. When she isn't writing or fulfilling her PTA duties, she loves to spend time with her family, sing with her sister, play tennis, and throw lavish dinner parties with outrageous menus. She lives in Southern California with her terrific husband, amazing teenagers, and two crazy dogs.